Yellow Hair

By

Andrew Joyce

Yellow Hair

eBook ISBN: 978-09981193-0-4
Softcover ISBN: 978-09981193-1-1

Published by William Birch & Assoc.

Dedicated To

Ben Dorson

who once saved my life

With Thanks To:

Emily Gmitter
My Editor

Little White Dove
Great-Granddaughter of Red Cloud

Asun Quintana

&

The Lakota Language Consortium

The Dakota Calendar:

Moon of Frost in the Tipis (January)

Moon of Dark Red Calves (February)

Moon of the Snow-Blind (March)

Moon of Red Grass Growing (April)

Moon When the Ponies Shed (May)

Moon of Making Fat (June)

Moon When Cherries Are Ripe (July)

Moon of Black Cherries (August)

Moon When Calves Grow Hair (September)

Moon of the Changing Season (October)

Moon of Falling Leaves (November)

Moon When Deer Shed Their Horns (December)

Author's Note

Yellow Hair documents the injustices done to the Sioux Nation from their first treaty with The United States in 1805 through Wounded Knee in 1890. Every death, murder, battle, and outrage depicted herein actually took place—from the first to the last. The historical figures that play a role in my story were real people and I used their real names. I conjured up my protagonist only to weave together the various events conveyed in this fact-based tale of fiction.

This *is* American history.

The Journey

Chapter One

FROM THE BEGINNING, the sea ruled that part of the planet. The wind rippled its waters. The sun warmed its surface—below lived myriad species of sea creatures and numberless varieties of sea grasses. Great mountains dotted its depths, patiently awaiting their time to be caressed by the wind and warmed by the sun.

At long last, the time came for the ocean to retreat. Slowly, over countless millennia, it made its way to the south. When finally the land was dry, a chain of mountains bordered it to the west, and to the east, a mighty river.

Soon, new species of life emerged—life that did not breathe water to survive. They had lungs to inhale the air. Gone were the fins that propelled the fish. These creatures had appendages that moved them about on the dry land.

These lifeforms started out small. But over time, they grew in size. Eons later, they became the Great Thunder Lizards. The earth was their domain. They would reign forever.

But then the earth grew cold.

With the Thunder Lizards gone, the smaller species promulgated the earth with their progeny. *They* now ruled that part of the world. There were herds of bison from horizon to horizon. Uncountable numbers of elk, antelope, and deer.

Eventually the first of the two-legged creatures arrived. They were a species that had developed elsewhere on the planet. They came down from the North carrying their homes on their backs and herding hitherto unknown species of four-legged animals.

In only a short while, the offspring of the two-legs had populated the great plains of the continent. By then they had broken up into different tribes, and on occasion made war with one another. They hunted the buffalo, elk, and deer for sustenance. They scratched at the earth and planted seeds in the rich soil that had once been the bottom of a sea.

They lived that life for 10,000 years until men from the South arrived. They wore iron helmets and iron upon their breasts. Their skin was white, not the color of a human being's. They called the people of the plains "Indians." They called themselves conquistadors and they brought with them an animal no one had ever seen before. It stood fifteen hands high and could be ridden long distances or used to carry packs.

The conquistadors did not stay long. The winters on the plains were too severe for them. They did not like the cold—they had come from a warmer clime. But they left behind a few horses that soon multiplied into many, many thousands.

Next came more White Men, but from the East this time. For the most part, they were solitary men, hunting the pelts of small animals. The Indians welcomed them to their land and traded for blankets and the iron implements used for cooking. Later, they traded for "noise sticks."

The men from the East called them guns.

Afterwards, also from the East, came still more White Men. They were looking for a route to the big water that lies over the mountains to the west.

They had given time a name.

The year, as they called it, was 1804.

In 1811, White Men forged a trail across the plains that led over the mountains and to the sea.

In 1836, the first "horse canoes" were seen by the people of the plains. The horse canoes, or wagons, as the whites called them, carried entire families to the West.

By 1850, The Trail scouted out in 1804 by the whites known as Meriwether Lewis and his partner, Bill Clark, had carried many whites to the Promised Lands to the West.

The coming of the White Man would forever change the fortunes of the people of the plains—more often than not for the worse. Very few White Men had a positive influence on the Indians. But there were a few.

One of those men was Jacob Ariesen.

Chapter Two

JACOB ARIESEN was born on Ariesen's Two Acres in the year of our Lord 1830. His maternal grandfather had acquired the land for services rendered. At the time, it was not known by that name. The property came unto the Ariesen family when Jacob's father married Jacob's mother. After a while, folks started calling it Ariesen's Two Acres. In time, the land came to be referred to simply as The Acres. Jacob was never able to ascertain what services his grandfather had rendered—or to whom—that got him his plot of land located on the outskirts of Concord, Massachusetts.

At twenty, Jacob, a tall and gangly lad, stood six-feet, two-inches in his stocking feet. His pale yellow hair denoted his Dutch ancestry. A comely-looking young man, his eyes were his most pronounced feature; they were light blue, the color of the sky—the irises flecked with yellow throughout.

On the property stood a unique house; it was more a cellar than a house. Jacob's father had built it the year before Jacob's birth. He first dug a pit in the ground . . . eighty feet long, half as wide, and seven feet deep. He lined the walls with wood all around to keep the earth from falling in, laid a plank floor, raised a pitched roof covered with sod, and added partitions as the family grew. It was a good house, warm in winter and cool in the heat of summer.

At the age of ten, after the other children of the town had teased him, Jacob asked his father why they had to live in a house that was so different from those of his friends.

Mister Ariesen sat Jacob down and told him of the first Ariesen who had come to the new land that would one day become the United States of America. Back then it was called New Netherland.

"When the first Ariesen arrived, he had no time to build a proper house; he had to get his crops planted before it was too late in the season. Instead, he built a house like the one we now live in. It was supposed to be a temporary shelter. However, as time went on, your ancestor became aware of the benefits of living in such a house. Those first New Netherland winters were harsh and the Ariesen family was the only family that did not succumb to sickness in those years. Many families lost loved ones to pneumonia and the like.

"That was two hundred years ago and the Ariesens have lived in these *'ground houses'* ever since." He then added, "You tell your friends that the wind does not blow through your house in winter as it does theirs."

An innocuous man, Mister Ariesen earned his living by doing whatever needed doing in the town of Concord, from mending bridles and harnesses, to sweeping out back rooms. He had helped build more than one of the fine houses the rich seemed to prefer to a more utilitarian home.

He did not make a substantial living, though his family never went without the necessities. There was always food in the larder and his children were never cold in winter for lack of a winter coat. The coat may have had a patch or two, but it kept them warm. In short, Jacob's father was a good provider to his family.

He worked hard the year round and did not partake of the drinking down at the public house—at least not too much. He wanted his wife to have the fine clothes he saw other women wearing. He wanted to provide a better future for Jacob and his two younger sisters. That is why, in the winter of 1850, he announced to his family that he had sold The Acres and they were all going to California.

Taken aback and trying not to let her emotions prevail, Missus Ariesen simply asked, "Isn't that expensive?" The older of Jacob's two sisters burst into tears and declared that she was not going to leave all her friends. Jacob's youngest sister asked, "Where's California?" Jacob, he was just stunned.

Mister Ariesen explained that they had enough to get them to a jumping-off point in Missouri with plenty left over to provision them for the trek. He informed his family that a few months earlier there had been a gold strike in California at a place called Sutter's Mill. "There's gold, big as hen's eggs, lying on the ground just waiting to be picked up. So we're going to be among the first people out there before it's all gone."

Jacob's mother did what good wives did in those days; she resigned herself to her husband's wishes. Jacob's sister continued to cry. The younger of the two said, "As long as I can have a gold bracelet, I want to go." Jacob, once he got over his initial shock, thought that this would not augur well for the family.

They had a week before they had to vacate the house and property. With so much to do, no one thought to ask for the details of how they were going to get to St. Louis, the closest town to a jumping-off point.

A jumping-off point, the town from which the wagon trains departed, was the last outpost of civilization. The two main towns were Independence and St. Joseph, Missouri. But down to the public house, there had been talk of brigands working out of those towns.

"They are dangerous places filled with thieves and cutthroats who'd just as soon rob you and leave you for dead as look at you. If a man is foolish enough to traverse to and have commerce with either locale, then he deserves the fate that awaits him. Go to Westport, Missouri. It is a much smaller town, filled with God-fearin' people," declared Dan Varney.

How Dan Varney—who had never ventured more than thirty miles from Concord his entire life—knew this, he did not say. It was said of ol' Dan that he had an oracular way about him. In matters of great import, he was never wrong. Therefore, based on Dan's counsel, it was decided the family would go to Westport, Missouri.

In reality, each jumping-off town sent out word that the others were dark and dangerous places filled with all sorts of miscreants. Much money could be made from the people who flocked to Missouri each spring, and every town wanted more than its share.

In 1850, train travel consisted of making a portion of the journey by rail, detraining to catch a barge on a canal going in your general direction, and then perhaps hiring someone with a wagon to take you to the next set of tracks owned by a completely different railroad company. The moneyed hired private coaches. The last segment of train tracks terminated at the Pennsylvania-West Virginia border.

St. Louis was to be the family's first destination. Once there, the sojourners would catch a riverboat that would take them two hundred miles due west on the Missouri River. When the river turned north, the travelers would disembark and hire one of the waiting wagons to take them into Westport. In the spring, there were always wagons in the offing for the people who were coming to make the two-thousand-mile trek over the California-Oregon Trail. It was a very good business.

The week following the sale of The Acres went by quickly, but not as fast as spring was seemingly approaching. If the family arrived in Westport too late in the season, they would have to wait another year before making The Trail.

When the day arrived for the family to depart, more than a few townspeople turned out to wish them well on their journey. The menfolk held Mister Ariesen in high esteem. They all wished it were they who were starting off on the great adventure. The women clucked their tongues at such foolishness.

The trip to St. Louis took longer and was more arduous than expected. There were places that had no transport to the next set of tracks, and sometimes it took a day or more to secure a wagon. Once the family reached the final terminus at the West Virginia line, it took three weeks before they found someone willing to transport them and their meager belongings all the way to St. Louis.

Chapter Three

THE FAMILY ARIESEN arrived in St. Louis on 9 April 1850.

People swarmed through the bustling city. Wagons, their wheels caked with mud, crowded the streets. Mud seemed to be all the streets consisted of with the spring floods in full bloom.

The family's first consideration was to find shelter. Every hotel, boarding house, and yes, even the flophouses to which Mister Ariesen would never have subjected his family, were full. However, a gentleman hoping to sell a wagon and team, informed Mister Ariesen of a place to the north of town where he might be able to hire a tent by the day or by the week.

"Space," said he, "is in short supply. And it gets worse every day with all you greenhorns a-comin' in. No offense."

"None taken."

Mister Ariesen found his way to the tent city all right, but once there, he had the dickens of a time coming to terms with the proprietor. After fifteen minutes of back-and-forth haggling, the proprietor agreed to $1.50 per night, which Mister Ariesen saw as highway robbery. He left to collect his family, thinking: *This man must be one of the brigands Dan Varney had warned me about.*

On the way, he thought of his friend back in Concord, Hank Thoreau, who night after night preached his Gospel of Simplification in the public house. He remembered Hank once said, "The cost of a thing is the amount of what I will call life, which is required to be exchanged for it."

If Hank was right, then I sure as hell just exchanged a good portion of my life for a few days in an old leaky tent.

11

He gathered his family and shepherded them to their temporary home. Once there, he announced, "We'll be leaving in three days on the next boat. The faster we quit this evil city, the better."

Mister Ariesen relegated Jacob to watch over the women while he ran about St. Louis. Consequently, there was not much for Jacob to do but sit and think. And the more he thought, the more he dreaded what his father had in mind for the family.

Is Father even thinking clearly? A two-thousand-mile trek across a mostly unexplored continent is not a walk in a bower.

On the evening of the second day, Mister Ariesen informed his family that they would be leaving first thing the next morning. He had booked passage on the steamboat *Andy Jackson*, an old but dependable paddle wheeler. He did not tell them that the extra time spent in getting to St. Louis and the exorbitant prices one had to pay for everything had seriously depleted the family's coffers. They would have to get to Westport and provision before their money ran out.

Early the next morning, the Ariesens were on the deck of the *Andy Jackson*, headed west. Mister Ariesen breathed a sigh of relief as they left the sinful St. Louis behind.

As the paddle wheeler neared Westport, the people on her decks gathered at the bow to get their first glimpse at what would very shortly be the last sight of civilization they were to see for a half a year or more.

"Jacob, you collect your mother and sisters and meet me at the gangplank. I'll attend to the bags," enjoined his father.

The family assembled at the appointed place along with the rest of the passengers. The throng pulsated as people pushed and jostled—everyone wanting to be the first off.

While waiting for the gangway to be lowered, Jacob observed the carryings-on of the people below him on the dock. There were numerous hawkers and drummers selling everything from charms that would protect one from mountain fever to Doctor Dennison's Tooth Powder. People were milling about with seemingly no purpose other than wanting to see the next crop of emigrants and sizing them up as to how best to fleece them.

As the gangplank lowered, the family dutifully got in line for debarkation. As they stepped off the boat, Mister Ariesen said, "Jacob, take care of your mother and sisters. I've got business to attend to. Here's five dollars. Secure us a clean and decent place to board for a few nights. I'll find you when I've completed my business."

Jacob escorted his family to a waiting wagon and asked the man tending the horse if he was the owner.

"Yes, indeed I am."

"May I inquire as to the cost of transport to the nearest decent establishment where I and my family can find shelter?"

"For the paltry sum of fifty cents, I'll take you anywhere in Westport you and yours wanna go."

In 1850, fifty cents was certainly not a paltry amount of money to most people. The good folks of Westport, Missouri—two thousand miles from the California gold fields—had struck gold of another sort.

Jacob's first impulse was to walk into town rather than succumb to such chicanery. But after considering his mother and sisters, he deemed it inadvisable. So he helped the women into the wagon, handed their bags up after them, then climbed up and sat down next to the driver.

"Take us to a lodging house appropriate for my family."

"That'll be fifty cents . . . in advance."

"I'll pay you when we get there."

Something in the lad's voice caused the smile on the driver's face to do a slow fade.

Perhaps the tenderfoot should not be trifled with.

He shrugged and gave the reins a shake. "Let's go, Betsy."

Westport was even more congested than St. Louis—if that were possible. Jacob saw men and women scurrying hither and yon as though Judgment Day were upon them. There were many dry goods stores and a multitude of blacksmith sheds with their ceaseless banging as mules and horses were readied for The Trail. Many of the shops were nothing more than tents erected helter-skelter. Wagons filled with families were going in every which direction . . . the father at the reins, his wife beside him, and the children peering out the back flap at the wonderland that was Westport.

Jacob had been deep in thought when they pulled up to the hotel. The driver roused him from his contemplation by saying, "Here we are, folks, all safe and sound."

Jacob looked up at the building that stood before him.

Well, this looks decent enough.

He asked the driver to attend to their baggage while he helped the women from the wagon.

"Haulin' grips ain't included in the price."

Jacob was on edge, what with his father disappearing— not to mention this fantastic journey they had embarked on with all its inherent dangers. He was in no mood to argue.

"If you want to get paid, then you'll do as I say."

The driver decided not to press the point. He had the bags stacked up nice and neat by the time the family assembled on the porch.

Jacob told him to wait while he went inside to get change with which to pay him. The driver frowned but said nothing. Jacob traversed the lobby and informed the man behind the counter that he and his family would be staying for a few nights, but first he needed change of a five-dollar bill to pay the man who had brought them there.

The clerk smiled and asked, "You talking 'bout a short little fella, horse's name's Betsy?"

"Yes, that's him."

The clerk turned to a man sorting mail. "You hear that, Marvin? Ol' Charlie got hisself another one." Turning back to Jacob, he said, "You greenhorns should know by now there ain't no accommodations in all of Westport. Charlie's been doin' this for weeks. Haulin' you suckers into town, chargin' ya fifty cents and letting ya think there's a room to be had when there ain't none at any price."

Without comment, Jacob turned and walked back through the lobby. He exited the front door and stepped out upon the portico where ol' Charlie was waiting for his fifty cents. Jacob grabbed the man by the scuff of the neck and the seat of the pants and tossed him out into the mud at Betsy's feet. He gathered his family, brought them into the hotel lobby, and told them to sit while he tried to figure out what to do next.

He decided that the best course of action would be to go out and try to find his father. He announced his decision to his mother. Then what Jacob had feared since getting off the boat happened at that moment—mutiny! The older of his two sisters stood up and said, "If you think I am going to sit here like a bump on a log while you and Father go traipsing all about, you've got another think coming, Jacob Ariesen!"

Jacob looked to his mother for support, but all she said was, "If you go, take your sister with you like a good boy."

To his sister he said, "If you're coming, then let's go."

Chapter Four

JACOB AND HIS SISTER walked out of the hotel and turned right. Jacob had no idea where to start looking, but he thought that if they walked to the end of town and then back again, they would eventually find their father.

As they passed a small alley between two buildings, they heard a voice say, "Hey, Bub and Sis." Jacob turned to see from whence, and from whom, the call had come. A rather large man emerged from the shadows, and with a surreptitious glance in both directions, made a sign for Jacob to approach.

"Hey, boy, ya wanna buy yourself an Arkansas Toothpick? It was me pappy's. Had it with him when he was with Colonel Jackson back in '14. Got him a mess of Injun scalps with this blade."

Jacob had no idea what an Arkansas Toothpick was, but something inside him drove him nearer. The man pulled out a very large knife from his belt. "Ya ever seen a knife liken this? A measly five dollars is all I ask."

Jacob informed the would-be knife seller he did not have *that* measly sum, and started to leave when he heard, "That's a pert nice Sis ya got there . . . maybe we can come to some kinda arrangement."

Jacob stood motionless for a moment, saying nothing. After a few seconds, he said to his sister, "You go to that dry goods store we just passed and inquire into the price of flour, bacon, and the like. I'll meet up with you in a minute."

Jacob had business to conduct with the gentleman holding the knife, and a man's business affairs were no concern of womenfolk.

After his sister had gone, he said, "Yes, I think we can make a deal. May I see the knife?"

Jacob accepted the knife and looked it over carefully before asking, "What makes you think you can insult my sister with me standing right here?"

The large man grinned and said, "Ya gonna dirk me with my own blade, boy?"

Jacob moved with a swiftness that surprised them both. He grabbed the man's coat with his left hand and pulled him close. Holding the knife in his right, he stuck it up under the man's chin and pressed until a small rivulet of blood trickled down the brightly polished, silver-like blade.

"I asked you a question. What makes you think you can insult my sister with me standing here?"

"I didn't know she was your sister!"

"Then why did you refer to her as Sis?"

"It's just a sayin'. You know? Them's just words, mister . . . Bub and Sis. Just words."

"How about I kill you because I just don't like the way you look?"

Jacob drove the blade in a little deeper and added, "I'm keeping this knife in payment for the insult, and if I ever see you on the street again, I'm going to slit your throat with your own pappy's knife. Got it?"

"Yes sir. No offense intended."

"Now go back from where you came."

Jacob took a step back, staring the man in the eyes the whole time—daring him to do to something. Instead, the man turned and ran back through the alleyway. Jacob wiped the blood from the knife on his pants and slid it into his belt.

Stepping out of the alley, he saw his father across the street, but because of the mud, crossing over would be no easy task. He called to him to get his attention. Mister Ariesen held up one hand—index finger pointing skyward, indicating, *wait a moment*—then scurried up the street where he engaged a man in what looked like a heated discussion. To Jacob's amazement, his father hopped upon the man's back as a small child would do, to be carried in a game of piggyback. In that fashion, they started across the street—the man stepping gingerly through the mud.

While that was going on, Jacob went to fetch his sister. It was the first store she had been to in almost two months and she was reluctant to leave when bid to do so. But she finally relented and followed her brother out the door.

As they exited, their father reached the boardwalk. He alighted from his carrier's back, reached into his pocket, drew out a nickel, and handed it to the man. Men like that were plentiful in Westport in the spring. They made a fair living during the rain and flood months transporting people across mud-filled streets.

When the Ariesens met up, Jacob started to ask his father where he had been, but before he could get the words out, his father said, "Got us a team and wagon. Had to plunk down hard cold cash, but they will hold up on The Trail. We'll get the longest use out of them."

"What are our plans? When do we buy our outfit, and when do we leave?" asked Jacob.

"The train leaves in two-and-a-half weeks . . . the first of the month. That gives us plenty of time to get what we need and make ready."

Jacob apprised his father of the lack of living accommodations in Westport.

"Doesn't matter squat. There's a staging area on the outskirts of town. We'll camp there until we leave. It'll give us good practice for The Trail."

"What about tonight?"

"Made a deal with the gent I bought the team and wagon from. We can camp a night or two behind his blacksmith shop, where the wagon is now."

18

Jacob started to ask another question but his father cut him off. "Jacob, I'll tell you all you need to know later, but for now, let's gather your mother and sister and get something to eat. I'm sure they're about ready."

Reaching the hotel, they found Jacob's youngest sister playing in the street making mud pies. Her mother sat on the portico watching over her.

The only place to eat that was not jammed to the rafters, seeing as how it was suppertime, was a groggery. A cheap drinking establishment that also served food. The family had their evening meal and proceeded to the blacksmith's shop to behold their home for the next seven or eight months. When Jacob saw the wagon, he was surprised at its size. It was nothing but a farm wagon with a cover! He had expected something larger, much larger. Something with heft, and he said as much. "Wouldn't it be better if we had a Conestoga instead of this little thing?"

"You can't control a Conestoga as you can this beauty. Look here, Jacob, underneath. It's got a kingpin so the front wheels can pivot."

Jacob got up from beneath the wagon and looked it over. It measured ten feet long and four feet wide, with a toolbox secured to one side and a water barrel on the other.

He next inquired about the team.

"They're grazing at the smithy's house. Got us six of the finest oxen you ever saw. Unlike mules, a team of oxen can pull a wagon through mud like it was paved with cobblestones. And they'll eat anything. You don't have to haul feed for them like you'd do for mules and horses. Just can't beat oxen on the trail."

That night the women slept in the wagon and Jacob and his father slept underneath. When everyone had settled in for the night, Jacob asked what the plans were for the next day.

"Tomorrow we start buying supplies. What we purchase, we'll bring back in lots. Your mother and sisters will stay here to keep an eye on things."

The next morning, they set out to provision up. The previous day, the man who would lead the wagons to the western sea, Jamison Cody, had told Mister Ariesen the amount of each item needed for the journey.

Cody, better known around Westport as Big Jim, had advised that they carry at least 200 pounds of flour, 150 pounds of bacon, 100 pounds of beans, 30 pounds of sugar and dried fruits, and 20 pounds each of coffee and salt. "That's all ya gonna be living on for six months," said Big Jim. He also added, "You run outta somethin' and it's gonna cost you to re-up at one of the trading posts along the way. Hell, a pint of flour will cost ya a dollar, when you can git it here for four dollars a barrel."

On The Trail, the diet consisted mainly of hoe-cakes— dough cooked over an open fire secured on the end of a stick—bacon, and beans. "We got us buffalo the first third of the way, but then it's gonna be hoe-cakes, beans, and bacon until you hate the sight of 'em," informed Big Jim.

Mister Ariesen and Jacob spent the day buying supplies and hauling them back to the wagon where the women packed them away, being careful to distribute the weight evenly. Two days later, the Ariesens were ready to move on to the staging area north of town. Jacob and his father started to lead the oxen, but after only a few steps, his father shouted, "Damn! I forgot something. Jacob, run down to the first dry goods store you see and get a bottle of linseed oil. Here's fifty cents. Also get a peppermint stick for each of your sisters and one for yourself if you want."

Linseed oil was rubbed into the cotton covers of the wagons in a vain attempt at waterproofing, but the covers still leaked to a certain degree. The peppermint sticks were to mollify Jacob's sisters who had been in a cranky mood all day.

Jacob returned, handed the candy to his sisters who sat next to their mother on the driver's seat, and stored the linseed oil in the wagon, behind the tailgate. His task completed, he walked to the front of the team and took hold of the lead pair's yoke. His father stood opposite, his hand also upon the yoke.

"Let's get going," said Mister Ariesen.

With those words, the family Ariesen started on the first leg of their two-thousand-mile journey—the five miles to the staging camp on the outskirts of Westport, Missouri.

Chapter Five

THE ARIESENS left the blacksmith's shop at dusk. By the time they neared the staging camp, it was full dark. Nevertheless, they had no trouble knowing where to go; they could see the campfires from a mile away.

Arriving at the edge of the camp, Jacob lit a lantern to search for smooth ground suitable for sleeping.

After he found an appropriate locale, his father goaded the oxen over and said, "Give me a hand unyoking these beasts. From this point onwards, they come first. For without them we are dead."

Once the oxen had been unyoked and hobbled, the family dined on hardtack and beans; the oxen grazed on nearby sage. The sleeping arrangements were different now because their supplies filled the wagon. The women slept under the wagon, the men on the ground next to them, one on each side.

The next morning, Jacob awoke to a cacophony of sounds. Now that it was daylight, he could see there were thirty or forty wagons spread out over a two-square-mile area.

His father was already out and about on one of his forays of discovery. Jacob was left to inquire at their nearest neighbor as to the location of the privy. He learned there were two trenches on opposite sides of the encampment, one for the men and one for the women. His perplexed expression won him additional information. "East for the women, west for the men."

Jacob took the information back to his mother and offered to escort her and his sisters to the convenience. "Don't be silly, we're going to have to start fending for ourselves sooner or later. You can't hover over us for two thousand miles." He knew she was right, so he headed for the west side of the camp.

He returned to find his mother in the process of filling the coffee pot with water. She asked if he could find enough wood for a fire. At first glance, it did not look likely, but he set off to see what he could find.

The area was well played out as far as firewood went. When he returned with his meager findings, his sisters were arranging stones in a circular pattern to encompass their fires.

While Jacob waited for the fire to get a start, a broad-shouldered man of about forty years, with sun-burnt hair hanging to his shoulders, approached. The lines in the man's face bespoke a rugged, outdoor life. His steel-gray eyes seemed hard, but were somewhat softened by his smile. He stuck out his hand and said, "Howdy, the name's Jim Cody. I'll be takin' ya'all to the other side of this great big land of ours. Where ya headed? California or Oregon?"

Jacob put his hand in the big mitt of a hand that was Big Jim Cody's and shook it saying, "We're going to California."

"Who's your old man?"

Jacob told him who his father was and added, "My father conversed with you two days ago."

"Oh yeah, the Yankee gent. Is he around?"

"At the moment I do not know where he is."

"That's okay, son. When he returns, tell him thar's a little business him an' me gotta talk over."

As Jacob watched the retreating figure of Big Jim disappear among the wagons, the smell of coffee reached his nostrils. With a shrug, he went to join the women.

After his breakfast of coffee and pan-fried biscuits, he decided he would scout around to see how the other emigrants built their fires, because there sure as hell was no firewood to be had.

"Will you and the girls be all right if I mosey around for a spell?"

"The girls and I will be fine; we have plenty to keep us busy. You go and have a good time."

He walked the camp, nodding to those he met along the way. At length, he saw a man starting to light a fire and approached him. "Morning, sir," said Jacob.

With a start, the man turned to face him and exclaimed, "Land sakes alive, boy, you nearly sent me to perdition. Aught not sneak up on a man like that!"

"I'm sorry, sir. I just wanted to inquire as to what fuel you are using for your fire."

"It betokens you've not been here long with a question like that."

"No, sir, we just arrived last night."

"Buffalo chips."

"Excuse me, sir?"

"I said *buffalo chips*; the plains is full of 'em. Easy to start burning, no smell, and they make a dandy fire. Most around here has been used up, but a mile or so out, they're as far and wide as the eye can see."

Jacob asked the man if he could watch him start the fire. He had never seen anyone light dung before.

"Sure, boy, you watch me. I might just learn ya somethin'."

With his chips piled in a pyramid fashion, he stuck a lighted stick into an opening at the base.

"That's all there is to it, boy. Where you saw me put the flame will now catch, and in a few minutes, we'll have us a dandy fire. But they burn so fast, you're gonna need a couple of bushel baskets of 'em just to cook a meal."

Once the fire got a good start there was an even flame. Amazingly, there was no odor! Jacob made up his mind right then and there to go and get a supply of chips for his family.

24

He was returning from his second chip-collecting expedition when he saw his father approaching. He hailed him, and together they walked into camp. Jacob discharged his load and informed his father of Big Jim's visit earlier in the day.

"Yes, we have a pecuniary matter to settle."

"In what respect?"

"Big Jim does not lead people across a continent for nothing. Each wagon going to Oregon pays him fifty dollars, and each wagon going to California pays thirty dollars." Jacob asked why the difference. "Well, when we get to Separation Pass and turn off The Trail, we'll be on our own. Big Jim will continue west with the people going to Oregon. It's a matter of miles. The more miles he guides you, the more you pay."

The following two weeks were uneventful. Days were spent sitting around waiting for the grass to grow tall enough to feed the oxen. They would not be going anywhere until they were sure that their stock could be fed.

After thirteen days of waiting, word spread that Big Jim had asked for every man, woman, and child to assemble at noon the following day. The news caused quite a stir. It was the talk of the camp that evening around the buffalo chip fires.

"You think we'll be leaving anytime soon? Is that what he wants to tell us?"

"Maybe."

"About time, any more sittin' around, all our supplies will be used up. The grass looks high enough to me."

"I don't think he has anything to say, probably just wants to hit us up for more money."

So went the conversations around the different campfires well into the night.

The next morning, long before the appointed hour, people started to assemble south of the encampment. Jacob and his family arrived just before noon and were relegated to the back of the crowd. There seemed to be about a hundred and fifty people present.

Big Jim strode into the crowd and made his way to an uncovered wagon. He climbed up, held up his arms high in the air and said, "Let's have some quiet, folks, let's have some quiet."

When things had quieted down, Jim said what he had to say.

"Looks like we got ourselves a fine boodle of folk here; seems like everyone showed. Alrighty, I got me some things to tell ya. An' I'll say 'em in no particular order. First of all, I'm not out for your approbation. You good folks hired me to git you to where ya wanna go, an' with the good Lord's help, I aim to do just that.

"We pull out in the mornin' at first light. We've got thirty-two wagons. To cut down on the dust, we'll roll four abreast of eight wagons each, separated by 'bout one hundred feet. Every day the lead of each column will change. The wagon at the end will take the lead, an' the lead will fall back one. This way you'll get a break from eating dust every eighth day.

"I expect you menfolk to be abstemious while on The Trail. Liquor just leads to trouble, like fights and even worse. Last year I had to hang a man who got drunk an' killed a fella over a woman. I'd rather not have to do anything of the sort this go-round. Let me make this clear, I am the law from the time we leave 'till we git to where we're goin', an' anyone breakin' my law or shuckin' his duties will answer to me."

Jim paused for his words to take effect before continuing. "We're all leagued in our common purpose. Be mindful of your dross, others have to live with ya for the next half year. If you flag, we cain't stop and wait for ya to catch up, so keep 'em moving. We gotta make it over them mountains afore the onset of winter.

"Thar will be very little laving on The Trail; water is too important. An' all you folks at one time or 'nother will be at your nadir. That's to be expected, but be mindful that others are countin' on ya to pull your share. An' anyone thinkin' of any hugger-muggery out thar or if ya think ya can gull me . . . well think again.

"Make no mistake about it, not all of ya are goin' make it; some are gonna die. Those that are a-dyin' will have to be left behind so that the rest of us don't join 'em. Seems harsh, but it's gotta be done for the good of the train. Mountain fever is our worst look-out. Nothin' to be done for the poor souls that git it.

"Watch out for your wagon wheels. Next to mountain fever, bein' run over and crushed is your next best chance of meetin' up with your maker. You greenhorns, careful with your guns. Had two men shoot theirselves last trip, one died. An' any man-jack of you caught molestin' womenfolk will git a bullet in the head from me personally.

"We're takin' the Platte-Sweetwater Trail. Done it afore, an' if ya'all mind me, most of ya will make it through. Last time we made Oregon in a hundred sixty-five days. They tell me those that left us at Separation Pass made it to California in a hundred an' thirty-five. That's it, folks, see ya at gloaming."

The mountain fever Big Jim referred to was a catchall term used to describe all ailments encountered on The Trail. Nevertheless, the number one killer of those who traversed The Trail was cholera. In 1850, the year of the Ariesen family's trek, five thousand deaths in the young United States would be attributed to the disease. It was not known at the time that the cause of cholera was contaminated water.

One hundred and forty-four souls heard the words spoken by Big Jim Cody that day. Every one of them about to emigrate to another land.

The lands west of the Mississippi were not part of the United States. Even California, in the spring of 1850, was not a state. California would not become so until 9 September 1850. Technically, the United States owned that part of the American continent west of the Mississippi River since the purchase from France in 1803. However, the United States Supreme Court, in the Johnson v McIntosh decision of 1823, ruled that Indians had a right to "occupancy and possession."

The next morning found the Ariesens in the second column, third from the lead. Everyone eagerly awaited the arrival of Big Jim so the journey to the Promised Land could commence. They did not have long to wait. If nothing else, Big Jim Cody was punctual. He rode up astride a large black mare he had named "Sweetheart on Parade," and she was easily one of the finest horses the good Lord ever made.[1]

Big Jim sat straight and proud as he inspected the four columns, making sure they were evenly spaced. After nodding his head in approval, he raised his right arm, and in a forward, arching motion he said, "Follow me."

With that one action and those two simple words, Jim Cody's infamous train that departed in the spring of 1850 from Westport, Missouri, and traveled into legend, started west, putting into play events that culminated in the largest mass execution in the history of the United States.

---

[1] Homage to John Stewart, Poet/Songwriter

28

The Trail

Chapter Six

IT WAS A GOOD START, but an inauspicious beginning. Within a mile of Westport, the formation of the columns broke down. A few wagons were tangential to their column but at right angles. Others bumped into their neighbors' teams. Mules refused to move after a short distance. One wagon toppled over.

Big Jim expected and planned for such contingencies. He had seen it all before and knew that no amount of talking would ready greenhorns for The Trail. He considered the first two days as "shake down" days.

"The best way for them greenhorns to learn anything is by letting 'em make thar own mistakes."

By day three, the four columns would be straight and proper or there would be hell to pay. As an incentive, Big Jim told the men that if they could not control their teams and keep up, they would be left to fend for themselves.

Neither the control of the animals, nor the slow pace, not even the sun, which beat down mercilessly with its scorching heat on man and beast alike, came anywhere close to the discomfiture caused by the pernicious dust. It hung in the air like a fog that would not dissipate. It lay upon the lips, invaded the mouth—it permeated everything. It filled one's eyes until they were red and raw from the grit. It filled the nostrils and forced the emigrants to breathe through their mouths, which filled their throats with the damnable substance. Even though the wagons were covered and the end flaps securely fastened, the contents were coated with a half inch of dust within days of leaving Westport.

Inside the wagons, the children lay on their backs and watched dust mites dance in and out of the shafts of sunlight that poured in through the small holes in the cotton covers. At first, the women would take great care to remove the dust from their hair and to shake it from their clothes at day's end. However, by day five, the women, like the men and the livestock, took the dust in stride. Except for a few short hours after a rainstorm, the dust was a constant companion on The Trail, along with the long days and the burning heat.

Big Jim had informed his charges that each day at dusk the train would halt for the night, no matter the miles traversed. The first day the train barely made eight miles, half of what it should have. That was to be expected. Big Jim knew the emigrants would do at least fourteen miles the next day, and then they would settle into a routine of twenty miles a day. Twenty miles per day was a little optimistic on Big Jim's part. If everything went smoothly, the goal of twenty miles could be achieved. However, things seldom went smoothly on The Trail.

Every seventh day was to be a day of rest—not for the people, but for the animals. On those days, the emigrants would work at repairing their wagons and equipment. Most of them had to learn how to hitch and unhitch their wagons in addition to handling the livestock. The people who made up Big Jim's train of 1850 were easterners, city folk. Store clerks, sellers of dry goods; just plain folk looking for a better life for themselves and their children.

On the first night, as the Ariesens were setting up camp, Big Jim sauntered in. "Saw how you folks handled it today, not too bad. But tomorrow we're doubling the distance. So be prepared."

Mister Ariesen declared, "Yes, sir. We aim to keep up our part. You'll never have to slow for us."

"Well, that's just fine, Mister Ariesen. Glad to hear it."

The next morning, before the sun made its appearance, Big Jim went from wagon to wagon getting the emigrants moving. He knew that, after the ordeals experienced the day before, the poor souls would rise from their beds upon the ground with the sensation of having battled their way out of perdition. Nonetheless, he showed no pity towards those he was to lead to the sea; they had another five or six months of the same—or worse—ahead of them.

The second day went more smoothly than the first. The train made fifteen miles. From the third day onward, Big Jim made damn sure the required twenty miles—or close to it—were covered before stopping at the end of each day. Still, problems of an individual nature did arise during the first week.

Many families had overloaded their wagons, and their teams could not haul such weight. Not to mention the strain put upon the axles and wheels. By the second day, many had come to the realization that personal possessions, even family heirlooms, were not as valuable as food and other items that were essential in making this once-in-a-lifetime trek across a continent. As a result, furniture, wardrobes, and trunks holding fine clothing littered The Trail. One wagon threw out a cast iron stove. Even food had to be jettisoned by families that had overstocked. Piles of flour and bacon were strewn about for five miles or more.

The Ariesens were traveling light. Their forty square feet of wagon space contained no superfluous items. As trains of the past had done, Big Jim's train of 1850 left its dross behind on its march westward.

By the evening of the fifth day, all the emigrants had learned to manage their teams sufficiently to start circling the wagons at night to provide a corral for the livestock.

The next day they encountered the buffalo. The herd extended as far and wide as the eye could see, stretching to the horizon and back again. Mile after mile, the train passed the great herd. None of the people who made up Big Jim's train had ever seen such a sight. In fact, very few people had ever seen so many animals congregated in one place.

The menfolk could not wait to get the wagons circled and take care of their livestock. They were in a hurry to shoot buffalo, not as a food source, but for the sport of it.

The women prepared the evening meal that night while the men went out "hunting." They slaughtered hundreds of the beasts. When each man had killed twenty or thirty, they wearied of the diversion and returned to camp for their supper.

Mister Ariesen had not joined in the hunt; he did not possess a rifle. Missing out on the fun had frustrated him to no end and, at length, he resolved to do something about it at the earliest possible moment.

After they had eaten, Mister Ariesen told his family that it was high time they got to know their fellow travelers better. "Think I'll mosey on over and get acquainted with Mister and Missus Johnston. Figure we can palaver for a spell. Why don't you join me, Jacob? It would be the neighborly thing to do."

While Missus Ariesen and the girls cleaned up the supper dishes, Jacob and his father walked over to the Johnston camp.

As they approached, Mister Johnston came out to meet them.

"Howdy, Mister Ariesen . . . Jacob."

"Howdy, Johnston," replied Mister Ariesen. "Thought we'd come over and visit for a spell."

Johnston smiled and said, "Come on in, folks, and meet the family."

Once seated around the fire, Mister Johnston made the introductions. "You know my missus, Clara. And these are our youngsters; Seth, Simon, and Phoebe. She's our baby."

"Mighty nice brood you got there, Johnston. You've seen my girls around. They're both the apple of their daddy's eye. The oldest is fifteen, the other is nine. Jacob here hits his majority this summer."

"Why, that's right nice; congratulations, Jacob."

"Thank you, sir."

After a while, they bid the Johnstons a goodnight, "Nice to have met up with you good folks. Come by our camp tomorrow, and I'll introduce you to the rest of my family," invited Mister Ariesen.

The Johnstons readily agreed.

As Jacob and his father walked back to their own camp, Mister Ariesen said, "We should visit the six other families in our column, get to know everyone. We'll need each other's support before this trek is over."

The next day was the first day of rest since leaving Westport. The Ariesens' wagon was in good repair, so Mister Ariesen had plenty of time to search out and meet new friends. He returned at mid-morning and spoke to his wife.

"Us men of the second column have decided to have one big fire for the noon meal rather than each family cooking over individual fires. Everyone is contributing their fair share of chips. We'll all bring our own food and cook it together. It will give us a chance to get to know one another a little better. Besides the Johnstons, who you know are from New York, there are the Mortons from New Jersey, the Walters from Pennsylvania, the Winstons who are also from New Jersey, and the Blairs from New York. Then there's the Garnetts and Suttons who are Missourians. Should be quite a conflux."

At mid-day, the families of the second column gathered for their first communal meal. The men carried in bushel baskets of buffalo chips. The womenfolk brought the food and wore their finest habiliments. They had inveigled their men to fetch the clothes from beneath the pounds of food stock in their wagons. Fine clothes were the last thing the women thought they would need on The Trail. Such items were buried deep within the wagons. However, for this particular confluence, and this one time only, the women wanted to look their best. Actually, only seven of the eight women of the second column wanted to show off their finery. One thought it foolish to dress up on the prairie. Jacob's mother came from sensible Yankee stock.

The children, as children do in all times and all locales, played games. The game of the moment was one in which a youngster tossed a buffalo chip, as one would sail a pie tin through the air, to another youngster who would catch it and then return it in like manner.

The meal consisted of buffalo meat, boiled rice, coffee, dried fruits, vegetables, and vinegar pickles. The last three items were an essential part of the emigrant's diet for the prevention of scurvy. Those who did not bring along such items usually came down with the disease by the time they reached the mountains.

After eating, the men and the women split into separate camps as men and women have done since the beginning of time. The women gossiped about the ladies of the other columns. The men, in between telling lies to one another, told of their history and the reasons for them being at that precise location at that precise moment in time. In other words, the men told each other of their hopes and of their dreams.

Mister Ariesen did not want anyone to get any ideas. Rather than tell his real motive for going to California, he told the men that he and his family were planning on become farmers. Yet, he need not have bothered with the lie. His wife had told the other wives the reason for their journey, and they told their husbands. His fear that some would want to go to the gold fields was off the mark. No one was going to be dissuaded from his own particular dream, gold or no gold. Each man had uprooted his family from a safe and relatively secure life for a dream. And come hell or high water, that dream was going to be realized.

That afternoon, after the Ariesens returned to their camp, Mister and Missus Ariesen compared notes as to what they thought of their traveling companions and their motivation for making the trek. Jacob's father started the conversation by stating, "Well, you know Morgan Walters is from Pennsylvania, but did you know he and his family are Quakers?"

Yes," responded his wife, "Missus Walters told me, and they have four children, two boys and two girls."

Mister Ariesen did not think *that* information very relevant, so he pressed on, "That Jonas Garnett was rather grum, I thought."

"His wife told me they're going to Oregon looking for farmland."

"That's what he said alright, but I don't know. He seems to be hiding something."

So it went for the rest of the afternoon until it was time to round up the children and start preparing supper.

Chapter Seven

BY THE END OF THE SECOND WEEK, the emigrants had settled into the daily routine of getting up before first light, building a fire, and preparing breakfast, followed by hitching up their teams, breaking up the circled wagons, and heading west. Six hours later, the train would stop for the noon meal—usually coffee, cold beans, and bacon—after which they headed westward once more. By the time they stopped for the night, most of the people were too tired to worry about anything fancy for supper. Boiled rice and hardtack usually sufficed. All were fast asleep on the ground soon thereafter. There was no sleeping in the wagons. Wagons were for the outfit—to carry the things that would sustain them on their journey.

The days stretched into weeks.

To break up the monotony, the emigrants not tasked with goading or driving a team would walk along with others of their column and talk as the hours and the miles passed. Sometimes the men would attend to the business of moving the team along, allowing the women to walk as a group and talk amongst themselves. At other times, the women handled things while the menfolk palavered about all the places they had never seen, like California and Oregon.

Mister Ariesen, being a naturally loquacious man, got to know his column mates quite well. There was the aforementioned Benjamin Johnston from New York with his wife Clara and their three children. He had owned a small printing shop in New York City where he printed handbills, pamphlets, posters, and bookplates. He had specialized in lithography. In the course of one of their many conversations, he mentioned to Mister Ariesen, "Did you know that back in 1768, Jean Baptiste LePrince discovered a way of achieving tone on a copper plate without the hard labor of mezzotinting? His technique was revolutionary. What he did was . . ."

His discourse was hastily cut off by an uninterested Mister Ariesen.

"I find that fascinating, Johnston, but I've got to get back to my team."

• • • • •

The view through the shop window never changes—the pedestrians, the horse-drawn carts, the wagons. It is the same, year in and year out. The shop is sweltering in summer. In winter, the ink freezes. Benjamin Johnston has been working on a procedure for the development of lithographic plates to print photographs onto paper. After two years of trying, the process, even with its many refinements, just will not work. A process will eventually be found, but not by Benjamin Johnston, and not for another twenty years. Mister Johnston owns the shop. It is better than working for another, but not by much, what with the rent and the cost of supplies.

It is late in the summer of 1849 when Mister Johnston throws up his hands in disgust and waves the white flag of surrender. On this steamy, hot August day, Benjamin Johnston calls to his wife Clara to come down from their rooms over the printing shop; he has something he wants to tell her.

As Missus Johnston descends the stairs, her husband says, "I am giving up on my process. No one will ever be able to reproduce and print photographs onto paper." In a sharp tone, he adds, "Look at that window. Look at that grime! How many times a week do you have to wash that damn thing?"

Misunderstanding Benjamin's meaning, Clara says, "I'm sorry, dear. I'll clean it right away."

"No, no, sweet Clara. That is not what I meant at all. I'm just frustrated with the whole setup. The boys have no open spaces in which to play and are forced to breathe the dust of the streets. No, Clara, I've had it! I want to live where the boys can run and play without fear of being run over by a drunken fish peddler's horse cart."

Clara Johnston had no idea her husband felt as he did about living in New York. She had never before heard him speak in such a fashion.

"So what do you have in mind, dear?"

"There's land, and plenty of it, out in Oregon. With what we've got saved and what I can get for the shop, we can outfit and go out there this spring. What do you say?"

Clara has also worried about the boys playing in the streets.

"For the sake of the children, I say that you are the man of the family and where you go, we will follow."

That night, the family Johnston gathers in their little parlor above the printing shop. Assembled are Mister and Missus Johnston, the two boys—Seth, who is eleven and Simon, who is nine—and Phoebe, age three. Mister Johnston tells the boys that in a few months' time they will take leave of New York City and make a new life for themselves in Oregon.

As children are wont to do, they became frightened by the idea of leaving their familiar surroundings. Seth says he will not go and Simon follows his older brother's lead. Together they swear they will never leave New York City. Phoebe is too young to understand the goings-on. Mister Johnston is an old hand at being a father; he simply declares, "This family is Oregon-bound, end of discussion!"

The shop has been up for sale for almost four months now and there have been no serious inquiries. Mister Johnston is starting to fret. Without the money from the sale, there will not be enough to get to Missouri, outfit, and stake them to a new life. This day finds Mister Johnston turning out handbills for Barnum's American Museum when a man walks in and introduces himself as Thomas Samuels. He inquires if the shop, as he has heard, is indeed for sale.

The upshot is that a deal is struck. However, Samuels wants immediate possession of the shop and the rooms above. This turn of events prompts Mister Johnston to alter the family's plans. He decides to make the journey to St. Louis in the dead of winter, believing that temporarily relocating within New York City would seriously deplete the family's funds. He reasons that things will be less expensive in Missouri.

The Johnston family spends Christmas Day at an inexpensive boarding house. On 26 December 1849, they set out for St. Louis. Mister Johnston has bought a wagon and horse. The wagon is not covered, but even if it were, the flimsy cotton covering found on farm wagons would not afford much, if any, protection from the cold. There will be time enough to get it covered in Missouri.

When the winter winds blow at a frightful pace and the weather is too severe for travel, they find temporary shelter wherever they can. It takes them seventy-two days to arrive in St. Louis. They are ensconced in the city on 2 March 1850. The town is crowded and the streets filled with people.

A dreary little man wearing a tow shirt emerges from the assemblage, approaches Mister Johnston within moments of the family's arrival and asks, "Neighbor, mind if I inquire as to which town you good folks be jumping-off from?"

"How did you know we were jumping-off from anywhere?"

"No offense, mister, but you folks got greenhorn written all over ya. Just wanted to give ya a little free advice, that's all. Be leery of Independence and St. Joe. Them towns fleece you greenhorns somethin' terrible. I ain't tryin' to sell ya nothin'. It's just I hate to see you emigrants get taken, that's all."

"Well then, what town would you suggest?"

"Ain't but one town treats folks like you right, and that be the town of Westport. Good day, neighbor. Hope I've been of some assistance."

Having offered his advice, the little man, who is in the employ of the town fathers of Westport, withdraws and amalgamates back into the array of bodies from which he had emerged.

Taking the man's word as gospel, Mister Johnston purchases tickets for himself and his family on the *Andy Jackson* for her next trip going north on the Missouri.

In Westport, the horse is sold, a team of oxen procured, a covering for the wagon obtained, and provisions purchased. Asking about, Mister Johnston finds that there is a one-and-a-half to two-month wait before a train leaves for Oregon. A man named Jamison Cody will head that train.

After a two-day search, Mister Johnston locates Mister Cody. They reach an agreement and Johnston pays over his fifty dollars. Cody tells Johnston to take his kit and kith to the staging area north of town and wait. "You'll know when it's getting near time to set out; the grass and sage will be tall enough to sustain your team."

The Johnstons are among the first families at the encampment. Time passes quickly and on the first day of May, the Johnston family finds itself in the fifth position of column two of Big Jim Cody's train that departed Westport, Missouri, in the spring of 1850.

Chapter Eight

MISTER ARIESEN RETURNED to his wagon and relieved his son from the chore of guiding the team. Jacob walked to the back where his mother sat on the tailgate and climbed up beside her.

"How are you doing?"

"Just fine, dear. I only wanted to rest for a spell. The walking wears me down some."

While they were speaking, Morgan Walters walked up.

"Afternoon, ma'am. Howdy, Jacob. Just thought I'd go up and chew the fat with Mister Ariesen for a while."

"That's nice, Mister Walters, and how are Missus Walters and the children this day?" asked Missus Ariesen.

"Just fine, ma'am, thank you for enquiring. I'll tell the missus you were asking after her." He finished speaking, ambled around the wagon, and headed towards the team.

"Afternoon, Mister Ariesen. Not too hot for you today, is it?"

"No sir, Mister Walters. But these mild days, I fear, are short in number. June and July's right around the corner."

"They surely are. By the bye, I was just speaking with Johnston; seems he was a printer. He was telling me the story of lithography. How it was invented by a Frenchman about sixty years ago. I found his knowledge of printing and its history quite fascinating."

"Yeah, he was telling me some such tale," affirmed Mister Ariesen somewhat indifferently. "What was your profession, Mister Walters, if you don't mind my asking?"

"No, not at all. I was . . . and maybe I still am, a saddler."

"Now I find that quite interesting. I always wondered how saddles were made."

43

"If you'd like, I would be happy to tell you right now as we walk."

"Sure, I'd like nothing better, and seeing as there's no place I've got to be at the moment, I've got all the time in the world." Both men chuckled at Mister Ariesen's attempt at humor.

"First, I always ask the person ordering a saddle what kind of horse it's intended for. Different type horses have different back structures. For instance, a gaited horse's backbone differs from that of other horses. And it's a real challenge to build for mules with their down-sloped backs.

"Then I build a wooden "tree" from layers of wood glued together. It's got to be steamed to put the rocker, or curved shape, in it. Next, I attach the stirrup bars and wrap the tree in the seat area with webbing. After that, I attach the webbing to billets and sew them together. It's pretty simple when you know how. The hard part is keeping up with the specific demands of individual riders. Any questions?"

"No, I think you explained it pretty well. Even a young boy could have followed that." Mister Ariesen was thinking that it was too bad he was not a young boy. If truth be told, he sure had the dickens of a time understanding half of what Mister Walters had said.

"Well, nice talking to you, Mister Walters. If I ever need a saddle, I'll know just how to make one. Now I think I'll have Jacob relieve me for a bit, so I can visit with Ed Blair. Want to come along?"

"No, thanks. I'm going to spell my wife for a while."

• • • • •

Morgan and Emma Walters are descended from Quaker stock. They live in Lancaster, Pennsylvania, with their four children: William, the oldest at fifteen; Hattie twelve; Ella ten, and Albert six.

It is the winter of 1850. Morgan Walters sits in his workshop looking out the window at the freshly fallen snow. He is thinking that there is no finer sight in all of Christendom than virgin snow upon the ground of the countryside.

After his moment of contemplation, he goes back to his work—a special-order saddle for Missus Dexter. Her daughter's sixteenth birthday is next week, and along with a horse that is safely hidden in old man Crowley's barn, the saddle is to be the daughter's birthday present. Missus Dexter is not a bad woman, but her incessant interfering in his work has started Mister Walters to thinking if there may not be more to life than sitting in a small workshop all day listening to people tell you how to apply your craft.

When he was young, Morgan Walters' dream had been to sail around the Horn and into unchartered waters.

Where did the years go?

He is now thirty-seven years old and owns a good and prospering business. He has the dearest wife in the world and four wonderful children. But in his heart of hearts, he is lacking something. Life has become dull for Morgan Walters.

A week later, the saddle for Missus Dexter's daughter has been delivered and all thought it his finest work. The snow outside his window is no longer pristine. It is dirty and muddy along the wagon tracks.

Wagon tracks? Wagon tracks! That's it!

At that moment, a plan evolves in Morgan Walters' mind.

We're going to Oregon or maybe California. I've heard tales about land out west just ripe for the taking. What an adventure! One in which my whole family can partake. I must speak with Emma about this right away.

However, it takes Morgan a few days to work up the courage to broach the subject with his wife.

The moment arrives when Emma is tidying up around the shop. Morgan remarks, "You know, I've been thinking. Don't you feel that life has turned a little stale for us? I mean the day-to-day drudgery, the routine. Do you know what I'm talking about?"

"Morgan Walters, if you have something to say, then say it. Don't waste my time and yours by beating around the bush."

"Emma, you know me so well."

"Well, Mister Walters, what is on your mind?"

"What is on my mind, Emma, is I think we should go out West, maybe California, where we can get some land. I can still make saddles, but they'll be for working horses. I'll be able to ply my craft without interference from people who don't know the first thing about saddle making. Those vaqueros in California only want a well-made saddle. They won't be coming in for fittings every other day. I hear that saddles have to be brought in by ship, and the cost is exorbitant. There will be a need for my craft as more and more people emigrate out there."

"Just one minute, Mister Walters. I let you have your say, now you hear me out. Are you proposing we uproot our children, our lives, and our livelihood for a dangerous six-month odyssey across this great big continent?"

"Well . . . Emma . . . I reckon I am."

"Morgan, I'll have to sleep on it. A decision like that will take some thinking about. Come, dinner will be ready shortly. Why not close for the day? After dinner we can go for one of those long walks like we used to, remember?"

A smile plays across Morgan Walters' lips as he affirms, "Yes, I remember those walks quite well. I also remember what we did as soon as we were out of sight of your father's house."

Blushing, Emma Walters leaves the room.

That evening, Morgan and Emma take their romantic walk. By the time they return, Emma has agreed to allow Morgan to follow his dream.

Time passes swiftly. There are matters to address and outstanding orders to complete. The house must be put up for sale and travel arrangements to St. Louis have to be made, among the myriad other things that need looking after.

It is now the middle of March, and Morgan Walters is in his shop putting the last of the family's personal items into crates that will be shipped in advance of the family's departure. He has nailed the lids shut on all but one. As he is about to do so, in walks his good friend Hiram George carrying a musket, a powder horn, and two leather pouches holding ammunition.

"Morning, Hiram."

"Morning, Morgan. I see you are just about ready to depart."

"Well, not just yet, not for another ten days. These crates are going ahead of us. The journey from here to St. Louis is no walk in the park. I figure it's best to travel light."

"Reckon you're right. Speaking about it being no walk in the park, there are savages out on the plains where you'll be traveling. I know your thoughts on violence, you being a Quaker and all, but you might be called upon to defend Emma and the children and I know you don't have a gun, so I brought you this."

Mister George holds out the musket horizontally in both hands. At first, Morgan is dumbfounded; he does not know what to say. The good people of his community know his views on firearms and their use. Still, the man before him is offering something of great value out of the goodness of his heart. To refuse the gift would also be against his religious precepts. Morgan accepts the gun with heartfelt gratitude and places it, along with the horn and pouches, into the last open crate before nailing it shut.

Today is the day of departure for the Walters family. They will travel by train to its terminus, and from there travel by coach to St. Louis. The railroad company has just instituted a coach service to St. Louis from where the rails end at the West Virginia border. It will operate for sixty days a year to accommodate the people flocking to Missouri each spring. It is a new service and not yet widely touted; very few people know of it.

The Walters family arrives in St. Louis on 7 April 1850.

As is the case for all newly-arrived emigrants, a jumping-off town must be chosen. Because Independence and St. Joseph are more widely known, Morgan chooses Westport as their point of departure. He believes it will be less crowded. The throngs in St. Louis annoy him to no end.

Once in Westport, Morgan learns that Big Jim Cody is the man to see concerning arrangements for the trek to The Promised Land. After he and Cody meet and settle the financial matter, Jim advises the family on the things needed for their outfit.

It takes them five days to procure the required items, including a wagon and livestock. On 17 April 1850, the family starts out for the staging encampment.

Thus, the family Walters found themselves in the fourth position of the second column of Big Jim Cody's train that departed Westport, Missouri, in the spring of 1850.

Chapter Nine

AFTER WALTERS' DEPARTURE, Mister Ariesen walked to the back of the wagon and spoke to his son. "I'm going to visit Ed Blair. So why don't you handle the oxen for a little while."

Jacob jumped off the tailgate and walked slowly westward—toward the oxen.

In the meantime, his father had reached the Blair wagon.

"Howdy, Mister and Missus Blair. Thought I'd stop by for a visit."

"Glad to have ya," said Mister Blair from beside his team.

"Yes indeed, Mister Ariesen," chimed in Missus Blair from up on the driver's seat.

"Mind if I walk along with you for a spell?"

"That would be right nice," replied Mister Blair.

"You know, I've just been talking to Johnston and Walters. Good folk they are."

"From what little contact I've had with them, I would have to agree."

Mister Ariesen continued, "They've been telling me of their work. Johnston was a printer and Walters made saddles for a living."

"You don't say? What did you do before starting this trek, Mister Ariesen?"

"Me? I was a jack-of-all-trades . . . and a master of none."

Both men enjoyed a hearty chuckle over that bit of wisdom.

"So, what's your profession, Mister Blair, if I might ask?"

"I was nothing special. I worked for a rich man in Albany, New York. I was a coachman. Actually, I was the head coachman. My wife, Polly, worked for the household also. She was the housekeeper. She had charge of all the female servants. She ran a tight household. In fact, she ran two tight households, ours included."

"A coachman, you say? What exactly does a coachman do? Just drive the coach from point to point?"

"Well, it's a bit more than that. As I said, I was the head coachman, and there was a second. The way it worked was I drove the coach with the team of two horses, and the second drove the one-horse coach used by his wife."

"Sounds like a good set-up."

"Yes, but being a servant kind of wears on one's soul. I had a lot of responsibility. I was in charge of the stables and the grooms. But with the responsibility come some advantages. We had a suite of rooms above the stables. It wasn't a bad life, but a man's got to stretch out. Go for the prize. You get what I'm saying?"

"Sure I do. We all are going for the prize. That's why we're here. By the way, tomorrow's our day of rest, or perhaps I should say our livestock's day of rest. Why don't we convene another community meal? We can palaver more then."

"Sounds like a good idea, Mister Ariesen."

• • • • •

It is 17 April 1844. The rain falls hard into the coachman's eyes, making it difficult to see the road ahead. He would have slowed long ago if he and the horses did not know the road so well. The left rear wheel dips into a rain-filled pothole—the second time in as many minutes—which brings a tapping from inside the coach. The master is telling his coachman to be more careful. It is a well-worn code between master and servant. The master does not like to be jostled about in his fine coach.

When they arrive at the house, the master does not wait for the coachman to alight from his seat and open the coach door. He opens it himself and steps out into the rain. Making for the dryness of the portico, he shouts over his shoulder, "That's all for tonight. Be here at 9:00 a.m. sharp!" Without further comment, the master vanishes into his fine, big house.

The coachman's duties are far from over. First, he must bring the coach to the courtyard where he and a groom will unhitch the team and put them in the stable. Then they will push the coach into the coach house. It is the groom's duty to attend to the horses, drying them and feeding them. Edward will have to clean the coach inside and out.

When Edward's work is finally finished for the night, he trudges up the stairs that lead to the rooms above the stables that he and his wife Polly inhabit.

Though it is late, Polly awaits her husband's return with a pot of hot cocoa to warm him on this cold and damp night. As Edward enters their front room, Polly inquires, "How did Mister Courtland's meeting go?"

"Based on his mood, I'd have to say not so well."

"Come, have some cocoa and get out of those wet clothes. You'll catch your death."

"Yes, dear. I'll be back as soon as I change."

Edward returns with a strange look in his eyes that Polly notices immediately. She asks, "Is anything wrong?"

"Let me sit down and marshal my thoughts. Then I'll tell you what I've been thinking on for some time now." Polly does not press her husband. Instead, she pours out the cocoa and sits down to take up her darning while waiting to hear what Edward has to say.

Edward finishes off the last of his cocoa and puts the cup down. "Polly, I don't know about you, but I dislike being a servant."

"Yes, but times being as they are, we are lucky to have a roof over our heads. And we both have good positions."

"It's just not good enough. When I was younger, I didn't mind the bowing n' scraping so much. But I'm thirty years old now, and I've made up my mind that within a few . . . a very few . . . years, we are going to improve our lot in life.

"I was thinking, Polly. You heard tell of the emigrants going out to Oregon and California where the land is free. Well, that's what we're going to do. I've been asking around and if we saved every penny for a few years, we could have enough to buy the necessities and then join with other families on the trail west. What do you think?"

Polly expresses her thoughts thusly: "It may take some getting used to, but seeing as we have no children yet, it may be a good thing. We're both young and strong. The journey shouldn't bother us none. Then, when we raise our family, it would be as our own masters. Yes, Edward, the more I think on it, the better your idea sounds."

Starting this night, 17 April 1844, the Blairs start to save for the journey of a lifetime.

It is now the evening of 30 October 1845. Edward paces frantically in the stable courtyard as two grooms look on. Upstairs in their rooms, with the help of the downstairs maid and the cook, Polly is about to give birth to the couple's first child.

The call soon comes down from the railing, "It's a boy, Mister Blair. A fine healthy boy!"

Edward thinks this is great news indeed, but his only words are, "And Polly, how is she doing?"

"Fine, Mister Blair, just fine. Why don't you come up and see her and your son in about fifteen minutes? We'll be ready for you by then." Edward turns to the grooms who had weathered the "crisis" with him and shakes their hands.

It is a few weeks before Edward thinks back to Polly's words of eighteen months previously ". . . *seeing as we have no children* . . ." and he wonders if having the child will make a difference in Polly's resolve to go west. He hesitates to broach the subject. He starts by asking, "How is little Aaron today?"

"He's doing just fine. My, he gets bigger and bigger every day. I never thought babies grew so fast. And every day he gets to look more like you."

That tact got him absolutely nowhere, so Edward has to come right to the point. "Polly, remember when we decided to go out to Oregon and you said because we had no children you thought it a good idea?"

"Yes, Edward, I remember."

"Has Aaron's birth changed your mind about going?"

"I have been waiting for you to bring up the subject, you silly man. The answer is yes, it does make a difference. We figure on having enough saved by next year, but I think putting an infant through the rigors of crossing a continent would be cruel. When Aaron is three, then we will go. Do you agree?"

"Yes, yes, I thought you might have changed your mind about the entire endeavor."

"No, dear. Let's keep saving, and we'll have just that much more to start our new life when we do leave."

It is a very cold February day and looks like it might snow. Once again, Edward Blair paces the stable courtyard, though this time he is alone. It is much too cold for anyone to join him. Edward is shortly put out of his misery when the call comes down from on high, "It's another boy, Mister Blair!"

Once again, the journey is postponed.

The second son, Isaac, will be four when the family starts for St. Louis. During the extended waiting period, Edward finds and reads pamphlets about The Trail. He is intrigued with the jumping-off cities. Without really knowing why, Ed Blair chooses Westport as their final destination before hitting The Trail.

The Blairs make Westport on 20 April 1850.

On the first day of May, they find themselves in the sixth position of the second column of Big Jim Cody's train that departed Westport, Missouri, in the spring of 1850.

Chapter Ten

ON THE THIRD DAY OF REST, the members of the second column met for their noontime meal. The women were the first to arrive at the large encirclement that was to be their cooking fire. The men and boys were out collecting chips.

Missus Winston sat down next to Jacob's mother and after an initial hesitation, she asked, "How are you finding The Trail, Missus Ariesen?"

"Oh, it's not so bad."

"I understand you hail from Concord, Massachusetts."

"Yes. Where do you folks come from?"

"A small town in New Jersey, Parsippany is its name. My husband worked in a local, or as you good folk from New England would call it, a public house."

"Missus Winston . . ."

"Please call me Martha."

"Well, Martha, I was just thinking that you and your husband are so young, and I notice you have no children. What made you pack up and leave your home?"

"John, that's my husband, he was very unhappy with his work. The late nights, the drunken revelry night after night just took its toll on him. We decided two years ago to go out to Oregon."

As Missus Winston finished speaking, her husband walked up with a basket filled with buffalo chips.

"Hi, Martha. Howdy, Missus Ariesen."

"John, I was just telling Missus Ariesen why we left New Jersey."

"We couldn't leave soon enough to suit me!" declaimed her husband.

• • • • •

The smoked-filled room with its raucous laughter and the incessant drone of many men speaking all at once is more than John Winston can stand. He is twenty-three years old and has been working in the tavern since he was eighteen. It is the evening of 3 July 1848, and the men seem to have a head start on the Independence Day celebration. Were he not recently married and a man of responsibilities, he would walk out the front door, never to return.

Later, after cleaning up the dross of the night, John bids the owner of the tavern good evening and walks the half mile to the little house he shares with his bride of six months.

Martha is waiting up for him as she does every night. This night she notices the worn look on his face.

"John, is anything the matter? You look drawn."

"I'm all right. It's just that I can't seem to stomach working down at the local much longer. I'd like a job that doesn't entail cleaning up the swill of drunkards every night."

"Well, what is it you think you would like to do?"

"I don't yet know. But I promise you this . . . before another year has passed, we'll be in different circumstances."

Four months later, John still has not found a way out of the unhappiness he feels about his lot in life. It is November 1848. The harvest moon is the brightest he has ever seen. Its beams shine through the front window and cut through the thick tobacco smoke, highlighted by the dim light in the room.

The moonlight falls upon a solitary figure sitting at a table by the window. He looks a lonely individual among the many men engaged in their pre-holiday revelry. John has never seen him before, but, for some unbeknownst reason, he feels compelled to speak to the man who sits alone, bathed in moonlight.

John serves drinks to the other patrons while keeping a watchful eye on the stranger. In spite of his natural reserve and despite the fact that the man's glass is practically full, John approaches, ostensibly to inquire if he may replenish his drink. He wants to speak to the gentleman; he does not know why, but he is drawn to the man as a moth to flame.

"Sir, may I get you another ale?"

"No, thank you, sonny. This will do for now."

John acknowledges the refusal, yet does not leave. Noticing the boy's reluctance to depart, the gentleman asks, "Yes, what is it? What are you looking at?"

"I'm sorry, sir, but there is something about you. I don't know what it is, but I feel I either know you or you have something of great importance to impart to me."

The man says nothing; he sits looking up at the boy until John says, "I'm sorry. If you wish nothing more, I'll leave you to your thoughts."

"No! Don't go. Please sit and stay a while."

"I am sorry, sir. The proprietor does not allow me to sit with the patrons."

"Nonsense, boy, you do as I tell you. Now sit. I'll handle any trouble that arises."

John sits down and the stranger says. "So, you think you know me or that I'm some kind of messaging angel sent here to impart the wisdom of the ages to you? Don't bother answering, boy, I'm only funnin' with you. My name's Jess Clanton and I hail from Westport, Missouri. I'm in the dry goods business. Just been up to New York setting up new sources of supply. My train came off the tracks about a mile back. So, while they get things straightened out, I thought I'd mosey on over here and be comfortable."

In 1848, train derailings were a common occurrence, and because of the slow speed were not as catastrophic as they would later become.

Clanton continued, "What's your handle, son?"

"John, sir, John Winston."

"You're a young lad. What's your dream in life?"

"Well, sir, I don't rightly know. I was just married."

"Congratulations."

"Thank you. I guess I'm looking to improve my station in life so I'll be a better provider and someday a good father."

"So, you've got no idea how to go about 'bettering' yourself?"

"No sir."

"Have you ever heard of Oregon and the Oregon Trail?"

"I know Oregon is out California way, but what is the Oregon Trail?"

"Son, the Oregon Trail is opportunity a-knockin' at your door. Every spring, emigrants flock to Westport and use it as their jumping-off point to adventure and riches, not to mention a new life. Did you know that there is land for the taking out there? Free land, boy. Free land!"

"How do I get some of this free land?"

"Just by goin' out there and claiming it for yourself.

"There are men who will guide you across the continent . . . for a fee. But first you'll need a wagon, a team, and provisions for about five to six months. Then you just go and get yourself some land. Look here, if you ever decide to follow the sun, use Westport as your jumping-off point. And be sure to come and see me at Clanton's Dry Goods Emporium. It's the biggest in town. I'll outfit you properly, and I'll help you with your other needs as well. Think it over."

After downing his ale with two swallows, Clanton says, "I have to go. They *must* have that damn contraption back on the tracks by now."

The stranger who calls himself Jess Clanton leaves money on the table and walks out, leaving John Winston with much to think about.

The clanging of the closing bell cannot come soon enough for John. He wants to get home and tell Martha the news. They are going to go to Oregon and become farmers!

John is so excited about the venture, his enthusiasm transfers to his wife. Rather than wait while the needed funds are skimped and saved, and with the audacity of youth, they decide to work their way to Westport.

Within a month, they start south. They are young and do not think about the rigors they will encounter along the way. As they make their way to Missouri, they find work, saving the money they earn. It takes the Winstons thirteen months to arrive in Westport. The date is 23 March 1850.

Their first stop is Jess Clanton's dry goods store. It's the busy time of the year, and Clanton is taking care of customers for the better part of an hour before there is a lull in the traffic and John has an opportunity to approach him.

"Hello sir. Do you remember me? I'm John Winston."

Clanton looks up from what he is doing and says, "No, don't reckon I can place you."

"Last year, up in Parsippany, at the local, when your train came off the tracks, you said you'd help me get outfitted for the Oregon Trail."

After a moment's hesitation, Clanton declares, "God sakes almighty, you were a skinny lad back then! You've sure grown a mite since I saw you last."

"Yes sir. I'd like you to meet my wife.

"Martha, this is Mister Clanton, the man I've been telling you about."

"Glad to meet you, and welcome to Westport."

"Thank you," replied Martha.

Jess Clanton tells one of his clerks that he will be gone for a short while.

"Come on, folks. Let's get us some coffee."

Once seated in the nearest flapjack establishment, Clanton addresses John. "Well, you took my advice, so now I reckon I'm kinda responsible for you and your missus. How much money do you folks have?"

"Nearly four hundred dollars, sir."

"Not enough, but you're getting there. You can stay at my place until we get you outfitted. Then you can get your 'sea legs' at the staging camp. John, you look healthy enough, you can work at the store to help pay for your provisions.

"Don't you young folk worry; we'll get you started westward. By the way, tonight you'll meet my brother-in-law. He's the man that will be taking you west. His name is Jamison Cody, Big Jim to his friends . . . of which he has many. He has a train leaving in about two months. I think we can even get Jim to waive his fee in your case. We'll just call it a family courtesy."

Which is how John and Martha Winston found themselves in the eighth position of the second column of Big Jim Cody's train that departed Westport, Missouri, in the spring of 1850.

Chapter Eleven

JACOB WALKED UP with his basket of chips and nodded toward John and Martha Winston. To his mother he said, "Is there anything I can get for you?"

"No, dear. Why don't you invite the Garnetts to join us? They seem a bit shy, always keeping to themselves."

The Garnetts had quite the little horde of children. Abigail was the oldest at eighteen, followed by Jonas Junior, fifteen, Elisabeth eleven, Alexander nine, and Virginia, the baby, five years of age.

Jacob approached their camp and spoke to Mister Garnett. "The folks over at the big fire would like you to join them."

Missus Garnett started to say something but her husband brusquely cut her off. "That's right neighborly of ya folks, but we attended the last one. We ain't much for mixin' with folk. No offense, son. That just be us."

"Well, sir, I kind of agree with you. There are just too many people over there. Mind if I join you for a spell?"

Missus Garnett spoke before her husband could say anything. "Can you stay and have dinner with us?"

"I'd like that."

Garnett said nothing. He busied himself building his fire.

Jacob retrieved his basket of chips and carried them over to the Garnett's camp. He handed them to Jonas, saying, "I understand you folks are from Missouri. Whereabouts?" Garnett ignored him, pretending to be busy stacking the chips. So it was up to Missus Garnett to answer Jacob's query.

"We're from Columbia. It's in the middle of the state, halfway between St. Louis and Kansas City. We was

61

croppin' . . . you know sharecroppin' . . . until my husband thought we should better ourselves for our children's sake. Croppin' is hard work and we don't want them growing up poor like us."

"Is sharecropping really that tough?"

That was more than Garnett could endure.

"Boy, you don't know what 'tough' is till you break your back farmin' forty acres, and year after year you got nothin' to show for it. The deal was the owner and I would split the proceeds fifty-fifty at the end of each year. He would supply the land and the money needed for plantin'. We was to supply the labor. But when ya don't own title to the crops themselves, and ya git cheated every year, there ain't nothin' ya can do 'cept swallow ya pride and take what's given ya. We was robbed every year for fifteen years straight!"

• • • • •

He has been in the field since before first light. He stands behind a mule. Harnessed to the animal is a plow. In turn, he is harnessed to the plow. The sun that beats down upon his thin frame is unforgiving. Sweat pours from his face. Over the years, his skin has turned a dark brown—he has aged before his time.

By the position of the sun, he knows his woman will soon be calling him to his noon meal. However, he must turn one more row before stopping. He has to get his crop planted.

As he fights with the plow to keep the furrows straight, he thinks.

Here I am, forty-two years of age and not a red cent to my name that I can call my own. Hell! This mule, this plow, even the house I live in belong to another man. A man who robs me every year. And if I dare say anything or call him out on it, me and mine would be tossed off this land faster than I could say 'Jack Robinson'."

Nearing the end of the row, he hears his woman call him to dinner.

Upon entering the house, he smells freshly baked bread, which reminds him of his childhood. In spite of himself, he smiles.

Hearing him in the front room, his wife comes out of the kitchen and suggests he wash up, adding, "I know how hot it is out there. I've made you some lemonade to cool you down. It's on the table. Dinner will be ready in a few minutes."

He walks through the house and out the back door to where a pitcher and basin sit on a small table. He bends down over the basin, picks up the pitcher, and pours water over his head. Grabbing the cake of soap off to his right and using the water in the basin, he washes his hands and face. Once the ritual is complete, he tosses the spent water and soap onto the dry, brown soil that surrounds the house. He goes inside and takes a seat at the kitchen table.

After placing his dinner before him, his wife sits down opposite her husband.

"All right, Jonas, tell me what you're thinking. You haven't been yourself for months. And that look on your face is enough to scare the bejeebers outta ol' Mister Scratch hisself. What is it, dear?"

"I'm plumb tuckered out, that's all."

"Look at me, Jonas. It's me . . . Mary. Your wife. I can read you like a book. Now let's have it."

Jonas softens and looks into his wife's eyes.

"We've been croppin' for near on fifteen years and where's it got us? We don't own no more today than we did the day we was married. And now we got a flock of offspring to consider. Miller, he keeps us just poor enough so I hafta keep on workin' for him. He knows there's nothin' I can do, we need this house. If not for it, where would we be?

"Lately, I've been figurin' out how much we've been cheated out of over the years by that no-account mudsill. I figure it's about eight hundred dollars . . . eight hundred and seventy-five, near as I can reckon. With that money, we could go to Oregon, git us some land of our own. Git a new start. Our children would have it better than what life handed us. And you, Mary, if we stay here much longer, you'll wither and die before your time, what with takin' care of me and the children and what ya do up to the big house just to help ends meet."

Jonas Garnett is not a man of long and fiery speeches. His wife has not heard him so passionate in a very long time. She reflects on what he has said, then replies. "Yes, Oregon would be wonderful for the children, but where would we get the wherewithal to get there?"

"I've been a-thinkin' on that too. I figure we're owed somethin' from Miller and I aims to git it. And I don't give a jugful on *how* I git it."

The date: 13 November 1849 and Jonas Garnett's crop has just been harvested. As in years past, it is handed over to the titleholder. Miller surveys the wagons filled with the product of another man's labor and turns to his tenant. "Hot damn, Jonas! This has indeed been a bumper crop all right! You sure got the touch, but I tell you that every year. Still, it doesn't make it any less true. See you in a week to ten days with your share of the proceeds. Of course, you know that there have been added expenses, like when your little Virginia took sick. The doctor wasn't cheap, but we did what needed doing."

Garnett knows that the doctor is a friend of Miller's and had not charged him. It is at that instant that Jonas Garnett knows for certain where he is going to get the money to leave his indentured servitude behind.

It is now 27 February 1850. The time: 11:20 p.m.—a moonless night. Jonas Garnett is walking the road that leads from the house he occupies with his family to the big house occupied by Miller. A few years back, and quite by accident, Jonas discovered where Miller hid his assets.

Just before Christmas, 1847, Miller had asked Jonas if he would like to earn a little extra money building a bookcase for his study. Being as how it was Christmas time, Jonas readily accepted the commission.

While installing the bookcase, he stepped upon a loose floorboard. Thinking he might repair it and maybe earn an additional fifty cents, Jonas probed the board and it sprung open revealing a steel box. Out of curiosity, he withdrew the box to inspect its contents.

The cash and gold coins that stared back at him started his heart a-racing. Not at the sight of so much currency and gold, but because he feared if anyone were to walk in at that moment, they would think him a thief. He hastily put the box back into its resting place and replaced the floorboard. That was three years ago.

Jonas arrives at the big house and finds it silent and dark—as expected. He goes to the study window and opens it to effect his ingress. Once inside, he knows just where to go and what to do. The floorboard easily springs open, the box still hidden within.

Jonas Garnett is not a thief; he has come only to extract what is rightfully his. He had the foresight to bring a small tallow dip with him, and this he lights. Since his last tally of eight hundred and seventy-five dollars, Jonas has figured that Miller cheated him out of an additional seventy-five dollars for this year's crop, which makes it nine hundred and fifty dollars that he is owed. He has brought a piece of paper with him, giving the amount taken and why. He plans to leave it in the box.

Taking the currency in hand, he counts out nine hundred and fifty dollars and puts the rest back into the box. He is just about to place in the receipt when he hesitates.

It may be days, or even weeks, before the money is missed. We'll need time to git to St. Louis, and then to a jumping-off town. Once on The Trail, I don't give a dang who knows about it. It's my money. I earned it by the sweat of my brow. Miller stole it from me. Let any man say different!

The receipt goes back into his pocket.

The Garnetts reached their jumping-off town of Westport and found themselves in the first position of the second column of Big Jim Cody's train that departed Westport, Missouri, in the spring of 1850.

Chapter Twelve

JACOB sat at the Garnetts' fire while Missus Garnett and Abigail prepared the food. He spoke with the Garnett children, mostly with Jonas Jr.

"Well, Jonas, what are you going to do when you get to Oregon?"

"Me and my father are gonna start a farm. He says we're gonna be gentlemen farmers."

"Do you know what you'll be growing?"

"Not yet. He says we've got to git there first. You know, git to know the lay of the land."

About then, dinner was called.

After eating and helping with the cleanup, Jacob thanked the Garnetts and bade them a good afternoon. He walked over to the big fire and sat down beside his mother and father.

Looking up from sewing a patch on one of his sister's dresses, his mother asked, "How are the Garnetts? Did you enjoy your meal with them?"

"Yes, Mother, they are very nice people. Even Mister Garnett, once he lets his guard down."

His father chimed in, "I don't know, seems there's something off there."

Missus Ariesen promptly replied, "Mister Ariesen, where is your Christian love for your fellow man?"

For once, her husband had no ready reply.

The people whose wagons needed no repairs were milling about the large fire and talking to one another. It was a nice respite from the previous six days of drudgery and the never-ending dust.

Mister Ariesen was fighting with a hoe-cake, trying to keep it from falling off the stick and into the fire. He did not have much luck with hoe-cakes. He usually burnt the outside while the inside stayed doughy and uncooked. Nevertheless, this day he intended to get one of the little buggers cooked—and cooked properly—if it killed him. So intent was he on his fight with the hoe-cake that he did not notice Nate Morton walk up and sit down beside him.

"Afternoon, Missus Ariesen, Mister Ariesen . . . Jacob."

After his wife and son responded in kind, Mister Ariesen said, "Sorry, I didn't see you come up. How's the missus?"

"She's doing fine. She's over there speaking with Missus Sutton. Where are your lovely daughters?"

"They're around here somewhere. I think they fell in love with the little Blair boy. You know females. No matter the age, they're gonna mother someone."

"Reckon you're right," replied Nate Morton.

As the battle between Jacob's father and the hoe-cake intensified, Nate Morton ruminated aloud, "I kind of wish it would rain. At least it would cut down on the dust for a little while."

Mister Ariesen was so preoccupied with keeping his bread on the stick and not letting it fall into the fire, he took a moment before responding. At length he said, "Big Jim tells me the storms out here on the plains can be pretty rough. The wind and lightning . . . hail as big as a man's fist. But I know what you mean about the damn dust. I must have swallowed a pound of it since we left Westport."

He finished speaking and withdrew his bread—it was burnt black as usual. He threw it into the fire, issuing a soft "damn" under his breath. He turned to Nate Morton and said, "Mister Morton . . ."

"Call me Nate, everyone does."

"Okay, Nate. I see besides your family, you're traveling with a man."

"He's my wife's brother. We went into this venture together. He's all right, I like him."

"Just a second, Nate, let me get another cake. I'm going get one of those damn things cooked if it takes me all night."

●●●●●

9 October 1849, a cold and blustery day. The men with the block and tackle pull and heave the stone figure that is to adorn the edifice before them. The wind is of such a high velocity that the load, as heavy as it is, sways back and forth at a twenty-degree angle.

When the figure is three-quarters of the way up the building's side and almost to its perch, the knot on the line suspending it slips. The one half-ton of limestone comes hurling to earth and crashes not twelve inches from one of the men who, until a moment ago, was lifting the now smashed gargoyle into place.

The man's fellow workers rush to him. One exclaims, "Nate, you all right? That damn thing missed you by a cat's whisker!"

The man's name is Nathaniel (Nate) Morton. He is thirty-seven years old and a fixer mason. His job is to lift accouterments, such as gargoyles, saints, or what have you, to the top of new buildings. Once in place, he affixes it with mortar and grout. Nate has been a "fixer" for nine years. Prior to that, he was a quarryman, splitting the rock and removing it from the earth. His dream was to become a banker mason, carving statues in the workshop. However, the near miss has crystallized something that had been fomenting inside of him for a long time. Now that the statue is no more, the men decide to call it quits for the day and go home early.

When Nate arrives, his wife Rebecca (Becky) is alarmed. "You didn't lose your job, did you?"

69

"What makes you think that?"

"Well, you've been sort of moody of late and I had a feeling it had something to do with your work and now here you are, home early."

"No, I didn't lose my job. We quit early because there was an accident and the statue we were to place on the Bonner Building was destroyed."

Nate had decided not to tell Becky the nature of the accident. He does not want to worry her needlessly.

"But you are right. I am frustrated with my work. Eight long years breaking my back in the quarry, and now almost ten years hauling tons of rock up to the top of buildings. I am not a young man anymore."

In an effort to change the subject, he asks, "Where are the girls?"

Nate and Becky have two beautiful daughters, Maddie, who is nine years old, and Carrie, who is six.

"They're out with Ham."

Ham is Hamilton Richards, Becky's brother. He works as a clerk for the City of Newark in the Department of Roads and Public Works.

Becky does not press the matter. Instead, she tells Nate to go wash up and relax while she prepares dinner. Then she thinks of a better plan, "Why don't you go down to the local and have an ale. On your way back, you can stop in at Harriman's Bakery and get something sweet for dessert."

Nate, thinking that is a capital idea, readily agrees. After washing up, he leaves for the local.

Just outside the front door, he runs into his brother-in-law who has Maddie and Carrie in tow. Or it may be the other way around; Nate is not exactly sure.

"Hello, Daddy," the girls say in unison.

"Hello, girls. Why don't you go inside and help Mother with dinner? I want to speak with Uncle Ham for a while."

As soon as the girls are in the house, Nate says to his brother-in-law, "Come with me. Let's go have an ale and talk."

Hamilton Richards is, if nothing else, a man who never refuses an offer of libation.

They enter the drinking establishment, order their ales, and seat themselves at a table in the far corner of the room.

Ham says, "You look vexed. Is anything wrong?"

"I'm unhappy with my work. Down at the shop, they tell me to be patient . . . that my time will come. But I know that every banker in that shop has at least another ten or twelve years left in him. I'm sure as hell not going to be hauling stone up the side of buildings when I'm nearing my fiftieth year. No sir, that is not going to happen!"

After taking a long pull on his ale, his brother-in-law says, "I'm on the same train as you. Those sons of bitches down at the Department ain't dying fast enough to suit me. Hell, I'll be well along in my dotage before I'm offered any advancement."

For a few minutes, the two men sit in silence, drawing on their ales.

Suddenly, Ham slaps his open palm down upon the table, jarring Nate out of his thoughtful contemplation. "I got it! I know where a man can be his own man, where there's land just waitin' to be claimed. Nate, we gotta go to California."

"What do you mean? Sail there? We can't afford to do that."

"No, we take the California-Oregon Trail. A man I work with, his brother did it two years ago and he just got his first letter from him last week. The brother tells of all the space that's out there. Between the two of us, we can claim two sections. That's three hundred and twenty acres! We can pool our money. I can talk to Jonesy tomorrow and get some of the details on how his brother did it. What do you say, Nate?"

"I've got to do a little thinking on this. You have no responsibilities, but I have Becky and the girls to think of. I have to talk it over with Becky first, but you find out what you can from your friend."

The following night after dinner, while Maddie and Carrie ready themselves for bed, Nate, Becky, and Ham sit around the kitchen table as Ham tells of his discussion with his co-worker, Jones.

"First of all, his brother said he went to St. Louis and from there to a jumping-off town, which is where you outfit and leave from. He also said that although it wasn't all peaches and cream—sixteen people died from mountain fever along the way—they had good luck and made it to California in four and a half months. He tells his family he's happy and damn glad he made the journey."

Nate turns to Becky and asks, "Well, what do you think?"

"What do I think? You know darn well, Nathaniel Morton, that if you decide to go to California, the rest of us would have to pack up and go along if we wanted to or not." Taking a moment to catch her breath, Becky continues, "Look into the matter and see what it will take. I'm not against going if we can afford it and it's not dangerous for the girls."

Nate smiles at Becky, takes her hand, and says, "You're a good woman, Rebecca Morton."

Either through happenstance or the vagaries of fate, the Mortons, along with Hamilton Richards, found themselves in Westport, Missouri, on 1 May 1850, in the second position of the second column of Big Jim Cody's train as it traveled into legend.

Chapter Thirteen

MISTER ARIESEN came back with a new hoe-cake and said to Nate, "My wife is making up some batter for flapjacks. Thought we'd griddle us up a batch. We'd be pleased if you and yours would join us."

"If you're sure we won't be obtruding."

"Hell no, glad to have you. My missus is making plenty. I see your missus is still speaking with Missus Sutton. Invite the Suttons over too. I don't know Al Sutton all that well. This will give us a chance to get to know one another."

"Sounds like a good idea. I just need to slap some grease onto my hubs. The damn dust is caking there bad and getting into the axles. I'll extend your invite to the Suttons and I'll be back before the griddle gets hot."

As Nate walked away, Mister Ariesen's hoe-cake falls off the stick and into the fire.

● ● ● ● ●

"Here comes Smith. You know what that means; we'll be loading his lousy cotton well-nigh into the night. I tell you, Al, there ain't no rest for the wicked."

Al can only agree with the man who spoke those words. There is indeed no rest. He does not know about the wicked, but he knows there sure as hell ain't no rest for Alfred Sutton. This he knows only too well, but that is about to change.

Smith strolls up to Captain Allison, Master of the *Andy Jackson.*

"Evening, Captain. Got room for my cotton this trip?"

"How many bales?"

"Just forty. I bought 'em outta Woodbine's warehouse. He had 'em left over from last season."

"Sure, we can take 'em."

Al hears this and groans inwardly. He was looking forward to getting home to his wife and son. At least he won't have to put up with this sort of thing much longer.

He thinks back to the winter of '45 when he made his momentous decision. It was a cold day in February, and the bags of grain going on the *New Orleans* were just about stored when the captain shouted, "Sorry, boys. Someone made a mistake. It's all gotta come off. We're going south and the gent wants his goods up in Davenport. Can't see how we can go in two directions at once."

That was the proverbial straw that broke the back of the proverbial camel for Alfred Sutton.

That night, on his way home, he thought of all the cargo he had loaded on board the various boats going upriver carrying the emigrants on their way to Oregon and California.

Upon arriving home, as tired as he was, the first words to his wife were: "Is Teddy still up?"

Teddy is Theodore, their three-year-old son.

"No, dear. I fed him and put him to bed a while ago. I didn't know what time you'd be home."

"The way they run that dock, it's a wonder I make it home at all."

"Would you like your dinner now?"

"Not right now, Cassie. Let's talk for a minute."

"What's on your mind, Al?"

"For the past three years, I've been loading emigrants and their gear onto boats going west on the Missouri. I've seen all kinds of people, young, old, some even going by themselves with no family. But one thing they all had in common was the look in their eyes. It was a look of hope, of a new beginning, of a better life ahead. And I've been

74

thinking if they can do it, why not us? Please, Cassie, before you say anything, hear me out. I've got it all figured. If we cut down on a few things and start saving a little each week, we could have enough saved in four or five years to get us to Oregon, with enough left over for a good start.

"I know a man who works out of Westport. He leads a train west every spring, his name's Cody. I'll write him to see how much we'll need to outfit. And Captain Allison—you know him, he's the captain of the *Andy Jackson*—I'm sure he'll give us passage to Westport. Alright, Cassie, now what do you think?"

Cassie Sutton is, as most women are, one smart cookie. When a woman sees that her man has his mind set on something, the only thing to do is go along. Therefore, she answered Al's question with a question of her own, "How long did you say we'd have to save?"

That was five years ago.

After years of scrimping and saving, they have their bankroll—their grubstake—to a new and better life. This Saturday when Al gets his pay, that will be the end of dockworker Al Sutton and the beginning of Alfred P. Sutton, Esq. and Oregon landowner.

Al helps load the bales of cotton, but his mind is on the verdure of his Oregon land.

A week later he, Cassie, and Teddy find themselves on the deck of the *Andy Jackson*. Captain Allison has given them free passage as a sort of going-away present. They will disembark at Westport.

In the last letter received from Mister Cody, he stated that he would meet the family at the dock and get them started with their outfitting and provisioning. Once properly outfitted and provisioned, they will go to the staging camp. The date is 20 April 1850. In eleven days, they will find themselves in the seventh position of column two of Big

Jim Cody's train that departed Westport, Missouri, in the spring of 1850.

There were, of course, other families on Big Jim's train of 1850, but these seven—Johnston, Walters, Blair, Winston, Garnett, Morton, and Sutton—were leagued with the Ariesens . . . for better or for worse.

Chapter Fourteen

THE NEXT DAY, the emigrants were up and on The Trail before dawn. They had miles to cover.

With the sun directly overhead, they stopped for their noon meal. The families sat in the shade of their wagons eating cold food. Dark clouds hugged the far horizon off to the northwest, and lightning could be seen in the clouds. However, the storm was too far away for any thunder to be heard. The emigrants looked skyward with eager anticipation and watched the clouds come their way as they prayed for a rain that would give them respite from the omnipresent dust, if only for a few hours.

However, Big Jim knew the dangers of a thunderstorm on the plains. There was nothing to attract the lightning except the people, the animals, and the wagons. As the families made ready to continue the day's march, Big Jim rode from column to column telling each that when the storm broke, everyone was to stop where they were and get into their wagons—fast.

The air cooled, the wind picked up. The drop in temperature was a welcome relief to the people of the train. Black clouds now covered the sun. Wind blew the dust away. A few minutes later, the first drops fell. At first it was a light rain, just a few drops here and there. Then the wind increased to an almost gale force and the heavens opened.

The families halted their teams and scrambled to get into their wagons. Jacob and his father had applied the linseed oil while at the staging camp, which kept most of the rain out. Lightning hit all around, followed by claps of thunder that made the emigrants jump. It was a frightful experience.

As the Ariesens huddled in their wagon, they could feel it sway from the force of the wind. The cotton cover rattled; the end flaps fluttered tumultuously. Jacob chanced a look out the back and saw the tall prairie grass bent over in a horizontal position, parallel to the ground. Just then, a lightning bolt struck nearby and the family felt the excessive discharge of electricity. The resulting thunder clap was so loud that Jacob's youngest sister started to cry. Her mother took her to her breast in an effort to soothe her. But her words of comfort were lost within the turbulence of the storm.

When they thought the tempest had hit its full intensity, a resounding *BANG* was more felt than heard against the side of the wagon. Then another . . . and another. The sound built up slowly until it was a steady drumbeat. It was hail, and with the hail, the storm raged harder than ever.

An hour after the assault commenced, when it seemed the fury would never cease, a calm descended on the train. A light rain still fell, but the men were beginning to emerge from their wagons to see what damage the storm had caused. Big Jim rode to each column and said to all within hearing distance, "Alright men, check your wagons, but we move out right away. We've already lost too much time."

There was only one hitch in Big Jim's plan. The storm had turned the floor of the prairie into a slough. The wagon wheels had sunk into the soft mire, some as much as eighteen inches. The teams struggled mightily to move their loads, only to have the wheels, after moving an inch or two, fall back to their original position. If the wagons could only get a start, the teams would be able to keep them moving. It would be slow moving, but on The Trail, you moved or you died.

Jim saw his people sloshing around helplessly without the faintest idea of what to do. With a deep sigh and a shake of his head, he rode to the head of each column and told the men to stop beating their animals. It was not doing any good. He ordered the women and children from the wagons and told the men to wait for him at the lead wagon of their respective columns.

Once they had assembled as ordered, Jim went from column to column and said the same thing, "Listen gents, the only way you're gonna git your wagons a-movin' is by pitchin' in and workin' together. We're gonna move one wagon at a time from each column. We start with the lead here. The owner takes care of the team and four of you men git back thar at the tailgate. You other three, each take a wheel. Thar's no need to beat the livestock, just makes the mules ornery and does no good at all with the oxen. We got eight strong men here; we'll git 'em movin'. Tell your womenfolk and young'uns to stay outta the way. This can be dangerous work. Them wagon wheels can crush a man's bones to powder, and it's easy to slip in this muck. After she gits up a head of steam, turn the team over to your missus. Then ya' all git yourselves back to the next wagon, and do the same gall darn thing all over agin."

On that day, the lead wagon of the second column belonged to Benjamin Johnston. The men did as ordered— Johnston with the team, the others going where Jim had directed. Walters, Blair, Winston, and Garnett at the tailgate. Morton took the left front wheel, Sutton the right, Mister Ariesen on the right back wheel.

• • • • •

Johnston prods the oxen; the four men at the back put their shoulders to the wagon and push with all their might. The three other men grab onto the steel rims of the wheels, and pull and jerk, trying to free them from the mud. It is hard to get a footing and push at the same time. However, little by little, the mire gives way and there is a sucking sound as the wheels start to turn. At first, it is only an inch, but slowly, as the oxen tug at their load and the men push, the wagon starts to move.

As the wheels come around, mud sticks to the metal rims making them slippery. The men on the wheels have to grab onto the spokes to get traction. After a few feet, the wagon bogs down again.

Watching the drama is Benjamin Johnston's eleven-year-old son, Seth. Like many boys his age, he considers himself far too grown up to be with the women and children. Looking at the struggling men, he thinks to himself, *I can help. There's a free wheel; someone should be on it. That will make the wagon go faster.*

His mother, occupied with his little brother and sister, does not see Seth walking through the muck, heading to the left rear wheel. Nobody observes him. The men at the back of the wagon cannot see him because of his height, and Morton, on the front left wheel, is facing forward.

Seth approaches the wheel, which is as tall as he is, but that does not dissuade him. He spits on his hands, rubs them together as he has seen men do, and grabs hold of a spoke. Just at that instant, the two back wheels that were the cause of the stall slide out of the mire, and the wagon rolls free. The movement is so quick and unexpected that Seth has no time to let go of the spoke. The momentum flings him forward and he falls into the mud. As he lies prone on the ground, and before he can raise himself, the rear left wheel rolls over his head. No one sees it happen. No one knows it has happened until the end of the wagon passes the recumbent body of little Seth Johnston.

The first person to notice is Jonas Garnett. He's looking down trying to keep his footing when he sees the motionless body. Immediately he yells, "Halt!" and goes to the boy. Hearing the command to stop, the men on the wagon look to Garnett. Benjamin Johnston, Seth's father, looks back. The women and children, who are congregated three wagons back, look forward. What they all see is Jonas Garnett kneeling over a small, prostrate body.

Jonas reaches down, raises Seth out of the mud, and gets his first look at the damage the wheel has done. Involuntarily his eyes close and his head turns away in disgust.

By now, the other men are standing in a circle around Garnett and the body of the boy. The stirrings and the murmurings of the men bring Garnett out of the daze caused by the horror that he holds. He opens his eyes, looks up into the solemn faces of the men standing over him, and gently lowers Seth back onto the ground. He stands and walks back to his wagon and his family without saying a word. For at that moment, Jonas Garnett has a powerful need to be with those he loves.

As Garnett walks away, Big Jim rides up to the circle of men and says, "What's the hold-up here?" The men move aside to allow Big Jim to see for himself what the hold-up is. After seeing the body, Jim looks to his left and sees Benjamin Johnston walking toward him. He dismounts and stands in front of Johnston blocking his progress, but then thinks better of it and lets him pass.

Until Johnston reaches the body, he has no idea that it is his son. As he looks down, he recognizes the clothing and slowly the realization creeps over him that what he is looking at—that horrible sight—is Seth. He drops to his knees, falls forward so that he is on all fours with an arm on each side of the boy, his hands in the mud, his head hung low. The only thought going through his mind at that moment is the day Seth was born and how proud he was to have a son. With that thought, he pushes himself up onto his knees, takes Seth to his bosom and cries.

Big Jim sees Missus Johnston hurrying toward her husband and thinks it advisable she not see what he is holding. He makes his way through the sludge to head her off. Taking her gently by the arm, he turns her around. At the same time, he calls to Missus Sutton and Missus Blair, who are nearby, to come and take charge of the woman.

Missus Johnston will not be deterred. She pulls her arm free from Jim's grasp and runs as fast as she can, considering the mire, to join her husband. Missus Sutton and Missus Blair decide between themselves to take charge of the other Johnston children until such time that their parents come to call for them.

The people of the other columns were starting to approach the scene. Big Jim went to them and said, "Please, folks, give them their moment." He did not have to ask twice, for every parent was thinking the same thing.

But for the grace of God . . .

They took their children by the hand and slowly walked back to their wagons. There would be no more miles made that day.

After unhitching his team, Mister Ariesen approached Big Jim and asked if it would be all right for the men of the second column to dig Seth Johnston's grave.

"Sure, Mister Ariesen, but make it deep enough so the wolves don't dig him up."

"What do we do for a coffin?"

"Wrap him in a blanket and pin it shut. That's the way it's done out here."

The women of the second column went to the Johnstons who were still kneeling in the muck of that godforsaken prairie, holding one another and looking to the sky. As the women got close, they heard them praying.

". . . and forgive us our trespasses as we forgive those who trespass against us and lead us not into temptation, but deliver us from evil. Amen."

They remained at a respectful distance until the Johnstons were finished. Missus Garnett, after a moment's hesitation, went over to them and very softly and gently said, "With your permission, we would like to lay Seth out for a proper burial. You have two other children that need you right now. Please let us take care of him for you." Missus Garnett's kind words brought the Johnstons around. They both had been miles away in their own thoughts.

Clara Johnston looked up at Mary Garnett and said, "Thank you." She lifted herself from the ooze, followed by her husband. As Benjamin Johnston rose, he nodded to Missus Garnett in acknowledgement of her kindness.

Clara and Benjamin clasped hands and walked back towards their wagon to be with Simon and Phoebe.

The women of the second column did their job. The men did theirs. Within the hour, Seth Johnston was entombed on the great plains of the American Continent— the first death of Big Jim Cody's train that left Westport, Missouri, in the spring of 1850.

Chapter Fifteen

THE MORNING dawned on a dry and dusty prairie. The emigrants were listless. The events of the previous day had drained the energy from the people of Big Jim's train. He had told them before leaving that Death would be a fellow traveler on The Trail. He had seen it demoralize an entire train once, which led to more deaths. If he did not address the matter, the fabric that held his train together would unravel, little by little.

It was time to rally his people.

Jim went from column to column spreading the word that there was to be a meeting at the lead wagon of the third column. When all had assembled, he rode up and sitting his horse, he began to speak. "Listen up, folks! Yesterday's complexion is bound to affect ya, but ya gotta pocket what happened. I'm a-tellin' ya . . . it's gonna happen again afore we reach Oregon, so don't chafe 'bout it. I'm sure Mister and Missus Johnston would agree with me that if we don't cover as many miles as we can every day, we'll all die out here. They got two young'uns they need to git to Oregon. You folks got young'uns of your own that you need to git to Oregon . . . or California."

Drawing a deep breath, he continued, "We're already three weeks out an' we're nowhere near Chimney Rock. That's where the plains end an' the high plains start. After that is Independence Rock. We gotta make it by the fourth of July to beat the winter snows of the Blue Mountains. But the most dangerous part of The Trail lies just ahead. It's the rivers, the South Platte, the Green, an' the damn Republican. Sorry, ladies, forgot myself."

The Republican River was not named for the political party by the same name. That did not come into existence until 1854. The river was so named for a band of the Pawnee Nation known as Republicans, though they referred to themselves as *Chaticks-si-Chaticks*—Men-of-Men.

Big Jim continued. "The Republican snakes around worsin' than a real snake. Parts of it go by different names, but it's all the same water. Two-year back, thirty-seven people drowned crossing the Green River. So I need you folk in sharp form an' payin' attention. Thar'll be some bridges an' ferries, but they'll cost ya 'bout the same as an ox—sixteen dollars. Don't mean to throw no fright into ya folks. Just lettin' ya know we got us some miles to cross. An' we best be doin' it as though our lives are at stake, 'cause they are. So folks, git your animals hitched and let's move out. We leave in half an hour."

Jim slipped his horse and walked over to where Mister and Missus Johnston stood with their children. "Morning, folks. Sorry I had to call ya out just now, but I figured if they all knew ya folks were buckin' up for the sake of your young'uns, then the rest would do the same."

Mister Johnston said, "We understand, and we want to thank you and the rest of the train for the fine burial you all gave Seth."

"I'm just glad we had the time."

When someone died on The Trail, there was no time to stop and conduct a formal burial with a gathering and words spoken. The train could not be slowed for anything—ever—not even Death itself. When someone died, kinfolk or a friend dug the grave while the train moved on. If someone was dying, say of cholera, from which there was no hope of recovery, that person was left along The Trail, either alone or with a "watcher." A watcher stayed with the dying person until death set in. With cholera, it was always soon, within hours. The watcher would dig the grave, bury the person, and then catch up with the train. Sometimes the grave was dug while the person was still alive—as they watched the digging of his or her own grave.

Within Big Jim's prescribed timeframe of half an hour, the train was once again moving westward.

Jacob was handling the team. His father had some business to conduct with Mister Walters. Mister Ariesen was vexed because once they hit the high plains, the buffalo would be no more, and still he had not had his chance to slaughter his fair share.

In a previous conversation, Walters had spoken of the gun that he had no use for, the one his friend Hiram George had given him. The one that was the last thing placed into the packing case.

Mister Ariesen approached the Walters' wagon and walked up to Morgan Walters, who was goading his oxen.

"Howdy, Morgan."

"Howdy, want to walk along for a spell?"

"That's my intent. Also wanted to do a little talkin'."

"Terrible thing what happened to the Johnston boy."

"Yes, it was. Makes you appreciate your children all the more."

The two men walked in silence for a while until Mister Ariesen spoke. "Morgan, you remember telling me about that gun of yours, you know, the one your friend gave you?"

"Yes, I remember."

"Well, I was just thinking if you might want to sell it, seeing as how you've got no use for it."

"I haven't given it much thought. True, I got no use for it. I don't hold much with killing; and that is all a gun is good for."

"Listen, Morgan, enough of this dilly-dallying around. I'm gonna acknowledge the corn and come right to the point. I would like to buy your gun if you'll sell it to me."

"Mister Ariesen, you may have the gun, I don't want it. I'll unpack it for you when we stop for dinner."

True to his word, Morgan Walters unpacked the musket while his wife prepared the noon repast. He handed it and the ammunition, along with the powder horn, over to Mister Ariesen who was practically giddy with excitement. That evening, he was finally going to go buffalo hunting.

He thanked Mister Walters and walked back to his wagon. Passing Jacob, he told him that once the train was moving again, he was to handle the team. He then proceeded to the back of the wagon and climbed up over the tailgate, bringing his newfound prize with him.

As the wagons rolled westward, Mister Ariesen loaded the gun in anticipation of the hunt.

Once the musket was loaded, he laid it on the sacks of flour that rested against the left side of the wagon. He was now ready for the Great Hunt. He mistakenly thought the gun only half-cocked. However, it was fully cocked.

When a sufficient number of miles had been covered that day, Big Jim called for a halt. After the wagons were encircled and the teams unhitched, the women started preparing supper for their families. The men went about the business of inspecting their wagons for any repairs that might be needed.

Mister Ariesen left his son building a fire—his wife and daughters fixing the family's supper. He had buffalo to hunt. He eagerly walked to the back of his wagon, untied the flaps, and reached in for his gun.

He grasped the barrel with his left hand and pulled the musket toward him. As it slid in his direction along the sacks of flour, the trigger caught on the corner of the last sack. The ball entered his heart—he was dead before he hit the ground.

The report of the shot was heard throughout the camp, but a stray gunshot was a common occurrence. The men were always taking pot shots at buffalo or low-flying birds. Nonetheless, Jacob knew instinctively wherefrom the shot had originated and ran to the back of the wagon where he found his father lying on his back, eyes wide open . . . staring into eternity.

Before Jacob could think or act, Big Jim rode up and took in the scene. He knew instantly how the man had died. He dismounted, muttering under his breath, "Damn fool."

Pushing Jacob aside, he knelt down on one knee.

More for the boy's sake than anything else, he went through the motions of inspecting the wound. After a moment, he stood and faced Jacob. "I'm sorry, son, but you're now the head of your family. Ya best be gittin' back to your mother and sisters, they'll be a-needin' ya. I'll handle things here."

Jacob was numb as he started for his mother and sisters.

Because the wagons were in close proximity to one another, the body was not visible from inside the enclosed circle. As Jacob walked away, Big Jim called to Winston and Sutton who were two wagons back talking to one another, "Come over here a moment, boys, I wanna talk to ya."

The two men reached Big Jim and he stood aside to reveal the body. "I need ya to ready him for his earth bath." He told John Winston to get a blanket to wrap the body in and ordered Sutton to stand by until Winston's return and stop anyone heading that way before they could see the body.

In the meantime, Jacob arrived at his family's fire. His mother was stirring a pot of rice, and his sisters were laying out the tin plates and eating utensils. He sat down next to his mother without saying a word and stared into the fire. One of his sisters walked up with a hoe-cake and a stick. Jacob thought of his father and all the trouble he had had cooking hoe-cakes.

Big Jim walked the encampment. He was not idly walking about; he wanted to know if word had gotten around about the death. He figured if it had, someone would approach him and ask him to confirm it, but no one did.

Carrying a blanket, John Winston returned to Alfred Sutton and what once was Matthew Ariesen. The two men spread it on the ground and rolled the body onto it. Sutton was folding the ends over when John Winston said, "Don't you think it would be proper to close his eyes and fold his arms over his chest?"

In spite of the circumstances, Sutton had to smile. The boy was right.

When did you, Al Sutton, become such a hard man that you'd bury a person with the sight of his own death still in his eyes?

"Yes, John, it's the least we can do."

The two men were finishing their preparations when Big Jim returned. He watched them pinning the ends of the blanket closed before saying, "Word of this hasn't gotten about yet, an' I don't want it to until I can have my say. Boys, this is what we're gonna do. First, you tell no one of this, especially your women. Next, we're gonna pick him up, put him in his wagon an' leave him there until it gets good and dark and the rest of the camp is asleep. Then we'll bury him. In the morning, I'll tell the rest of the train what happened."

John Winston spoke up. "Excuse me, sir, but aren't we going to have the family at the burial?"

"Sure, that will be fine. When the time comes, you fetch 'em."

Jacob sat transfixed in front of the fire; he had uttered not a word since sitting down. While he gazed into the flames, his thoughts were on the day his father told him of the first Ariesen to come to America and the history of the house they lived in. He smiled inwardly at the memory.

"You just tell your friends that the wind does not blow through your house in the winter as it does theirs."

Jacob slowly surfaced from his contemplations and took in the scene before him. His mother, whom he loved dearly, his two sisters whom, in spite of the usual sibling squabbles, he also loved. How was he going to tell them of the death of the man who had looked after them for all these many years? He decided to wait until after supper; they would need their strength.

As Jacob was making his first decision as head of the family, Big Jim walked up and said, "Mind if I speak to ya private-like?"

When they had walked a few feet from the fire, Jim said in a low voice, "We've put him in the back of your wagon for now. I don't want word of this to git around until I had my say, which will be in the morning. After dark, we'll bury him. When we're ready, the Winston boy will fetch ya. I suggest you keep your family outta the wagon until you tells 'em. Might be kinda a shock to 'em, seeing him lying there like that."

Jacob went back to the campfire and asked his mother, "How long before we eat?"

"Supper's ready now. Go and see if you can find your father, he's probably lost all track of time, hunting those buffalo of his." It never crossed her mind that she had heard only the single gunshot.

Jacob sighed and said, "Father said to eat without him."

When the Ariesens had finished their evening meal, and the girls were washing the eating gear in a bucket of water, Jacob asked his mother to walk with him. He did not want his sisters to hear what he had to say. He led his mother to the back of their wagon.

"Mother, something horrible has happened." That is as far as he could go before faltering. After a moment's hesitation, he thought to himself, *If I am to get this family to California, I must be strong.*

He faced his mother and said, "Your husband . . . my father . . . is dead."

Chapter Sixteen

IT TOOK A MOMENT for his mother to comprehend the words her son had spoken. In that brief instant, she went from not understanding, to the hope that somehow he was mistaken, and finally to the acceptance that his words were true. She stood looking at Jacob and noticed that the yellow in the iris of his eyes were now golden-orange in color. They were reflecting the light of the setting sun.

How beautiful, she thought and then she simply asked, "How?"

As Jacob explained the circumstances of his father's death, he opened the rear flap and showed his mother the blanket-wrapped corpse of her husband. He informed her that the burial would be held later that night, after the camp had gone to sleep.

Missus Ariesen stared for a few moments at the bundle in the back of their wagon—her thoughts her own—before saying, "I must tell the girls. Please come for me when it's time to put him to his rest."

After it grew dark, Big Jim sought out Al Sutton and said, "Git Winston and some diggin' tools and meet me at the back of the Ariesen wagon. Oh yeah, and bring a lantern."

The men arrived with the tools and found Big Jim and Jacob waiting for them. Jim gave his orders: "Git out thar and dig a grave for the man and git yourselves far enough away from camp so ya don't wake nobody. Make sure it's at least four feet deep or he'll be scattered all to hell and back come morning. The boy and me will tote him."

Winston and Sutton disappeared into the night. Big Jim turned to Jacob and asked, "Is your mother ready for the burial?"

"Yes, she's with my sisters. They'll be here in a few minutes."

"Okay, boy, let's git him to his final resting place."

As the men were placing Matthew Ariesen in his grave, Jacob's mother and sisters walked out of the darkness. The girls hugged their mother about the waist, one on either side. They had all been crying, but as they approached, there were only residual sniffles.

While the family huddled together over the grave, Winston, Sutton, and Big Jim stood a respectful distance away. After a few moments of silent thought, Missus Ariesen looked into the shadows and said, "You men were his friends. Will you please join us?"

The three walked into the light of the lantern. Winston still held the pick, and Sutton the shovel.

Jacob, as head of the family, said, "This is from Exodus, Chapter 10, verse 17." From memory, he spoke these words: "Now therefore forgive, I pray thee, my sin only this once, and entreat the Lord your God that he may take away from me this death only."

Jacob finished his recitation, bent over, picked up a handful of dirt, and threw it into the grave and onto the blanket-covered body of his father. His mother and sisters did likewise.

Winston and Sutton took turns filling in the grave while Big Jim Cody held the lantern. The Ariesens slowly and sadly walked back to their wagon.

The following morning while the emigrants were preparing their fires, Big Jim walked to the center of the camp and called all the men to him. He told them of the death of Mister Ariesen, and how it had occurred. He added, "It would be best if ya don't keep your rifles loaded. Ya never know. One of ya young'uns might git to it, ya just never know. Now go and tend to your fires and eat. We've got miles to cover."

Within the hour, the four columns of Big Jim's train were once again westward bound.

The Ariesens and the Johnstons did not have the luxury of properly grieving for their dead. They had to press on. They could grieve privately, but The Trail had to be traversed. The Trail was all. The Trail would take others if miles were not left behind every single day.

When they stopped at noon, and while Jacob's sisters were out collecting chips for their fire, Jacob spoke with his mother. "Do you think we should still go to California? Maybe Oregon would be better. I never did want to go after gold."

"Jacob, you are now the man of the family. You must make the decisions for all of us. But if you are asking my advice, I will tell you what I think."

"Yes, Mother, please. I need guidance."

"Your father is not dead. I see him in you when you smile. I see him in your sisters when they laugh. He lives in my heart. It was his desire that we go to California. I do not want you to live his life. You must live your own. But why not go where he was taking us? When we get there, then you can decide what we will do."

"Thank you, Mother. I'll be back in a moment to build the fire for you."

Jacob had something he needed to know, and the only man who could answer his question was Big Jim Cody. Jacob saw him sitting at one of the fires and walked over. "Hello, Mister Cody."

"Hey, boy, why not sit a spell. We've got a lot of miles to go 'afore the day is spent. Might as well rest while ya can."

Jacob squatted on his heels and asked, "When we split up at Separation Pass, how will we know the trail to California?"

"Thar's only one pass through them mountains so ya cain't git lost. Once ya come down from the mountains, the trail is clearly marked. If that ain't enough, just follow the sun. It'll lead you right into California. And don't worry. You won't be alone. Nine other wagons will be turning off with ya."

Shortly thereafter, the wagons were rolling again. The hours turned into days. Each day was like the last. The scenery did not change. The dust never retreated. Every day, the sun beat down mercilessly.

On the fifth day after the death of Jacob's father, when the train had stopped for the night, Big Jim addressed his people. "Tomorrow we come up to our first river crossing. Thar's a ferry, but as I've said, it'll cost ya. The river is at peak height, there'll be no fording. If ya *was* fool enough to try it, ya'd lose your wagon fer sure. Maybe even your livestock, not to mention your fool necks. We'll cross by columns, startin' with column one. Then we'll go in order. Now git somethin' to eat, and git a good night's sleep. 'Cause loadin' your wagons and team onto them ferries is the stuff to try men's souls."

The four columns of the train set out at first light in a northwesterly direction. The emigrants were excited about the upcoming crossing.

Just before noon, the earth rose up a little, giving the people of the train their first sight of the Republican River, or as the Pawnee called it, the *Kitkehahki*. There was a small shack sitting upon a rise overlooking the river. The shack was the domicile of one William J. Travis—the proprietor of the ferry. He was also known as Crazy Bill because living alone out on the plains for four years had changed him, as it would have any man.

Big Jim rode up ahead to Bill's shack and hollered, "Anyone about?"

From inside the shack came the reply, "Where in tarnation ya reckon I'd be?"

A grizzled beard poked itself out the door, followed by a small man of about two score years. He was short, very thin, and walked with a limp favoring his left leg. When he saw the black mare and the rider astride her, he said, "Well, if it ain't ol' Jim Cody hisself. What brings ya to this neck of the woods?"

In answer, Big Jim pointed east. Travis looked in that direction and said, "I see ya got yourself another flock of emigrants."

Jim slipped his horse and said, "We've got 'bout an hour afore they git here. Whatcha got to drink?"

"I reckon I can rustle us up a little somethin'. Let's go inside and git outta the sun."

An hour later, the two men emerged from the shack to await the train. When Jim saw that it was still at least fifteen minutes out, he mounted his horse and said to Bill, "I gotta speed 'em up. I want 'em all across fast. I still plan on making miles today. Git your barge ready."

Big Jim got his train to the river and told the men of column one, "Ya can eat when ya git to the other side." To the people of the other three columns he said, "Ya can eat while we move the first column across. No fires. We ain't got time; we got miles to cover."

Bill Travis went from wagon to wagon collecting his fare of sixteen dollars from every man who wanted to avail himself of the ferry. Seeing the swollen and fast moving river up close, the men paid what was asked, albeit begrudgingly. Sixteen dollars was a fair amount of money, especially to people who were out to start a new life and needed every penny to sustain them until that new life took hold.

After collecting his fares, Bill walked up to Big Jim who was looking at the barge Bill Travis called a ferry. It was rectangular, one hundred feet long and fifty feet wide, with railings two inches in diameter on all four sides made from river birch branches. The longer railings on the sides were permanently affixed, while the ones on the ends were removable for getting the wagons and teams on and off.

Bill asked, "Notice the improvements?"

"Looks 'bout the same. A mite bigger, that's all."

"Them's the improvements. I can now git eight wagons and teams on her. Makes for less pullin'. I ain't as young as I used to be. The setup works this way, Jim—four wagons and teams abreast at the front and four behind 'em at the rear."

Jim frowned. He did not think eight wagons and teams could fit on the ferry and said so. Bill responded, "Not long ago, I had a train come through here. Loaded eight wagons and teams every time. Mite crowded, but I got 'em all across without no trouble."

Big Jim shrugged and said, "Alright, it's your ferry."

The first wagon had a minimum of trouble ascending the dirt ramp and getting onto the ferry. Once it was in place, the other seven wagons followed suit. In spite of Big Jim's doubts, the ferry did accommodate all eight wagons—barely. Because of the lack of space, the families were confined to the back of the wagons, while the menfolk sat in the driver's seat. Big Jim crossed with the first column. The crossing was uneventful, as it was with columns two and three.

While the first three columns were crossing, a mile upstream an old river birch stood poised on the edge of the riverbank, just where the river made a sharp turn from flowing east to flowing in a more southerly direction. For weeks, the fast-moving water had been eating away at the soil beneath the tree. River birches are known for their multiple trunks; this one had three. Together they measured ten feet across.

Just as Bill started out from his side of the river with the eight wagons of column four, the soil gave way under the old tree, which fell into the maelstrom that was the Republican River that day. The tree landed in the water with a mighty splash and was momentarily submerged. When it bobbed back to the surface, it commenced its ride down river with the trunk facing south.

At the exact moment that the birch started on its journey, Bill had the ferry about a quarter of the way across the river. As they reached the mid-river mark, the tree came around a bend and collided with the ferry. The resulting jolt caused the front wagon on the opposite side—the one closest to the left railing—to move slightly, which precipitated the left rear wheel to slip over the edge. The railing broke, and the wagon did a slow slide into the water, dragging the team of oxen with it.

The weight of the wagon as it slipped into the river, dipped the ferry to a precariously steep angle and the right side rose into the air. When the ferry rebounded, the two wagons on the right edge crashed through the railing and slid overboard. They became entangled with the line Bill Travis was using to pull the barge across and he was dragged into the river. The ferry was now free from its tether and spinning out of control. It moved downriver— tossing wagons, teams, and people into the cold waters of the Republican.

The weight of the stores and the emigrants' personal possessions caused the wagons to sink immediately, also pulling the livestock under. After a few moments, the wagons bobbed to the surface. Some of them with only the top half of their cotton covers showing, but most of them were on their sides. Those that were inside were trapped under hundreds of pounds of supplies.

The emigrants on the far shore watched in horror as the ferry sped downstream. The first man to take action was

Big Jim, followed by Jacob Ariesen. Jim mounted his horse and said to the men, "Git your ropes and follow me." Before he had finished speaking, Jacob was running downriver, rope in hand. Big Jim galloped past him and shouted, "Ya git the first one ya see. I'm goin' farther down to git 'em as they come by."

Jacob ran until he saw a man struggling to reach the shore. He ran to a point a hundred yards downriver and waded into the water until he was waist deep. As the man came his way, he threw one end of the rope out into the river. In desperation, the man lunged and got a hold of it just before he would have been swept out of reach. Jacob hauled him in and helped him to shore.

"My wife, my children . . ." the man kept repeating over and over again.

"Don't worry, Big Jim is downriver. He'll get them."

By then, other men were running past looking for someone, anyone, to throw a lifeline to. However, there was no one else to be seen—only wagons floating on their sides and animals thrashing about in their harnesses or yokes trying to stay afloat.

Big Jim rode until he saw a woman in the water trying to make it to the far shore. He hailed her, but to no avail. Either she did not hear him or her panic was so great that she stayed fixated on the spot on the shore that she was trying to reach. He knew the river was the stronger of the two, and that she would never make it. Without another thought, he slipped his horse and splashed into the icy waters.

When he reached her, she tried to climb upon him as though he were a boulder in midstream—a place of safety. Compared to Jim, the woman was small. However, her fear gave her strength and she fought his attempts to grab hold of her. He finally had to grab her by the hair and make for shore pulling her in that fashion.

He emerged from the raging water to find two men waiting. As they took charge of the woman, Big Jim jumped on his horse and rode downriver looking for someone else to rescue. He saw no one . . . alive. But there were plenty of dead bodies lining both banks.

Are they all dead?

Presently, Jim came upon the ferry lodged up on shore. The line that had once anchored it to both banks was entwined with an arm. Attached to the arm was Crazy Bill Travis—his eyes wide open, seeing nothing. Like all good captains, William J. Travis had gone down with his ship.

The dead numbered thirty-one, not counting Bill Travis. Men, women, and children—entire families—were either floating downriver or lying on its banks. There were only two survivors. Charlie Hicks, the man Jacob had saved, and Molly Smith, the woman Big Jim had saved.

Mister Hicks sat huddled, wrapped in a blanket, repeating the same four words he had first spoken as Jacob pulled him from the river, "My wife, my children." Missus Smith sat by a fire and said nothing.

It took the emigrants three days to collect and bury their dead. Not all the bodies were recovered. Four were never found. Big Jim was for moving on and leaving the dead where they lie. Not because he was unmindful of the emigrants' feelings, but because he knew that if the train dawdled for whatever reason, they would not make Independence Rock by July 4th.

If they did not make that deadline, many more would die in the mountains when the snows came. Nevertheless, Big Jim Cody knew the collection and burying of the dead was something the people of his train had to do before they could move on, so he helped with the burials and said not a word.

With the dead buried, the train made ready to leave. That's when Charlie Hicks announced that he was not going to leave his family.

Before anyone could stop him, he ran to the river and swam—with some effort—to the far side. Once on dry land and pointing toward Bill Travis' shanty, he shouted across to the other emigrants, "I'm stayin' right here in this shack! I will not leave my wife and little ones."

Big Jim walked up to those staring across the river at the retreating figure of Charlie Hicks and said, "Come on, folks, we're movin' out. He's a grown man. He knows his own mind."

Missus Smith rode with the Winstons.

Chapter Seventeen

BIG JIM CODY'S TRAIN that departed Westport, Missouri, in the spring of 1850 once again headed west. It was now down to three columns of eight wagons each. Down to one hundred and ten emigrants from the one hundred and forty-four that had started out on a trek across a continent.

Big Jim was worried. The river catastrophe took place on June 4th, which meant he had a month to get his people to Independence Rock if they were to be assured of crossing the Blue Mountains before the first snow. Yet, Independence Rock was eight hundred miles away. Making twenty miles a day, with every seventh day a day of rest, would mean they would not get there until July 14th, providing nothing else happened to delay the train.

There were a few more river crossings ahead, but they were all small rivers and easily fordable. Fifty miles before Courthouse Rock, the Republican would have to be traversed again, but by the time the emigrants reached it, the water should have slowed. In addition, Big Jim knew of a narrow crossing point; there would be no need of a ferry.

The next two weeks were uneventful. The train averaged nineteen miles a day and the emigrants were slowly getting over the shock of losing a fourth of their number. Jacob and his family took the days as they came. All days were the same. Up before daybreak, walk for six hours, stop for an hour to eat, then walk six more hours—or seven, if Big Jim deemed not enough miles had been covered—then stop for the night and do the exact same thing the next day.

After fourteen days, the train reached Courthouse Rock, so named because it reminded the first emigrants of the St.

Louis courthouse. Twelve miles to the west stood Chimney Rock, whose name should be self-explanatory.

The train camped at Courthouse Rock that night, and the next day they made eighteen miles. Big Jim halted the train six miles west of Chimney Rock. There was a source of water at that locale and water barrels were getting low.

The emigrants were too tired from the day's march to carry bucketsful of water back to their wagons. It was an individual decision on each man's part, but they all decided to refill their barrels the next day.

In the morning, the women prepared the meals and the men toted the water back to their wagons. In doing so, they brought Death into the bosoms of their families. Death, which had stalked the train since its departure from Westport, was now firmly entrenched within Big Jim's train that departed Westport, Missouri, in the spring of 1850.

This time, Death took the guise of cholera, or "mountain fever" as the emigrants referred to the disease. The water the emigrants had just put into their barrels was teaming with the *Vibrio cholera* bacterium.

Not all the emigrants had need of refilling their barrels. Four wagons of the first column and two of the third did not replenish their water supply. All the wagons of column two, save the Ariesen's, refilled before leaving camp that morning. Jacob was preoccupied with hitching up the team and forgot about filling his water barrel.

The train moved out at dawn.

As the sun rose and climbed higher into the sky, it cast long shadows of the emigrants and their wagons. The day wore on and the sun rose higher still. The shadows shortened and the heat of the prairie increased, causing the emigrants to become thirsty. One by one, they went to their water barrels to slake their thirst.

While Jacob was goading his oxen, his mother walked up to him and said, "The girls and I are going visiting. I'm going to the Winstons. I want to see if there is anything I can do for poor Missus Smith. Jane will be with the Blairs. She adores their youngest boy, little Isaac. Nine years of age and already she's practicing to be a mother! And Mary will be with the Garnetts' oldest daughter, Abigail. They've become fast friends. So if you need us for anything, you'll know where to find us."

Missus Ariesen and Molly Smith walked alongside the Winston's wagon, occasionally drinking from their water barrel. Jacob's sisters did the same with the folks they were visiting.

By the time the train was ready to stop for the noon meal, the first of the emigrants were starting to feel the effects of the cholera bacteria. In the second column, Nate Morton was the first. While leading his team, he felt such sharp abdominal pains that he fell to his knees.

When Nate stopped goading his oxen, the animals halted their advance, which halted the advance of the wagons to the rear of his. Jonas Garrett, who was in the lead, continued on until Jonas Jr. told him the rest of the column had stopped. He halted his oxen and walked back to see what the trouble was.

Big Jim looked back and noticed that the second column was not moving. He stopped the other two columns and went to see what was holding things up. He rode up to a knot of people surrounding Nate and saw Becky Morton wiping the sweat from her husband's brow. Jim dismounted, walked up to those gathered around the Mortons, and said, "Git back to your own wagons. We're stopping here to eat." Then he asked Jacob, "Will ya tell the other columns?"

"Yes sir," replied Jacob.

Big Jim knelt down and asked Nate what was wrong. Becky answered for her husband, "We don't know. He has cramps and he's been heaving."

Jim stood and looked about. He saw Ham Richards standing close by with the two little Morton girls. "Help me git him to his feet and we'll put him in the shade of his wagon. He'll be more comfortable there."

They got Nate situated and Big Jim looked out over the makeshift campsite and sighed. He knew mountain fever when he saw it. Soon others would be coming down with the debilitating sickness; mountain fever never affected just one person. He told Becky to keep Nate comfortable and that he would be back presently.

It was just high noon.

Jacob arrived back at his wagon to find his mother laying out biscuits, bacon, and beans left over from the previous night's meal.

"Where are the girls?"

"They're eating with their friends," answered his mother.

The news bothered Jacob. Why, he did not know. The trepidation he had felt back in Concord when his father first told the family that they would be going to California was now as a bell ringing in his head.

Jacob expressed his concern to his mother. "I think the girls should be with us, something is not right. I cannot explain it, but I'm getting them." Without awaiting her response, he went in search of his sisters.

He returned with the girls in tow to find their mother sitting on the ground bent over in pain. Jacob knelt down on the grass next to her and asked what was wrong. "I don't know. All of a sudden I had cramps in my stomach, got sick, and started to vomit."

Jacob told Mary, the older of his two sisters, to get a blanket and spread it out under the wagon. He helped his mother to stand, walked her over, and helped her lie down. After making sure that she was as comfortable as possible, he said to his sisters, "Look after her. I have to speak with Mister Cody."

He found Big Jim sitting in the shade of a wagon looking pensive. Seeing Jacob he said, "Squat, son. Ya got somethin' on your mind?"

"Yes sir. I sure have. Is what affects Mister Morton mountain fever?"

"I'm sorry to say so, but yes, it is."

"Well, my mother has it also."

Jim sighed and said, "I'm sorry, but you're a man now, so I'll level with ya. Them that gits the fever usually don't recover. Some do, but very few. I'm a-just sittin' here waitin' to see how many come down with it this go-round. I've seen it before. It hits outta nowhere. Within twelve hours, usually a lot sooner than that, them it hits are dead."

"Is there no medicine for the illness?"

"If thar is, I ain't never heard tell 'bout it."

Jacob stood and started back to his wagon, but Big Jim stopped him in mid-stride by saying, "Son, it's almost an hour we've been sittin' here, an' by all rights we should be movin' out in a few minutes. But we're not gonna do that. Ya hear them moans and cries out thar? That's more of my people being struck down with the fever. I figure by four o'clock, them that's comin' down with it will have it. So an hour after that, I'm movin' them that's healthy a few miles up trail. It's gonna be a night of death. Them that's healthy are my responsibility. Them that's dyin' are God's. I've got to git this train over the mountains afore first snow or the rest of 'em will die. I don't reckon you'll leave your ma, but I just wanted ya to know why we're leavin'. I'll ride back in the morning to check up on ya. And just one more thing, son. Build yourself a big fire tonight. The wolves will be comin' in after the dead."

106

Jacob arrived back at his wagon to find both his sisters ill, the younger one crying out in pain. He got them onto blankets and sat down next to his mother to watch her and his sisters die. He had never felt so helpless in his life.

A few hours later, Big Jim walked up and asked, "How ya farin', son?"

Jacob looked up at the big man and said, "My sisters are dead, and my mother will soon join them."

"I'm real sorry. Just wanted ya to know we're movin' out. Only six families came through the attack. Only six! I'll ride back in the morning afore we start the day's march. I want to unhitch the livestock. It would do no good to leave 'em in harness. Don't think they can survive a winter out here, but at least they'll have a couple of months of good grazin'. Best to ya. I'll be seein' ya in the mornin'."

"Please wait, Mister Cody. There is no need for you to return. I will take care of the livestock. I will also attend to the dead. You may believe me when I tell you no wolf will touch a member of your train."

"Alright, ya seem to have grit. Catch up with us as soon as ya can. But I don't know how you're gonna bury eighty bodies an' keep the wolves at bay. Just remember wolves gotta eat too. Oh, I almost forgot, Mister Richards is stayin'. Says he's gotta bury his dead. His sister, her husband, an' the young'uns are all gone."

Actually, the number of stricken emigrants totaled eighty-eight. Not all were dead as of yet, though they would be, come the morrow.

Whilst Big Jim walked away, Jacob's mother grabbed him by the arm and said something. She was too weak to speak above a whisper. He had to bend down to hear her words.

"My beautiful firstborn, do not mourn us. Your father is here; I can see him standing right behind you. He is waiting for me; he looks different. He is the young man that I married. He told me the girls are with him, and that he has a home waiting for us."

Saying those words took the last of Anika Ariesen's strength. She slowly closed her eyes and left her body. Jacob tenderly covered her with a blanket as he had done with each of his sisters.

It was only after his mother's death that Jacob noticed the cries of those dying around him. He stood and looked at the bodies lying in the tall grass, some moving, some still. He looked to the west and saw the pitiful vestige of Big Jim's train as it moved out. *Only six wagons out of thirty-two.* Riding in those wagons were twenty souls who still had a dream, and still needed Big Jim Cody to get them to the Promised Land.

For the second time that day, the sun cast long shadows of the emigrants and their wagons. In the morning, the shadows had been before them. Now, like many of their fellow emigrants, the shadows were behind them.

Chapter Eighteen

PONDERING THE RECEDING TRAIN, Jacob was roused from his thoughts by Hamilton Richards walking up with a bottle of whiskey in his hand. "So you're staying too?"

"Yes. I am staying."

"Well, have a snort. This day has been a hell on both of us. Anyway, I'm not much of a water drinker. I had a case of this stuff hidden in the wagon. I always said whiskey will quench a man's thirst far faster than water will."

Jacob politely refused Mister Richards' offer of libation, by saying, "Not now, thank you. I must bury my dead."

"Alright, Jacob. I'll help you bury yours, and then you can help me bury mine. The unpleasant work will go faster that way. Let me get a pickaxe and shovel. I'll be right back."

Left to himself with the cries of the dying reverberating in his head, Jacob knelt by the body of his mother and said a prayer. "Please, Lord, let it be true that my mother did indeed see my father, and that they and my sisters are with You in Heaven this day."

Hamilton soon returned with the entrenching tools, and the work of burying their dead commenced. By the time the seven bodies were resting in their graves and a few words had been spoken over them, it was getting dark. Jacob faced Hamilton and said, "We've still got a long night ahead of us. First, we have to unhitch the livestock and set them free. There are sixteen wagons, not counting yours and mine. You take eight and I'll take eight. We should be finished before full dark."

"But how are we going to keep the wolves from the dying and the dead? Are you planning to bury over eighty bodies before sundown? That will take days, and by then the wolves will surely have gotten to some of them."

"I have an idea. I will tell you about it later, but first we need to wait for those that are going to die to die. Come morning, when it is all over, we will take care of the dead. But tonight we must keep watch. We will take whatever can be found in the wagons that will burn and start two or three large fires; we'll keep them going all night. So let's start unhitching, it's getting late."

After the animals had been freed, the two men set about making three fires among the wagons. They sat up throughout the night keeping them going and listening to the sounds of the dying. As the night wore on, the cries of the afflicted lessened and became feeble until the only sound heard was the crackling of the fires. When the sun once again made its appearance, Jacob and Hamilton looked at one another, nodded, and set about doing what had to be done.

During the night, Jacob had conveyed his plan to Hamilton. He told him of something he had learned from a man who lived in Concord. He had described the funeral rites of the people of India. How they place their dead on funeral pyres and burn the bodies until they are nothing more than ashes. At first, Hamilton balked at such a notion. "What about the resurrection of the dead? That's blasphemy!"

"No," said Jacob. "I thought the same thing, but it was explained to me that the body turns to dust after a few years anyway. So what is the difference if it turns to dust or ashes? It's all the same in the end."

Jacob's plan was to put the bodies in their own wagons, douse the wagons with lantern oil, and set them ablaze. By the time the wagons burned down to embers, there should be nothing left for the wolves. Hamilton finally saw the merit in Jacob's plan. Besides, digging graves was hard

110

work. After a meal of cold beans and biscuits, the two men set about the business of burning the dead.

The day wore on and the sun beat down upon them as they toiled at their gruesome task. They quenched their thirst, each in his own way. Jacob from his water barrel, Hamilton from his whiskey bottle.

After burying their own dead the day before, they were left with eighty-one corpses to deal with. By noon, they had just about completed their task. Only four more bodies lay in the grass, the Blair family—Edward, Polly, Aaron and little Isaac. Hamilton was about to suggest they stop for something to eat, but then realized the work of lifting dead bodies onto wagons had robbed him of his appetite.

After the Blairs were in their wagon, Jacob took a drink from their water barrel rather than walk the fifty or so feet to his own wagon. It had been a tiring morning's work. Seeing Jacob ladling the water to his mouth, Hamilton said, "That looks refreshing. I think I'll bend my rule about water just this once and join you."

Thus, the last two of the ninety left behind took the cholera bacteria into their bodies.

It was time to set the wagons afire. Jacob had decided to take care of columns one and three first, saving column two until last. They went from wagon to wagon and found the supply of lantern oil. Pouring it throughout the wagons, they set them on fire—one by one.

When it came time to set fire to the wagons of column two, Jacob hesitated. "My father considered these people his friends. Perhaps we should take a moment to remember them, maybe say a few words."

Hamilton agreed, "Let's start at the back and work our way up."

They had moved their own wagons about a quarter of a mile up trail to separate them from the fires and in readiness to move out once their work was done. However, it was getting late, so Jacob suggested they finish the job at hand and head out first thing in the morning.

"No use starting out an hour before dark."

"You're right, Jacob. Let's get this last task behind us so we can rest. I'm spent, what with all the work and no sleep last night."

By coincidence, the wagons were in the same order as they had been on the day the emigrants left Westport. The last wagon in line was the Winstons', the newlyweds. Jacob poured the oil onto the bodies of John and Martha, struck a match and touched it to the oil. Within seconds, the cotton cover was ablaze. Jacob looked upon the makeshift pyre and said, "John Winston told me of his dream, his hatred of working in a public house, and of the love he had for his wife. At least they are together in eternity."

The next wagon was the Suttons'. The oil poured, the wagon set on fire. Jacob turned to Hamilton and asked, "Did you know them? I barely spoke with him and not at all with his wife."

"Yes, I spent many an hour jawboning with Al. He loved his wife and his little boy, Teddy. He was a dockworker, and as much as he loved his family, that is how much he hated the docks. I do not believe there are any docks in Heaven. That should soothe his soul."

At the Blair wagon, Jacob spoke. "Ed Blair was a coachman, but he referred to himself as a servant. He and his wife Polly saved for five years to make this trek. They wanted a new life as masters of their own fate. At least he died as a free man."

They then moved on to the Johnston wagon. While watching it burn, Jacob said, "Mister Johnston was my father's first friend on The Trail. He was a printer, but what he wanted more than anything else was wide-open spaces in which to raise his children. His son Seth went ahead to prepare a place for the family. Now Benjamin Johnston is with his wife, Clara, and his children. They are in a place that is nothing but wide-open spaces."

At the Walters' wagon, Jacob hesitated. He was not sure how one should speak for those of the Quaker faith. Hamilton cleared his throat and said, "Morgan Walters was a man of peace. I heard that he was also a damn good saddle maker. Of course, I heard it from him, but it must be true because Quakers don't lie. Morgan and his wife, Emma, had four beautiful children. They must be a comfort to him and Emma at this very moment."

The first wagon of the column and the last wagon to be set afire belonged to the Garnetts. Jacob spoke this time. "I think of the bitterness contained within the soul of Jonas Garnett. The man worked hard all his life, but I wonder if he ever saw the fruits of his labors with a clear eye. Like the rest of the people of the train, he wanted something better for his children than what he had. But did he really have so little? Perhaps now he knows of the richness of his life, and the bitterness has left him. I pray so."

As the wagons burned, the two men walked to their own wagons. They were tired; it had been a long day. They sat side by side in the shade of Jacob's wagon, their backs against a wheel, neither one wanting to eat. Hamilton brought out a bottle of whiskey and offered it to Jacob. This time he accepted the offer and took a long pull. "I just want to get the taste of death out of my mouth."

"Amen to that," responded Hamilton.

They sat in the grass and passed the bottle back and forth as they watched the sun move towards the horizon. After a few moments of contemplation, Hamilton said, "You know, those were some nice words you spoke back there. It started me thinking of Nate and Becky, not to mention the loves of my life, Mattie and Carrie. Poor old Nate, he spent years chipping rock out of the earth, then more years hauling that same rock up the sides of buildings. He was happy doing so until recently. The rock was not his life. His life was Cassie and the girls. The first thing he did every night when he came home was ask for his daughters. He was a good father."

Jacob nodded and said, "My father was also a good father. He worked hard, sometimes doing jobs that were disagreeable just so we would not do without. I think the only reason he wanted to find gold in California was so we—my mother, sisters, and I—could have more. It's just too bad he didn't realize that we had everything we needed. We had a loving home, and that's more than some folks can say."

The western sky burned orange—the white clouds turned purple and pink, moving Jacob to observe, "God does move in mysterious ways. Here we sit surrounded by death, but look at His majesty in that sky."

Hamilton shrugged and said, "Pass that bottle over here."

After doing so, Jacob suggested, "We should unhitch our teams and it would be best to do so before dark."

Hamilton agreed, "Sure, let's do it. I'm ready to hit the hay. I've been too long without sleep. I'm feeling kind of low."

What Hamilton was feeling were the first effects of mountain fever.

• • • • •

Big Jim was hell-bent on getting his train to Oregon before any other disasters befell it. Only one of the six remaining wagons was originally destined for California. However, after some discussion, it was decided the emigrants of that wagon would accompany Big Jim to Oregon. Once there, if they so desired, they could proceed down the coast to California. It was deemed safer than making their way through the mountains alone.

The first stop of any significance was Fort Laramie, situated between the North Platte and Laramie Rivers. It was originally known as Fort William, named for the man who erected it, William Sublette. However, in 1834, the United States Military purchased it and renamed it Fort Laramie after the French fur trapper Jacques La Ramie.

The next destination of any mention was Independence Rock. They were fifteen days late in arriving. Big Jim knew that would not bode well for his train. He could only hope and pray that the snows were late in coming that year.

Big Jim Cody had gotten his flock to the Elkhorn Mountains, at about eight thousand feet, when the final adversity befell his train. It was in the form of a severe snowstorm. When the storm had passed, there were drifts seven feet high. They could not progress up the mountain, nor could they go back down.

Jim scouted a place to camp. He found it in the form of a rock outcropping. He huddled his charges against the wall and built a fire for them. They stayed huddled and cold for two days, waiting for the snow to melt enough to traverse the pass and descend on the other side.

On the third day, when the snow showed no sign of giving way, Jim thought some fresh meat might bolster the emigrants' spirits. Therefore, he picked up his gun and went looking for game.

While he was away, a woman wandered from the makeshift camp looking for warmth. She was not thinking right or she would have known that the only source of heat was the small fire Big Jim had managed to make in spite of having nothing but damp wood to work with.

When he returned, Jim saw that she was gone and immediately went in search of her. He followed her tracks in the snow, and had gotten only a few hundred feet when he heard a woman's scream. He knew right away from whence it came. He had scouted a cave a few days earlier

115

in the hope that it might present shelter and warmth for his bedraggled group. Upon entering, he discovered a very large grizzly bear starting its yearly hibernation. Jim knew that next to a she-bear protecting her cubs, there was nothing more dangerous than disturbing a grizzly while it is hibernating.

Jim made his way as fast as he could through the thick covering of snow. Just as he entered the cave and his eyes adjusted to the dim light, he saw the grizzly, now standing erect on its hind legs, take a swipe at the woman's head, removing her scalp in one fluid motion. For a moment, he stood transfixed as he watched her crumple to the ground— her white skull turning red as blood poured over it.

Jim did not have his gun with him, but he drew his knife and flung himself upon that mighty monster. The bear's first swing missed. Big Jim had ducked in time, which gave him the opportunity to get inside the bear's arms and sink his knife into its neck. It went in deep. When steel met bone, the bear gave out with a prodigious roar. It lashed out at Big Jim, connecting with—and removing— his face. But Jim did not give up the fight. Even though he was now blind from the blood pouring into his eyes, he fought as a man of his stature was expected to fight. But in hand-to-hand combat, no man is a match for a grizzly.

The bear made short work of Big Jim Cody that day. When the fight had finished, the pile of meat that lay upon the floor of the cave could hardly be taken for anything human.

Without Big Jim to fend for them, the small group of remaining emigrants slowly froze to death. So ended the trek of Big Jim Cody's train that left Westport, Missouri, in the spring of 1850.

Some say that greed brought down the hand of God upon the emigrants. Yet, only a few souls were out for gold. Fate . . . God—whatever you want to call it—

116

descended on all alike. All of Big Jim Cody's train were marked for death.

All save one.

• • • • •

With their teams unhitched and hobbled, Hamilton turned to Jacob and said, "I'm sleeping in the wagon tonight. Got myself a bed fixed up in there. I'm through sleeping on the ground."

"All right, Hamilton, but I like looking at the stars as I fall asleep. I'll see you in the morning."

Before bedding down for the night, Jacob walked over to the graves of his mother and sisters and stood for a few moments in silent prayer. He then lay down next his wagon and fell asleep looking at the uncountable stars that filled the night sky and listening to the crackling and popping sounds of the burning wagons.

To the south, a band of Dakota Indians were returning from a retaliatory raid against the Pawnee. The daughter of the war chief looked to the north and saw great plumes of smoke rising into the air. She rode her pony to her father and asked, "Father, what is that?"

"I do not know, daughter, but we will cross that place tomorrow, then perhaps we will know."

The Dakota

Chapter Nineteen

AS THE WARRIORS came over the rise, they saw in the distance the white cotton covers of the two unburned wagons. The girl pointed and exclaimed, "Look, horse canoes!" Her name was Fighting Woman—the only female member of the war party.

The war party consisted of eighty braves of the Mdewakanton Dakota, their war chief, Big Eagle, and his daughter, Fighting Woman. Big Eagle wore leggings, no shirt. In his hair, he wore two feathers of the eagle, denoting bravery.

The warriors wore moccasins and breechclouts or leggings, nothing more. All wore coup feathers in their hair or carried them on their coup sticks. Fighting Woman wore leggings and a deerskin shirt. Her raven-colored braid fell to the middle of her back. She was a good-looking woman with high cheekbones and a strong chin. She stood almost six feet tall. Her most outstanding attribute—the one that set her apart from all the other women of her tribe—were her blue eyes, accounted for by the fact that her maternal great-grandmother had married a French fur trapper. At eighteen winters, she could ride and shoot as well as any man in her village.

The Indians drew near and saw that there were more wagons than just the two they had seen from the bluff. But all the others had been put to the torch. Riding slowly past the still-smoldering ruins, they observed that a few had been incinerated completely—their wheels eerily standing upright, alone, attached by their metal axles. Between the wheels lay human remains, the gleaming white skulls reflecting the bright sunlight.

The majority of the wagons had not been completely consumed by fire. Only their cotton covers were gone, revealing the terrible sight of partially incinerated men, women, and children lying on their backs, staring skyward toward their Heaven. Some, with their lips burned away, smiled macabre smiles. Their white teeth stood in sharp contrast to their blackened bodies.

The nearby livestock gave an unnatural feel to the location. The peaceful, pastoral background of oxen and mules contentedly grazing, surrounded by the abhorrent sight of half-burned bodies, made some of the Indians want to flee this "place of death." They were already uneasy because they were south of their homeland. They believed that a south wind brought sickness. That the south was a land of death, and when you died, your spirit went south. Nevertheless, they were soldiers; they followed their war chief through the horrifying tableau.

Fighting Woman asked her father, "Do you think it might have been the Pawnee that did this terrible thing?"

"I do not think so. If it were the Pawnee, why would they go to the trouble of putting the bodies in the horse canoes? Nothing has been taken." He pointed to a partially burned wagon with sacks of flour lying beneath it. "And the animals . . . they would not still be here if a war party of Indians had done this."

They gradually made their way to the two unburned wagons and came upon Jacob. He was unconscious but alive. Fighting Woman slipped her pony and ran to him. She knelt down and looked at the dying *Wasichu*, this White Man, with the yellow hair. In an instant, she decided that Hín Zi—Yellow Hair—would not die; she would see to it!

Big Eagle ordered two of his braves to look into the unburned wagons and see what they contained. In one, they found the body of Hamilton Richards; in the other, nothing but food stock.

The braves talked of rounding up the animals and herding them back to their village. One brave suggested that anything of value found in the wagons should also be taken.

"The animals, we will take, but touch nothing from the horse canoes. We do not know what killed these people," said Big Eagle.

He had lived forty-five winters; most of his braves, only half that. He was their war chief—they would defer to his wishes.

At length, Big Eagle told his braves to mount their ponies; it was time to move on. Fighting Woman stood and looked down at Jacob for a long moment. Turning her gaze to her father, sitting his horse with the sun to his back, she shielded her eyes from the glaring sun, and declaimed, "We cannot leave him here alone. Yellow Hair must not die!"

"If it is the wish of *Wakaŋ Taŋ'ka* that he dies, he will die. If it is the wish of *Wakaŋ Taŋ'ka* that he lives, he will live."

"No, he *will not* die! I will not allow it!" cried Fighting Woman.

Her father, the great war chief Big Eagle, looked down at his daughter and sighed; how he loved her. Before he spoke, he thought back to the day she had come into his life. At first, he had been disappointed that it was not a male-child he had sired, but when he saw her for the first time, he was glad that he had fathered a girl-child. He nicknamed her Suni. The name in itself meant nothing, merely a term of affection—a name that would be between father and daughter only. That was how it had been for eighteen winters. She would allow no one but her father to call her Suni.

Big Eagle gently said, "He cannot travel, and even if he could, we do not have a pony for him."

Fighting Woman responded, "I will stay with him, and when he is well enough, he will ride my pony and I will walk."

Once again, her father sighed. He knew his daughter only too well. If she had made up her mind to stay with the *Wasichu,* there was little he could do about it. Of course, he could have two—no, it would probably take four—of his braves hold her, while a fifth tied her hands and feet. She could then be flung over her pony and brought back to their village like a freshly killed deer. However, Big Eagle said only, "Suni, if you were a man, you would obey your war chief. But follow when you can." He had no fear for her safety; he knew she could take care of herself as well as any one of his braves.

Fighting Woman stood for a moment watching her father and the war party as they headed northeast, herding the livestock. She then went rummaging through Jacob's wagon. Having found what she was looking for, she covered him with two blankets, thus taking the first step in saving Jacob Ariesen's life.

For five days and five nights, she stayed with him. He could not eat, but Fighting Woman forced him to drink as much water as possible. The medicine man of her village had once told her that water is the mother of all life. At night, she slept next to him to keep him warm. She touched nothing from what she called "the horse canoe of death," the wagon that held the body of Hamilton Richards. She drank water and secured food only from the Ariesen family wagon.

On the sixth day, she awoke with a start. Her patient was up on one arm and looking down at her. He said nothing when her eyes opened; he just continued staring at her. Her first impulse was to back away in embarrassment. After a moment, Jacob said, "Are you real? I have been dreaming of you." When she did not answer, he asked, "Do you speak English?"

Fighting Woman stood up and vigorously brushed the prairie dust from her shirt and leggings before answering. "I speak your tongue; my people have traded with the Americans and English for many winters now."

"I am an American . . . a hungry American."

"Yes, you are an American . . . *Isantaŋka* in my tongue. I will feed you, but first you must bathe. Remove your leggings and shirt. I will find you new ones in your horse canoe."

Disoriented and confused, he scrutinized the captivating, beautiful, blue-eyed Indian girl standing over him who was telling him to take off his clothes before she would feed him. He shook his head as if to clear it. At length, he said, "Who *are* you?"

"My name is Wíŋyaŋ Kićizapi, daughter to Waŋmdi Taŋka of the Mdewakanton Dakota. But you may call me Suni."

"Well, Suni, can you tell me what has happened? The last thing I remember was going to sleep. I remember getting sick. Wait . . . I had mountain fever! I should be dead!"

Fighting Woman drew herself up to her full five-foot, eleven-inch height before saying, "You are not dead because I would not let you die. Now take off your coverings and bathe; you smell like a dead buffalo. If you want to eat, you must bathe."

Jacob did not understand, but when the girl had gone to the back of the wagon, he disrobed and quickly wrapped himself in a blanket in an effort at modesty. The girl soon returned and handed Jacob a pair of pants and a shirt. "While you bathe, I will start a fire, then you shall eat. We must be on our way; my father may worry of me."

Once again, Jacob shook his head in confusion. "Your father?"

Fighting Woman simply said, "We will talk while you eat." She abruptly turned her back on him and walked away. Jacob mentally shrugged, walked over to the water barrel on his wagon, and first drank his fill, then used the cup to pour water onto himself.

Once he had made himself as presentable as possible, he dressed and walked to the other side of the wagon where Fighting Woman was frying bacon over a fire of buffalo chips. He sat down on his heels and said, "Smells good, I feel like I haven't eaten in days."

"You have not eaten in five sleeps that I know of."

While Jacob waited for the bacon to cook, he looked out over the plain at the half-burned wagons, and the horror of what had happened to his family and the others came flooding back into his consciousness. He suddenly remembered Hamilton Richards and asked Fighting Woman, "Was there another White Man here when you arrived at this place?"

"Yes."

"Well, did he say anything before he left?"

"No."

"He said nothing at all, he just left?"

"He did not leave. Can you not smell him over there?" said Fighting Woman, pointing to the wagon in which lay the body of Hamilton Richards.

No need to go over and look inside because, as the girl has said, I can smell him from here.

Fighting Woman placed the frying pan between them and said, "Eat."

Jacob picked up a piece of bacon and, as he chewed, he asked, "Can we talk now?"

"Yes, we may talk, but first tell me of what has happened here."

Jacob explained to the girl, who called herself Fighting Woman, about the train coming down with mountain fever, and of his and Hamilton's effort to burn the bodies before the wolves could get at them. He finished with, "I guess we did not do a very good job of it."

126

Fighting Woman responded, "Good enough."

Jacob asked where she had come from. She told him of the war party, how they had been attracted by the smoke of the burning wagons and how she had stayed behind to care for him.

Jacob was hungry and could have eaten all the bacon, but left half of it in the pan. When she saw that he had not eaten it all, she asked, "Did you not say you were hungry? Why do you not eat what I have cooked?"

"I was saving some for you."

"I have dried deer meat; I will eat as we go."

"That is the second time you said we are going somewhere. I am going to California. Is that where you are going?"

"Are you going to walk to this Californ with no food, no water?"

"It's California, not Californ. I will take my wagon."

"Will you also pull your horse canoe?"

"Horse canoe?"

"Yes, over there with the *Wasichu* in it."

"You mean my wagon. No, I have a team to pull it." As he said so, Jacob noticed for the first time the animals were gone, even his and Hamilton's hobbled teams. "Where are our animals?"

"They are gone."

"But mine and the Morton's teams were hobbled; they could not have gone far."

"My people took them to our village. But I have given in return."

"You had no right. And what do you mean, you have given?"

"I have given you back your life. I think *Wakan Taŋka* wanted you somewhere else, but I would not let your spirit leave your body."

It was then Jacob realized that this Indian . . . this girl . . . had saved his life. If not for her, he too would be as bloated and odorous as Hamilton Richards. He turned to Fighting Woman and said, "I am sorry. Thank you for my life, though I don't think it was worth your time. But what do we do now? I see you have only one horse."

"You are too weak to walk; you would not get far. If you are ready, we will now leave. You will ride on my pony and I will walk." Jacob started to protest, but she cut him off by saying, "I must get to my village. I cannot leave you here or you will die. You are not strong enough yet, so you will ride. When you are able to walk, I will ride and you will walk."

I won't get far if I start walking west. For now, my only hope is to accompany this Indian girl. Perhaps we'll meet a train or other White Men along the way.

Then the realization came to him.

I never wanted to go to California to begin with; I have no family, no ties, I will go with this girl!

"Your name is Suni, is it not?" asked Jacob.

"Only you and my father may call me Suni. To all others, I am Fighting Woman."

"Well, Suni, my name is Jacob and it is my deepest pleasure to have met you."

"No, your name is Híŋ Zi, Yellow Hair in your tongue. Get on the pony, we leave now."

"Wait, Suni; let me get some food out of my wagon."

"There is no need; I will supply what we eat."

"But I have to do something for the man in the wagon; the wolves will be at him."

"Get on the pony. We leave now!"

Because of his weakened condition, Jacob could not dig a grave. He could barely stand, so he acquiesced to her demand. But first, he retrieved the knife he had taken from the man in Westport; he might have need of it.

He mounted the girl's pony while thinking, *Yellow Hair?*

Chapter Twenty

FIGHTING WOMAN took the lead and walked in a northeasterly direction, following The Trail made by the war party a week earlier. To Jacob she said, "My father and the others should be back in our village by now, but for us, it will take ten sleeps to get there."

"Ten sleeps?"

"Yes, ten nights and we will be in my village."

The first day they covered fifteen miles. Fighting Woman did not hurry; she knew Jacob was too weak to travel at a face pace. With the sun sinking in the west, she had Jacob dismount. With war club in hand, she jumped on her pony and raced away at full gallop.

She had trained her pony to chase down small game on the prairie. She approached a prairie rabbit, leaned off her pony and struck it with her club. She repeated the maneuver three additional times and returned to Jacob with four rabbits. She told him to collect buffalo chips while she skinned and dressed the kill. When Jacob returned with his last burden of chips, Fighting Woman said, "This meat will last us two sleeps."

Jacob had many questions he wanted to ask, but his every query was met with, "We will speak another time."

"Just answer me one question," he implored.

"What question?"

"Who is this *Wakan Taŋka* that wanted my spirit to leave my body?"

"*Wakan Taŋka* is the Great Mysterious, the Great Mystery, the life that is in all things. Your people call him the Great Spirit."

"You mean God?"

"Yes, now do not speak."

Jacob wondered if all Indian girls were as taciturn as Suni.

On the morning of the third day, Jacob thought he was strong enough to walk. When told by Fighting Woman to mount the pony, he refused, telling her that she should ride and he would walk. Instead of arguing, Fighting Woman looked Jacob in the eye and said, "We will see." Within a few hours, Jacob realized he had underestimated his recuperative powers. However, rather than give the girl the satisfaction of knowing that she was right, he continued on. That is, until he collapsed and passed into unconsciousness.

When he came to, it was getting dark and Fighting Woman was nowhere in sight, though he knew she would be back. Her belongings were on the ground next to him. Jacob surmised she had gone hunting. So he thought he would make himself useful, and went out to collect the buffalo chips that would be needed to cook whatever game Fighting Woman was sure to bring back.

It bothered Jacob to be dependent on a girl, even an Indian girl, for his survival. But at the moment, he had no alternative. The cholera had taken its toll.

As he stacked the chips, he thought, *I guess I'll just have to put myself in her hands until I'm stronger*.

Fighting Woman returned with two birds, a variety unfamiliar to Jacob.

Still on her pony, she looked down and held them out, "Take these *wakiye*. We will eat them tonight. Tomorrow you will ride. We have lost enough time because of your foolishness."

Jacob made no reply at that time. Later, while plucking the feathers of the unidentified birds, he said, "I am sorry I slowed you down today, but tonight while we eat, will you please tell me of yourself and of your people? I don't even know what tribe you are with."

130

For the first time since he had known her, Fighting Woman smiled—a small smile, but nevertheless a smile—before saying, "*Damakota!*—I am Dakota!"

They did not speak during dinner, but afterwards, as they lay in the grass looking up at the bright firmament, Fighting Woman began to speak.

"Dakota means ally. There are four tribes within the Dakota: the Yankton, the Yanktonai, the Lakota, and the Santee Sioux. The first three tribes live in the West. We, the Santee Sioux, inhabit the East. Within the Santee Sioux are four bands: the Mdewakanton, the Wahpeton, the Sisseton and the Wahpekute. My people are of the Mdewakanton.

"We received the name Sioux from the Chippewa and the French. The Chippewa called us *Nadonessiou*, which means adder, or enemy. The French shortened the name to Sioux. But we are Dakota!

"Many winters before my time, we lived at Knife Lake, *Isaŋtamde* in my tongue. We were called the *Isaŋyati*, which in your tongue means Dwelling at the Knife. From that, the *Wasichus* called us the Santee Sioux. Yet we are Dakota!

"I will tell you one other thing of my people. I will tell you how we came to be in this world. Then, no more questions until we reach my village.

"In the beginning, before the creation of the Earth, the gods resided in the sky and humans lived in darkness. Chief among the gods is Ta'kuwakaŋ, the Sun, who is married to Haŋyetuwi, the Moon. He has one daughter, Wohpe. And there is Old Man and Old Woman, whose daughter, Ite, is wife to Wind, to whom she gave four sons, the Four Winds.

"Of the other spirits, the most important is Inktomi, the devious trickster. Inktomi conspired with Old Man and Old Woman to increase their daughter's status by arranging an affair between the Sun and Ite. His wife's discovery of the affair led Ta'kuwakaŋ to give the Moon her own domain, and by separating her from himself, created time.

"Old Man, Old Woman and Ite—who was separated from Wind, her husband—were banished to Earth. Ite, along with her children, the Four Winds, and a fifth wind—the child of Ite but not of Wind—established space. The daughter of the Sun and the Moon, Wohpe, also fell to earth and later resided with the South Wind. The two adopted the fifth wind, who is called Wamniomni.

"Alone on the newly formed Earth, some of the gods became bored. Ite prevailed upon Inktomi to find her people, the Buffalo Nation. In the form of a wolf, Inktomi went beneath the earth and discovered a village of humans. Inktomi told them about the wonders of the Earth and convinced one man, Tokahe, to accompany him through a cave to the surface. Tokahe did so and, upon reaching the surface, saw the green grass and blue sky for the first time. Inktomi and Ite introduced Tokahe to buffalo meat and showed him tipis, clothing, hunting clubs, and bows and arrows. Tokahe returned to the underworld village and appealed to six other men and their families to go with him to the Earth's surface.

"When they arrived, they discovered that Inktomi had deceived Tokahe. The buffalo were scarce; the weather had turned bad, and they found themselves starving. Unable to return to their home, but armed with a new knowledge about the world, they survived to become the founders of the Seven Council Fires."

Jacob asked, "The Seven Council Fires?"

"Yes, *Oćeti Šakowin* . . . the Mdewakanton, the Wahpeton, the Wahpekute, the Sisseton, the Yankton, the Yanktonai, and the Lakota," responded Fighting Woman before turning away from Jacob and falling asleep.

The next night as they ate, Jacob prevailed upon Fighting Woman to tell him more of her people. With a sigh, she told him of White Buffalo Calf Woman.

"After Tokahe led the six families to the surface of the earth, they wandered for many winters. Sons were born and sons died. Winters passed, more winters than could be counted. This was before *Oćeti Šakowiŋ*. Then we were not Dakota. Not until White Buffalo Calf Woman did we become Dakota.

"Two scouts were hunting the buffalo when they came to the top of a small hill. A long way off, they observed the figure of a woman. As she approached, they saw that she was beautiful. She was young and carried a *wakiŋ*. One of the scouts had lustful thoughts and told the other. His friend told him that she was sacred and to banish such thoughts.

"The woman came up to them and said to the one with the lustful thoughts, 'If you would do what you are thinking, come forward.' The scout moved and stood before her and a white cloud covered them from sight.

"When the woman stepped from the cloud, it blew away. There on the ground, at the beautiful woman's feet, lay a pile of bones with worms crawling in and among them.

"The woman told the other scout to go to his village and tell his people that she was coming, for them to build a medicine tipi large enough to hold all the chiefs of the nation. She said, 'I bring a great gift to your people.'

"When the people heard the scout's story, they constructed the lodge, and put on their finest clothing, then stood about the lodge and waited.

"As the woman entered the village, she sang:

'With visible breath I am walking.
A voice I am sending as I walk.
In a sacred manner I am walking.
With visible tracks I am walking.
In a sacred manner I walk.'

"She handed the *wakiŋ* to the head chief and he withdrew a pipe from the bundle. On one side of the pipe was carved a bison calf. 'The bison represents the earth, which will house and feed you.'

"Thirteen eagle feathers hung from the wooden stem. White Buffalo Calf Woman told the chiefs, 'The feathers represent the sky and the thirteen moons. With this pipe, you shall prosper. With this pipe, you shall speak with *Wakaŋ Taŋ'ka*. With this pipe, you shall become the People. With this pipe, you shall be bound with the Earth for She is your mother. She is sacred. With this pipe, you shall be bound to your relatives.'

"Having given the pipe to the People, and having said what she had to say, she turned and walked four paces from the lodge and sat down.

"When she arose, she was a red-and-brown buffalo calf. She walked on, lay down and came up as a black buffalo calf. Walking still farther, she turned into a white buffalo and stood upon a hill. She turned to bow in the four directions of the four winds and then she vanished.

"Before White Buffalo Calf Woman, we were as animals. Because of White Buffalo Calf Woman, we honor our mother the Earth; we honor our parents and our grandparents. We honor the birds of the sky; we honor the beasts of the earth. We know that *Wakaŋ Taŋ'ka* resides in all animals, in all trees and plants and rocks and stones. *Wakaŋ Taŋ'ka* is in all. We know that *Wakaŋ Taŋ'ka* lives in each of us. Because of White Buffalo Calf Woman, we have become Dakota."

When she had finished speaking, Fighting Woman smiled at Jacob for the second time since he had awakened from his illness. She then frowned and said, "Enough talk, it is time to sleep."

That girl should smile more often. She has a beautiful smile.

Chapter Twenty-One

THREE MORE DAYS WOULD PASS before they reached Suni's village. During that time, she was as reticent as ever. The only words she spoke to Jacob were short commands. "Wake up." "Collect buffalo chips." "Build a fire." "Go to sleep." And a few other words when it suited her.

As they approached her village, the older children and a few of the women came out to see the *Wasichu* that Fighting Woman had brought back from the raiding party. The women giggled amongst themselves. Captives were supposed to be women, not men. The younger children stayed in their tipis peering out at Jacob with fear showing on their small faces. Their parents had used White Men as a threat. As in, "If you don't behave, I'll let the *Wasichus* get you." Indians did not have wardrobes for a White Man to hide in, nor a bed to hide under, but many an Indian child was convinced that a White Man lurked in the darkness on the far side of their tipi at night, awaiting a chance to devour them.

Being on horseback for ten hours a day for ten consecutive days did not help Jacob's efforts to convalesce. He was still weak. At the edge of the village, Fighting Woman told him to get off the pony and sit under a nearby tree while she spoke with her father. For a moment, Jacob was tempted to tell her that he was finished taking orders, but then thought better of it. The ground beneath the tree did look inviting. There would be time enough when he felt stronger to let her know that he had had it with her bossy ways. For now, he would do as he was told, but only because he was too weak to put up much of a fight.

Once Jacob was sitting on the ground with his back against the tree, Fighting Woman scattered the women,

135

telling them to take their children and go to their homes where they belonged.

She reached her tipi and hesitated for a moment before entering. Because she was an only child, her father had let her do pretty much as she pleased as long as her actions brought no shame to his lodge. Her mother had died when she was quite young and Big Eagle had not taken another woman. It had been just the two of them. As a result, they had grown closer than most fathers and daughters of their band. When Fighting Woman was younger, she had always said she would never marry; she did not desire to be a wife, she wanted to be a warrior. Big Eagle heard those words and secretly smiled. He knew she would one day be a good wife and mother. As she stood before her tipi, she did not know of her father's thoughts back then. She only knew that it was going to be hard to tell him what was *now* in her heart.

She took a deep breath, pushed aside the skin covering the opening, and entered. She saw her father sitting in his place of honor and said, "*Dećiya atkuku wauŋ.*"

Big Eagle put down the piece of dried buffalo meat he had been chewing and responded, "I can see that you are here, daughter. Why have you been so long in coming? I was about to send men out to look for you."

She looked down at the earthen floor of her home and said, "Yellow Hair, I mean the *Wasichu,* did not awaken for five sleeps. Because of his weakness, I had to walk my pony with him on her."

Big Eagle, in spite of himself, let a small smile play across his lips. "Come, daughter, sit here by me. I have not seen you for half a moon. I was worried that the Pawnee might have followed our trail and found you. Now all is right; you are home. So tell me of this *Wasichu*. What do you intend to do with him now that you have brought him here?"

"When I have made a warrior of him, I will marry him and be his woman."

Big Eagle was not surprised at his daughter's declaration. However, as her father, he had some questions that needed to be asked. "You know when you marry you will have to take on the duties of a wife, and sooner or later the duties that come with motherhood. There will be no more warpaths for you."

"Yes, Father, I know. But Yellow Hair is my destiny."

Big Eagle *was* taken aback by that statement. "What do you mean?"

"Father, do you remember when I was of ten winters how sick I was? I lay for eight sleeps near death."

"Yes, Suni, I have not forgotten that time. It was The Winter Of The Great Buffalo Hunt."

"I had a vision then, but I was afraid to tell you or anyone. Girls are not supposed to have visions, only boys and men. But now I will tell you of my vision." Big Eagle said nothing. He nodded at his daughter, relaxed against his backrest, and waited.

Not looking at her father, but off to his left as though once more seeing her vision, Fighting Woman spoke. "I was in terrible pain, but I could not speak to tell of it. Just as I thought that it would be better to die than endure the pain any longer, a handsome brave appeared next to me and said that if I would go with him, the pain would stop. He held out his hand; I took it and stood up. As soon as I was standing, the pain vanished. I turned to look down and saw a girl of my winters lying where I had just been. I asked the brave, 'Who is that?' 'She is you,' was his answer. Then he told me I should go with him, that he had something of great importance to show me. I was afraid to leave myself, or that part of me wrapped in the buffalo skins. 'You will be all right, both of you. When you return, you will be well; there will be no more pain.'"

After a moment's hesitation, she went on. "The brave was handsome, and he seemed so kind that I went with him. We did not walk; we floated up through the top of the tipi as though it was not there. Shortly, we were among the clouds, and he pointed to a white cloud that had only one side. He told me he was going to show me my future, and I was to remember what I was about to see because it was important for my people. Upon the cloud, I saw myself learning the ways of a brave. I learned to ride, to hunt, to make bows and arrows.

"As I watched, the brave said, 'You will learn these things in order to teach another who will come to you during your eighteenth winter. I will now show him to you as he will look then.' The vision faded from the cloud and was replaced by a vision of a *Wasichu* with yellow hair. He lay on the ground under a horse canoe. As I watched, that vision disappeared and was replaced by another. It was of a woman . . . it was me. She was in a tipi, but it was not our tipi. She was a woman of about thirty winters. Then a boy-child of about ten winters entered. He ran up to me and said something that I could not hear. I shook my head as if to say no. Next, the one with the yellow hair entered the tipi. But he did not look the same. He was dressed as a brave. His hair was long and braided. He wore eagle feathers in his hair, and was painted for war. He walked over, kissed me, and ruffled the boy's hair. Smiling at us, he walked out of the tipi. For some reason that I cannot explain, I knew he would not be harmed in battle.

"Then the handsome brave took hold of my hand and said it was time to go back. He said that if I stayed away from the part of me wrapped in the buffalo skins for too long, I would not be able to return. We descended from the clouds and floated once again through the top of the tipi. I awakened to see you looking at me with tears in your eyes. As the brave had said, the pain was gone and I was well again. The man in my vision was the same man we found in that place of death; he is the man that I have brought to our village."

Big Eagle said nothing for a few minutes. Finally, he asked, "What do you want to do now?"

"Father, Yellow Hair is still not well. I must get him strong so that I may teach him our ways. When he becomes the man I saw in my vision, I will become his woman."

"Suni, you have always known your own mind. I have encouraged you to follow your own path. Are you sure this is where you want to go?"

"Father, it is where I *must* go. There is one other thing that the handsome brave said to me that I have not told you. He said what Yellow Hair and others of our tribe do while alive will not do much to alter the destiny of the Dakota, but long after we have gone south to the world of the dead, their deeds will have secured for the Dakota a place in this world. He said that the *Wasichus* would at long last come to realize the greatness of the Dakota."

"Suni, have you asked the *Wasichu* what he wants?"

"It does not matter what he wants. It is our destiny."

Big Eagle could only shake his head and say, "Go and get your *Wasichu*. I will speak with Taoyateduta, our chief. If Little Crow says he may stay, then he will stay. If Little Crow decides he must leave, he will have to leave. However, I will speak on his behalf."

Fighting Woman leaned into her father and kissed him on the cheek. Without saying another word, she stood and left the tipi.

She found Jacob where she had left him. He was fast asleep. She looked down on him as a loving mother would look upon her sleeping child. Of course, Fighting Woman would not have let Jacob see the expression of love on her face, not yet. First, she had to get him well, and then she had to make a man of him—one worthy of her. Because of her vision, she knew that, in time, it would come to pass.

She knelt down and shook him by the shoulder. He awakened with a start, looked about him, and then looked at

Fighting Woman. "I was just dreaming of lifting dead bodies into the air where they caught on fire."

"Yes, it is a terrible thing to see one's friends and family die, but you are a man, and men do not let such things bother them." Fighting Woman had just given Jacob his first lesson in the ways of the Dakota.

"Come now, we will speak with my father."

After ten days with Fighting Woman, Jacob was getting used to obeying her commands without question. He had been dependent on her while they traveled to her village. If not for her, he would have starved during the journey. Nevertheless, when he was halfway to a standing position, he sat back down and said, "Suni, there is much that I owe you, but from this moment on, I will not take orders from you."

Standing over Jacob with her arms folded, Fighting Woman let the slightest smile escape before she again frowned.

This is what I've been waiting for—Yellow Hair to treat me as a woman.

"If you want to eat tonight, you will speak with my father." She turned away, but before leaving said, "Follow when you are hungry."

Damn her, I am already hungry.

He raised himself and ran to catch up.

Fighting Woman held back the skin covering the entrance to the tipi and motioned for Jacob to enter. He saw a man, a big man, directly in front of him. He was sitting on a buffalo hide on the ground—or floor. Jacob was not sure if the ground inside of a tipi was called a floor or not. It was his first time inside a tipi.

The man spoke. "*Ekta mitawa ounyaŋ ikieiyuśkiŋ.*"

"My father welcomes you to his lodge," translated Fighting Woman.

Jacob asked, "Does he speak English?"

"Only when he has to. Sit down, I will bring food."

All of a sudden, Jacob lost his appetite sitting in front of the father of the girl with whom he had spent ten days and nights without anyone else present. He was thinking, *Shotgun wedding.*

Big Eagle was thinking, *What a sorry excuse for a son-in-law.*

Neither man spoke. Jacob fidgeted; Big Eagle looked sullen and stared at Jacob. Finally, to both men's relief, Fighting Woman returned with three portions of food. After having placed a bowl in front of each man, she said, "Have you two gotten to know one another?"

In unison, they stammered, "Yes." That made them smile. The ice was broken. Big Eagle was the first to let out with an uproarious laugh. Then Jacob followed with a hearty laugh of his own. Fighting Woman looked at them and thought, *Men!*

As they ate, Big Eagle asked questions. He wanted to know where Jacob came from, how he got to the place where they had found him, and what had happened to the people. When he asked what his plans were, Big Eagle received a withering look from his daughter. A look Jacob missed because he was answering the question. "I don't know. My entire family is gone. I have no home to go back to. I guess I'm free to do as I please."

Fighting Woman smiled at Jacob's response.

Big Eagle took pity on his daughter and said, "You are welcome to stay here in our village for as long as you wish. I will talk with our chief. I am sure he will invite you to be our . . . our . . . Suni, what is the word I am trying to say?"

"I think, Father, you want to say *guest.*"

"Yes, that is it. Our band would like you to be our guest. After I speak with our chief, I will secure a place for you to stay while you are here. It would not be proper for you to stay in this tipi seeing as how Suni is a maiden."

They finished eating and Fighting Woman brought out a pipe. She handed it to her father and said to Jacob, "I will go and speak with Heȟáka Wa'kitapi. He is our *pežihuta wičasta* and he will make you strong." Smiling at her father, she turned and left the tipi.

"Mister Big Eagle, what is a *pežihuta wičasta?*"

"A *pežihuta wičasta* is a medicine man."

"You know, Mister Big Eagle, your daughter should smile more often."

"Yes, Yellow Hair, I think so too."

"Sir, my name is Jacob, not Yellow Hair. I don't know why Suni insists on calling me by that name."

"If she wants to call you Yellow Hair, be Yellow Hair. Make your life easy. I have known her for eighteen winters. I am bigger and stronger than she; still I do as I am told," said Big Eagle with a smile.

He then asked Jacob why he had addressed his daughter as Suni. "Because she told me that is what I should call her. She said only you and I may address her as such."

Nodding his head, Big Eagle said, "Looks as though you are one of the family, like it or not." He then raised his pipe and put a lighted stick to the contents. After drawing smoke through the stem, he reached out to hand it to Jacob.

"No, thank you, sir. I do not use tobacco."

Blowing smoke into the air, Big Eagle said, "It is not tobacco. It is the bark of the red willow. This pipe is holy. You see the five ribbons hanging from it? The black is the West, where the Thunder Beings live. They bring us the rain. The red is the East, where the morning star lives. The East gives us light. The yellow is for the South, the summer. It has the power to grow. The white ribbon is the cleansing wind from the North. The eagle feather signifies the Father. The sky is Father. On the mouthpiece is buffalo hide to signify the Mother. The earth is our mother."

When he had finished speaking, Big Eagle again held out the pipe to Jacob. This time Jacob accepted and drew on the holy pipe.

He coughed as he handed it back to Big Eagle.

Chapter Twenty-Two

BIG EAGLE rose and said to Jacob, "I will inform Little Crow of your presence. Before I come back, I will see Tataŋkabdoka Ptéčela. His granddaughter, who he raised, just married a man of the Wahpekute and Short Bull cannot stand the man's mother. He refuses to live with them. He lives alone and if I tell him you will perform the tasks that a son would do, he may allow you to live in his lodge. We shall see. You wait here. Suni will soon return."

Jacob sat thinking. He had nowhere to go, and no one to go to. Should he stay with the Indians? Should he go west or perhaps back East? Pondering these questions, he slowly came to the realization that he liked Big Eagle and, God help him, he even liked Suni. In the few moments he had been left to himself, he made up his mind to stay with the Dakota—at least for the time being.

About then, Fighting Woman entered the lodge. "Looking Elk will see you in the morning. Where is Father?"

"He went to speak with your chief and to find me a place to live. I have decided to stay for a while."

"That is good, Yellow Hair."

"You may call me Yellow Hair, but please don't call me late for dinner."

Fighting Woman did not understand, "What is that you have said?"

"Never mind, it was only a joke. You know ... ha ... ha."

No, she did not understand, but she let it pass because she was pleased she would not have to fight with him to stay.

Big Eagle returned and announced, "Little Crow has extended the friendship of the Dakota to the guest of Fighting Woman."

He went on to say that Short Bull thought it a good thing to have a young man in his lodge, someone to do the heavy work even if he was a *Wasichu*. "Short Bull does not speak your tongue; Suni will speak for you."

After thanking Big Eagle for the efforts on his behalf, Jacob left with Fighting Woman for Short Bull's lodge.

As they walked through the village on that first night, Fighting Woman explained that if he were to live among the Dakota, he must become a Dakota. "You must learn our language and the ways of a brave. Boys are taught from birth how to be Dakota, but you are already a man; you will have to learn quickly. Living with Short Bull is good. It will help you to learn our language."

When she had finished speaking, she stopped short and asked, "How many winters are you?"

By now Jacob knew what she meant by winters, but he still had to think before answering. "It was the beginning of June when I took sick; you told me I was out for five sleeps, and it took us ten sleeps to get here. I will be twenty-one winters next month, which should be in a few days . . . I mean sleeps."

"'Month', what is month? Do you mean the Moon When Cherries Are Ripe?"

The Dakota labeled the months by moons. July was the Moon When Cherries Are Ripe. Jacob answered in the affirmative that in the Moon When Cherries Are Ripe, he would be twenty-one. In the white culture, one became a man upon reaching his majority, twenty-one. In the Dakota culture, a boy became a man once he experienced his Vision Quest, when he would seek an animal spirit that would protect him for the rest of his life. Some boys went on their Vision Quest as young as fourteen winters.

As they walked on, Fighting Woman thought, *I have much work ahead of me before Yellow Hair becomes a Dakota and the man of my vision.*

Presently they arrived at Short Bull's tipi.

A wizened old man of sixty-five winters, Short Bull had been quite the warrior in his day and had the coup feathers to prove it, most of them first coup. The battles had taken a toll on the man. He walked with a pronounced limp and had multiple scars on most parts of his body where arrows—and a few musket balls—had penetrated. However, living to the ripe old age of sixty-five winters had mellowed the once-fierce warrior, as it did all men.

Short Bull heard Fighting Woman's greeting of "*Deḉiya wauŋ Mi'ye*," and immediately went to the entrance of his tipi, threw back the skin, and gave her a smile that would have been dazzling if not for the fact that most of his teeth were missing. When war club meets teeth, the war club usually carries the day.

"Come in, come in," exclaimed Short Bull in the Dakota language, "and bring your *Wasichu* with you."

Continuing in his native tongue, Short Bull bid Jacob and Fighting Woman to be seated and offered them something to eat, which Fighting Woman declined on her and Jacob's behalf.

"This is Yellow Hair. He has much to learn and, with your help, he will learn our language. He has been ill; he may be weak for a while, but when he is well, he will be of help to you. We thank you for taking him into your lodge. Remember, he does not speak our tongue, so be patient with him."

In the morning when Fighting Woman and Looking Elk arrived at Short Bull's tipi, they found Jacob and Short Bull sitting and staring at one another.

"Thank God you're here," said Jacob. "I cannot understand what he wants me to do."

Short Bull said, "Fighting Woman, your *Wasichu* is not very bright. He does not understand the words a child should know."

Fighting Woman stared at both men with a look of exasperation. Finally she said, "Yellow Hair, I will start teaching you our language today." She next directed her attention to Short Bull. Reverting to her own language, she told him, "He will quickly learn our tongue, but you must be patient. You can help teach him by pointing to what you want and saying the word for it. Now, what is it you wanted him to do?"

"Simply to take my hatchet and go chop firewood."

"Short Bull, if Yellow Hair had said the same thing to you in his tongue, you would not understand his words. You should have picked up your hatchet and told him the word for it, and then taken him and shown him what it is you wanted." She looked around the tipi, saw Short Bull's hatchet and picked it up. Holding it out to Jacob, she said, "This is oŋspedaŋ. Short Bull wants you to get firewood. He will show you where it is. Then you cut it into small pieces for his fire. But first, Looking Elk has some medicine for you. Drink it. It will make you strong."

After Looking Elk had administered his potion and left, Fighting Woman took Short Bull by the hand and then Jacob. She walked them out of the tipi. To each she said the same thing in his own language, "You two start acting like grown men." Then to Short Bull she said, "Show him what it is you want done and he will do it." To Jacob she said, "Do what Short Bull asks of you. After you two have eaten, I will return and we will begin your lessons."

As the two men walked away, Fighting Woman once again exclaimed, "*Men!*"

Every day for the next moon, Jacob grew stronger. He was a good pupil and he had a knack for languages, or at least for the Dakota language. He and Short Bull had warmed up to one another considerably since that first day. Every morning after Jacob finished his chores, Fighting Woman would come and school him in the language of the Dakota. In the afternoon, she would teach him how to ride a pony into war, and the different ways to ride while hunting buffalo or rabbits and other small game.

By the end of the first moon since coming to the Mdewakanton village, Jacob was dressing as a brave. Fighting Woman had made him a breechclout, leggings and a set of moccasins. His skin was getting brown from the sun and his hair was getting long. When he asked Fighting Woman to cut it, she replied, "A brave needs long, braided hair to hold his coup feathers."

As Jacob became more proficient in their language, members of the village got to know him, and the little children were no longer afraid of him. At first they followed him with only their eyes. As their hearts grew braver, they followed him at a distance. One day Jacob stopped suddenly, turned to the children following him, and motioned for them to come closer.

They stood frozen, not knowing whether to run or act brave and stand their ground. The youngest of the group approached and looked up at the tall *Wasichu*. Jacob sat down on his heels and asked the youngster his name. The boy did not answer. He stood transfixed, staring at Jacob's yellow hair. Tentatively, he reached out to feel it and Jacob allowed him to do so. In a matter of seconds, all the other children crowded around him, touching his hair. From that day on, the children of the village referred to him as Uncle Yellow Hair.

By the end of the second moon after his arrival in the village, Fighting Woman no longer spoke to Jacob in English, only in her own tongue. She knew the time had come for him to become a Dakota. "The four things that make a man a man are bravery, fortitude, generosity, and wisdom. You will find that the fourth grows out of excellence of the first three." Fighting Woman went on to say, "You have asked me many times what coup feathers were, and I said that I would tell you when the time was right. Well, the time is now.

"First coup is striking an enemy at close range with a coup stick. Second coup is killing your enemy. However, just because you have first coup does not mean that you are entitled to second coup. Anyone may rush in, kill the enemy, and claim second coup. First coup feathers are much more desired than second coup feathers. For to claim first coup—to attack the enemy in hand-to-hand combat—shows true bravery," explained Fighting Woman.

"After you have struck the enemy, yell your name and say, 'I have overcome this one'. After the battle, you will need witnesses to claim coup. That is why you shout your name. If you are wounded or rescue a comrade, you claim third coup. Capturing a horse is fourth coup. If you have witnesses to your deeds of bravery, you are awarded your coup feathers at *Wakté-gli*. The Kill Dance is the celebration after a victory where you will tell of your courage."

As far as Jacob knew, he had no enemies. If he did, killing them or knocking them off a horse with a war club would not be the way he would go about settling such matters. He conveyed those thoughts to Fighting Woman who simply said, "Cowards are not welcome by the Mdewakanton." She also informed him that their enemies were his enemies as long as he resided with them.

"The Chippewa are our worst enemies; we have been at war with them for many, many winters. It is they who drove us from Lake of the Knife. They are still trying to drive us from our land. I know that you will fight when the time comes. Enough for now. It is late; we must go to our lodges. Tomorrow, Looking Elk will tell you of our religion."

Jacob walked with Fighting Woman to her tipi and paid his respects to Big Eagle. Whilst he walked back to Short Bull's lodge, the little boy who had first approached him came to him. Jacob looked down at the little fellow and said hello.

"Uncle Yellow Hair, where are you going?"

"I am going home."

It occurred to Jacob that he had not thought of Short Bull's tipi as "home" until that very moment. It stunned him.

Yes, it is my home. Short Bull has treated me as a son.

He smiled, knowing that once again he did indeed have a home.

Jacob became mindful that he had never bothered to ask the boy's name since their first encounter. The youngster had walked with him many times and had never said much more than "Uncle Yellow Hair." Jacob got down on one knee and again asked the child his name.

"I am called Running Close. When I am big, I will go on the warpath and get many coup feathers. Then I will have a new name."

Fighting Woman had told Jacob that male children usually did not keep the name given them at birth. After his Vision Quest, a boy's name might be changed. Or, after a young brave had distinguished himself in battle, his father might give the brave his name as an honor, taking a new name for himself. Fighting Woman was an exception. Until her fourteenth winter, she was known as Red Eagle Woman. However, in The Winter Of The Falling Snow, she followed a raiding party that had set out to steal horses from the Chippewa. She did not know exactly what she was going to do when they met the enemy. But she did know she wanted to participate in some way. She thought it unfair that men should have all the fun.

Before they could reach the Chippewa camp, the raiding party was attacked. Red Eagle Woman, without thought, charged into the battle wielding a tomahawk. She embedded it in the skull of the first Chippewa she met. Unwilling to release her hold on her weapon, she was pulled to the ground by the weight of the dead Chippewa as he fell from his pony. Her head hit a boulder, knocking her unconscious. After the Mdewakanton prevailed, they found her still holding onto the tomahawk embedded in the Chippewa's head.

The braves returned to the village with Red Eagle Woman still unconscious and brought her to her father's lodge. Big Eagle had not been on the raid. There was to be no fighting, just the stealing of horses in the night. Seeing his daughter, he feared the worse, but when told she was alive and had a strong heartbeat, his anguish turned to anger. The brave carrying Red Eagle Woman placed her on her skins and Big Eagle sat down and waited for his daughter to regain consciousness.

By the time the Kill Dance was underway, Red Eagle Woman was sitting up, rubbing her head, wondering what had happened. Her father was patient; he wanted her fully awake before he scolded her. But before he could do so, a brave that had been on the raid called out, "*Dećiya wauŋ Miʼye?*"

"Of course you may enter my lodge. You are always welcome," replied Big Eagle.

The brave asked Big Eagle if he would allow Red Eagle Woman to attend the Kill Dance and tell of her coups. She had two—first and second. Big Eagle's first thought was to throw him out of his tipi, but when he saw the sparkle in his daughter's eyes, he relented. "She may do as she wishes; I am only her father," he said with a smile.

At the Kill Dance, when the time came for her to receive her feathers, two braves stepped forward, and each, in turn, told how they had found her with the dead Chippewa. Little Crow asked Red Eagle Woman to stand and approach. He handed her two feathers, one for striking the enemy and one for killing him. He then asked her to recount her coups.

She stood in silence for a moment, looking dazed. She looked to her father for help. He shrugged as if to say, *This is your doing, not mine.*

At length, she said, "I am sorry, I remember nothing. The last thing I remember is kicking my pony; I wanted to get into the fight before it was over."

All those assembled burst into laughter, even her father.

Big Eagle walked over to Little Crow and after a few moments of discussion, Little Crow sat down while Big Eagle remained standing. He held up his hands for silence. When all eyes were on him, he said, "Little Crow and I have decided that my daughter has earned herself a new name. She may have her choice of two. Choose your name, daughter. Is it to be Forgets Woman or Fighting Woman?"

That was his and Little Crow's way of chastising her for going on the raid in the first place. They knew what name she would choose, and from that day forward, she was known as Fighting Woman.

Chapter Twenty-Three

JACOB RETURNED HOME that evening to find Short Bull sitting in his usual place, working on an ear of corn, doing the best he could despite his lack of teeth.

"Good evening, Grandfather. If you would like, I will prepare us food."

"No, Yellow Hair. This will do for me, but you eat something."

"Maybe later. If I may, I would like to talk with you."

"We talk every night. Why so formal this night?"

"I would like to speak to you about your youth."

"I should warn you that there is nothing old men like more than speaking about their youth."

Jacob smiled and sat down opposite Short Bull.

"I would first like to speak of war."

"My favorite subject," responded Short Bull.

"I want to know why the Mdewakanton fight the Chippewa generation after generation. I am told you have been at war with them since you were a boy."

"Yellow Hair, we have been at war with the Chippewa long before I was born."

"But why? You do a raid, they retaliate. They steal horses, you steal horses. It never ends. What is the point?"

Short Bull put down the corn—he was not making much headway with it anyway—and picked up his pipe. He took his time getting the bowl burning, using the time to think. Finally, he said, "There is more to it than what you see. You look at things as a *Wasichu*, which is how it should be. However, you must understand our way of life. There is nothing more important to us, to both men and women, than bravery. A woman will have nothing to do with a man if he is not brave. Members of our village will shun a man who is cowardly in battle."

"But ..."

"No, let me finish. The only way to prove bravery is in battle. Yes, one can be brave during a buffalo surround. Some bulls can be dangerous, but it is not the same as facing a man who wants to kill you. My people need to go on the warpath to allow the young men who have not yet been in battle to prove their bravery.

"Wait while I reload my pipe. I am happy you do not use tobacco; it leaves more for me."

Once he had refilled and lit his pipe, Short Bull continued, "You see that stick over there with the feathers hanging from it? That is my coup stick and those are my coup feathers. Without them, I would have to live with my granddaughter and the man she married, not to mention that terrible mother of his.

"Because I was once a great warrior, I do not go hungry. The women bring me the corn and other things they grow in the summer. Men will put aside a choice piece of meat and give it to me when they return from the hunt. I will tell you, Yellow Hair, that there is no better feeling in this world than yelling '*Hoka hey*' and galloping right up to your enemy and touching him with your coup stick."

While Short Bull was speaking, his pipe had gone out, but he did not relight it. He stared at the bowl, lost in thought. Perhaps thinking of past battles and the praise and admiration he had received at the Kill Dances afterwards.

Coming out of his reverie, Short Bull looked up from his pipe and said, "One more thing makes a man fight."

Jacob, thinking the conversation at an end, had been about to leave. Instead, he sat back down and asked, "What is that?"

"Hatred."

"How can you hate people you do not know?"

"It is very easy. When a raiding party enters your village, kills your son or your mother or your best friend, the hatred rises from within."

"Perhaps you are right. I once threatened a man for insulting my sister even though she did not grasp the meaning of his words."

Short Bull smiled his toothless smile, "I am old now and some of the hatred has left me. The older I get, the less I hate."

The next day, as Jacob and Fighting Woman walked to Looking Elk's lodge, Running Close came up to them holding out a small knife. Not much more than a toy, but it did have a steel blade.

"What is this?" asked Jacob.

"It is for you when you go on the warpath, Uncle Yellow Hair."

Jacob took the proffered knife, inspected it and said, "Will you not need this when you yourself go on the warpath, my little friend?"

"When I am old enough and ready to battle our enemies, you can return it."

Jacob smiled at the boy who had become his friend, thanked him, and told him he would always carry the knife. Running Close grinned from ear to ear and ran back from where he had come. Fighting Woman watched the exchange between the two, thinking that Yellow Hair would make a good father.

They arrived at Looking Elk's tipi to find him waiting outside. To Fighting Woman he said, "You will not be needed. Yellow Hair and I have things to discuss that do not concern women."

Looking Elk's words did not anger Fighting Woman. She knew of what they would speak—she had told Looking Elk the previous day what she wanted him to say to Yellow Hair. Nevertheless, she pretended to take umbrage at his declaration, raised her chin in the air, turned from them, and walked off with a smile that neither man could see. Looking Elk and Yellow Hair watched her retreating figure for a moment before Looking Elk said, "Come; let us walk among the trees."

They reached a clearing in the woods and, wasting no time, Looking Elk got down to business. "It is the Moon When Calves Grow Hair. Soon it will be the Moon of the Changing Season. Then we will fold our tipis, put our children upon pony drags, and go hunt the buffalo. We live in this village only during the warm moons when the women can grow corn and turnips, when men can hunt the deer and the elk. The buffalo feed us in winter; the village nourishes us in summer."

By now Jacob was wondering what Looking Elk was leading up to. He did not have long to wait. "Yellow Hair, before we go to hunt the buffalo, you must attend to your Vision Quest."

"Vision Quest? What are you speaking of?"

"Before you can become a man, you must seek an animal spirit that will protect you for the rest of your life."

"I am already a man," asserted Jacob.

"If you are to be a member of our band, you will seek your vision," said Looking Elk. He started to walk away but stopped. Turning back toward Jacob, he said, "You have little time; when you are ready, I will prepare you."

He left Jacob standing alone in the clearing, in the woods, and in confusion.

Fighting Woman was waiting for Jacob when he returned to Short Bull's tipi. He entered and she looked at him expectantly, yet he said nothing. He sat down, seemingly lost in thought. After a few minutes, Fighting Woman asked if there was anything wrong. Rather than answer her question, Jacob asked one of his own. "Where is Short Bull?"

"He went to visit his granddaughter. What is troubling you, Yellow Hair?"

"I wish everyone would stop thinking me as less of a man because I do not follow your ways. Looking Elk tells me I cannot be a man unless I have a Vision Quest."

Fighting Woman walked over to Jacob and knelt down. Taking both his hands in hers, she looked into his sky-blue eyes and said, "The Vision Quest was my idea. I am sorry. I know you are a man. You are the man I love, but our ways, I believe, will make you a better man."

Jacob was surprised, to say the least. Not once in the three moons he had known her had Suni, in word or deed, indicated feelings for him. He looked at her kneeling before him, and for the first time saw her as a woman. He noticed that she was not dressed in her customary breechclout and shirt. She was wearing a deerskin dress. In addition, her hair was not braided; it fell—no, it *cascaded*—down over her shoulders and shimmered in the light of the fire.

This girl . . . this woman . . . is beautiful!

He wanted to kiss her; however, his Yankee upbringing kept that impulse at bay.

For a minute, they sat looking into one another's eyes. At last, Jacob said, "Suni, if *you* want me to have a Vision Quest, I will do it. Tell Looking Elk I am ready."

Fighting Woman, not having been brought up as a Yankee, kissed Jacob full on the mouth before running out of the tipi.

Women! thought Jacob.

Fighting Woman collected Jacob from Short Bull's lodge the next morning and escorted him to Looking Elk's tipi. When they arrived, he was again waiting for them outside where he addressed Fighting Woman, "I will speak with Yellow Hair alone. You go and get Chetáŋ Okáwiŋȟya." When she had gone, Looking Elk pointed to his tipi and motioned for Jacob to go inside.

Once seated, Looking Elk told Jacob of the Vision Quest. "The Vision Quest was given to us by White Buffalo Calf Woman. It is sacred. You will first take *inipi*. The sweat bath will cleanse your body. Next, you will be taken to a place of solitude; you will wear only your breechclout and moccasins. You must not eat until you have had your vision. You will pray to *Wakaŋ Taŋ'ka* to send you a vision—it usually comes on the third or fourth day. Once you have your vision, the *Wichasha Wakaŋ* will interpret it for you. Then you will be Dakota, even though your hair is the color of corn."

The sweat bath not only prepared boys for their Vision Quest, it also helped in the prevention and cure of ailments, and was part of the Dakota religion. Braves took a sweat bath before major ceremonies and before going on the warpath. A sweat lodge consisted of an *éistinna*—a small hut—built from willow saplings covered with skins to let in the least amount of air. A depression dug in the center of the hut accommodated heated stones over which water was poured. At the conclusion of the sweat bath, the brave would immerse himself in the cold water of a river, lake, or stream.

Looking Elk finished speaking just as Fighting Woman entered with a man of forty winters. He was tall and broad in the chest. He looked more a warrior than a *Wichasha Wakaŋ*.

Looking Elk spoke: "This is Circling Hawk. He is a dreamer, a man who dreams sacred dreams. He also interprets the dreams of others. After you have your vision, he will tell us what it means."

Looking Elk turned to Fighting Woman and told her that she must leave. "This is no place for a woman."

In the past when men tried to exclude her from their activities, be it hunting or war, Fighting Woman would jut out her jaw and inform them that she could do anything they could do, and do it better. However, in this instance she was facing the only two men of her village, the medicine man and the *Wichasha Wakaŋ*, who knew of things that she did not.

Therefore, she kept her mouth shut—for once. She smiled at the three men and left without a word.

Looking Elk declared it was time for Jacob to go to the river and heat the stones for his sweat bath. Purified, he would immerse himself in the cold water of the river before being taken to a holy place where he would remain until *Wakan Tanʹka* sent him a vision.

When, four days later, Jacob had not returned, Looking Elk went in search of him and found him lying on the ground, staring up at the sky.

I should have known that the Wasichu could not follow the way of the Dakota. The fool is near death from having not eaten.

He looked down into Jacob's eyes and what he saw was not a half-starved *Wasichu*, but a man in the throes of ecstasy.

"Did you have your vision?" asked Looking Elk.

"Yes."

"Then why did you not return to the village?"

"I wanted to think on what I saw."

"It is not for you to interpret your vision. It is for the *Wichasha Wakan* to do so."

"Yes, that is true, and I welcome his wisdom in helping me understand my vision. *Wakan Tanʹka* spoke to me. His words were trying to reach my spirit. Now they have."

"When did *Wakan Tanʹka* speak to you?"

"Yesterday."

"After not eating for three days, you stayed another day to 'think'?" asked Looking Elk incredulously.

"Yes. But I will go with you now. It is time that I became a Dakota. We will see what Circling Hawk has to say."

Jacob stood and smiled at Looking Elk. "It is a beautiful day. I thank you for coming to bring me home."

Looking Elk held back as Jacob started down the path that led to the village. He stared silently at the retreating White Man for a long minute.

Either all Wasichus are crazy . . . or something extraordinary happened with this one.

Chapter Twenty-Four

JACOB RETURNED to Short Bull's tipi, cleaned himself, and ate. A short while later, Circling Hawk and Looking Elk called out for permission to enter. Jacob answered, "Short Bull is not here; however, come in, my friends. I have ears for what you have to say."

When seated opposite Jacob, the two men looked at one another, both thinking, *Is this the same Wasichu we sent into the woods only four days ago?*

Jacob pulled out Short Bull's pipe, filled it with red willow bark, and said, "White Buffalo Calf Woman has shown us the way. In remembrance of her, we smoke the sacred pipe."

Circling Hawk could contain himself no longer.

"What do *you* know of White Buffalo Calf Woman?"

"Until yesterday, only what Fighting Woman has told me. But now, I understand. Now I know what she was trying to tell the Dakota."

"You, a *Wasichu,* know what White Buffalo Calf Woman was '*trying*' to tell us?" asked an incredulous Looking Elk.

Jacob caught the sarcasm in the man's voice but ignored it. "I only know what *Wakaŋ Taŋˊka* has told me."

"If I may ask," inquired Looking Elk rather sardonically, "what is it that *Wakaŋ Taŋˊka* has told you?"

Jacob, reverting to the parlance of the *Wasichu,* said, "I thought you would never ask."

The boy born Jacob Ariesen—now the man called Yellow Hair—spoke. "White Buffalo Calf Woman told the Dakota that *Wakaŋ Taŋˊka* resides in the sky, in the earth, the trees, plants, and grasses, and rocks. Is that not so?"

Looking Elk, after a quick glance to Circling Hawk, replied, "Yes. That is true."

Yellow Hair then went on. "*Wakaŋ Taŋ'ka* lives in all of the Dakota. Is that not also true?"

"Yes, Yellow Hair. That is also true," answered Circling Hawk.

Yellow Hair continued, "*Wakaŋ Taŋ'ka* is in *all* living things, is that not true?" Both men nodded in agreement.

Yellow Hair pulled on the pipe and blowing smoke into the air said, "Then, it stands to reason that *Wakaŋ Taŋ'ka* lives in the Chippewa, the Crow, the Flatheads, the Pawnee, in all the people; yes, even in the *Wasichus*."

He stretched out his hand offering the pipe. The two men seated in front of him, both of whom were older and wiser than he, looked at one another before Circling Hawk reached out to accept it.

"What you say is true, Yellow Hair. *Wakaŋ Taŋ'ka* lives in all of us," countered Circling Hawk. "But if it were not his wish that we war with the other people on his earth, it would not happen. It is not for us to discern *Wakaŋ Taŋ'ka's* plan for us."

Having said his piece, the *Wichasha Wakaŋ* drew on the pipe and handed it to Looking Elk.

Looking Elk accepted the pipe and spoke, "What was your vision, Yellow Hair?"

"I was on a prairie. The grass was tall; it reached up to my waist. I had a bow and a full quiver of arrows across my shoulder. In my right hand, I held a lance that was much taller than I. From the lance hung a single eagle feather. I stood alone, and for as far as I could see, there was only prairie.

"A black cloud covered the sun, allowing only one ray of sunlight to pass through. It fell just before me. From the light stepped a beautiful woman wearing a white deerskin dress. She came to me, took my hand and pointed to the sky. 'The father lives there.' She pointed to the earth beneath our feet, 'Our mother.' Letting go of my hand, she walked to the place where she had first appeared, sat down in the grass and I could see her no more. From that place arose a white buffalo. "The buffalo spoke to me. 'Everything on the earth is of *Wakaŋ Taŋ́ka*. From the dirt upon which we stand, to the smallest rocks, to the prairie rabbits, to the elk and deer of the woods, to the wolves on the prairie and to the bears that live on the mountains. *Wakaŋ Taŋ́ka* lives in the Dakota. *Wakaŋ Taŋ́ka* lives in all, including your enemies.' She then changed into a great mountain lion whose head stood above the tall grass. It sprang at me. Without thinking, I raised the lance and the mountain lion was impaled upon it."

A moment passed before Circling Hawk spoke, "I will tell you the meaning of your vision. Yes, *Wakaŋ Taŋ́ka* lives in everything of the earth, including our enemies. What the woman, the buffalo, and the mountain lion were trying to tell you is that, when it comes time to defend yourself, you will fight . . . and you will kill if you have to."

Circling Hawk stood and walked to the entrance of the tipi. "There will be a ceremony celebrating your vision. At that time, you will be accepted into the Mdewakanton band of the Dakota. A new name is usually given to one who has completed his Vision Quest. However, since you are older and already have the name given to you by Fighting Woman, you will remain Yellow Hair." Turning, he left the tipi.

Looking Elk stared at Yellow Hair for a long moment before he spoke. "Will you be going with the young braves on the next raiding party?"

"Yes," answered Yellow Hair, "I will go to prove my courage. I will get first coup, but I will leave second coup to others. I will not kill."

Looking Elk shook his head and said, "Did you not listen to Circling Hawk? Did you not hear his words?"

"I heard his words. Perhaps the time will come when I will have to kill, but I will not kill to steal a horse."

"You are still young. I know you will learn our ways; it was in your vision."

Yellow Hair thought for a moment before speaking. "That is a fence I will climb when I get to it."

"We Indians say, 'That is a path I will walk when I come to it'. We have no fences on our land."

There were no fences on the Mdewakanton land that day. However, they were coming, and so were the *Wasichus*.

That night, Yellow Hair became a Dakota.

Chapter Twenty-Five

IN THE DAYS that followed, Yellow Hair and Suni spent much time together, hunting deer and other game. It was during those hunting excursions that Yellow Hair fell in love with Suni. She had loved him from the moment she first laid eyes on him. Indeed, she had been in love with the *Wasichu* with the yellow hair since she was a child and first saw him in her vision.

Suni taught Yellow Hair how to make a bow, how to choose the green wood—ash was the best. She showed him how to bend the sapling against a tree and tie it off to two stakes on either side of the tree until it dried in the desired shape. She also taught him how to string a bow with the sinew of buffalo legs, how to make arrows and give them true aim using the feathers of the turkey. In no time, Yellow Hair became proficient in the use of a bow and arrow.

One day they stopped to rest in a small glade. They had been stalking a deer, but lost it when the wind changed and the deer caught their scent. With Suni lying flat on the ground looking up at clouds through the trees, and Yellow Hair lying next to her, up on one elbow looking down into her eyes, he asked her about the Mdewakanton ritual for marriage.

Suni smiled, as women do, and answered his question with a question, also as women do. "Are you thinking of getting married?"

"Yes, I thought it time I settled down. Do you know any eligible women in the village? I would prefer one whose father owns many ponies."

Suni sat up. Her first impulse was to hit Yellow Hair in the chest with her fist, but thought better of it when she saw the grin on his face and the laughter in his eyes. She decided to play along.

"There are three ways a man may take a wife. First, if her father will not permit the marriage, the man can run away with her and live in another village. Or the father can give him the woman. But the best way is for the man to buy the woman from her father."

Yellow Hair had to think about that. "Why is buying the woman the best way? Would it not be better to get her without paying?"

Suni answered, "It is not best for the man, it is best for the woman. For the rest of her life, she can say that her husband loved her so much that he paid for her."

"How much does a woman cost?" was Yellow Hair's sensible question.

"It depends on how many ponies the man has."

"I have no ponies, so the woman I marry will never know how much I love her."

"Do you love her very much?" asked Suni.

"Yes, I do. She saved my life and has taught me the ways of her people. She is blessed by *Wakaŋ Taŋ'ka* with good looks and a strong body. And she has the most beautiful eyes I have ever seen on a woman."

Suni threw her arms around Yellow Hair and kissed him. Yellow Hair, not accustomed to the way Indians outwardly showed affection, tried to disentangle himself. But Suni would not let go. There was to be no more hunting that day.

They returned to the village late in the evening, Suni dragging a reluctant Yellow Hair by the hand. "Come, you can speak with my father tonight. We can be man and wife as soon as he gives me to you."

"Perhaps I can speak with him tomorrow. It is late and I do not want to disturb him."

Like any man in any culture, Yellow Hair was hesitant to approach the girl's father. "I have no ponies to offer him."

"Do not worry. I will tell my father to give you one of his."

"I think Short Bull might be waiting for me. He expects me to build the fire."

"Yellow Hair, do you want me or do you not?"

"Of course I want you. I want you to be my wife."

"Then be quiet and come with me."

He knew he would have to beard the lion in his den. He would have to face Big Eagle sooner or later. And Suni had decided that it was to be sooner rather than later. He stood erect, squared his shoulders and said, "Take me to your father."

When all was said and done, Yellow Hair thought, *That was not so bad.*

Not only did Big Eagle not throw him out of his tipi, he gave him, at Suni's insistence, a young sorrel pony named Catcher-of-the-Wind, so named because of his speed.

After they received Big Eagle's blessing, Suni walked part of the way to Short Bull's tipi with Yellow Hair. "Just think, this is your last sleep with Short Bull. Tomorrow you and I will sleep together in my father's lodge."

Yellow Hair stopped in his tracks. "I had not thought of that. We should have our own lodge, but until we do, we can live with Short Bull. I am sure that he would not mind." Yellow Hair was thinking that it would not be easy to act in a married way with Suni's father sleeping only a few feet away.

"It is not right that we sleep with Short Bull. He is not family. I know what you are thinking, but do not worry. Tomorrow night we will sleep in our own tipi. In the morning, we will cut pine poles for our lodge. For now, we will find skins here in our village. Next moon we go to hunt the buffalo; we will have fine new skins then. I am a good hunter, but you will be a great hunter, my husband." She kissed her man and ran off in the direction of her father's lodge. Yellow Hair looked after the running figure of the girl he loved until he lost sight of her in the darkness. As he walked on to Short Bull's tipi, he felt as though his feet never touched the ground.

Suni was at Short Bull's lodge before the sun had come up, and before Yellow Hair and Short Bull were awake. Without asking permission to enter, she went into the tipi and shook Yellow Hair awake.

He opened his eyes and beheld the love of his life standing over him with an axe in her hand. His first thought was, *She must have changed her mind about marrying me!*

As the fog of sleep left his head, he heard, "Come, it is getting late. We must cut the poles for our tipi."

"Is the sun up yet?"

"No, but we must get an early start if we are to sleep in our own tipi tonight."

Like women everywhere, Suni could not wait to be in her own home, with her own man. And like most women, she would make it a loving place, one that her man would want to come home to.

The conversation had awakened Short Bull who grumbled, "Go with her, Yellow Hair, and let an old man sleep in peace."

Suni ultimately got Yellow Hair up and outside where their horses were waiting, Suni's pinto and Yellow Hair's sorrel. "I have brought our ponies because it is too far a walk to the pine woods."

Yellow Hair hesitated before mounting his pony. Looking up at Suni, mounted and ready to go, he asked, "What about something to eat first? I am hungry."

Pointing to the skin hanging from his rawhide saddle, Suni said, "We have food; you can eat while we ride." Yellow Hair thought that once they were married, he would have to start asserting himself. But he did want a tipi of their own as badly as Suni, so he got on his pony and followed her out of the village.

While they rode north, Suni spoke of their tipi and how she would provide a good home life for the two of them. In the Dakota culture at that time, the women ran the household. They had no voice at councils, but they influenced their men within the lodge. That influence translated into tribal decisions made by the men.

Yellow Hair asked a question that had been on his mind since he walked out of Short Bull's tipi. "When is the ceremony?"

Suni looked perplexed and asked, "Of what ceremony do you speak?"

"Our marriage ceremony, of course."

"My dear husband, we have been married since last night when my father gave me to you."

Now it was Yellow Hair's turn to look perplexed. "You mean we do not get married by the medicine man or a holy man, something like that?"

"No, why would we? We are the only ones that matter."

"Then why did you not stay with me last night?"

"For two reasons, Husband; you did not want to stay in my father's tipi, and Short Bull did not invite me into his. But tonight we will sleep together in our own lodge."

"So we are married right now?"

"Yes, as I have said, since last night."

Yellow Hair kicked his horse and galloped into the woods.

It was now Suni's turn to think that Yellow Hair had changed *his* mind about marrying *her*. She was not about to let him off that easy. She spurred her pony forward and followed. When she caught up, she found him dismounted and sitting under a tree. She jumped off her pony, and standing over him, with hands on hips, she said in a not-so-soft voice, "If you think you can give me back to my father you are ..." That's as far as she got. Yellow Hair reached up, took her by her right hand, and pulled her to him.

Now they were both on the ground and Yellow Hair said, "You are my wife. You are no longer Fighting Woman, you are Suni." He kissed her. And as the eastern sky turned gray and the last of the stars faded away, they made love for the first time.

Afterwards, they lay entwined in each other's arms. "That was wonderful," said Suni, "but I think it would be better in our own tipi. You are the man. When you say it is time to get our lodge poles, then we will get our lodge poles, and not before."

Yellow Hair sighed.

It is going to be tough breaking this filly.

Winking at her, he said, "Let us go. *You* have to get our tipi up before dark." It was women's work to erect and dismantle the tipis when the village moved.

Working jointly, they had their pine poles cut and were back in the village by the time the sun hung directly overhead. Suni had managed to secure enough skins to cover the poles, with a few left over to sleep on.

So it was, in The Winter Of The Lone Elk, during the Moon When Calves Grow Hair, Yellow Hair and Suni started their life together.

Chapter Twenty-Six

THE VILLAGE was set to move to the plains at the end of
the Moon of the Changing Season to hunt the buffalo. It was
a seasonal trek for the Mdewakanton. For five moons, they
lived off the buffalo. When the Moon of the Snow-Blind
arrived, they would migrate back to the banks of the
Minnesota River at the southern end of the Minnesota
Territory. During the winter moons, they also replenished
their stock of buffalo leg sinew, used for bowstrings and
sewing. They would render the hooves for glue used for a
myriad of purposes, such as securing fletches to arrows and
repairing clay pots. The skins were used to cover tipis, to
sleep upon, and to wear in winter.

Because of the impending move, the people were in a
high state of anticipation and none more so than the children.
Running Close followed Yellow Hair and Suni when they left
in the mornings to gather the ash saplings for the making of
arrows. Many arrows were needed in the hunting of buffalo.
If an arrow hit bone, it could break at the tip or fracture along
its length. Yellow Hair put Running Close to work scouting
the woods for appropriate saplings. The little boy relished the
responsibility and ran from sapling to sapling asking Uncle
Yellow Hair if they were any good for the purpose at hand.
As a reward for his help, Yellow Hair made a small bow and
four blunt arrows for the boy. Thenceforth, wherever Yellow
Hair went, Running Close was not far behind.

One morning, Suni decided to stay in the village, so
Yellow Hair headed for the woods alone. Before he had gone
very far, he heard the familiar cry, "Uncle Yellow Hair! Wait
for me!" He knew without turning around that Running Close
was hurrying to catch up. However, when he did turn around,
he saw not just one child, but five. When they reached him,

171

Running Close said, "This is my brother, Brown Wing, and his friends. They wanted to meet you." Brown Wing was of nine or ten winters, as were his friends.

Yellow Hair said hello to the boys, and asked the other three their names. "Breaking Up," answered the tallest. "I am called Against Something When Crawling," piped up another. The last to speak informed Yellow Hair that his name was Killing Ghost.

"Glad to meet you fine young men. Are you ready to hunt the buffalo?" They all assured him that indeed they were ready, if only their parents would allow them to participate. Yellow Hair asked if they would like to join him and Running Close in the collecting of saplings for arrows.

Brown Wing declined the invitation, explaining, "We are on an errand for Breaking Up's father."

Yellow Hair and Running Close collected their quota for the day and returned to the village. They cut the saplings, whittled down and notched both ends. Then they chipped, knapped, and lodged the arrowheads into the cleft at the head of the arrow. Finally, the flights were cut and glued to the shaft. It took all afternoon, but with help from Running Close, Yellow Hair had thirty arrows more to add to the over two hundred he and Suni had already made.

He was collecting his tools when Suni walked up with her hands behind her back.

"Are you two men finished for the day?"

"Yes, we have made many arrows today," responded Running Close.

"That is good because I have something for my hard-working men."

From behind her back, she brought out two sheaths to hold knives. The larger of the two, over eight inches long, had a yellow orb painted on its face. Four lines surrounded the orb . . . two vertical, two horizontal.

"This is for carrying your knife, Husband."

Yellow Hair had been using the belt he had worn since leaving Concord to secure his knife. Because he kept it finely honed, he had complained to Suni that one day he was going to cut himself if he was not careful.

He reached to his left, pulled the knife from his belt and handed it to Running Close. From his right, he took the little knife that Running Close had given him and asked him to hold that also.

"You see, I told you I would always carry it with me."

After removing the belt, he inserted it through slits in the sheath. He put the belt back around his waist, took his knife from Running Close, and slid it into its new home.

"It is a perfect fit. How did you know?"

"I traced the knife onto a deerskin late last night while you slept. I painted the image of Ta'kuwakaŋ, the sun, to protect you, my husband." Yellow Hair beamed a broad smile and kissed his wife in way of thanks.

Suni then handed Running Close the smaller sheath. "See if your knife will fit this."

The smaller sheath also had an orb painted on it. However, it was white and smaller than the one on Yellow Hair's.

"On this I painted the wife of Ta'kuwakaŋ . . . Haŋyetuwi, the moon."

Running Close slipped the little knife into the sheath; it fit perfectly.

Yellow Hair looked at Suni and winked. To Running Close he said, "Why not hold that for me. As you can see, I have a knife of my own. I think my little nephew should also have a knife. You never know when you may need it. Bring it back tomorrow and I will put a sharp blade on it for you."

Running Close smiled and said, "I know how to sharpen it. My brother has taught me." Without saying another word, he took off running. Presumably to get a strip of rawhide so he could proudly wear his knife in its new sheath. After a few steps, he halted and turned back, "Woman of Uncle Yellow Hair, I thank you for this gift." And then he was gone.

As Yellow Hair collected his tools, he said, "Woman of Uncle Yellow Hair, I also thank you for this gift." When he had everything in hand, he put his free arm around Suni, and together they walked to their lodge.

Because the weather was turning cold, the next morning Suni and Yellow Hair stayed wrapped in their buffalo skins longer than they normally would have. Being in love and enjoying each other's company had nothing to do with it. Not much!

Eventually Suni said, "Have I married a lazy man who wants only to sleep all day?"

"I have not been doing much sleeping since we have been married."

"Get dressed, Husband. We need more arrows for the winter. We leave in seven sleeps."

"We can make the rest in two sleeps. How about staying here all day?"

"We also need pine poles for pony drags to carry our tipi and the buffalo meat we will be bringing back."

"Half a day at the most."

Yellow Hair was not serious about staying in. The conversation, although it varied somewhat, was one they had often since becoming husband and wife.

Once the word play was out of the way, they got out of their warm and comfortable buffalo skins and dressed. The last item Yellow Hair put on was the belt with his knife hanging from it.

"While you prepare the food, I will see if Short Bull needs help with his firewood. I will be right back." He started to leave, but walked back to where Suni was braiding her hair, and kissed her.

Just then, they heard the screams of women and what sounded like war cries. Yellow Hair told Suni to stay in the tipi while he went to see what was going on. Stepping outside, he could not believe what he saw. Running through the village were Indians not of his band. And they were painted for war!

Before he could think of what to do, Suni was standing beside him with her war club in hand.

"They are Chippewa. Take this."

She continued, "I am only a woman. I will wait here for your return. You will have no trouble telling the Chippewa from our braves because they are the ones painted. Our men have not had time to put on paint."

It was hard for Suni not to rush out and crack a few skulls with her war club or put a few arrows into a hapless Chippewa or two. But if she had, the men of the village would have teased Yellow Hair about needing a woman to fight for him.

Yellow Hair held the war club and looked about, wondering what to do first. He did not want to kill. Maybe he should use the club only to disable. It was then he saw Running Close, knife in hand, running toward a painted Chippewa.

He dropped the club and ran, trying to head the boy off.

Running Close got to the Chippewa before Yellow Hair could stop him. The brave slapped the knife out of his hand and hit him on the side of the head with the flat of his tomahawk, knocking Running Close unconscious. He picked the boy up by his ankles and swung him into a small outcropping of rock, smashing open his head. Blood and brains splattered onto the Chippewa. Dropping the boy, he picked up his tomahawk and started to hack away at Running Close's neck. He was trying to decapitate him, so Running Close would have to wander the spirit world looking like the body he had left behind.

Yellow Hair was now only a few paces away, and as he ran, he saw red. Not metaphorically speaking, he actually saw the color red. It momentarily obscured his vision.

He was not aware that he had drawn his knife, but there it was in his hand when he reached the Chippewa. The brave was so intent on the horrendous act he was performing that he did not notice Yellow Hair until it was too late. Without hesitation, Yellow Hair grabbed the man's hair and pulled his head back, exposing his throat. Yellow Hair's knife sliced through the skin so thoroughly, it almost severed head from body.

As the Chippewa's blood pooled on the ground, Yellow Hair knelt down on one knee and dipped the index and middle fingers of his right hand into the blood. Using the warm liquid as war paint, he painted himself for battle. Picking up the brave's tomahawk, he went looking for more Chippewa to kill.

The first Chippewa he saw was fighting hand-to-hand with a Mdewakanton brave. Yellow Hair stuck his knife into the back of the Chippewa and withdrew it without finishing him off. He knew the man was as good as dead, but he would let his fellow Mdewakanton claim second coup. He was not looking for coup feathers; he was looking to kill Chippewas.

He saw that the fighting was thickest over by Short Bull's tipi and headed in that direction. It did not matter if the Chippewas he encountered along the way were fighting with a member of his tribe or not; they all received a thrust from his knife or a blow from the tomahawk, sometimes both. He did not stay to watch them die, but he would not leave until he made sure they were headed in that general direction. He fought with such ferocity that others could not help but notice, even though he did not call coup.

Passing a tipi, Yellow Hair heard a woman's scream. He entered and saw a Chippewa brave advancing towards the mother of Running Close. He yelled to get the brave's attention and then set upon the Chippewa like a madman, swinging the tomahawk and knife until he backed the startled brave up against the wall of the tipi. The Chippewa raised his war club in defense, exposing his belly, into which Yellow Hair plunged his knife, moving the blade left to right, eviscerating the man.

By the time the Mdewakanton drove the invaders from their village, Yellow Hair was a vision from hell, covered in blood. The blood he used for war paint had dried and turned a brownish-black color and was starting to flake from his skin. The fresher blood from his kills was still crimson.

He stood in the middle of the village holding his knife and the tomahawk, surrounded by people who had seen or heard of his exploits. Red blood dripped, one drop at a time, from the tip of the downward-pointing blade onto the green grass upon which he stood.

He did not notice the people milling about him. With no more Chippewa to kill, he thought of Running Close, and wondered how to tell the child's mother about her youngest son. It was not until Suni rushed to his side that he dropped the knife and tomahawk and allowed himself the luxury of crumpling to the ground. He was spent.

Suni immediately summoned two of the nearest braves to carry him to her tipi, but Yellow Hair refused their help. "No, I can walk, and there is something I must do." He retrieved his knife, rose to his feet, took Suni by the hand, and together they walked away from the murmuring crowd.

Chapter Twenty-Seven

YELLOW HAIR brought the body of Running Close to his mother and told her that he would attend to the funeral scaffold. The boy's father was not around to build it. He had been killed during a raid against the Chippewa two years previously.

After speaking with Running Close's mother, whose name was Plenty Eagle Feathers, Yellow Hair went to the river to be cleansed of the blood that covered his body—Chippewa blood. He sent Suni ahead to their lodge to prepare food. He was at a loss to explain it, but he was hungry. He thought he should be sick rather than hungry. The events of the morning were a blur and he had trouble remembering his actions. The only image that was clear in his mind was the death of Running Close.

Later that day, Big Eagle came to see Yellow Hair.

"May I enter your lodge?"

"Yes, Father, please come in," answered Suni.

Once seated across from Yellow Hair, Big Eagle asked, "Are you wounded?"

"No. I am fine. How many Chippewas did our braves kill?"

"We found twenty-four bodies. But they may have carried some of their dead away."

"Of the Mdewakanton, how many dead, how many wounded?"

"Eleven dead, including your little friend, and eighteen wounded. There would have been more of our people killed if not for you. In the heat of battle, one does not look about to see what others are doing. But many saw you kill without calling coup. From those I spoke with, I judge you, by yourself, killed eight Chippewa. How many you wounded, I do not know."

Yellow Hair whispered, "I wounded none. I wanted only to kill."

"It would seem that way," agreed Big Eagle. "I have spoken with Looking Elk. He told me that, after your vision, you said that you did not want to kill. But he knew you would because it was foretold in your vision. Is that right?"

"Looking Elk and Circling Hawk are wise."

Big Eagle nodded. "Now that I know you are all right, I will go. There will be a council tonight and Little Crow would like you to attend. I will come for you when it is time."

Suni walked outside with Big Eagle. "Father, I am worried about Yellow Hair. He sits and does not speak. I have to speak to him twice before he will look at me with those blue eyes of his, and then he says nothing."

"Do not worry, daughter. It was his first battle and his first coups. He saw his little friend killed. Give him time. After all, he is a *Wasichu* and not used to our ways."

"No, Father, he is Dakota."

"Have him ready when the sun leaves the sky. I will come for him then."

A few minutes after Big Eagle left, there was another call from outside the tipi. "May an old warrior enter the lodge of Yellow Hair?"

Roused from his thoughts, Yellow Hair smiled. "Come in, Grandfather. You are always welcome."

Short Bull nodded to Suni as a way of greeting and said to Yellow Hair, "My son, you are the talk of the village."

Yellow Hair stood and pointed to where he had been sitting, "Please, Grandfather, take my seat. In my lodge you are an honored guest."

Once the two men were seated, Suni announced that she was going to see Plenty Eagle Feathers. "I will tell her that you are coming to build the funeral scaffold. I will stay with her until you come." Bidding farewell to Short Bull, she left the lodge.

Wasting no time, Short Bull got down to business. "What did I tell you about the hatred coming from deep inside? From what I saw take place outside my tipi this morning, you were full of hate. I heard about Running Close. I am sorry. Is that where the hatred sprung from?"

Yellow Hair looked at the old man who had taken him into his lodge and treated him as a son, and felt ashamed. "I am young. You have the wisdom that comes with age. You, Looking Elk, and Circling Hawk tried to tell me the ways of men, the way that I am. But I would not listen."

"Yes, we have all told you of things of which we know. Although we have given you our knowledge, we can never give you our wisdom. Wisdom comes from experience. Experience builds upon experience until one day you find that you have acquired a certain amount of wisdom. You are young and you have had an experience today. That experience will be but one lodge pole in your tipi of wisdom. Do not be hasty; wisdom, for most men, comes in its own time."

"I have a funeral scaffold to build. Would you like to come along and help?"

"I am honored that you have asked."

Yellow Hair went to the spot where Running Close had been killed and searched the ground. He walked back and forth a few times before he found what he was looking for.

"What is that?" asked Short Bull.

"It belongs to my friend. I am going to return it to him so that he may take it with him on his journey." He held Running Close's little knife.

On the way, Short Bull stopped at his lodge and got his hatchet. "We will need this."

When they arrived at the tipi of Plenty Eagle Feathers, she was wrapping the body of Running Close in a deerskin. She acknowledged the men by saying, "I was saving this skin for *my* death."

"One moment, Mother," said Yellow Hair. He knelt down and slipped the little knife into the sheath that Suni had made, which still hung from the boy's waist.

As the two men walked into the woods to get the scaffold poles, Short Bull asked Yellow Hair, "Have you ever built a funeral scaffold before?"

"No, but I am sure you will show me how."

"We must build it near an elevated spot. It is our people's way. The women will stand on the higher ground, wailing and singing their lamentations. If Running Close had been older and a warrior, his mother and the other women would sing his death song, telling of his courage in battle and the brave deeds that he had performed."

By the time the two men returned, Plenty Eagle Feathers had finished sewing the skin together, in effect waterproofing the body. She sat on the ground next to her son's body, holding a large lock of hair. Yellow Hair gave an inquisitive glance toward Suni. In answer to the silently asked question, Suni said, "The hair belongs to Running Close. Our women take a small piece of the body to show their grief, sometimes some hair, sometimes a finger."

Yellow Hair thought nothing of it. He was now Dakota; their ways were now his ways.

Brown Wing, Running Close's brother, was there and asked of Yellow Hair, "May I help build my brother's scaffold?"

"Yes. It is only right that you take part."

The sky was darkening as they finished the scaffold and placed the body of Running Close upon it. Suni mentioned to Yellow Hair that he should go and meet her father. "He will

181

be waiting to take you to Little Crow. I will stay here. Come for me when you are finished."

Yellow Hair thanked Short Bull and Brown Wing for their help and went to find Big Eagle.

The meeting with Little Crow and the council took place outside, around the council fire. It did not take long and Little Crow did most of the talking.

"Yellow Hair, please come over and sit by me. I have heard of your bravery today."

Yellow Hair looked uncomfortable. He wished everyone would just drop the matter. He was not proud of what he had done. However, to voice his feelings would bring shame onto Big Eagle and Suni, thus he said nothing.

Little Crow continued, "We will observe the mourning period of four sleeps, then we will have a Kill Dance. At that time, you will be given your coup feathers."

"I did not call coup. I thought one needed witnesses to receive the feather?"

"That is true. But some of your coups were witnessed, and those witnesses will speak at the Kill Dance. They will tell of what they saw, as is our custom."

Yellow Hair nodded his understanding.

"After they speak, you will tell of your bravery. I might suggest that, before the Kill Dance, you make yourself a coup stick on which to hang your feathers. We believe that you have eight kills, but only four were witnessed. For those four, you will receive coup feathers. Three moons ago, I welcomed you to our village. I now welcome you to our band and our tribe. You are truly Dakota."

The council, or at least that part of it that concerned Yellow Hair, was over. Little Crow and his council still had to decide on when to mount a raid to punish the Chippewa for that morning's attack.

On the way to fetch Suni, Yellow Hair came across Short Bull. "I followed you, and standing outside the light of the fire, I heard Little Crow tell you to make a coup stick." Holding out *his* coup stick, minus the feathers, Short Bull said, "I want you to have this. It has served me well in many battles, but I have no more use for it. Please accept it."

Yellow Hair reached out and took the stick. "I thank you, Grandfather. I promise to never bring shame to you for giving me this." There was nothing else to say. Short Bull left for his lodge and Yellow Hair went to retrieve Suni.

Four days later, the village assembled for the Kill Dance. After the initial singing and dancing, Little Crow stood to announce that the council had decided to forgo a retaliatory raid on the Chippewa for the time being. "Instead, we will prepare and leave to hunt the buffalo in seven sleeps."

The news brought some of the younger braves to their feet with shouts of protest. They wanted to attack the Chippewa camp.

Little Crow asked for quiet and then spoke, "There will be a time to avenge our dead and wounded. It grows colder by the day. We are short of meat. We must hunt the buffalo. The old, the young, and the sick cannot feed themselves. Would you leave your mothers and sisters to go hungry?"

The young braves grew quiet, and one by one, they sat down.

It was now time to award coup feathers. Because of Yellow Hair's unique status within the Mdewakanton, Little Crow had decided to award his feathers last. Witness after witness recounted what they saw. Recipient after recipient told of their deeds of valor. At length, it was Yellow Hair's turn. He did not want to stand before the entire village and be lauded for killing. He had concluded that, yes, killing is necessary at times, but to celebrate it afterwards is not right. Though he would kill again, he would never speak of it, and he would never call coup.

Yellow Hair stood in front of the big fire, before the assembled people of the village, as his first witness spoke.

"I was in my tipi. A Chippewa brave was about to attack me with his war club. Just then Yellow Hair ran in shouting. The brave turned on him, but Yellow Hair had no fear. He charged in and killed him." So said Plenty Eagle Feathers, mother to Running Close.

The next witness stood and told his story. "I was fighting hand-to-hand when Yellow Hair came up and thrust a knife into the Chippewa's back." Holding up his right hand with thumb and forefinger separated by an inch, the witness continued, "About this much of the knife came through the brave's chest. It must have pierced his heart because he stopped fighting and fell dead to the ground."

The third witness recounted what he had seen. "I had just come out of my tipi to see what all the screaming and yelling was about when I saw Yellow Hair, painted in red war paint, run up to a Chippewa brave and swing a tomahawk that he held in his left hand. It landed on the man's neck and went in deep. The man fell to the ground, but he was still moving. Yellow Hair knelt down on one knee and, with the tomahawk, hacked at the man until he stopped moving. Without calling coup, he ran off to where the fighting was the thickest."

Yellow Hair was staring at the ground. He was unable to look at his fellow Mdewakantons.

The final witness spoke. "First I would like to thank Yellow Hair for saving my life. I was fighting a Chippewa and called first coup. Then I made the mistake of looking around to see if anyone had witnessed my coup. That is when the brave struck me with his war club. It was only a glancing blow, but it did knock me down. As he was coming in to kill me, Yellow Hair appeared and grabbed one of the man's braids. Pulling his head back, Yellow Hair drove his knife deep into his throat. He withdrew the knife, picked up a tomahawk he had dropped and started to walk away. I yelled my thanks. He turned and looked at me, but he did not say a word. He seemed to look right through me."

Yellow Hair continued to stare at the ground.

Little Crow stood and held up his hands for silence. "Yellow Hair, you will now tell us of your coups."

Yellow Hair slowly raised his head, looked at Little Crow, then at the people sitting around the fires. "I have been told of the time four winters back when my wife, Fighting Woman, was awarded the only coup feathers ever given to a woman of our band. I have been told what she said that night. I am sorry, but I must also say the same. I do not remember that day, or at least that morning. I left my lodge and saw my friend killed. The next thing I knew I was standing in a circle of people covered in blood. That is all I know."

No one made a sound, no one spoke a word. Then, out in the darkness where the firelight did not reach, a few chuckles were heard, then a laugh here and there. Within moments, the entire assemblage was roaring with laughter. Everyone thought it funny that both husband and wife—who had fought so bravely—could not remember their coups. Even Little Crow laughed so hard, tears flowed from his eyes.

Slowly the laughter subsided and Little Crow stood. To Yellow Hair he said, "Here are your feathers. Also for you, the feather of the eagle. When worn in your hair, it denotes bravery of the highest order. Not many men wear this feather; it is an honor, but you have earned it."

After the awarding of the feathers, the Kill Dance continued. The Mdewakanton Dakota celebrated their victory over the Chippewa.

A week later, they struck their tipis, placed their belongings and small children upon pony drags, and trekked southwest to hunt the buffalo.

For the eastern Dakota, who were also known as the Santee Sioux, which consisted of the Mdewakanton, the

Wahpekute, the Sisseton, and the Wahpeton, it was to be the last buffalo hunt.

The *Wasichus* were coming.

The Seeds of Rebellion

Chapter Twenty-Eight

THE SIOUX, or the Dakota, as they were then known, first laid eyes on a White Man exactly one hundred and ninety-seven years to the day prior to the Little Bighorn, their greatest military victory over the *Wasichu*. The date: 25 June 1679. It was not a band of braves or a chief that first glimpsed the *Wasichu*. It was two young boys who should have been tending the corn crop with the women but decided to go fishing instead.

The two youths, both of ten winters, walked the path that led to Lake of the Knife. One carried a net, the other a coiled strip of rawhide. They would use the net to catch the fish, and the rawhide to string them together. "I bet we catch so many fish our fathers will allow us to go fishing every day instead of staying with the women," said the first child, whose name was Fast Wolf.

Fast Wolf's friend, Little Deer, expressed his thoughts on the matter. "We are too old to stay with the women."

The boys were so intent on their discussion that, when they came around the bend in the trail, they did not see the *woniya sica* right away. However, after a few steps more, they looked up and saw the bad spirit. It looked almost human, but instead of hair, its scalp was covered in fur, as was the lower half of its face.

It was tall, at least twelve hands high, and its skin was not the color of a human being's. The *wowinihaŋ*, or monster, saw the boys and smiled, probably to lure them to their destruction. It held up a hand and said something only another *wowinihaŋ* could understand.

The boys did not wait around to be devoured. The net and the coil of rawhide lay on the path. The boys themselves were hightailing it back to their village to warn the people.

Seeing the boys turn and run, the *wowinihaŋ* shrugged and hefted the large sack that hung from its left shoulder. From its right shoulder hung an iron stick with what looked like a block of wood attached at one end. At a leisurely pace, the monster followed the path on which the boys had just fled.

Fast Wolf and Little Deer ran into the village shouting that there was a *wowinihaŋ* in the woods and it had tried to eat them. The people were amused. Some smiled tolerant smiles. Others laughed out loud. Still others shook their heads at the foolishness of children. That is, until the monster himself walked into the village.

This particular "monster" had a name. Daniel Greysolon, Sieur du Lhut. He was from a land far to the east, a land called France. He had traveled many moons to find the Dakota; he had business to discuss with them.

As Sieur du Lhut strode into the Dakota village, the women stayed close to their tipis, the children stayed close to their mothers, the men stayed where they were, but all eyes followed the monster.

Of course, he was not a monster, but a man. However, he was a type of man the Dakota had never seen before. What sort of man has hair on his face and skin of such a pale color?

He reached the center of the village and spoke in the Ojibwa tongue. "I have come to trade with you."

A few understood what he said and they told the others.

Sieur du Lhut laid the sack on the ground and reached inside. He withdrew a large knife with a razor-sharp edge. Next, he pulled out a steel kettle and metal eating utensils. Again and again he reached into the sack, and each time he pulled out a new wonder until the sack lay empty. Sieur du

Lhut picked up the knife and said, "I would speak with your chief."

By now, a crowd had formed around him. The women were looking at the metal implements used for cooking and the men were looking at the brightly polished steel blade of the knife.

Shortly thereafter, the crowd parted as two men approached. The younger of the two spoke in the Ojibwa tongue.

"I am Tataŋka duta—or Red Buffalo, as the Ojibwa would say. And this is Šuŋka ska—White Dog. He is our chief. I will speak for him."

Sieur du Lhut extended the knife toward White Dog. "I give you this in friendship."

Red Buffalo translated as White Dog accepted the knife. It was a beauty. The blade, nine inches long; the handle—made of deer bone—five inches. White Dog turned the knife over and inspected it from every angle, finally testing the blade with his thumb.

Sieur du Lhut took a green twig from his side coat pocket and offered it to White Dog. Speaking to Red Buffalo he said, "Tell him to slice the knife through the wood."

Holding the twig in his left hand and the knife in his right, White Dog brought knife to wood, cutting the twig cleanly in half. He smiled and instructed Red Buffalo to tell the stranger to collect his gear and follow them. He was to be an honored guest of the village.

Once they had smoked the sacred pipe, the men got down to business. Speaking through Red Buffalo, White Dog asked, "What do you want, stranger?"

"I am called Sieur du Lhut and I want to trade with you and your people."

"You have such wondrous things. What have we that you desire?"

Sieur du Lhut removed the fur cap from his head. "This is beaver pelt."

White Dog replied, "I know what it is."

"I desire the pelts of the beaver and the fox. There are also two other animals, but I don't know the words for them in the Ojibwa tongue. In my tongue they are called ermine and sable. If we come to an understanding, I will go into the woods and show you the animals of which I speak. What I propose is that this autumn and winter your people trap as many of the animals as they can. In the spring, I will return for the skins with canoes filled with blankets, things made of iron, knives, and hatchets. But I have saved the best for last. If you will follow me outside, I will show you something that will make the Dakota a mighty nation. With what I am about to show you, the Dakota will easily defeat the Ojibwa, the Huron, *and* the Ottawa." Picking up his musket, he held it out to White Dog. "This will win many battles for the Dakota."

Once outside, Sieur du Lhut walked to the edge of the village and pointed to an old birch. As he aimed his musket, he said "Think of that tree as a man."

People were milling about trying to observe what the stranger was doing. Sieur du Lhut asked Red Buffalo to tell everyone to stand behind him. He did not want to shoot anyone by accident. It might interfere with his trading plans. It might also considerably shorten his life.

With everyone clear, Sieur du Lhut squeezed the trigger. The loud report frightened some. Red Buffalo, who was closest to Sieur du Lhut, jumped at the noise. White Dog gave no indication of fear or surprise. He simply asked, "Are loud noises supposed to defeat our enemies?"

"No, but this will." Sieur du Lhut went to the birch and pointed to the hole the ball had made. Taking out his knife, he dug the ball from the tree and handed it to White Dog.

"If that little ball can do that to a sturdy tree, think what it can do to a man."

White Dog was thoughtful for a moment and then looked at the inquiring faces of his people who had crowded in close to see the musket ball. To Red Buffalo he said, "Tell the . . . the . . ." and looking at the man with the pale skin, he said the word for the first time in the Dakota language, "Tell the *Wasichu* he will stay with us for a while; there are many things of which we must speak."

Sieur du Lhut stayed in the village for half a moon. During that time, he taught White Dog how to load and fire the musket. White Dog wanted to trade for the musket before Sieur du Lhut left, but the trader politely explained that it was needed for the return journey.

It was agreed that they would trade muskets, balls, and powder, plus knives, hatchets, and other goods for the pelts of the beaver, fox, ermine and sable. How many pelts per musket would depend on the quality of the pelts.

Sieur du Lhut would return in nine moons with many men and canoes to carry away the skins harvested during that time. He left at the end of The Moon When Cherries Are Ripe and would return during The Moon of the Red Grass.

The British knew the man Sieur du Lhut by his Anglicized name Duluth. The same Duluth for which a city in Minnesota was named.

So ended the first encounter between the *Wasichu* and the Dakota. The Dakota thought they had made a good bargain, and perhaps they had, but it was still a bargain with the devil.

After Duluth, other *Wasichus* came to trade. Still others came and stayed the winter to do their own trapping. Every year brought more of the *Wasichu*. Three winters after making his pact with Duluth, White Dog was killed in battle by a ball fired from a musket held by an Ojibwa brave. Duluth had traded the musket to the brave in exchange for eighty beaver pelts.

Forty winters after Duluth walked into White Dog's village, the Ojibwa, also known as the Chippewa, drove the Isanyati Sioux, as the French called them, from Lake of the Knife. They migrated south and eventually settled along the Minnesota River on the fringes of the Great Plains. They continued to trap and sell furs to the French and then to the English. Later they would trade with men from a new country to the east . . . the United States.

One hundred and twenty-four winters after the death of White Dog, the Isanyati Sioux had their first dealings with officials from the United States. The treaty signed at that time and subsequent treaties forced upon the Dakota would portend the demise of a way of life that had held them in good stead for ten thousand years. In the end, the Dakota would be reduced from a nation of fierce, independent people to a people dependent on hand-outs from the ones who stole not only their land, but also their dignity.

Chapter Twenty-Nine

THE MAN looks at his reflection in the mirror, his gaze directed at the single yellow bar that decorates each shoulder of his dark blue tunic. So intent are his thoughts that he does not hear the woman as she enters the room.

Smiling, the woman says, "Admiring ourselves again?"

"Oh, hello, Clarissa. No, I was wondering how I would look with captain bars on my blouse."

"I think you would look just fine, Lieutenant Pike."

"Why, thank you, Missus Pike."

In the summer of 1805, Lieutenant and Missus Zebulon Montgomery Pike, Jr. have been married for four years. This is his eleventh year in the army; he started out as a raw cadet in his father's old regiment. He and his wife are "regular army," moving from posting to posting along the frontier of the new country known as the United States. Like all young men, he wants a taste of action and adventure. Instead, he is assigned to handle the logistics and payroll of the various forts to which he has been sent.

Continuing the conversation, Clarissa Pike asks, "What did General Wilkinson want to see you about?"

"Clarissa, you will not believe this, but I have a command. I have orders to find the head waters of the Mississippi and to secure a treaty with the savages west of the river. If I succeed, I may get those captain bars yet. Six years as a lieutenant is a mite too long in my estimation."

"I believe you can do anything you set your mind to, Lieutenant Pike. But why a treaty? That land is a wilderness; no one but a savage can live there."

"The way it was explained to me is that, since President Jefferson bought all that land from France, we should at least know what's out there. My orders are to procure land in order to build a string of forts. Also, the Indians are trading with the English and we want to get them to trade with us. President Jefferson does not want the English in our back yard."

Clarissa Pike thinks President Jefferson foolish to have spent so much money on land no one can live on. *Fifteen million dollars—for a wasteland!*

But she keeps those thoughts to herself. After all, she is the wife of an officer in the United States Army. It would not help his career if she were overheard criticizing the Commander-In-Chief.

"I came in to tell you that dinner is ready. Come, you can tell me when you have to leave and what you might need so that I can pack for you."

Over dinner, Lieutenant Pike tells his wife that his contingent will be leaving as soon as they have provisioned.

"Probably in about three weeks; stores have to be brought in."

Clarissa knows that her husband will be away for at least eight months and she is not happy about that. However, she is pleased that Zeb has finally been offered a chance to prove himself. Then she remembers something. "What about that nice Mister Lewis your father introduced us to last year in Washington?"

"You mean Meriwether Lewis?"

"Yes, that's the man. Didn't he tell us that the President was sending a surveying party out West with him heading it?"

"Yes, he and Bill Clark. They left a few days later. That was over a year ago and no one has heard from them since. As I've told you, the President is getting anxious to know what's out there."

196

The President of the United States wants the country to have a presence west of the Mississippi, and Lieutenant Zebulon Pike is determined to help establish that presence.

It takes six weeks before Lieutenant Pike and his contingent are ready to leave. Since General Washington's time, there has been one axiom that has held fast in the American Army, and that is: "Hurry up and wait."

• • • • •

It is the morning of 9 August 1805. The sun has not yet risen on the Mississippi River as a keelboat leaves St. Louis, headed north. At its bow are three men: Lieutenant Pike, Sergeant McLaughlin, and the scout and interpreter Harley. It is not known if Harley is his given name or his surname. If he has another name, no one had ever heard it spoken. He is a grizzled ex-trapper who has spent many years among the Sioux. Sergeant McLaughlin is an Irishman with a fondness for spirits—the liquid kind. Behind the three men are ten soldiers and the supplies needed for the expedition.

Forty-three days later, on 21 September 1805, Harley informs Lieutenant Pike that they are entering Sioux territory and that they should make camp and then go to the Mdewakanton village and speak with their chief to get the lay of the land.

Lieutenant Pike calls to his sergeant, "Select two men to accompany us and issue them the gifts we brought for the savages. Harley and I will proceed to their village whilst you set up camp."

On this day, the American flag was first raised over the land of the Sioux.

As they set out for the village, Harley speaks to the lieutenant. "I heard you refer to the Indians as savages. I hope you don't make the mistake of thinking that you will be dealing with simple men. Their chief, Little Crow, is twice the man either one of us pretends to be."

"I plan to carry out my mission to the best of my ability. The savages—excuse me—the *Indians* will be treated fairly." The two men do not speak again until they are approaching the Sioux village.

The Little Crow to whom Harley referred is the grandfather of the man who welcomed Yellow Hair to his village.

"Alright, Mister Pike. Time to earn your army pay. Just do as I tell ya and ya won't offend nobody. When Little Crow offers you the pipe, accept it, take one pull and return it to him. And are you going to wear that cutlass? You know there ain't no chairs out here? It's gonna be mighty hard sittin' on the ground with that thing stickin' out."

"It is not a *cutlass,* Mister Harley, it is a saber. It is part of my uniform. Now please lead the way without further comment. Your job is to guide and interpret. Your advice concerning my attire is not required."

"It ain't 'Mister' Harley, just Harley."

Harley wishes he were still trapping instead of guiding this fool lieutenant. But what with the French and the English, and now with the Americans on the scene, there just are not enough animals to go around anymore.

The four men walk into the center of the Sioux village where they stop in front of a large tipi. "This is Little Crow's lodge," says Harley. "I'll go in and speak with him. You stay here and enter when I call. But leave the two soldier boys outside . . . *you* bring in the presents. A chief will only parley with another chief."

Harley goes to the entrance of the tipi where he calls out in the Dakota tongue, "May an old friend enter the lodge of Little Crow?" There is an affirmative answer from within. Harley pulls back the skin covering the entrance and disappears inside.

He is gone for what seems like a long time. Pike is just about to enter the tipi when Harley sticks his head out. Seeing Pike's intent, he says, "Mister Pike, you were just about to sabotage your own mission. Don't never enter an Indian's lodge unless you've been invited. Now let's get you and those presents inside."

Once the introductions are made, the gifts given, the pipe smoked, and food offered (but declined), it is time to get down to business.

Lieutenant Pike, speaking through Harley, tells Little Crow that he has come to buy land for the purpose of setting up trading posts, and that the Americans wish to trade with the Sioux. They will offer more for their furs than the English. "To establish these forts, or trading posts, we will need land, land with timber nearby. And we'll pay for it in gold."

Speaking to Harley, Little Crow says, "What use have we for the yellow iron? Ponies make a man wealthy, not that which is stolen from the earth."

Pike takes out a ten-dollar gold piece and shows it to Little Crow. "You see this? This and many more we will give you. Once the posts are established, you and your people can use these to purchase blankets, knives, hatchets, food and even horses. With the posts right here on your land, you will not have to wait a year for the traders to return in the spring."

Pike finishes with, "We do not require much land, and you have so much. The little you sell us will never be missed."

If Pike thought he would get a quick yes or no from Little Crow, he was mistaken. Little Crow's mind seems to be somewhere else. He says nothing. Instead, he reaches for his pipe, fills it with tobacco, and smokes. He is thinking what would be best for his people.

After a few minutes, Pike looks inquiringly at Harley. The unspoken question: "What is he doing?" Without saying a word, Harley holds a hand up towards Pike. The meaning: "Just wait." And wait they do.

Minutes later, Little Crow sets down his pipe and says, "It is not for me alone to decide. I speak only for the Mdewakanton. I will call a council of all the chiefs. It will be held in three sleeps."

Pike hears the translation from Harley and does not know if he is one step closer to those elusive captain bars or if they have just evaded him once again. Thinking to get a jump on things, he tells Little Crow, "While we wait for the other chiefs to arrive, I'll survey appropriate locales for the forts. When you are ready to parley, send for me and I will come. We are camped east of here."

As they leave the village, Harley says to Pike, "You know, giving beads and blankets to Indians is rather old-fashioned. I think you would have made more of an impression if you had given Little Crow a musket and some powder."

Pike agrees. "Those gifts were the idea of some jackass in the procurement office, not mine. Hell, I'll give him *my* gun if I can return with a signed treaty."

For the next three days, Pike scouts for the best locales to build the forts. Although he had told Little Crow they were to be trading posts, in reality the American intent is to establish a military presence. There will be a small trading post within each fort run by a "trader." However, that is of a secondary concern to the Americans.

On the fourth day after meeting with Little Crow, Pike and Harley are summoned to the Mdewakanton village. Upon arriving, they are introduced to the other chiefs of the Sioux: Mato-Tamaheda (Lean Bear) of the Wahpeton, Iśta hba (Sleep Eyes) of the Sisseton, Mazo'Hota (Gray Iron) of the Wahpekute, Tataŋka-haŋska (Long Buffalo) of the

Yanktonai, Ite Wakiŋyaŋ (Thunder Face) of the Teton, and Wamdi duta (Scarlet Eagle) of the Yankton.

After the formalities are attended to, Pike tells the chiefs the same thing he had told Little Crow three days earlier. Though he does add, "I now know we will require approximately one hundred thousand acres. That will include the right-of-way between the three proposed forts and the surrounding lands for access to timber and water. Each fort, or I should say trading post, will be twenty miles apart."

The Indians do not know what an acre is, let alone one hundred thousand of the damn things. Pike presses on regardless. "I believe the land to be worth two dollars per acre. Hence, the United States of America will pay you $200,000.00 for a ribbon of land sixty-six miles long."

The long and short of it is that the chiefs agree to sell a small portion of their land to the *Wasichus*. There are smiles and handshakes all around until Pike takes a piece of paper out of his coat pocket and says, "I have taken the liberty of drawing up the treaty beforehand. Now all that is needed is for us to affix our signatures to the document."

That causes a problem. The Indians tell Pike that their word should be enough. To put their mark on paper would mean that they are not men of honor—that they will keep their word only because of the mark. In the end, only two of the seven chiefs, Little Crow and Lean Bear, sign the treaty.

In what was to be a precursor to all future treaties with the Sioux, the amount was not written into the agreement. It was left blank so that the Senate could fill in the amount during the ratification process. However, the Senate changed the amount from $200,000.00 to $2000.00, which meant that the Sioux were to be paid two cents per acre, not the two dollars agreed upon and promised. The amount turned out to be irrelevant. The Sioux never were paid for the land. It would be fourteen years before the United States came to build the forts on the land they had stolen.

• • • • •

The next encounter the Dakota had with *Wasichu* officialdom was in 1806 when Pike returned and tried to enlist the Dakota's allegiance to the American cause vis à vis the British. Perhaps because a year had gone by since the signing of the treaty and no payment had been received, it is not surprising that Little Crow responded to the entreaty by saying, "We know the English. They have treated us fairly. You American *Wasichu* are unknown to us. We will wait to see if you can keep your word before we pledge ourselves to you."

As to Lieutenant Pike, he reported that he had found the headwaters of the Mississippi. He had not. While trying to climb the mountain that would come to bear his name, Pike's Peak, he got himself stuck in the snow half way up and had to descend. He never did make it to the summit. When he was exploring and mapping the Southwest for the United States government, the Spanish captured him and held him prisoner for a year. During the war of 1812, while leading a charge against York—now known as Toronto— he was killed. But he died as a brigadier general.

In 1815, at the Portage des Sioux, the United States signed peace and friendship treaties with the Mdewakanton, the Teton, the Wahpeton, and the Yankton bands. A year later, the rest of the Dakota Nation signed identical treaties.

In 1819, the US Army finally showed up to build the first fort provided for in the treaty of 1805. The fort, originally named Fort St. Anthony but renamed Fort Snelling, would one day be used as a prison to house the Dakota.

In 1825, the Treaty of Prairie de Chien was signed in an effort to stop the warring between the Dakota and their enemies. A boundary was set to keep the tribes apart. However, the wars continued, so the Americans proposed another treaty. Under that treaty, the Dakota ceded a twenty-mile strip of land to the United States. It was to keep the Indians apart. In return, the Sioux were to receive cash and tools. As usual, the payments were slow in coming, if they came at all, and the tools were of an inferior quality.

In 1832, the United States gave the twenty-mile strip to the Winnebagos. Naturally this did not sit well with the Dakota. Little Crow, who had signed the 1825 treaty, saw the giveaway as treachery on the part of the Americans.

Up to that time, the Dakota had signed four treaties with the United States. In not one of them did the Americans live up to either the spirit or the letter of the words written within those documents.

Five years later, in 1837, the Americans wanted an additional five million acres of Dakota land, Santee Sioux land in particular. Knowing it would be a hard sell, the government brought twenty-six chiefs to Washington to show them the might and majesty that was The United States of America.

The government proposed paying one million dollars for the acreage in installments over a twenty-year period. Part of the payment was to be in the form of farm equipment, medicine, and livestock. Intimidated, the Indians signed the treaty and went home. The United States immediately laid claim to the lands. It took a year for the first payment to arrive.

The significance of the 1837 treaty lies in the fact that it was the first time "traders" were allowed to lay claim to the Indians' payments without any proof that money was owed . . . and without consulting the Indians. Monies were subtracted from the imbursements and paid directly to the traders.

In 1849, the Territory of Minnesota was created. Overnight, the Dakota went from living on their own land to inhabiting land within a United States territory. Once Minnesota became a territory, the pressure from the *Wasichus* to acquire land to accommodate the ongoing and significant influx of immigrants became great indeed.

Chapter Thirty

LATE IN THE MOON OF THE SNOW-BLIND, the Mdewakanton broke camp and started back to their summer hunting grounds. The buffalo hunt had gone well. Yellow Hair had learned how to skin a buffalo and how to use its stomach in which to boil the meat; he learned about the myriad other uses of the beast, as well.

As Suni and Yellow Hair rode side-by-side, one pony drag carrying their tipi and belongings, the other stacked high with dried buffalo meat, Yellow Hair spoke. "These last few moons have been quite an experience. Never in my life did I think I would participate in a buffalo surround."

Suni looked at her husband with pride and said, "My husband, you have done well. You have killed as many buffalo as any man."

"You know what surprised me most about the hunt?"

"What was there to be surprised about? I told you everything. I did not forget anything."

"You did not tell of the children running to my kill, watching me skin the animal and before I can get the skin fully pulled off, rushing in to take the liver. I would turn to see a child with a big smile on his face, holding the still-warm liver. Then he would devour it as I had the half-cent peppermints my father used to buy me when I was a child."

"Yes, pulling a liver or a kidney out of a just-killed buffalo and eating it while it is still warm is what a child looks forward to before the hunt. I remember getting in my father's way as he skinned and cut meat because I could not wait to get to the liver."

I have taught him well. He is a respected warrior and hunter. I have told him many things, but what I now carry in my heart I do not know how to say. But it must be said.

She reached out her hand.

"Take my hand, Husband, there is something you must know."

Yellow Hair stretched out his hand and Suni took hold of it. She envisioned herself telling Yellow Hair what she had to say, then spurring her pony and galloping away to let him ponder her words, but there would be no galloping . . . not with a drag tied to her pony.

Holding her man's hand, but not looking at him, Suni said, "Soon there will be a time that I will no longer be able to hunt with you. I will be like the other women of our band. And I will no longer tie my pony's tail for war. Soon you may desire a second wife."

Yellow Hair let go of his wife's hand, and reaching over, he placed a finger under her chin, and raised her head until she was looking directly into his eyes. "What is this nonsense you speak? Yes, in the future, I will go on the warpath and you will stay home, as it should be. I will hunt, but I always liked hunting with you. Especially when we took breaks under a tree. As for another wife," and here he smiled, "I think one is trouble enough."

Remembering what transpired under the trees, Suni blushed. She straightened her back and said, "My husband, I am with child."

Though she did not gallop off, she did kick her pony to pick up its pace and rode in front of her husband without looking back.

Yellow Hair sat on his pony with a stunned look on his face that slowly faded, to be replaced with a broad grin. With a shout of joy, he too kicked his pony and caught up with his wife.

• • • • •

The Mdewakanton band of the Santee Sioux returned to their summer camp and the women prepared the earth to receive the seeds of the vegetables grown the summer before. The men went out in hunting parties, and for the first time since she was of fourteen winters, Fighting Woman did not accompany them. Nor did she mind staying behind with the women, which surprised her greatly. Her thoughts were on the life she carried within, not on stalking deer. The hunting parties returned and told of scarce game, and of seeing more and more *Wasichus* where once there had been only deer and elk.

The animals they depended on for food were being hunted by the *Wasichus* or driven away by their presence. The people of the village were alarmed at the scarcity of game. Little Crow and his council met to discuss the diminishing food supply and what could be done to slow the advancement of the *Wasichu* onto their lands.

At the same time that Little Crow was meeting with his council, another meeting was taking place to the north, in the capital city of St. Paul. The territorial governor, Alexander Ramsey, was meeting with Luke Lea, the Commissioner of Indian Affairs, who had been sent out from Washington to help with "The Indian Problem."

With his back to the room, looking out the study window at his children playing in the yard, the governor said, "I appreciate your coming all the way out here, Mister Lea, to help us with our problem. We will need the support of Washington if we are to avoid war with the savages. Every day more immigrants pour into the territory and settle on land that the Indians supposedly own. The Indian agent hears complaints daily from the Indians concerning settlers living on their land. He tells me he fears some of the wild young bucks might cause trouble if things continue as they are."

"Washington, or I should say, the President, is acutely aware of your problem, Governor Ramsey. I assure you that your letters have not gone unread at the White House.

That is why I am here, to help you in any way I can," replied the Commissioner of Indian Affairs.

Ramsey knew the Commissioner was pacing behind him. He could hear the click, click, click of his peg leg on the wooden floor. Lea had lost a leg fighting the British in 1814. Ramsey turned from the window to face his guest.

"The answer is easy, Commissioner. We just need more land. We've got a few thousand savages laying claim to millions of acres that are just ripe for settlement."

Lea interposed, "I have been authorized to purchase up to twenty-five million acres at a cost to the Treasury of three million dollars, more or less. May I suggest you summon their chief and I'll make the offer? Three million dollars is a lot of money."

"First of all, there are four bands, or tribes, and each band has sub-bands, each with their own chief. They may be reluctant to sell more of their land to the United States. From what I hear, we have not exactly honored our past commitments. And if payment is made, there is not much left after the traders take what they say is owed them."

"Well, Governor, we'll just have to persuade them that selling us their land is in their own best interest. It should not be too hard. After all, they're just ignorant savages. If we have to deal with four or eight chiefs, then so be it. You know the situation out here better than I do. What do you suggest?"

Some Commissioner of Indian Affairs, thought Ramsey. *Just another political appointee who doesn't know the first thing about the Sioux.*

Aloud he said, "I suggest we divide and conquer. We'll have two confabulations. At each, we'll dicker with only two of the four main bands at a time."

It was decided in April of 1851 that there would be two convocations with the Santee Sioux in the summer of that year. Preparations were made, word sent out to the chiefs, and champagne ordered from the East.

• • • • •

Halfway through the Moon of Making Fat, two soldiers of the United States Army rode into the Mdewakanton village with a message for Little Crow. They could not speak the language of the Sioux; therefore, the chief sent word for Yellow Hair to come and interpret their words.

The soldiers took one look at Yellow Hair and their jaws dropped. Here was a White Man dressed as a savage, if you could call it being dressed. He wore only a breechclout and moccasins. The more senior of the two, a lieutenant by the name of Murray, blurted out, "My God, man, where did you come from?"

Yellow Hair did not respond to the Lieutenant's query. Instead, he asked him his reason for coming. Still the Lieutenant persisted.

"What is a white man doing running around half naked in an Indian camp?"

Yellow Hair looked hard at Lieutenant Murray and said. "I am Dakota. Now state your business. You are in the presence of Little Crow, chief of the Mdewakanton. He has met with the President of the United States and many generals. They consider him a friend. One word from him and you will be a private when you get out of the stockade, *if* you ever get out. Now I'll ask you once again, what is your business?"

Taken aback, the Lieutenant said, "We have been sent to invite Little Crow to meet with the Territorial Governor and the Commissioner of Indian affairs at Mendota. The Wahpekute will be there also. The Governor and Commissioner have something of great importance to discuss with both chiefs. If Little Crow agrees to come, an escort will be provided. The exact date has not yet been set, but it will most likely be the first week of August."

Yellow Hair conveyed the message to Little Crow, adding that the *Wasichu* chiefs wanted to meet with him and the Wahpekute chiefs in a moon and a half. Little Crow sighed and slowly shook his head before saying, "It seems the Americans want more of our land. It is the only time we hear from them. Tell the soldiers that I and my council will attend."

After the soldiers had left, Little Crow asked Yellow Hair to stay for a moment; he had something to say. "With so many *Wasichus* coming into our country, I think it is time that I learn the American tongue. Will you teach me how to speak the *Wasichu* language?"

"Little Crow, I would be honored, but I am out hunting daily. Every day we have to go farther and farther from the village to find game. I was thinking that, since Fighting Woman stays in the village, she could teach you. She taught me your language."

"That would be fine. Tell her I would like to start tomorrow. Now there is one more thing I would like your help with."

Yellow Hair sat expectantly, waiting to hear the request. Little Crow spoke. "Do you read the *Wasichu* words that are written?"

"Yes, Little Crow, I can read."

"It would be good if you went with us; their treaties I cannot read. To date, we never seem to receive what has been promised."

"Even though I was born a *Wasichu,* I am now Dakota in body and spirit. I wish never to return to the land of the *Wasichu.* I will do anything I can for the Dakota in general and the Mdewakanton in particular. But there is one that my allegiance must be given to first. Fighting Woman is with child and is expected to give birth at the time of the conference. So my chief, I must decline your request. I may be needed here."

"You may think you are all Dakota, but I think you still have some *Wasichu* blood in you. Having children is woman's work. But that is all right. I will have Big Eagle speak to the *Wasichu* chieftains on our behalf."

• • • • •

It is the first day of the Moon of Black Cherries in The Winter Of Loss. It is a calescent day in the Mdewakanton village. The skins that cover the entrances to many of the tipis are lifted to allow an in-sweep of air that funnels up and out of the opening at the top of each tipi. The overwhelming heat is oppressive. The sun is almost overhead and most of the people are immobile. The children, of course, are active and playing their games. The chief and the men of the council are away negotiating a new treaty with representatives of the Great Father in Washington.

An old man walks up to the lodge and asks permission to enter. Instead of getting the reply he expected, he hears a woman say, "Short Bull, this is no place for a man. If you are looking for your friend, he is down by the river. I think you should go to him; he may need you." As the old man turns to leave, he hears a scream from within the tipi.

He finds the one he seeks by the riverbank, pacing back and forth.

"Yellow Hair, I see that it is Fighting Woman's time."

Thankful for the distraction, Yellow Hair complains to his friend.

"I am not allowed in my own lodge, and at a time like this!"

Trying not to smile, Short Bull says, "Come, let us walk. I will tell you the ways of the expectant father."

211

As they walk along the rippling waters, Short Bull collects a handful of small stones. Stopping to face the river, he throws the stones—one at a time—into the flowing water.

"I may not look like it, but I have fathered three children, two boys and a girl. They are all gone now, the tragedies of war. What I am trying to tell you, my friend, is that the time to worry is after they get here. What is going on in your lodge at the moment is not meant for men to be a part of. When the women want you—when your child has arrived—you will be sent for. Being brave in war is nothing compared to what you are going through now. I think the feather of the eagle should be given to first-time fathers."

Short Bull puts his hand on Yellow Hair's shoulder and adds, "Let us go back and await the call from the women. It is too bad you do not use tobacco. This is a good time for the pipe."

As they make their way back, Plenty Eagle Feathers runs up to them and exclaims, "Yellow Hair, you have a boy child!"

Yellow Hair's legs get weak. He has to sit down on a nearby boulder.

"When can I see Suni?"

"She is waiting for you, and so is your son."

"I like the sound of that . . . 'my son'." He jumps up and runs off towards his lodge, shouting "I have a son!"

Short Bull and Plenty Eagle Feathers break out in big grins before laughing out loud. The child is a fine and healthy boy. He is named Wakiŋyaŋhotoŋ Cístiŋna—Little Thunder.

And the Yellow Hair lodge knows peace and happiness.

Chapter Thirty-One

THE PROCESSION stretches back a quarter of a mile. It marches at a slow pace in an effort not to kick up too much dust. However, the pace is to no avail; it is the hot, dry season. Leading the procession is William Murray, actually Lieutenant William A. Murray, a recent graduate of West Point and who, on behalf of the United States, had extended the invitation to the Mdewakanton and the Wahpekute. He is on his first posting. He and his wife, the former Mary Chandler, look forward to the adventure that will be their lives together.

Lieutenant Murray is escorting the Mdewakanton to the conference at Mendota. On the *Wasichu* calendar, the date is 1 August 1851. Behind Lieutenant Murray and his soldiers ride the Mdewakanton men, Little Crow, and his council. Behind them walk their women, children, and dogs. They have been traveling for two days. Soon, Lieutenant Murray will have completed his mission. Mendota is coming into sight.

The *Wasichu* tents are set up and waiting. They are grand affairs, suitable for the station in life of those who will inhabit them. The Wahpekute are already in camp, their tipis arranged in a circle, denoting the hoop of life.

Except for the soldiers, there are no *Wasichu* in sight. Little Crow is in full regalia—a war bonnet with eagle feathers cascading down his back, shirt and leggings made of deerskin, the claw of a bear strung around his neck.

Thinking something might be amiss, he asks Big Eagle to inquire of Lieutenant Murray why the chiefs of the *Wasichu* are not there to meet them. "I see only soldiers."

"The conference does not start until tomorrow. The representatives of the Great Father will be here in the morning. I've been ordered to show you every consideration. If there is anything you need, you have only to ask." Before speaking further, Lieutenant Murray points to a large tent with two soldiers guarding it. "Over there are the food stocks. You may send your people to collect anything that is available. I was told your needs and those of the Wahpekute were anticipated. You should lack for nothing."

Having been assuaged of his fears that the conclave may have been some sort of trap, Little Crow tells the women to unload the tipis from the drags and set them up. He sends H'da ye yaŋ́kay (He Runs Rattling) and Hiŋhaŋkaġa duta (Red Owl) over to the soldiers guarding the food to secure provisions for the night.

● ● ● ● ●

As the Wahpekute and Mdewakanton sit around their fires discussing what they might expect from the *Wasichus* the next day, in a stone house not five miles away, three men sit in front of a fire of their own. They are Alexander Ramsey, Luke Lea, and Henry Sibley. Sibley is a fur trader of some repute. They, too, are discussing the next day and what their plans might be.

Sibley: The problem as I see it, gentlemen, is how do we get the Indians to sell their remaining lands in the territory?

Lea: We tell them that, because their game is vanishing and the prospect of starvation is on the horizon, we are willing to help them by buying their land.

Sibley: But it is because of us, the White Man, that their game is disappearing. The Indians know that, they're not stupid. Regardless of what you may think, Mister Lea.

Lea: Mister Sibley, we have an Indian Problem, *and* we need their land to accommodate the immigrants that are flowing into the territory every day. It has been decided in

Washington that the best way to solve both problems is to acquire their lands and use their money to turn them from savages into farmers. There are only a few thousand savages . . . alright, Mister Sibley, I see that look on your face, from now on I'll refer to them as Indians . . . there are only a few thousand Indians in the territory, and it is Washington's intent to turn them to farming. Once the land is ours, each Indian family will be given eighty acres and the annuity owed them for their lands will be paid mostly in farming tools, seed, and whatever else farmers need. We will teach the Indians how to farm. The cost for those hired to teach them will be deducted from future annuities. It's a brilliant scheme, gentlemen. We open up a whole new territory for settlement and turn savages—I mean Indians— into law-abiding farmers, using their own funds.

Sibley: Mister Lea, for a Commissioner of Indian Affairs, you sure don't know much about Indians. You ever met one?

Ramsey: Alright, gentlemen, let's not get personal. There is too much at stake here. If we cannot convince the Indians to sell, we may have to call in the army to protect the settlers. Remember, more than a few of the immigrants are squatting on Indian land. The Indians are not going to starve to death without putting up some sort of fight. If we fail to obtain a signed treaty granting us the lands owned by the Sioux, it may mean war; so let's devise our plan without further acrimony.

The men talk into the night. In the end, it is decided that the best approach is to tell the Indians that the Great Father in Washington is only interested in their well-being and has decided to buy their lands so that they will have the wherewithal to purchase food from the traders at the Agency. If that does not induce the Indians to sell, then the *Wasichus* will imply that their lands can be taken from them at the point of a gun.

• • • • •

As the sun rises over the small plain adjacent to the
Minnesota River that will host the conference, the first of
the *Wasichus* start to arrive. Settlers from the surrounding
countryside have loaded themselves onto the family wagon
and are showing up in droves. The Santee Sioux watch with
interest and wonder why the *Wasichus* are in such a festive
mood.

The morning progresses and more soldiers appear. They
go about setting the stage for the impending congress. Ten
chairs, placed halfway between the tents of the *Wasichus*
and the tipis of the Sioux, are arranged in a semi-circle
facing the tipis. They will be filled by lawyers from The
Bureau of Indian Affairs, a few land speculators, and the
main negotiators, Alexander Ramsey, Luke Lea. The
traders will be represented by Henry Sibley.

When the sun is directly overhead, in ride the
Wasichus; they ensconce themselves in the largest tent and
send for Lieutenant Murray.

"Lieutenant," says Alexander Ramsey, "please extend
our felicitations to Little Crow, Red Leaf (Wapa ŝa, chief of
the Wahpekute), and their headmen. Invite them over for a
glass of champagne before the conference begins."

"Yes sir."

The tent proves too small to accommodate everyone.
Little Crow's council consists of fourteen; Red Leaf's,
eleven. Therefore, the group adjourns outside where the
chairs have been set up.

With the *Wasichus* in the chairs and the Indians seated
on the ground, the mess sergeant and two orderlies hand
out glasses of champagne.

"May I propose a toast?" announces Ramsey. "To our
brothers, the Sioux."

Big Eagle translates Ramsey's words and adds, "It looks like we are in trouble. When a *Wasichu* calls you "brother," better look to your ponies and see if they are all still there."

With the pleasantries out of the way, Commissioner Lea suggests they get down to business. He stands and makes a long-winded speech. In effect, he says that the Great and Generous Father in Washington is willing to buy all their land so they will have money to purchase food and supplies from the traders at the Agency. He speaks for fifteen minutes.

When his peroration is over, Big Eagle rises to interpret his words.

"They want to steal more of our land" is all he says. Commissioner Lea did not understand what Big Eagle had said. Nevertheless, he is crestfallen that his oratory has been so succinctly condensed.

The negotiations take three days. The Indians do not want to sell more land to the *Wasichus,* let alone all their remaining land. If they did want to sell land, they certainly would not sell it to the Americans who have not once lived up to a treaty.

In treaties past, the Indians and the representatives from Washington would agree to terms. When the treaty got back to Washington, Congress would alter the terms— always to the United States' benefit—and hold the Indians to a treaty they had not agreed to. To make matters worse, if one band signed a treaty, all other bands of the same tribe were expected to adhere to it under penalty of reprisals from the United States Army.

The Sioux remind Lea and Ramsey that the Treaty of 1837 was abrogated after the signing. Ramsey is affronted by such accusations and says, "*This* treaty *will* be adhered to."

Still the Sioux refuse to sign.

217

Ramsey decides to try a new tact.

"You know, if the Great Father wants your lands, all he would have to do is send in his soldiers. He has many. They are like the leaves on the trees and you are few."

Commissioner Lea is a bit more blunt. "If you do not sign, your present annuities may cease altogether."

Hearing Big Eagle's translation, Little Crow looks to his council and says, "We have a knife to our backs. If we do not sign, the little gold we see each year will not be paid. We either sign and hope the Americans, for once, keep their word, or their soldiers will come and take our land."

Little Crow and Red Leaf confer, and decide the best course of action is to sign the treaty.

Before signing, Little Crow asks, "If we sell our land, where will we live?"

"We will set aside land for the Santee Sioux only. It is called a reservation and it will be along both banks of the Minnesota River, twenty miles wide, ten on each side and seventy miles long. It will stretch from the Cottonwood River northwest to Lake Traverse and will be yours until the grasses no longer grow," answered Commissioner Lea.

Commissioner Lea offers $1,000,000.00 for their lands. To the Sioux, $1,000,000.00 or $10,000,000.00, it was all the same. They have no concept of the dollar. Even if they did, they do not expect the Great Father to live up to his end of the bargain.

When Sibley hears the amount offered, he rises and asks Commissioner Lea if he might have a word with him in private. Granting Sibley's request, Lea asks, "What is it, what do you want?"

"I want you to offer the Indians more money. We traders have to make a living too. The more they got coming to them, the more us traders can deduct. And I won't forget you when I'm doing the deducting."

218

Commissioner Lea smiles and winks at the stout trader.

Instead of the four cents an acre the Sioux were originally offered, they are offered six cents an acre for land that was worth at least a dollar an acre. In the end, the amount specified on the treaty was $1,410,000.00. The Santee Sioux never did see all of the monies promised. In fact, in the end, they saw very little of what they were owed.

Knowing they had no choice, Little Crow and Red Leaf affixed their marks, followed by their councils. They signed two copies, one for Washington and one for themselves. Sibley and the other traders had the chiefs sign another paper, telling them it was a third copy. That was a lie. The Indians had actually put their mark to a document stating that they owed certain amounts—alleged debts—and that the signees pledged to pay those debts. It also authorized the government to pay the traders directly from all future annuities. No receipts were needed, no proof whatsoever. Whatever the traders said was owed, was owed. It became known as the Traders' Paper.

The Sioux could expect their first payment—what was left after the traders got to it—in one year's time. However, the land speculators and the settlers were on the land and building houses before the Wahpekute and Mdewakanton could strike their tipis and return to their villages.

One year later, there was a new outrage in the offing. The Senate finally got around to ratifying the treaty. During the process, the provision calling for a Sioux homeland vis à vis the reservation was struck from the document.

Governor Ramsey asked for a meeting with Little Crow and Red Leaf to explain the Senate's action. Red Leaf traveled to Little Crow's village on the appointed day and together they awaited the arrival of Governor Alexander Ramsey. The man who had said to them, *"This* treaty *will* be adhered to."

Ramsey arrived and was shown the courtesy and respect that all who visited the Dakota were shown. Little Crow had learned the *Wasichu* tongue by then and Red Leaf had spoken English for years; no interpreter was needed. The three men retired to Little Crow's lodge where they smoked the sacred pipe before getting down to business.

"My friends, something has come up and I need you . . . no, I *ask* you . . . to sign an amended treaty to the one we signed last year."

Little Crow looked at Red Leaf and Red Leaf returned the look.

What are the Wasichus up to? We have no more land, what can they possibly want from us now?

Ramsey explained that the clause establishing a reservation for the Sioux had been eliminated from the treaty. He had come to have them sign an amended treaty.

The *Wasichu* spoke fast and loose. He told the chiefs that everything would be worked out in time, that the land was theirs, but it might take a while for the government to put it in writing. Red Leaf asked the obvious question. "Why is not the ownership of our land in the paper you have brought today, the one you want us to place our marks on now?"

It was a pertinent question, and right to the point. The truth of the matter was that the *Wasichus* in Washington did not know where else to relocate the Sioux. It was thought best to allow them to live on the banks of the Minnesota River—for the time being. The Indians could always be moved elsewhere when that land became desirable to the whites.

Resigned to the inevitable, the chiefs made their marks on the amended treaty and the Santee Sioux settled along the south bank of the Minnesota River. The Sisseton and Wahpeton were farther north. The Mdewakanton and

Wahpekute set up their villages on the Redwood River to the south.

The United States established two agencies to manage the Indians. The first located at the confluence of the Minnesota and Yellow Medicine Rivers, known as the Upper Agency or the Yellow Medicine Agency. It would oversee the Sisseton and Wahpeton. The Lower Agency was located on the Redwood River and known as the Redwood Agency; it would handle the Mdewakanton and Wahpekute.

Five years later, the *Wasichus* were back. Now they wanted half of the reserve, the part on the north side of the river; almost one million acres. Though the reservation was not in the Treaty of 1851, and the United States could "legally" expropriate the land, it was thought a token payment would look better all the way around. After bringing Little Crow and the other chiefs to Washington, and after three months of negotiations and coercion, the Sioux were paid $266,880.00 for the land. About twenty-seven cents an acre for land assessed at five dollars an acre.

The Sioux did not see even that paltry amount. By the time the traders descended on the agencies waving their Traders' Paper, claiming alleged debts, there was nothing left.

As Little Crow left the signing ceremony, giving away the seventy miles on the north bank of the Minnesota River, the words of Luke Lea reverberated in his mind.

"It will be yours until the grasses no longer grow."

Chapter Thirty-Two

It Is The Moon Of Changing Season in The Winter Of The Lonely Deer—October 1858. There is to be no migration to hunt the buffalo this winter. There are no buffalo left to hunt on the eastern plains. Some of the Sioux have gone the way of the *Wasichu*. They have become farmers. They have adopted the dress of the *Wasichus*— pants and shirts—and have cut their hair. They are known as "Cut Hairs." Some call them "Corn Indians" or "Farmer Indians" because they raise crops, primarily corn. Those who adhere to the traditional ways of the Dakota are called "Blanket Indians."

Little Thunder has now seen seven winters. Yellow Hair and Suni are raising him in the old ways. He will not be a Cut Hair.

Little Thunder and Yellow Hair are down by the river testing Little Thunder's new bow that his father has made for him. Along with the bow, Yellow Hair has fashioned a quiver and six blunt arrows.

"But Father . . . why can I not have arrows that will kill game?"

"When you can hit what you are shooting at six times out of six, we will make you some hunting arrows. But for now you must practice. Soon I will be too old to hunt, and your mother and I will depend on you to feed us with the game that you will bring back."

"Yes, Father, you are old, but you and Mother will always eat as long as I can hunt."

Yellow Hair thinks that maybe, at twenty-eight winters, he is indeed getting old. Going out every day seeking game and finding less and less has made him feel old. As father teaches son the proper way to hold a bow and how much pressure to apply to the buffalo sinew, they look up to see Little Crow and Big Eagle approaching. Little Thunder shouts, "Grandfather, look at my bow. I am going hunting!"

Yellow Hair is surprised to see them. They had been gone for almost four moons. "When did you return?" he asks.

"The agent brought us back this morning," responded Little Crow. "We looked for you at your lodge. Fighting Woman said you were down here with the little one."

Big Eagle seems more interested in the doings of his grandson than anything else. After seeing the boy shoot a few arrows, he says, "I worry for our young ones. The old ways are going the way of the buffalo. Will my grandson be just another farmer living in a square lodge? The *Wasichus'* lodges are square! How can *Wakaŋ Taŋka* reside in a square lodge?"

Little Crow and Yellow Hair look at one another knowing what Big Eagle has said is true. The tipi is round because the father—the sun—is round. Because the mother—the earth—is round. *Wakaŋ Taŋka* lives in both.

Big Eagle holds out a hand to his grandson and says, "Come, let us go to your mother. As we walk, you can tell me what you have been doing while I was away."

Little Thunder collects his arrows and puts them in his quiver. As he and his grandfather, hand-in-hand, start for the village, he looks backward over his shoulder. "Father, are you not coming?"

"Not right now. I will speak with our chief first."

Yellow Hair watches the receding figures, then inquires, "What happened in Washington?"

"We return with bad news. The men in Washington have taken half the land left us . . . all the land north of the river."

Stunned by the news, Yellow Hair says, "They cannot do that! It was granted to us forever."

"It seems as though nothing is forever where the *Wasichus* are concerned. They promised payment, but I do not think we will see much, if anything, once the traders are done with us. It is a shame that, to live, we have to buy our food from them. All year long they make marks in their books and when our payment comes, they show their books to the agent. He then turns our gold over to them. We are fortunate to receive anything after a year of waiting."

Yellow Hair nods in agreement. "I once asked one of the traders at the Agency to see his book, but he would not show it to me. I wanted to see if he was writing down the price he told me my goods cost. He would not show me because he knew that I can read the White Man's language."

Little Crow shakes his head in sorrow. "Last year I went to Flandrau and complained to him about the trader's prices, but it did no good. All these agents—Murphy, Flandrau, Brown—they are all traders. It seems that after they enrich themselves at our expense, the government puts them as the Indian Agent over us. And that Flandrau, he was the worst. After Spirit Lake, he told me if we did not go on the warpath against Iŋkpaduta, he would hold out that year's annuity. If he did that, the traders would not sell to us and we would have starved. These are not good men. I find it hard to believe that *Wakaŋ Taŋ'ka* lives in any of them."

The Spirit Lake of which Little Crow spoke was known in the *Wasichu* culture as The Spirit Lake Massacre which took place in 1857—The Winter Of Tall Pines. Forty *Wasichu* were killed and four women taken captive by hostile Indians. Two of the women were subsequently killed and two were sold to friendly Indians who took them to the Agency and turned them over to the agent.

The Indians who perpetrated the killings were Dakota of the Wahpekute band. Their leader was Iŋkpaduta

(Scarlet Point). History tells us he was a thoroughly bad egg. However, history is often written by the victors.

Scarlet Point had not signed the Mendota Treaty and felt no obligation to abide by it. He and his people were Dakota. They did not live on a reserve and allow the *Wasichu* to feed them as if they were children or old men. They were warriors, they were hunters! They had no use for the *Wasichu's* gold.

• • • • •

It is The Winter Of No Elk—1854, as the whites count time. Scarlet Point sits in his lodge listening to Wakaŋhdi O'ta (Many Lightnings).

"I am telling you, your brother Sintomŋi duta is dead. So are his wife and five of his children. The whiskey trader, Lott, killed them. And now he has disappeared. He is nowhere to be found."

Scarlet Point cannot believe what he has just heard. "Just the other day I was playing with his youngest child, carrying him on my back, pretending to be his pony. When I left their lodge, they were gathering to eat. They were laughing and happy, even though food is scarce. Now I am told they are all dead at the hands of this *Wasichu* Lott?"

If Henry Lott had been anywhere in the vicinity, he would have had only hours to live and his death would not have been a pleasant one.

Because Scarlet Point does not know the whereabouts of Henry Lott, he decides to see if the *Wasichus* are indeed the men of honor and laws as they have claimed.

Scarlet Point stands before Major Stevens. "I demand justice for my brother and his family."

Major Stevens, who has no great love for Indians, wants this bugger out of his office, but he has been ordered to give lip service to the concerns of the savages. "What

225

can we do? Lott is gone. If he is ever located, we will bring him to trial."

"Then I will speak with the General if you will do nothing."

Stevens does not want to hear this. The Indian going over his head and bringing the General into it may be bad for his career. "Alright, we can indict him and try him in absentia. Do you know what that means?"

"Does it mean you will hunt him down and kill him?"

"No, not exactly. We will put him on trial. If he is deemed guilty *and* if he is ever found, then he will be punished."

"If . . . if . . . if! . . . If I had killed seven *Wasichus,* you would hunt me into the sacred hills. There would be no trial; there would be only my death."

In disgust, Scarlet Point leaves the major's office.

To protect his career, Major Stevens appoints Granville Berkley as prosecuting attorney. The trial is a farce. To show where he really stands in relation to the Indians, Berkley skewers Sintomŋi duta's head to a pole and places it over his house.

It is now The Winter Of Many Snows—1856, as the whites count time. Scarlet Point and his band have been living off the land as the Dakota have done since time immemorial. It is hard. To live, they must steal cattle and food from the *Wasichu* settlers. At one point, after a foray to obtain food, they are caught by the local militia led by a Captain Smith. Smith demands that the Indians turn over their firearms. It is winter and Scarlet Point tells Smith that his people will starve without guns to hunt with. It makes no difference to Captain Smith. He takes the Dakota's guns and leaves them to fend as best they can.

In the Moon of the Dark Red Calves—February 1857— one of the band tries to steal livestock from a *Wasichu.* He is shot, killed, and decapitated.

Scarlet Point and his people have had enough of the *Wasichus*. Though they are starving and forced to steal in order to eat, they have not killed anyone . . . yet.

A few weeks after the murder of his brave, Scarlet Point and his band reach Spirit Lake only to find the *Wasichu* living on its shores. The lake is sacred; *Wakaŋ Taŋ'ka* resides in the lake. No one may fish or even place a canoe onto its sacred waters. And here are the hated *Wasichu* living on its very shores!

It is bad enough what they have done to my people, but the affront to you, Wakaŋ Taŋ'ka, is unforgiveable.

It is the last straw for Scarlet Point. That is when the killings begin.

After the settlers are killed for desecrating the sacred waters, the army pursues the band. However, because of the heavy blanket of snow on the ground, the soldiers are forced to return to their fort. When Scarlet Point and his band come into the vicinity of the Upper Agency, Flandrau tells Little Crow to apprehend the renegades or risk losing that year's annuities.

Against his wishes and against his better judgment, Little Crow gathers his warriors and goes after Scarlet Point. It is the Moon of the Red Grass Appearing and the snow has abated. Yellow Hair is leading one group of braves while Little Crow and his men ride two miles to the east in an effort to outflank the Wahpekute. But the Wahpekute are not camped where they were thought to be. Yellow Hair and his men practically stumble upon them in the early morning.

A short battle ensues, but the Mdewakanton's hearts are not in the fight. They manage to kill three of Scarlet Point's men before retreating. Yellow Hair does not try to rally his men for another charge.

If Flandrau wants Scarlet Point, then let him send the army to capture him.

He sends out a scout to locate Little Crow. "Tell him that the battle is over and we are returning to the village."

Receiving Yellow Hair's message, Little Crow turns for home. After he reports to Flandrau, the agent harangues the Dakota chief to mount another expedition and go after Scarlet Point—all to no avail. Little Crow tells him he can do whatever he wishes concerning that year's annuity, but he and his men are going back to their lodges.

"The traders see all the gold anyway and all we see are strange markings in their black books."

He walks out of Flandreau's office feeling like a Dakota chief for the first time in a very long time.

• • • • •

That was one winter ago, and now Yellow Hair and Little Crow stand on the south bank of the Minnesota River. Yellow Hair inquires, "What do you need of me? If we have lost half the reservation, there is nothing I can do about it."

"Yes, I know. But I have to tell the people of our village, and I would like you by my side when I do so. I am afraid that the young braves might do something foolish. I know they yearn to go on the warpath. You are closer to their age and a much-respected warrior. If you counsel peace, they will listen. In me, they see an old man who gives away too much to the *Wasichu*. They have not seen what you and I have seen. The *Wasichus* bring me to Washington to demonstrate their might, and if that were not enough, this last time they took me and the other chiefs to New York, the great city. I have seen, as you have, that the *Wasichus* are as many as the blades of grass on the prairie."

That night, Little Crow informed his people of the *Wasichus'* treachery. As expected, the young braves were most unhappy about it and said so. He informed them that he had had no choice but to accede to the new treaty. The

228

young ones saw only a tired old man, and as they shouted for war, Yellow Hair stood up, and in the light of the fire, he told those assembled that Little Crow fought long and hard to preserve the north bank of the river for his people. "He spent four moons in Washington, away from his home and wives, fighting the *Wasichus.* But, in the end, the *Wasichus* were going to have our land no matter what."

"If they want our land, let them fight for it," shouted Mato Woŋahťake (Kicking Bear), a brave of twenty-one winters. Shouts of war went up from around the fire. The young braves were working themselves into a frenzy.

Raising his voice so that he could be heard over the shouts for war, Yellow Hair said, "You know me. You know that I am first into battle. I am not afraid to fight. Yes, we can attack the *Wasichu's* fort and we will be victorious. We can come back and have the Kill Dance, stay up all night telling of our coups, and in the morning go to sleep thinking that we have won the war over the *Wasichu.* But I tell you this. Within one moon, more soldiers than can be counted will descend on us. Little Crow and I have seen their numbers and they are many. They are as numerous as the stars in the sky. The Great Father can send thousands of his soldiers to kill us and our families."

Yellow Hair's speech had the desired effect. The hotheads cooled down and were reduced to mumbling among themselves.

Chapter Thirty-Three

A WINTER PASSES. There is less and less to hunt with the coming of every sunrise. Yellow Hair and Suni are in the woods with Little Thunder, searching for ash saplings with which to make the boy's hunting arrows. They watch him run from sapling to sapling as Running Close had done years earlier. Yellow Hair turns to Suni and says, "I thank *Wakaŋ Taŋka* that Little Thunder is only old enough to hunt muskrats. By the time he is big enough to hunt elk and deer, there will be none left. There may be none by next winter."

Suni takes Yellow Hair by the hand, "Come, let us not think of that now. Our son is waiting. See the smile on his face? He is about to hunt his first animal. That is what we should be thinking about on this day. A boy's first hunt is very important."

"You are right. Little Thunder will be a great hunter. He will learn from me as I have learned from you, my dear wife."

Little Thunder is getting impatient. "Father, Mother, hurry, it is getting late!"

• • • • •

Three winters later, in The Winter Of The Red Bird— 1861. A new agent was appointed to manage the reservation. His name: Thomas Galbraith. Although he referred to himself as Major Galbraith, he was not a major of anything. He thought the title would give him more authority over the Indians.

Galbraith was determined, regardless of the consequences, to institute the government's policy of turning the Indians from their traditional ways to farming.

Those who took the offer of land, cut their hair, wore the clothes of the White Man, and sent their children to the Christian missionary school would be treated differently than the Blanket Indians.

When food was in short supply, the stores at the Agency would give credit to the Cut Hairs on Galbraith's say so, while the Blanket Indians were told to hunt if they were hungry. The practice resulted in resentment toward the Cut Hairs from those who had not abandoned their tribal lifestyle and customs.

In the Moon of the Frost in the Tipis, in The Winter Of Distress—January 1862, the snow lay deep upon the land. There was no game to hunt. The people were hungry on the Dakota reservation. By the Moon of the Red Grass Appearing, the people had eaten their ponies and dogs to stay alive. They had been told all through the winter that relief was at hand, that the gold of the annuity would arrive any day. Then they would be able to buy food from the traders. But still, there was no gold.

If not for the war being fought in the East, the traders might have let some food out of the stores on credit. But rumors abounded that there might not be a payment that year. It was said the government needed all its gold to fight the War of Rebellion. General McClellan was losing battle after battle, even though the Grand Army of the Potomac had superior numbers to anything Lee could muster against it. So it was said at the agencies that winter.

• • • • •

The man and woman stand over their son, watching him sleep. The man speaks. "I am not going to raise my son in this manner. He goes to bed hungry when there is a warehouse filled with food not two miles from here. I have been reduced to trading my gun for food. And you, my beautiful wife, are forced to dig roots to feed our son. Now

231

I have no gun, and there are very few edible roots left. But we still have our ponies, those we will not eat! We will need them to get us to the western lands. I am told that there are still buffalo and elk on the western plains. The *Wasichus* have not yet settled there. We will have a few years to raise our son in the ways of the Dakota before the *Wasichu* arrives.

"Yes, my husband, this place is no longer for us. It is a prison, a prison where the jailer will not feed his prisoners."

As Suni and Yellow Hair discuss their future, a few Wahpeton from Yellow Medicine approach the Upper Agency intending to ask Agent Galbraith to open the warehouse and distribute food. They and their families are starving. The babies have distended stomachs; they cry out in the night from hunger.

It is the middle of the Moon of Making Fat. The Indian Agent listens to their plea, then tells them there will be no food allotment until the annuity arrives. "And when will that be?" asks Wakaŋ o żaŋ.

"Any day now," answers the agent. "Now return to your homes and be patient. No food can be given until the annuity arrives."

Fearing the Indians might return and cause trouble, Galbraith sends to Fort Ridgely for help. Two companies, totaling one hundred men led by Lieutenant Timothy Sheehan, are dispatched to protect the property and persons under the auspices of the United States Government.

As Agent Galbraith feared, the Dakota return in greater numbers. This time they do not intend to leave without food. Lieutenant Sheehan, knowing that his hundred men will not prevail if hostilities break out, persuades Galbraith to distribute a small amount of the food stock that he is hoarding in the warehouse. Galbraith relents and gives the Wahpeton only enough to keep body and soul together for a few days.

The young men of the Mdewakanton down at Redwood also have had enough. The morning after the Wahpeton received their small allotment, a voice calls from outside Yellow Hair's lodge. "Yellow Hair, it is I, Śake haŋ́ska. May I enter?"

"Yes, please come in." Long Claws enters and first sees Fighting Woman. He tells her that he is honored to be in her lodge. The young men of the village are in awe of Fighting Woman and Yellow Hair because of their many coups.

Long Claws sits down opposite Yellow Hair. "We have decided that the time has come to do something. We can no longer allow our mothers, our sisters, our little brothers to go hungry. We are forming a Soldiers' Lodge and plan to stop the traders from taking our gold when it comes."

Yellow Hair glances at Suni as he listens. He says nothing, but he wants to know what she thinks. He does not verbalize his question. A brave does not ask a woman's opinion in matters of this sort—not in front of another brave.

Suni knows the question on Yellow Hair's mind.

Do you think this is a good idea?

In response, she smiles and nods once. The interplay between husband and wife is subtle; Long Claws misses it entirely.

"First I must ask of who you speak when you say 'we'?" questions Yellow Hair.

"We are the young men of the Mdewakanton and the Wahpekute. The old men are like women. All they do is please the *Wasichu*."

"Why have you come to me?"

"We want you to lead us. None of us have been in battle, we have no coups. By the time we came of age, there were no more battles to be fought."

"How many are you?"

"At least one hundred and half that many more. Will you lead us?"

Yellow Hair is now of thirty-two winters and does not act as rashly as he did a few winters back. Before committing himself, he wants to meet with those that will form the Soldiers' Lodge.

"Call your braves together. We will meet tonight at the council fire. I will give you my answer then."

"Good. We will see you tonight."

Yellow Hair calls out as Long Claws reaches for the skin covering the entrance, "Tell me one thing."

"Yes, if I can."

"What do you plan to do after you get the gold from the traders?"

"I thought you knew. We plan to go to war. We want to kill all the *Wasichus*."

After Long Claws has gone, Yellow Hair says to Suni, "I will have to lead them. If I do not, they will get themselves killed and probably destroy the village. You know how the *Wasichu* blame all Dakota for the acts of a few."

Yellow Hair tells Little Crow of the meeting to take place that night and asks him to keep the older men and the women away. "I hope to lead them off the warpath, but if there are others looking on, they may feel they must cry out for war, or otherwise look like cowards."

Little Crow agrees. "See what you can do. If the *Wasichus* are attacked, Galbraith will call in the soldiers. The payment will be here any day, then this talk of war will be forgotten."

That night, one hundred and forty-six braves gather to hear what Yellow Hair has to say. The oldest is twenty-six winters, the youngest fourteen. The braves sit at the council fire talking among themselves. The mood is joyous. Occasionally a war whoop is heard. Yellow Hair sits by himself and says nothing. He is staring into the flames. He will say nothing until the men quiet down.

Slowly the noise subsides. When there is absolute quiet except for the crackling of the fire, Yellow Hair speaks. "My name is Yellow Hair. I was once a *Wasichu*, but now I am Dakota."

A cheer erupts. Yellow Hair holds up his right hand until again there is silence.

"What has been done to the Dakota cannot be forgiven. It is time to take action. I know how your young blood yearns for battle. How you dream of striking the enemy. How you want to kill those that have treated our people so badly. I too am angry, but getting ourselves killed and our village destroyed is not smart. I know you look around and see there are not many soldiers; that most have gone off to fight in the Great Father's war. You think that if we go on the warpath, there will be no one to oppose us but farmers. But I tell you this, the Great Father has many soldiers and, if we give cause, he can send many here to fight us and never miss them."

Yellow Hair stops speaking to let his words be understood. Then he continues, "Yes! I will lead you. Yes! We will take our gold from the traders and yes, we will take the food that is rightfully ours! But if I lead, you must follow. When we fight, it will not be in the old way. Coups do not matter when your family is hungry. We will not fight for coups. We will fight for food. We will fight for our dignity. We will fight because we are Dakota!"

The aggregation jumps to its feet and cheers. Some raise tomahawks or knives over their heads and shake them at the night sky. A few shots ring out. Yellow Hair stands erect, arms folded across his chest and looks at the young faces illuminated by firelight.

Eventually the cheering and whooping dies down. Yellow Hair tells the men to sit. "If I am to lead you, remember this. The Dakota do not make war on women and children. That was the old way." He sees a few nods of agreement, but not many—the old ways die hard.

"Tomorrow, Long Claws and I will go to the soldiers' fort. We will scout and learn if the soldiers will oppose us and side with the traders. This we must know before we can make our plan. Now go to your lodges and tie your ponies' tails for war. When we are ready, I will call for you. I promise it will not be long."

He sends the men on their way by shouting *blihéic iya po* (take courage).

The next day, Yellow Hair and Long Claws ride to Fort Ridgely to speak with Captain John Marsh.

When led into Marsh's office, Yellow Hair speaks. "Thank you for seeing us, Captain."

"Hell, man. I've been wanting to meet you since I first heard about the White Sioux with the yellow hair. You're kind of well-known in these parts, but no one ever sees you."

"Sir, I am Dakota and I have come to speak with you on a matter of some import. At least it is important to my people. There are some *Wasichus*, I mean whites, who think we Dakota are less than human. They think they can steal from us and leave us to go hungry. We have put up with it because we know we cannot win in a fight with the Americans. There are just too many of you."

Marsh interrupts, "You're an American, aren't you?"

"I told you, I am Dakota! Please allow me to finish."

"Yes, I'm sorry, go right ahead."

"We were forced, with a gun to our head, to sell our land. We were moved to a reserve. Then we had half the reserve taken from us. The men from Washington tell us we are well paid for our land and should have no complaints. They tell us we are treated fairly. I ask you, is it fair to threaten someone to sell something they do not

236

want to sell? Is it fair to offer three cents an acre for land that is worth over a dollar an acre? Is it fair to give our money to thieves masquerading as traders? Is it fair that we are now reduced to starving? Is it fair that our babies, our children, cry out for food? Is it fair that the food that could feed us lies in a storehouse and the agent refuses to give it to us because the men in Washington are late in sending our yearly payment for the land they have stolen from us?"

Yellow Hair abruptly stops speaking, looks straight into Captain Marsh's eyes, and waits for answers to his questions.

Before responding, Marsh shakes his head, then a broad grin forms on his face. "Sir, that was some speech. You ever think of running for Congress?"

Yellow Hair does not see the humor and is just about to say so when Marsh raises his hand. "Don't take offense. I was only joking. I happen to agree with you. Tell me, why have you come to see me?"

Yellow Hair is pleased at Marsh's attitude . . . pleased and surprised. "Sir, I have one, and only one, question for you."

"Alright, let's hear it."

"Will you send soldiers after us if we stop the traders from taking our gold this year?"

"You mean that's it? That's all you want to know?"

"Yes sir. That is all I want to know."

"The gold is yours; we will not come after you. My boys are soldiers, not collecting agents for the traders."

On the ride back to the reservation, Yellow Hair speaks to Long Claws.

"Pass the word that when the gold arrives and we are summoned to the Agency, for all to be ready for war. We will surround the traders. They will be there with their books as they are every year. We will put them under arrest, take their books, and we will burn them. We will tell

Galbraith that the gold belongs to us and we are taking it. Before we leave, we will tell the traders that if they want to continue to sell to us, the prices must be disclosed beforehand. If we do not like what they are charging, then I will go East and buy food and supplies with the gold. We will become our own traders."

Yellow Hair based his plan on the gold arriving within a few days. He had not counted on the dilatory nature of the bureaucrats in Washington.

Because of the war, the men at the Bureau of Indian Affairs dithered as to what form that year's annuity should take. Should it be gold or should it be bank notes? By the time they came down on the side of gold, the Dakota on the reservation were starving. The seeds of rebellion were planted, had sprouted, and were bearing fruit. War was about to break out.

• • • • •

On the morning of 4 August 1862, two braves ride into the Yellow Medicine Agency and ask for Lieutenant Sheehan. One of the braves informs Sheehan that, shortly, many more braves will be arriving and they will be shooting their guns into the air. The braves want to reassure the soldiers that the demonstration is to be a peaceful one. They are angry that so much food that is rightfully theirs stays behind locked doors while their people go hungry.

A few minutes later, hundreds of Dakota ride into the Agency whooping, shouting, and firing their guns. One group peels off and rushes the warehouse where the food is stored. Tate Hmiyaŋyaŋ (Round Wind) and Yellow Hair raise axes over their heads and bring them down on the warehouse door. It splits open and men pour inside. The other Dakota cover the soldiers with their guns. They outnumber the soldiers three to one.

Lieutenant Sheehan sees the Dakota are only after food and orders his men to stay their fire. But he has his orders. He knows the Indians respect the power of his cannons, so he has one aimed at the warehouse where the Indians are busy loading a wagon. That gets their attention and stops their endeavors. The soldiers and the Dakota stare at one another over the barrels of their guns. It is an impasse; Lieutenant Sheehan goes to find Galbraith.

"Listen Mister Galbraith ..."

"It's Major Galbraith."

Of all the pompous jackasses I've ever known!

"*Major* Galbraith, we have a situation here. The Indians are hungry, they outnumber my men and I do not believe they are going to leave this agency until they have secured what they have come for, or until they and many of my soldiers are dead."

"I am sorry, Lieutenant, but rules are rules. The food cannot be allocated until the annuity arrives. I've been very magnanimous by allowing food to the savages on a previous occasion. But this time I must be firm, no food! Especially not at the point of a gun. Why, I would lose all control over them if I were to relent now."

"How much control do you think you'll bring to bear with your scalp hanging in some Indian's lodge?"

Without waiting for an answer, Lieutenant Sheehan turns his back on Galbraith and calls to his sergeant, "Allow the Indians to finish loading that one wagon and then send a rider to the fort. Have him report to Captain Marsh what has happened here and ask him to come immediately."

Turning back to Galbraith, he says, "I'm taking it upon myself to allow the Indians to take just enough food to last them twenty-four hours. I will ask them to return tomorrow with their chiefs so that this may be worked out. By then,

Captain Marsh will be here and, thankfully, it will then be his problem."

In the morning, well before the sun is overhead, the Dakota ride into the Yellow Medicine Agency, led by Little Crow and Big Eagle from the Lower Agency and Medicine Bottle from the upper. Yellow Hair and Long Claws are along, but defer to the older men.

Andrew Myrick, the trader, is present along with the Agency's interpreter, Peter Quinn. There are also a few of the smaller traders, but because Myrick does more business than all of them combined, they will accede to whatever he says.

The *Wasichus* and the Dakota congregate in the Agency's office. Galbraith opens the meeting by stating imperiously, "I want it on the record that this meeting is taking place only at the insistence of the army. Now, what is it that you Indians want?"

Quinn starts to put Galbraith's words into the Dakota language when Little Crow stops him by saying, "We understand what was said. We also understand the meaning behind the words. You ask us what we want. I will tell you, Mister Indian Agent.

"We have waited a long time. The money is ours, but we cannot get it. The stores are filled with food, yet we go hungry. We ask that you, the agent, make some arrangement by which we can get food or else we may take our own way to keep from starving. When men are hungry, they help themselves."[2]

The smaller traders speak among themselves and then look to Myrick for guidance, but he sits impassively looking straight ahead, saying nothing.

---

[2] *A History of Minnesota,* By William W. Folwell, Vol. II, pg. 232, St. Paul, Minnesota Historical Society, Revised Edition 1961.

Galbraith, feeling that he must take charge—he cannot have a savage speak to him in such a manner—says, "You have been promised a payment this year and it will eventually arrive, but until it does, I cannot dispense any more of the food stores. If you had taken up farming, you would not be hungry. You notice that your brothers who farm are not starving."

Big Eagle can stand it no longer. "They are not hungry because you give them food! You want the Blanket Indians to know that if they cut their hair and wear the clothes of the *Wasichu,* then they too could have food from the stores that you say cannot be given out."

Galbraith replies. "Go back to your homes. The monies will be here any day now, then you can purchase food."

Myrick looks to the traders and says, "It's up to you now. What do you want to do?"

After conferring, the spokesman for the group says, "Whatever you say, we'll go along with, Mister Myrick."

Myrick stands and makes for the door without speaking. Galbraith stops him by saying, "I insist you give us your decision before you leave."

Turning at the doorway, Myrick looks directly at Little Crow and says, "So far as I am concerned, if they are hungry, let them eat grass or their own dung."[3]

Without another word, he walks out, leaving a very quiet room behind.

No one says anything for a few moments, but when Myrick's words sink in, when the Dakota realize that is the best that they can expect from the *Wasichu,* they stand and say a few choice words to Galbraith in their own language, which Quinn refuses to interpret.

Captain Marsh knows there will be trouble if he does not act in a decisive manner. His one hundred men would

---

[3] Ibid, pg. 233

241

be no match against a thousand hungry Indians fighting for the lives of their women and children. He goes to the Indians, who are now standing outside, and asks them to wait a moment before leaving.

He storms back into the building where Galbraith and the traders are still conferring and says in a very calm, but nevertheless, menacing voice, "I order you to release to the Indians enough food to last them for at least a week. Enough to feed all the Indians at both agencies. If any man-jack of you so much as looks at me the wrong way, I'll put the whole damn lot of you under arrest!"

Two weeks later, the day is 17 August 1862, or the middle of the Moon of Black Cherries in The Winter Of Distress, as the Dakota count time. The annuity gold is on the last leg of its journey. It is also the day that the Dakota, who are also known as the Santee Sioux, go to war against the United States of America.

The War

Chapter Thirty-Four

THE SUN has not yet shown itself over the horizon, though it will do so shortly. There is enough light for the four men to make their way out of their village at Rice Creek. Each carries an antiquated musket; they do not ride ponies. The four are on their way to hunt in the Big Woods to the north. They have not been eating very well of late because of Galbraith's stance on food distribution.

Their names are Kaomdei ye ye daŋ (Breaking Up) and Suŋgigidaŋ (Brown Wing). Their two friends are Nagiwe cakate (Killing Ghost) and Pazoiyopa (Runs Against Something When Crawling). All four are just past twenty winters.

The sun has crested the horizon by the time the four young men reach Little Crow's village where they make straight for the *wakpa* (river). Their intention is to borrow a *wáta* (boat) for the crossing and return it on their way back. As they near the riverbank, they see their old friend, Yellow Hair. Brown Wing yells out, "Yellow Hair, what is an old man like you doing up so early?"

Yellow Hair looks up from his work and sees four youths who are only ten winters younger than himself.

"This 'old man' is repairing his *wáta* so Fighting Woman, Little Thunder, and myself can cross to the north bank. We are going hunting; there is very little food in the village."

"Do you want to come with us?" asked Brown Wing.

"Where are you going?"

"Up to the Big Woods."

"No, we are going to stay close to the village; there is still some small game hereabouts."

As the four are getting into another boat, Yellow Hair asks them why they did not join the Soldiers' Lodge. Answering for himself and his friends, Killing Ghost says, "We do not want to fight. It is better to hunt."

Yellow Hair agrees and tells them that a fight is not expected. "Not with three hundred braves surrounding eight traders and Galbraith. We expect them to give us the gold and that will be the end of it. But you have the right idea. To fight the *Wasichus* will only bring disaster to the Dakota."

He places his foot upon the boat the four sit in and gives it a good shove out into the river. With a wave of his hand, he turns his back on them and resumes the task at hand.

• • • • •

Outside the town of Acton, Robinson (Robby) Jones sits on the steps that lead into his small store. He is thinking about how good life is. It is a Sunday morning, and though warm, it is not oppressively hot. He is not a particularly religious man, but on this Sunday morning he gives thanks for all the blessings the Good Lord has bestowed upon him. He has a wonderful wife and two fine children, Clara who is fifteen and her infant brother of eighteen months. True, they are adopted, but he could not love them any more if they had come from his own loins. After his family, Robby is thankful for his land. It is only a quarter of a section, but by gum, it is *his*!

Basking in the morning sunlight, thinking of what else he should be thankful for, he notices four Indians walking on the road that passes in front of his store. They distract him from his thoughts for only a moment. Indians are a common sight. They come to trade. Sometimes he and his wife will invite one or two to have supper with them. In fact, he knows many Indians he considers his friends, though these four are strangers. As they pass out of sight, he stands and goes into the store.

The Indians, seeing Robby sitting on his stoop, give him no more thought than he has given them. They are young. They do not remember a time before the *Wasichus* came. The whites are a familiar sight to them as Indians are a familiar sight to Robby Jones.

Entering his store, Robby tells Clara he is thinking about going over to the Baker place. His wife is there visiting. Seeing as how it's Sunday and trade will be light, he asks Clara if she can look after things.

A split rail fence demarcates Robby's land. At the northern boundary, a hen has built a nest and laid her eggs. Killing Ghost and Runs Against are arguing about who is the better shot. Brown Wing is thinking about how hungry he is, while Breaking Up eyes the ground looking for the right size stone to hurl at the next bird he sees, but instead he discovers the hen's nest.

"Look what I have found!" he shouts. The other three turn to see Breaking Up kneeling on the ground holding a hen's egg.

Killing Ghost excitedly says, "That belongs to a White Man, you should not take it."

The two get into an argument with Breaking Up finally calling Killing Ghost a coward.

"We will see who is a coward," counters Killing Ghost. "I will kill the White Man we just passed."

"I will go with you to see that you do," taunts Breaking Up.

It is decided. The four of them will go back to the store, and Killing Ghost will shoot the White Man sitting outside.

Robby sees the four Indians come back down the road and turn onto the short path that leads to his store. Speaking to Clara, he says, "Looks like we might get some business after all."

The Indians file up the steps. Killing Ghost is in the lead, with Breaking Up close behind prodding him with the barrel of his musket. Just before entering the store, Killing Ghost hesitates.

"Stop poking me. I know what I have to do and I will do it. Now watch me."

"Anything I can help you boys with?" Robby asks from behind the counter. Without replying to his query, the Indians start taking things off the shelves and putting them back in disarray. At length, Breaking Up says to Robby, "My friend here wants to speak with you," and pushes Killing Ghost toward the proprietor.

With a fatuous grin, Killing Ghost asks, "What is the trade for a sack of flour?"

Robby has run the store for a few years now and knows a paying customer when he sees one. The Indian standing before him is *not* a paying customer. He decides that he has wasted enough of his Sunday, he picks up his gun and says, "You boys decide on what you want and my daughter will take good care of you."

Turning to Clara he says, "I'll be at the Baker's. Your ma and me will be back in time for dinner. We'll be eating a little late today, about two o'clock I figure." He leaves the store, smiling at the Indians as he walks out.

The four braves are caught off guard. They look at one another, not knowing quite what to do. Suddenly, they rush for the door. Three of the four are down the steps, hurrying to catch up with Jones when Killing Ghost calls to them, "Wait, I have a plan."

He has stayed under the small ramada at the entrance to the store.

The three halt and wait as he descends the steps. "What is your plan?" Breaking Up asks scornfully.

"Follow me, let us see where he is going," answers Killing Ghost.

248

"I thought you were going to kill him," sneers Breaking Up.

"Did you not hear him say he was going to his neighbor's lodge? We may be able to kill more than just one White Man. Follow me."

"Why did you not kill him in his store?"

"I did not want to do it with the woman there."

Breaking Up looks to Runs Against and Brown Wing and says sardonically, "Do you think our brother will kill the White Man before we all grow old?"

Without another word, Killing Ghost starts down the same worn path that Robby Jones has just traversed; it leads into the woods behind the store. The other three follow him.

They reach the end of the path and find a clearing with a small hill at its center on which stands a farmhouse. Sitting under a white oak at the bottom of the hill are three men, one of whom is Robby Jones. The other two are Howard Baker, who owns the farm, and Varanus Webster, an immigrant from back East. Webster and his wife are living out of their covered wagon on Baker's land until they find some land of their own. Baker and his wife have two children—an infant and a boy seven years of age.

So intent are the men with their conversation that, at first, they do not see the Indians approach. Mister Baker is the first to take notice. "What have we here?" Turning in the direction of Baker's nod, Jones and Webster see the four Indians coming their way.

Before any of the White Men can say a word, Killing Ghost advances to Robby Jones and demands that they be given whiskey. To which Jones replies, "This is not my home, but even if it were, this is the Lord's Day. There is no drinking of whiskey on Sunday."

"The missionary told us of your Lord. He said every day is the Lord's Day."

"Yes, he was right, but Sunday is a special Lord's Day."

Killing Ghost turns to his compatriots and declares, *"Wasichu un waciŋhnuni waŋyaka niye!"* (You see, White Men *are* crazy!)

On the frontier, men were never far from their guns. The first thing the Indians observe is that each man has a gun within easy reach. Continuing in the Dakota language, Killing Ghost tells the other three that they must first disarm the White Men.

At that moment, Missus Jones walks up carrying a bucket half filled with water in one hand and a soup ladle in the other. Saying hello to the Indians, she puts the bucket down among the men, places the ladle in the bucket and says, "With all your jawboning, I thought you men would be parched by now." As she starts back to the house, Mister Baker asks, "What are you women doing up there?"

"Missus Webster and I are helping Ann with your dinner, Mister Baker, *and* we are also looking after your little ones," Missus Jones answers with a smile.

While the White Men are diverted, Breaking Up whispers in the Dakota tongue, "I know how we can disarm them. We will challenge them to a shooting contest; one shot each, but reload your gun as soon as you shoot. Watch them. If they do not reload, then after the last *Wasichu* has fired, we will turn our guns on them."

Breaking Up addresses the three men. "Would you like to see who is better at shooting, you White Men or us Indians?"

Howard Baker answers the challenge. "Sounds like a good idea. But I must warn you, there ain't a man within twenty miles that can out-shoot me. Let me get a couple of planks and draw circles on them. I'll nail them to this here oak. We'll each get one shot at fifty paces, the group that has the most holes within the circle of their plank wins. But only three of you can shoot. It would be unfair to have an extra shooter."

After the wood is secured to the tree and the fifty paces walked off, Baker tells the Indians that, because they are his guests, they may shoot first.

Seven men—three whites and four Indians—stand fifty paces from the old oak. The whites are thinking they'll show the Indians a thing or two. The Indians are not thinking of the contest. They are anxious, each hoping that when the time comes to fire at the whites they will have the courage to do so. Not one of them has ever killed another human being before.

Among the Indians, it does not matter who shoots first, so Runs Against stands up to the line, aims, and fires. He is so nervous, he misses the plank entirely and the White Men find it an effort not to laugh out loud.

The report of the first shot brings Missus Jones to the door of the farmhouse. She looks down the slight rise on which the house sits and sees that the men are having a shooting contest with the Indians.

Ann Baker calls to her, "What was that shot?"

"It's just men being men," she answers. Then adds, "I think I'll go back down there and tell Robby that we soon have to leave. We have our own dinner to prepare and the children will be getting hungry."

By the time Missus Jones reaches the bottom of the hill, the Indians have finished shooting and Mister Webster is just about to take the first shot for the whites. Not wanting to distract him, she says nothing.

In short order, Robby and Howard Baker each take their turn. After the last shot is fired, the White Men start walking toward the targets, with Missus Jones following. The Indians lag behind. Robby notices and says to his companions, "Looks like they're scolding the one who missed."

The Indians are in fact arguing, but not about a missed shot. Killing Ghost is saying to Breaking Up that he does not like the idea of killing a white woman. "It will be bad enough when the other *Wasichus* find out what we have done, but to kill a white woman!"

Breaking Up tells him that they have no choice. "She knows what we look like. She will tell the other whites and they will hang us from that tree," he says pointing to the oak. The other two, Brown Wing and Runs Against, stand back and listen to their friends. They are wondering what they have gotten themselves into. Breaking Up and Killing Ghost stare at each other for a long moment before Killing Ghost finally shrugs and says, "Death to all of the *Wasichu!*"

The White Men and Missus Jones are standing under the oak looking at the targets. The whites have easily won the contest. The men are smiling at one another, and Missus Jones is just about to tell her husband that they should be leaving when a shot rings out and Robby Jones falls to the ground.

Before Webster and Baker know what hit them, they too are on the ground—Webster dead and Baker dying. Things are happening very fast and Missus Jones does not have time to scream before a ball rips into her heart, killing her instantly. Up at the house, the two women hear the gunfire and, thinking it is more target shooting, go about their business.

It is not until Missus Baker's son looks out the window, sees the men and Missus Jones lying on the ground, and says, "Mommy, what is wrong with Daddy?" that they have an inkling anything is amiss.

Ann Baker had been rolling dough for biscuits. Wiping the flour from her hands, she walks to the window and sees the unbelievable sight of her husband and friends lying in the dust. She immediately takes hold of her boy and calls to

Missus Webster, "Please get the infant and come with me." Not waiting for a reply and with her son in tow, Missus Baker goes to the trap door leading to the root cellar and lifts it. She tells the boy to descend and wait for her. "Please hurry, Missus Webster. I will explain in a moment."

Missus Webster is slow in comprehending what is going on. However, she picks up the baby from his crib and walks to where Missus Baker is awaiting her. "What is it, Ann?"

Holding the door open, Ann Baker informs Missus Webster that there may be trouble, but she will explain its nature once they are all safely hidden in the cellar.

"Our husbands!" exclaims Missus Webster. "Are they all right?"

"Please, we must get into the cellar now!"

Looking into Missus Baker's eyes and seeing the fear within, Missus Webster, holding the infant, rapidly descends into the blackness of the Baker's root cellar followed by Ann Baker who closes the door behind her.

Down at the oak tree, Killing Ghost is speaking to Breaking Up, "I told you I would do it."

Breaking Up does not hear his words. He is too intent on the scene before him. Missus Jones and Webster are dead. Baker is alive, but bleeding badly. There is a pool of blood next to where he lies. He moans, but very softly. The more blood that flows from his body and onto the earth, the softer he moans. Robby Jones is a big man; the ball that hit him entered his chest but did not exit. He is alive, but barely. He has only minutes to live.

The Indians' thoughts now turn to escape. They are far from home in enemy territory. As soon as the bodies are discovered, the *Wasichus* will hunt them down.

"Let us go," warns Runs Against. "The *Wasichus* will be on us before we can leave this place."

After reloading their guns, the four take flight up the path they had walked down an hour earlier. In that one hour, the four young men changed not only their own destinies and those who were soon to die—they also changed forever the destiny of the Santee Sioux.

Chapter Thirty-Five

AS THE WOODS THIN, the Indians see Jones' store and the road that will lead them home and to safe refuge. Coming abreast of the store, Breaking Up notices Clara standing in the doorway. Without hesitating, he raises his gun, takes aim, and squeezes the trigger. The ball hits the girl in the chest, knocking her backwards into the store. She lies on the wooden floor, staring at the thick, overhead beams supporting the roof, and just before she dies, she wonders, *Why?*

That is also the question someone else wants answered. "Why did you do that?" shouts Killing Ghost.

In a calm voice, Breaking Up answers, "She could have told the whites about us." Then he adds, "We need horses. The next farm we come to, we will see what is there."

When Missus Baker hears no sounds above, no footfalls on the wooden floor, she decides to investigate and cautiously opens the trap door. The occupants of the cellar have been standing in total darkness; there had not been time to fetch a candle. She leaves the cellar, goes to a window, looks down towards the oak and sees the men and Missus Jones lying on the ground. The Indians are nowhere in sight.

She calls to Missus Webster, telling her to come up, but tells her son to stay hidden in the cellar and look after his baby brother. Together, the two women run down the incline to their husbands and friends. All are dead.

Ann Baker kneels down by her husband's body, cradles his head in her arms, and with tears flowing down her cheeks, she says, "We have to get some help. We have to make for the Olson place. They live just north of here."

While the two women hurry north for help, the four Indians are running south, hoping to find a farm with no one about and good strong horses either in the barn or in a field. Their only thought is to get out of the vicinity before the alarm can be raised.

Luck seems to be with them. Off to the right sits a farm and next to the barn are two horses harnessed to a wagon. The first to see the rig is Brown Wing. "Wait, look over there!" His exclamation halts the others in mid-stride. When they see what he is looking at, they group together and hunker down off the road.

Run Against asks nervously, "Do you think anyone is around?"

"Does not matter if they are or not," says Breaking Up, "we need those ponies. If someone tries to stop us from taking them, we will have to kill us another *Wasichu*."

With stealth, the four advance towards the barn. Breaking Up peers around its side to watch for anyone approaching. Brown Wing jumps up into the driver's seat and tells the other three to climb onboard. With Runs Against next to him and Killing Ghost and Breaking Up in the bed behind, Brown Wing drives the horses forward and out onto the road.

At that same moment, Missus Baker and Missus Webster reach the Olsen household. Seeing the state the women are in, Olsen has no doubt as to the veracity of their story. Turning them over to his wife to look after, he tells his twelve-year old son, Lars, to saddle the family horse and ride to Forrest City. "Tell the people what has happened and to send help at once." He then goes to the Baker farm to see the bodies for himself and to retrieve the children.

Word of the Indians' deeds starts to spread, to the northwest with Lars Olsen and due south with the four Indians. Lars reaches his destination first. The people of

Forrest City find it hard to believe that what the boy is saying is true.

The four Indians have no trouble convincing others that what transpired in Acton actually happened. When they make it back to their village at Rice Creek, they head straight for the lodge of Wicaho ocokayaduta (Red Middle Voice). He is their chief. On the way, they shout out to everyone they see that they have killed whites.

When told the news, Red Middle Voice's first thought was that the deaths would be attributed to his band as a whole; that everyone would have to pay the price for what the four young men had done. Not only have they killed White Men, but they have killed two white women. The four will have to be given over to the soldiers. And even then, Galbraith will think the rest of the band complicit in some way.

He was looking for an excuse to withhold this year's annuity. He probably knows it is not coming and this will give him the reason he needs for denying us our gold and supplies. It will not be only our band, but all the Dakota of the reserve will suffer and starve.

Red Middle Voice asks the four youths to retell their story. He wants to weigh his options. He needs all the details to make an informed decision. If it had not been for the killing of the women, a claim of self-defense might have been made. Many braves crowd around and listen intently. When the four are finished relating the events of that morning for a second time, a yell erupts from the crowd. "Death to the whites!"

Death to the whites! The idea intrigues Red Middle Voice. With the regular soldiers away fighting in the south and the fort poorly manned, this would be the ideal time to go to war. But he knows that his small band cannot do it alone. At most, they have perhaps one hundred warriors. Once they went on the attack, the state of Minnesota would form a militia, which, based on the number of *Wasichu* that have come in over the last few years, would probably number in the thousands.

There were nine villages along the southern bank of the Minnesota River in the summer of 1862. If all the bands acted in concert, a thousand warriors could be amassed to forever rid the land of the hated *Wasichu*.

The braves of Rice Creek were yelling for blood. Red Middle Voice was inclined to agree with the sentiment. Asking for quiet, he told his braves that they must enlist the other bands if they were to go to war. "Let us see what Shakopee and his braves have to say."

Shakopee's village was the next village to the south, located at the confluence of the Redwood and Minnesota Rivers. His braves were the most radical of all the bands. They supplied more men to the Soldiers' Lodge than any other village on the reservation.

Word of the killings had spread rapidly from band to band. When Red Middle Voice and his braves arrived in Shakopee's village, there were a hundred braves waiting for them.

Shakopee was of the same mind as Red Middle Voice. He was sure they all would pay a price for the actions of the four young men. He believed that, even if they turned them over to the army, Galbraith would find some way to punish them all.

More braves were arriving by the minute, all shouting for war.

The chiefs of the Lower Sioux assembled in Shakopee's lodge and spoke among themselves. It was decided they needed someone who could rally all of the Dakota. There was only one man that fit that description.

"Let us go and see Little Crow," counseled Shakopee.

By August of 1862, Little Crow had adopted many of the ways of the *Wasichu*. He was living in a square house built for him by Galbraith. He wore the clothes of the White Man, but he was not a Farmer Indian.

He had been to Washington twice; he knew nothing was going to stop the White Man from taking over the lands that had been the Dakotas' since time began. Still, he was the most respected chief of the Santee Sioux. He alone could unite the four bands for war.

When Shakopee, Red Middle Voice, and the other chiefs reached Little Crow's house, there were close to four hundred people encircling it. Most were from Little Crow's village, but a good number of the men were from the Soldiers' Lodge.

The chiefs entered the house and found Little Crow in his bed. The only light in the room came through the window from the fires outside.

Red Middle Voice said, "We have come to tell you what has happened today and to obtain your counsel."

"I have heard. Tell me the details."

Sitting on his bed, surrounded by the chiefs of the other bands, Little Crow listened with keen attention as Red Middle Voice reported what had happened up in Acton.

When the narration ended, Little Crow asked, "Why do you come to me? Am I supposed to tell you what to do?"

Red Middle Voice stepped forward so that Little Crow could see his face in the half-light of the room. "We know what to do. We will wage war on all the whites. We will drive them from our lands."

"And what do those who are shouting outside my house want?"

"To kill the whites."

Looking at the men's faces, their eyes reflecting the firelight coming in from outside, Little Crow noticed Big Eagle for the first time. "And you, my friend, do you also want to kill the whites?"

"No, I do not. Red Middle Voice and Shakopee are fools!" said Big Eagle.

It was hard to hear his words because of the war whoops and the shouting coming from outside. Knowing that most of the members of the Soldiers' Lodge hailed from Shakopee's village, Little Crow asked him, "Are those who are making all that noise from the Soldiers' Lodge?"

"Yes, and as you can hear, they are ready for war."

"Then should not their leader be present? Send for Yellow Hair."

"I know Yellow Hair has many coups, or would have if he ever called coup, but he is a *Wasichu*. He will not fight against his own kind."

"We are Indians; do we not fight against our own kind? Have you yourself, Shakopee, not killed many Chippewa? Was not your first coup feather given for killing a Winnebago? Yellow Hair may at one time have been a *Wasichu,* but he is now Dakota. He is as much Dakota as you or me. If nothing else, perhaps he can advise us what the *Wasichus* will do about the killings."

"We know what they will do. They will punish us all," said Red Middle Voice.

Shaking his head and sighing, Little Crow called to one of his wives. When she entered, he said, "See if you can find Long Claws outside and tell him that I want Yellow Hair. If you cannot find Long Claws, *you* bring me Yellow Hair."

The conversation did not lag while they awaited Yellow Hair's arrival. Shakopee stood looking out the window. In the firelight, he could see the smiles on the faces of the young braves. He saw the joy in their manner and the hope in their eyes. Turning back to Little Crow, he said, "This is our time. It has been a long time coming. Our people are starving, there is no game to hunt and the White Man holds our food and steals our gold. If we do not fight now, the Dakota will be no more!"

"Shakopee is right," offered Red Middle Voice.

Wabasha (Red Leaf) then spoke for the first time. "Are we to go to war to save four men who killed unarmed men and women?"

"We will go to war to save the Dakota," replied Red Middle Voice.

It was evident that there were two factions present, the chiefs who wanted war and those who counseled peace. No one in the room had any great love for the Americans, but a few of the men could see beyond their hatred to what a war would mean for the Dakota. One of those men was Yellow Hair.

"You sent for me, Little Crow?"

"Yes, Yellow Hair. Have you heard about the killings of the white settlers?"

"It is the talk of the village, but what need have you of me?"

"You lead the Soldiers' Lodge; did you not see your men as you entered?"

"I saw a few. I know they want war with the Americans."

Red Middle Voice intruded into the conversation. "Yellow Hair, will you lead the men of the Soldiers' Lodge into battle against the Americans?"

Yellow Hair, who had been standing just inside the door, walked slowly into the room. As he passed the chiefs, he looked each man straight in the eye. When he reached Red Middle Voice, he stood before him and said, "Fighting the Americans would be foolish, there are too many; we cannot win a war against them.

"If you men of the council vote for war, I will fight the soldiers that will surely come. But I make war only on soldiers, not on farmers, women, and children. I hear that

261

those killed today were unarmed farmers, a woman, and a girl-child. I am done."

Heads nodded in agreement with what Yellow Hair had said.

Sensing that he might be losing the consensus for war, Red Middle sneered, "Those that are against war are cowards."

Shakopee quickly agreed.

"Red Middle Voice is a fool," said Little Crow.

The talk went on with each chief weighing in with his thoughts for or against war.

"There are too many Americans."

"Now is the time to attack while they are fighting among themselves."

Still another counseled for peace because the whites had cannons.

Little Crow looked around the room. As he looked at the faces of the men standing before him, he realized that if he did not act as their chief, they would turn to another to lead them.

"I have led the Dakota for many winters. All you men who now stand before me, I have led into battle. I have proved my courage on the warpath." He took a deep breath before continuing, "I see that war is coming, though I counsel against it. I am your chief. I will lead you."

It took a moment for Little Crow's words to sink in. He was going to lead the Dakota into war! Shakopee and Red Middle Voice went to the window and shouted, "Kill the whites! Kill the whites!" Those outside heard the words and knew they were going to war, and a great roar went up from the crowd.

Wabasha, Big Eagle, Yellow Hair, and the others who had lobbied for peace were stunned. Later, Yellow Hair spoke with Big Eagle about Little Crow's decision for war.

"Do you think he changed his mind because Red Middle Voice called him a coward?"

"I do not know, but I do know this will not end well for the Dakota," answered Big Eagle.

"I believe you are right," concurred Yellow Hair.

Chapter Thirty-Six

18 AUGUST 1862—on this day, the war starts in earnest.

Two hours before dawn, Yellow Hair returned from the meeting with Little Crow and the other chiefs and spoke with Suni. "It looks like we are going to war."

Lying on their buffalo skin bed, Suni asked her husband, "Is it not good that we drive the *Wasichu* from the valley?"

"If we *could* drive them from the valley, yes, that would be good. But this land is now a state. I know you do not know what that is, but it means it is a part of the United States. I have spoken with the White Men down at the Agency. The Great Father's war is not being fought for the Negroes; it is being fought because half the states left the union. The President, I mean, the Great Father, will never allow the Dakota to take back their land."

Suni changed the subject. "Is my father leading his braves?"

"Yes, he feels it is his duty, though he counseled for peace."

"When does the war begin?"

"It begins at sunrise. The braves are going to the Agency to kill all whites and half-breeds. Some are even talking of killing the Cut Hairs."

"Are you going with them?"

"Yes, I need a gun and ammunition, but I will not make war on store clerks. After the braves have done what they set out to do, I will get what I need from Myrick's store. By then I do not think he will object. Only when the soldiers come will I fight."

With the sun rising over the Agency came two hundred braves, painted for war and led by Little Crow. They stopped in the middle of the settlement. Astride Catcher-of-the-Wind sat Yellow Hair. Little Crow pointed to various buildings and as he did so, groups of braves peeled off and surrounded them.

A few whites looked out their windows or stood in doorways wondering what the Indians were up to. At that point, no one was worried.

The largest contingent of braves had circled the storehouse that harbored the government food and supplies. Another surrounded the store of Andrew Myrick—the man who had told them to eat grass.

On a signal from Little Crow, his men opened fire on anyone in sight. Myrick ran out the back of his store in an effort to reach the relative safety of the woods. *Kaġa Tha'ta* (Wind Maker) saw him leaving and shot him. Almost before he hit the ground, half a dozen braves surrounded him. They took great satisfaction in seeing the fear in his eyes. One by one, each brave drew an arrow from his quiver, strung it and shot it into the still living body of Andrew Myrick. Just before he died, Ite duta (Scarlet Face) grabbed a handful of grass, stuffed it into Myrick's mouth and shouted, "Let *him* eat grass!"

Little Crow and Yellow Hair went behind the blacksmith shop where the corral was located and happened upon a number of braves trying to take the horses. They were fighting with three White Men who were hampering their efforts. Astonished at the scene before him, Little Crow asked, "What are you doing? Why do you not shoot these men? What are you waiting for?"

The braves promptly leveled their guns and fired, killing all three men. Turning to Yellow Hair, Little Crow said, "I think some of our people still do not know we are at war."

Yellow Hair glanced down at the three dead men and said, "If the braves do not know it yet, they will soon find out." He added, "Will you send out scouts to watch the fort and let us know when the soldiers come?"

"What makes you think the soldiers will come today?"

"I saw some whites making for the river. They will get to the fort and tell the soldiers what has happened here. If nothing else, the soldiers will see the smoke when you start burning the buildings."

Little Crow did not look pleased. "You should have said something. I would have sent men to stop them."

"You mean you would have sent men to kill them."

"Yes, of course we would kill them. Have I not said this is war?"

"They were mostly women and children. How many eagle feathers does a brave receive for killing a child?"

Little Crow heaved a sigh and said, "You are right. I did not want to go to war and now I may not be able to control the young ones once they have tasted blood. But what are you going to do, Yellow Hair?"

"I have to get a gun before they are all gone. Then I will seek out the braves that are attacking the farms and bring them to the river. We will await the soldiers at the ferry crossing. You should send scouts to watch the fort and report when the soldiers are coming. That is, if you agree with my plan."

"Yes, it is a good plan. Killing these clerks has been easy. But I believe the soldiers will be harder to kill."

"Perhaps, but remember, we will have the element of surprise on our side. Tell the scouts we will wait for them at the river, where the ferry crosses."

Everyone living at the Agency knew there was whole-scale slaughter taking place and all tried to escape. They were helped in that endeavor because, after the initial volleys, the Indians turned their attention to looting. In front of the storehouse stood eight wagons in a line. The wagons, up until a few moments ago, belonged to the traders. Now they were the plunder of war. The Indians loaded each wagon in turn with food stocks: flour, salted pork, corn meal, and the like. When fully loaded, they left for the village of the man who drove it.

While the Indians at the storehouse emptied it of its contents, others set about torching the buildings. A few whites had tried hiding, but when the buildings were set ablaze, they ran out into the open where Indians quickly dispatched them into the next world.

Because the Indians were so intent on gathering trophies of war, forty-seven people escaped and made it to the fort. The first arrived at ten o'clock in the morning. Some of the refugees had to take roundabout routes to avoid the Indians and did not arrive at the fort until much later.

The commander, Captain Marsh, had a hard time believing the accounts of the goings-on at the Agency. However, as stragglers arrived and told their stories, he gave more credence to what he had heard, although he still believed the outrages were conducted by only a handful of malcontents.

In the summer of 1862, the fort's entire contingent consisted of one hundred and thirty men. The day before the uprising, Captain Marsh had sent Lieutenant Sheehan and the fifty men of Company C to Fort Ripley, situated on the Mississippi River.

The first thing Marsh did was dispatch a rider to recall Sheehan. Then he assembled forty-seven men, issued them forty rounds each and one day's rations and marched toward the Agency. He did not think putting down a small uprising would take any great time or effort.

Yellow Hair left Little Crow, went to Myrick's store, and entered through the back door. The ground floor housed the store and a small storeroom. Myrick's living quarters were on the second level. The looting was just getting underway and the braves were too intent upon their labors to pay Yellow Hair any attention.

Myrick was the largest trader at the Agency, and even though most of his supplies were in the main storehouse, there were still ample pickings within the store. Yellow Hair, seeing there were no guns at hand, decided to look around upstairs.

There were two rooms at the top of the stairs. The one on the left faced the front and was obviously Myrick's bedroom. The door to the other room was closed. Yellow Hair went into the first room and looked under the bed; he saw only a layer of dust. Then he went to the wardrobe, opened it, and peered inside. No rifle, just a Sunday suit and a few shirts.

Turning his attention to the other room, he found the door locked. He started downstairs, thinking that he had dallied too long. He should be out there with the looters looking for a gun to claim. Then a thought presented itself.

Why is that the only locked door in the entire store?

He bounded down the rest of the stairs two at a time. When he reached the bottom, he saw Wićasta Ta'wa (His People) with a sack of flour over his left shoulder, headed for the door. "Wićasta Ta'wa, where is your gun? Can I use it for a short while?"

Stopping at the door and turning to see who had spoken, His People broke out in a big grin. "Some fun, huh, Yellow Hair? I have enough food stacked outside to feed my mother and me for two moons . . . maybe more!" His People had seen only nineteen winters and this was his first war.

"Yes, Wićasta Ta'wa, it is some fun. But I need your gun for a minute."

"Do you know where there are some whites hiding? Are you going to kill them?"

"I do not know. There may be people hiding upstairs, but I will need your gun to find out."

"Well, if you need any help killing whites, call to me. I have a pistol I took from Myrick's desk. It is on a shelf behind the counter."

"Thank you."

"This flour is getting heavy, I must go."

With pistol in hand, Yellow Hair went back up the stairs. Standing at the door, he aimed the gun at the lock. Before pulling the trigger, he thought about what His People had said. There might be someone hiding in the room. They would be scared and may have a gun. If he shot the lock off and pushed open the door, it might be the last act of his life. So he knocked and said in English, "If someone is in there, open the door. I will not harm you. It is me . . . Yellow Hair."

Everyone who lived at the Agency knew Yellow Hair and they all liked him. Well, almost all; Galbraith and Myrick did not like him all that much. Galbraith because he was trying to get the Indians to adopt the ways of the White Man and here was a White Man going in the opposite direction and becoming a savage. Myrick did not like him because he hated all Indians. It did not matter if you were born that way or became one by choice. His disdain for Indians was probably the main reason he was lying out back—dead—with a mouth full of grass.

When Yellow Hair received no reply, he aimed the gun and shot at the lock. The wood splintered, and what was left of the lock would never again impede anyone's ingress.

He pushed open the door and jumped back. There was no loud report of a gun. He gingerly looked around the door jam and saw that the room was empty except for three large boxes.

They bore no markings, and when he gave one a shove, it did not move. Whatever was inside was heavy. He drew his knife and was about to pry one open when His People and Tate Hmiyaŋyaŋ (Round Wind) burst into the room. Breathlessly His People asked, "We heard a shot. Are you all right?"

"As you can see, I am alone and unharmed."

When the two braves had caught their breath and calmed down, they noticed the crates. Round Wind asked, "What is in the boxes, Yellow Hair?"

"I do not know, but I was about to find out when you two came to my rescue."

Without further folderol, Yellow Hair took out his knife and pried opened the top of one of the crates. What he beheld astounded him and his two companions.

Rifles filled the boxes—new, breech-loading rifles—oil glistening on the barrels. Without saying a word, Yellow Hair opened the other two cases. One held more rifles. The other was filled with cartridges.

Round Wind looked down at the musket he held in his hand and made a face before hurling it to the floor. Taking one of the rifles and a box of ammunition, he said "I thank you, Yellow Hair."

His People also helped himself to a gun and a box of cartridges.

"I know you found these, Yellow Hair, but you don't mind if I take one for myself?"

"No, you are welcome to it, but I ask a favor in return. Actually two favors. We will need these guns to fight the soldiers, so do not tell others of them. And please go find Little Crow and bring him to me."

The two young braves were so pleased with their new guns that they would have carried Little Crow to Yellow Hair if he had asked.

Chapter Thirty-Seven

LITTLE CROW walked into the room, saw the guns, and with a broad smile, said, "Well done. These will be put to good use."

"Sooner than you think," said Yellow Hair. "We will need them when we meet the soldiers at the ferry. I must go and round up enough braves for the battle."

"What do you need?"

"Can you get me a wagon to carry the boxes?"

Yellow Hair got his wagon and His People and Round Wind helped load it. The crates were heavy, and it took the strength of the young braves to get them down the stairs and loaded onto the wagon.

Looking up at Yellow Hair sitting in the driver's seat, Little Crow said, "I will send braves to meet you at the river. You tell those that are roaming from farm to farm that we will stop the soldiers first, then they can rid the valley of settlers. Tell them those are the words of Little Crow, their chief."

Most of the braves had left the Agency after the looting and burning. Those with booty were in their villages. Those without took to the countryside in search of farms where they could kill more whites and get some spoils of war for themselves.

While traveling west on the main road, Yellow Hair came across burned-out farms with dead bodies lying in the yards. But he saw no Indians. Just as he was about to give up hope of finding men to recruit for the coming battle, he happened upon a war party that had surrounded a wagon of settlers. He drove up to the assemblage and heard the leader Hołipa (Hawk) say, "We are going to kill you all."

Yellow Hair saw Helen Carrothers. She was a friend of Looking Elk's, the medicine man. She spoke the Dakota language and had studied the healing ways of the Dakota. Looking Elk had taught her of the curative powers of different barks, wildflowers, roots, and herbs. Yellow Hair knew that if harm came to her, Looking Elk would mourn for her as though she were his own daughter.

Before he knew what was happening, the men of the war party started shooting the settlers. He jumped from the wagon, went to Missus Carrothers and told her to follow him. She hesitated and screamed, "My children!" It was then that he noticed the two young ones clinging to her dress. "Go! Jump in that ditch over there. I will bring the children."

Once he had the three of them lying in the trench and out of view, he stood to see what the braves were doing. The sight sickened him. He had been on many a war party, but he had never seen a Dakota act in such a brutal fashion. These were young braves who had never been to war. Boys brought up on tales of courage. But it takes not a brave man to smash a baby's head against a wagon.

Yellow Hair knew he could not save the other whites; the Indians were in a blood lust. But he was going to save Helen Carrothers and her children if it meant he would have to die in their stead.

After killing all the whites they could—the ones who had not run away—the Indians went to the ditch where Missus Carrothers was lying, shielding her children with her body. Yellow Hair stood over them.

Hawk spoke. "Yellow Hair, you know all the *Wasichu* must die. Stand aside. If it bothers you to watch, leave us. We know what we have to do."

"I know what you have to do. You have to come with me. You are needed to fight the soldiers that are coming. Can you stop killing women and children long enough to fight men? Men who will fight back and not run away as some of these farmers have done?"

Yellow Hair paused a moment, then continued, "This woman is a friend to Looking Elk. He does not want her or her children harmed. Are you, Hawk, going to go against the medicine man of our village? If you think you might, then think again. Because you will have to kill me first."

Hawk wavered for a moment. To save face he said, "Where are these soldiers? We will fight them. You may take the White Woman. If Looking Elk wants the woman, then he may have her as my gift."

Yellow Hair reached out his hand to Missus Carrothers and helped her stand up as he said to Hawk, "Send two men with this woman and her children to make sure they make it to our village safely. I will go with you. Little Crow has told me to bring you and your men to the river. It is there that we will meet the soldiers."

Hawk had seventy-five men with him and few had ponies. If they were to reach the river before the soldiers, they would have to start right away. Hawk drove while Yellow Hair, from the back of the wagon, dispersed guns and ammunition to the men without guns.

His task completed, Yellow Hair climbed up front and sat down next to Hawk. In silence, they traveled east to do battle with soldiers of the United States Army.

Meanwhile, Captain Marsh and his men marched west. Along the way, they met settlers making their way to the fort; they told of seeing farmhouses with dead bodies strewn about. Soon Captain Marsh and his men were seeing the dead for themselves.

Marsh's column slowed as it neared a still-smoldering farmhouse. When they reached the homestead, they saw a body lying in the yard.

Suddenly, a young boy rushed from the trees where he had been hiding.

He told Marsh of the attack on the Agency. How, when it started, his father had bundled the family—his mother, his sister, and himself—into a wagon and made a run for the safety of the fort. "We got only as far as this house when my mother couldn't go any further. You see, she was feeling poorly. The house was empty, so we went inside to rest.

"My father sent me to find water for my mother. As I reached the creek, I heard a shot and ran back. I got to within sight of the house and saw my father lying on the ground, surrounded by Indians. Other Indians were going in and out of the house. Then they all came outside and closed the door. One of them put the handle of a hoe through the loop so the door could not be opened. And then they set fire to the house."

The boy stopped for a moment and looked as though he was going to cry, but recovered and went on. "From inside, I heard my mother scream and my sister crying out for our father. Just then, the glass in a window broke and my sister tried to crawl out, but a brave shot an arrow at her, driving her back inside. As the fire grew, the screams became louder until all of a sudden there was quiet. That's when the Indians left. As soon as they were gone, I ran to my father. His throat had been cut. I tried to get to the door so I could get it open and let my mother and sister out, but the flames were too hot. I couldn't get close. I went to the window my sister had tried to climb out of and called to them. There was no answer. The other windows started to explode and black smoke was pouring through them. I heard someone coming and ran back to the trees. It was a small band of Indians who watched the fire for a little while before moving on."

Marsh told the boy to make for the fort where there were people who would look after him.

Before long, the soldiers came across the Reverend Hinman, a missionary from the Lower Agency. He tried to warn Marsh that he and his soldiers were greatly outnumbered, and that if he went as far as the Redwood Ferry, he would meet his match and then some.

"I thank you kindly for the warning, preacher, but this is army business. We will proceed. It is the work of only a few malcontents. We'll have them rounded up before suppertime. If they have retreated to their villages, the chiefs will hand them over. You continue on to the fort. You'll be safe there."

While Captain Marsh was busy patronizing Reverend Hinman, Yellow Hair and Hawk were making their way to Redwood Ferry. They kept the silence between them until they saw a man on the road coming their way. It was Šuŋka ska (White Dog).

Said Hawk: "He is a Cut Hair. We will kill him."

Yellow Hair looked over and said, "You like to kill unarmed men, don't you."

"He worked with the whites. He is a traitor. He and all Cut Hairs will die, armed or not!"

"Well, this one will not die. We have need of him. I will explain when we reach the river."

They came abreast of White Dog, and Yellow Hair told him to climb into the back of the wagon. White Dog had heard the shouts of "Kill the whites." He had also heard some call for the death of all the Cut Hairs and mixed bloods. That was why he was on the road going away from the Agency.

"No, thank you. I am going in the opposite direction," said White Dog.

"You better do what he says," interjected Hawk, "because if it was up to me, I would kill you where you stand."

"White Dog, come with us. No harm will befall you," assured Yellow Hair.

Nodding his head to Yellow Hair and without looking at Hawk, White Dog climbed into the back of the wagon.

Underway once again, Hawk thought long and hard before saying, "When I was a boy, I heard the stories of Yellow Hair. How he was first to ride into battle. That he could have had many coup feathers, but he never called coup. That he would knock the enemy to the ground, but would not kill him. At the Kill Dance, Yellow Hair would give witness to the coups of others, but would allow no one to give witness to his. I know you are a great warrior and that you are brave, but why do you not kill? Especially those that want to kill you."

"I do not think you will understand, but I will tell you why I do not kill. And by the way, I did not see anyone trying to kill you this morning, certainly not those women and scared farmers."

"They would have killed me with their presence. They have driven off the game and the buffalo that we need to live. They have taken our valley, our rivers, our lakes, and put us on a small strip of land. They have made us dependent on them for food. They do not pay us for our land and give our gold to the traders. They ..."

"Hold on, young Hawk. All that you say is true. If driving out a few farmers would get us our lands and our dignity back, I would be all for it. However, we would not have to kill them. We could round them up, take them to the border of our land and tell them that if they were ever to return, they and their families would be killed. If we could do that, I would be the first to join the rounding-up parties. But that is the talk of children. If we killed them or even expelled them, the Americans would send vast armies to our land and retake it with many Dakota dying as they did so.

"You are young and I admire your spirit, but the *Wasichus* are here to stay. You asked me why I do not kill. This is the reason. Because *Wakaŋ Taŋ'ka* lives within all. White Buffalo Calf Woman has told us so. I know it is the Dakota way to kill our enemies. I have killed many when it meant my life or theirs. But that does not mean I must rejoice in the killing by calling coup. Now let us talk no more until we reach the river. I have some thinking to do."

Chapter Thirty-Eight

WHEN THEY REACHED THE RIVER, one hundred braves were there waiting. Hiŋhaŋkaġa duta (Red Owl) was in charge.

"Little Crow sent us to meet you. He said we were to stop the soldiers from coming into our villages."

"Tell your men without guns to come over here. I have weapons and ammunition. Every man should have a gun and a pouch of bullets. Then I will tell you what I have in mind. But first, have you heard from the scouts?"

"No, we got here only a short while ago."

"Well, it does not matter; they will report long before the soldiers arrive."

After Yellow Hair had given out the remaining guns and ammunition, he went down to the river, accompanied by Hawk, Red Owl, and White Dog.

"The first thing we have to do is secure the ferry on the other side," said Yellow Hair.

He looked across the river, then back to Hawk and Red Owl and informed them of his plans.

"The soldiers will be coming to see what has happened at the Agency and they will have to cross at this point. We will hide behind that bluff over there; it will give us the high ground. When they cross the river and assemble on this side, we will attack."

"So why do we need White Dog?" asked Hawk.

"We need him because he will be the one to tell the soldiers that it is safe to cross over. He is a Cut Hair, they will trust him."

To White Dog, Yellow Hair said, "I want you to call to the soldiers and tell them that we are at the Agency and want to parley. Once they are on this side, you may leave."

As he was speaking, Yellow Hair noticed two braves on the far side of the river.

"I think those are our scouts. Hawk, you have some men get the ferry over there so the soldiers can use it. Red Owl, you and your men put your ponies among the trees and make sure they cannot be seen. Then get all the men out of sight behind the bluff. White Dog, you go up to the bluff and wait for me. I will come to you after I have spoken to the scouts."

The scouts crossed over and approached Yellow Hair. One of them said, "Little Crow told us to report to you."

"Yes, we have been waiting. What of the soldiers?"

"They will be here soon. Marsh is leading them. There are less than fifty and all are on foot."

"We will wait for them behind that bluff where you see White Dog standing. Go over and tell the others what you have told me."

Yellow Hair was sorry to hear that Captain Marsh was leading the soldiers. Marsh had always been fair with the Dakota. He hoped he would not have to kill him.

Everything was made ready. There was nothing else to do but await the soldiers' arrival.

The braves were anxious to go into battle. They were mostly young and had never fired a gun at another man before that morning. What happened at the Agency and the farms was not war, but slaughter. However, with trained soldiers firing at you, it could be called nothing else but war.

Yellow Hair spent the time walking amongst the men, talking with them to put them at ease. Again, he told White Dog where he wanted him to stand and what he was to say to Marsh. He wanted the soldiers to see White Dog as soon as they crested the last hill. That way they would be less likely to suspect a trap. White Dog would also act as lookout and inform him when he saw the soldiers.

Yellow Hair sat down next to Hawk.

This will not be like riding into a village and knocking a man to the ground. This will be pointing a gun at another man from afar and killing him. A man that woke up this morning with thoughts of his wife or his sweetheart in his head, not with thoughts that today was the day he was to die.

After what seemed an eternity, White Dog called down, "I see their blue coats. They are coming!" There was a cessation of all talk. Mouths became dry. Men licked their lips and looked to the man next to them to see if he was as nervous as they were.

When Marsh and his men were close enough to hear him, White Dog shouted, "Everything is all right over here."

Marsh responded, "What was the trouble?"

"There was some trouble between the Blanket Indians and the traders. But you can settle their differences. The Dakota are at the Agency waiting for you. I will go and tell them you are coming."

White Dog waved to Marsh and descended to the far side of the bluff where Yellow Hair waited for him. "You have done well. You are now free to go."

Marsh thought to himself that he had been right all along. The uprising was the work of a few drunken Indians, and now that they were sober, they sat at the Agency in fear of what he might do.

Think I'll let them stew in their own juices for a spell.

To his sergeant, a man named Bishop, he said, "Tell the men to relax for a bit. We'll move out in twenty minutes."

Over on the other side of the river, when the soldiers sat down instead of boarding the ferry, Hawk said to Yellow Hair, "I do not think your plan is working out."

"I do not think so either, but I have another plan."

"So do I. I say we attack the sons of dogs."

"That is my plan also."

Yellow Hair informed Hawk that they would go upstream to the northwest, cross the river, and work their way behind the soldiers. The soldiers would then be between them and the river with no place to run.

The Dakota, keeping low, went a half mile upriver and crossed to the northern bank where they quietly deployed to Marsh's rear. Before moving out, Yellow Hair had told Red Owl to take twenty braves and make his way to the southeast. This was to cut off any avenue of escape. It was Yellow Hair's aim to surround the enemy on three sides with the river to their backs.

• • • • •

Private Rollins has a thirst, which makes him reach for his canteen. As soon as he holds it in his hand, he realizes that it is empty.

Oh, damn! I forgot to fill it before we left the fort.

Being the resourceful chap that he is, he goes to the river to quench his thirst.

As he holds the canteen under the cool water and the air bubbles pop to the surface, he notices leaves and twigs floating by. Not just a few, but an abundance of such. As the canteen fills, he ponders the mystery of the leaves and twigs. What he comes up with disturbs him greatly. He casts a cautious eye to the far bank of the river. After a moment, he sees something that disturbs him even more than the leaves and twigs. They are hard to see at first, but if he looks closely enough he can see horses in the thicket—just back from the river. Over there by that bluff!

Private Rollins does not bother going to his sergeant; he does not think there is time. He goes directly to the Captain.

"Captain Marsh, I think we are being surrounded by Indians right at this very moment. They are crossing the river above us."

"Hold on, son. What makes you think so?"

"There are Indian ponies hidden in the trees on the far side of the river. And just now, I saw a whole mess of debris float by. Like when *we* cross a river."

"Show me where the horses are."

Yellow Hair is watching the interplay between Marsh and Rollins. When they walk to the river and Rollins points to where the ponies are hidden, he knows the time to strike is now. It is too bad—his men have not gotten to the south. But with the river at their backs, the soldiers are cut off on three sides and that will have to do.

A few soldiers are standing, trying to see what Rollins is pointing at. They are the first to go down when Yellow Hair gives the order to fire.

Seeing that the shots are coming from the east and the north, Marsh orders his men to run for the bushes and trees to the south. He does not have to tell them twice.

For the next three hours, the soldiers make their way southeast, always keeping within the cover of the trees. The Indians are taking pot shots at them the entire time. At length, the soldiers come to the end of the woods. There is only open ground before them. By then, the soldiers' numbers are diminished by half.

They had been firing at the Indians as they made their way and are now low on ammunition. If they do not take some sort of decisive action, and soon, the Indians will rush them when their ammunition runs out.

Captain Marsh calls Sergeant Bishop to his side.

"Our only avenue of escape is the river. We must make it to the other side. I will go first. When I reach the bank, start sending men across, four at a time. I'll cover them from the far side and you and the others cover them from here. You come over with the last group."

Marsh takes off his sword, removes his pistol from its holster, and holding both over his head, he wades into the cold, slow-moving river. All is going well; no one is shooting at him. As he nears midstream, he goes under. One moment he is there, and the next he is not.

His head comes to the surface—he has dropped the sword and pistol and seems to be struggling to stay afloat. He sinks again, but resurfaces a moment later. Sergeant Bishop tells two men to get out there and save the Captain. However, before they can reach him, he goes down for a third and last time.

The death of their captain causes the soldiers to be even more demoralized than they had been a moment ago. Sergeant Bishop tells them that their only hope is to wait until nightfall, then try to get back to the fort under the cover of darkness. He adds, "The Indians don't know we're low on ammunition, so conserve your fire and shoot only if one of the bastards is coming right at you. And then, only if you're sure of hitting him."

From a small hill overlooking the river, Yellow Hair watched Marsh walk into the water. It would have been easy to shoot and kill him at that point, but Yellow Hair told the braves to hold their fire. He did it for two reasons. One, he wanted Marsh to live, and two, if they fired on Marsh, no one else would attempt the crossing. Once the soldiers were waist deep, they would be easy to pick off. It would be like shooting fish in a barrel.

When he saw Marsh go under for the third time, Yellow Hair felt sadness for a man who had treated the Dakota with respect.

The Indians keep the soldiers pinned down and continue to whittle away at their numbers. When darkness finally arrives, Yellow Hair tells the braves that they had done all they could for the day. Better to return to their villages and rest for the next day's battle, which he is sure will be an attack on Fort Ridgely.

Chapter Thirty-Nine

THROUGHOUT THE AFTERNOON of that Monday, refugees continued to arrive at the fort. By sundown, their ranks had swelled to over two hundred. A few hours later, the first of Captain Marsh's decimated command began to arrive. Of the forty-six men that marched out of the fort that morning, fourteen made it back healthy and in one piece. Another eight came back with wounds of various degrees.

While Yellow Hair had Captain Marsh and his men at a disadvantage, Red Middle Voice, Shakopee, and their men roamed the countryside killing as many whites as they could find.

Not all the Dakota were at war with the Americans. Many saved the lives of white friends. One such man was named Chaska (Little First Born).

• • • • •

Word of the uprising finally reaches the Upper Agency at 1:00 p.m. on that first day of war. Most of those who hear the news refuse to believe that the docile Indians they have known for years could do anything of the sort. However, Dr. John Wakefield is not about to take a chance with the lives of his wife and two children.

Not wanting to alarm his wife, he tells her that as long as she is planning on visiting her sister, she should not wait two days for the stage, but make her way to Fort Ridgely that day. "I've arranged for George Gleason to take you and the children to the fort."

"John, tell me what's wrong. Why are you sending us away?"

"It's just that I've got a lot of work to do and it will be a little easier to get done if things are quiet around here."

Sara Wakefield knows that is not true; nevertheless, she obeys her husband and leaves with Mister Gleason. On the way out of the Agency, a shopkeeper informs them of the killings that morning at the Lower Agency.

"Take me right back home, Mister Gleason."

"Ma'am, that's just foolish talk that man was talkin'. We both know that the Indians in this part of the country are a peaceful lot. So don't worry your head none about it. I'll git you and the young'uns to the fort. Now please don't fret."

Later, they come across two Indians, Chaska and a man by the name of Hapa (Skin). Gleason pulls up the wagon to ask if they had heard anything about trouble down at the Lower Agency.

Hapa says, "No, we have heard nothing." Gleason bids them farewell and moves the horses along. Still feeling apprehensive, Missus Wakefield turns to look back at the Indians. She sees Hapa raise his gun and shoot. Gleason falls out of the wagon and lies on the ground, crying out in pain. Hapa reloads his gun and shoots poor Mister Gleason again, this time killing him. After reloading for a second time, Hapa takes aim at Missus Wakefield. As he pulls the trigger, Chaska grabs his arm, pushing it skyward; the bullet sails harmlessly over her head.

"The Wakefields are good people," says Chaska. "They have treated all Dakota with respect and kindness."

Hapa is furious that he has wasted ammunition. "All whites must die," he says indignantly. "All whites are bad. Better off dead."

"You must kill me before you kill her," declares Chaska.

Hapa shrugs. He does not think one woman and her children are worth the trouble of a fight with Chaska. The Indians get in Gleason's wagon; and with Sara Wakefield and her two children, head for their village.

True to his word, Chaska protects Sara Wakefield. At times it is close. Some nights Sara and her children have to flee into the woods and hide when the killing frenzy comes upon the braves. She witnesses many women killed. When Chaska is away, his mother makes it her responsibility to protect Sara.

• • • • •

By late afternoon, the people at Yellow Medicine were beginning to believe the reports that were coming in regarding the attack on the Lower Agency.

Little Crow sent men to Yellow Medicine to try to enlist the help of the Upper Sioux—the Sisseton and the Wahpeton. When his emissaries finally convinced the chiefs that the stories they were hearing were true, they called a council.

The council was a repetition of the one held in Little Crow's house the night before. Factions called for war, and factions called for peace. John Other Day, a leader of the Farmer Indians, argued for peace but to no avail.

In the end, those who wanted to go to war went to war, and those who did not went back to their farms or their villages where they hoped that, when the fighting was over, the soldiers could tell the peaceful Sioux from those that made war.

When it became apparent that some of the Upper Agency Sioux were going to join the fight, John Other Day left and rode hard and fast for the Agency. Arriving, he told his brothers to go house-to-house and bring all the whites to the brick storehouse. "Tell them that an attack is coming. Tell them that the war has come to Yellow Medicine!"

That night, as the whites huddled in the storehouse, John and his brothers kept watch outside for signs of the attack that was sure to come. For most of the night, it was quiet.

Then, just a little while before daybreak, out of the darkness came a group of braves. John stood his ground and faced his fellow Indians. He was much too respected for the braves to fire on him without a chief's sanction. Before he became a Farmer Indian, he had been one of the fiercest warriors of his band. No one had more coup feathers than he.

Things were at an impasse until a single shot rang out in the night, accompanied by loud whoops and cries of jubilation. The stores were being looted! For a moment, the braves surrounding the warehouse stayed where they were. They looked at one another and all had the same thought: *We are missing out on our fair share of the loot.*

After a moment's hesitation, they ran south to where the booty was located.

As soon as the Indians were gone, John called into the storehouse for the men to come out. He instructed them to get wagons and horses and to be quick about it. They were going to leave while the Indians were otherwise occupied.

As luck would have it, Galbraith was in St. Paul that night. He had escorted a company of volunteers who were on their way south to fight for the Union. If Galbraith had been at the Agency, the Indians probably would have attacked the warehouse first and left the stores for later. There was no one more hated than Galbraith. However, his wife was at the Agency and John knew what would happen not only to her, but to the rest of them if she was seen leaving in their company.

They discussed where they should go. Most argued for making straight for Fort Ridgely, but John said that is where they would be expected to go and that the Indians would be waiting for them along the road.

"The safest thing to do is go to St. Paul. There we can find help."

As Tuesday morning dawned, the refugees from Yellow Medicine started their trek north.

Counting John, there were sixty-two people who were hell-bent on putting miles between themselves and the Agency. The women and children rode in the wagons, the men walked alongside.

By then, word of the uprising had made its way to St. Paul. At nearby Fort Snelling, the two hundred twenty-five men of the Sixth Minnesota Infantry were under the control of Governor Ramsey. He promptly put Henry Sibley in charge and conferred upon him the rank of colonel. Sibley would also command the volunteer force Ramsey would eventually organize.

Sibley was ordered to take his men to Fort Ridgely and, along the way, save any settlers left alive.

• • • • •

The evening before Sibley accepted his commission, Little Crow, Big Eagle and Yellow Hair met in Little Crow's house. Little Crow was the first to speak.

"You did well today stopping the soldiers at the river."

"I did very little," said Yellow Hair.

"They never made it to the Agency or our village."

"I participated in stopping them from getting to the village because I have a family here. And after seeing the dead whites, especially the women and children, I think the soldiers would have shot any Indian they saw, regardless of age or gender."

Big Eagle spoke next. "Little Crow, can you not keep the young braves in line? Waging war on women and children is not the Dakota way."

"The ones that are doing so are mostly Red Middle Voice and Shakopee's braves. I have said to them many times to capture the women and children, do not kill them. We will need hostages when we sue for peace."

"Then why are so many dead?" asked Yellow Hair.

Little Crow answered with an edge to his voice. "Because they are young and they know no better! But enough of that, tomorrow we attack the fort."

"You and Big Eagle make the plans," interposed Yellow Hair, "I am going to my lodge. I have a wife and son waiting for me. If you attack the fort, I will fight. But you must first assure me that we will make war only on the soldiers. If you cannot control your braves, I will stay in the village with the women."

He bade goodnight to the two older men and left for his lodge.

There was silence for a moment after Yellow Hair's departure. At length, Big Eagle spoke. "He is right. When the whites see some of the things I have seen, they will punish all the Dakota. I saw a white baby nailed to a tree on my way back to the village. There were women without clothes lying in a ditch not a mile from here. I am almost ashamed to call myself a Dakota when I see things like that."

Little Crow affirmed once again, "Tomorrow we fight the soldiers at the fort. We will ride out at dawn. You, my old friend, are not as young as you once were, you better get some sleep."

"Before I take my old self off to my lodge, let me ask you . . . should we not have a council first?"

"Yes, we will have a council, but I want to have it on the plain in front of the fort so the soldiers will have time to worry. The scouts tell me there are no more than thirty or forty soldiers there. I want all the wild, young ones to know that we will kill only soldiers and that the whites in the fort will be taken captive and not harmed."

Big Eagle started to take his leave, but stopped at the entrance and said, "You also are not as young as you once were, my friend."

Chapter Forty

THE RISING SUN looked down on Little Crow and hundreds of his warriors as they advanced on Fort Ridgely. Two miles short of the fort, they halted in the middle of the prairie and held council.

Pointing to the fort, Little Crow spoke. "There are only forty soldiers over yonder. There are big guns and muskets for the taking. The scouts tell me there is a column of fifty soldiers on the march and they will be here in short time. We must attack now."

Next, Mato tamaheća (Lean Bear) spoke, "Little Crow speaks the truth, there is much we want and need at yonder fort, but there is still much more at the settlement down river. I say we attack New Ulm. I have spoken."

Mankato (Blue Earth) spoke. "We should heed Little Crow, attack the fort. The big guns we capture will keep the soldiers out of our valley. You will find no big guns and very few muskets at New Ulm."

After the other chiefs had their say, it was put to a vote.

Overwhelmingly, the vote was for an attack on New Ulm. It was a major defeat for Little Crow.

Those who had voted against an attack on New Ulm crossed the river and went north in search of farms to burn and pillage, not to mention white settlers to kill. The remainder, all but three, headed for the settlement with war whoops and much talk of plunder and of new wives to be had at New Ulm.

Little Crow, Big Eagle, and Yellow Hair remained on the prairie. At length, Big Eagle spoke. "What do we do now?" Yellow Hair, thinking that was a very good question, looked to Little Crow for an answer.

With a lowness of spirit, Little Crow answered, "Now we go back to the village."

Big Eagle nodded and rode northwest towards their village. Yellow Hair and Little Crow, without further words, followed in his tracks.

While they rode, Yellow Hair thought about the war that Red Middle Voice and Shakopee had inveigled Little Crow into leading.

Little Crow has no control over the braves. Where are Red Middle Voice and Shakopee this morning? They are probably off killing unarmed farmers and their families.

Little Crow was thinking along similar lines. They rode on in silence, both men lost in their own thoughts.

As they drew near his tipi, Yellow Hair was about to say something encouraging to Little Crow, but thought better of it when he saw the look on the chief's face. Besides, he himself did not feel very encouraged.

He entered his lodge and Suni asked him why he was back so soon. He told her about the young braves voting to attack New Ulm instead of the fort. Unexpectedly and quite forcibly he said, "This is not a war. This is madness! Yesterday I did what I had to do to protect our village, but now I see that people are dying for revenge. Some of the whites have been good to us. No, Suni, I will not make war on the *Wasichus* any longer."

He then asked about Little Thunder. "Where is the boy?"

"He is out with his friends looking at the captives who are being bought into our village. Did you not see the tipis that have been set up since last night? People from the other bands are coming here in great numbers."

"No, I did not notice."

"They think that when the soldiers attack, it would be better to have all the captives in one place."

Yellow Hair knew one thing for certain; he was not going to fight unless the village was attacked, and this he told Suni.

"I believe you are right, my husband. I have seen and spoken to the women that the braves have brought here. They tell me how they were compelled to watch as their husbands and children were slain. All I could think of was Little Thunder and how I would feel if someone killed him as I looked on."

Later in the day when the braves came back to the village, many carried the scalps of whites and some brought women. They were the braves that had gone in search of farms to plunder. Those that went to New Ulm came back empty-handed. The attack had failed. It failed because there was no leadership on the Indians' side. Each man was out for whatever he could get for himself.

The young braves with scalps asked Little Crow to call a Kill Dance.

"You will receive no feathers. Only cowards kill women and children," he responded. Instead, Little Crow convened a council of war during which it was determined that they would attack the fort the next day.

In the morning, Little Crow and his warriors set out for Fort Ridgely. Yellow Hair stayed in the village. By then, Lieutenant Sheehan and the fifty men of Company C had reinforced the contingent at the fort.

The Dakota were repulsed, mainly because of the soldiers' big guns. Little Crow went back the next day with double the braves, only to fail once again. The day after that, the Indians attacked New Ulm for a second time and failed for a second time.

By 26 August, a week after the failed second attack on the fort, Henry Sibley had amassed a fighting force of fourteen hundred men. Little Crow decided to move the village to Yellow Medicine, thinking it prudent to put some distance between his people and Sibley.

The Mdewakanton and Wahpekute struck their tipis and loaded them onto wagons and pony drags and headed north. It was a sorrowful procession. The women and children walked. Their captives, about two hundred in number, also walked. Among the captives were Sara Wakefield, her two children, and Helen Carrothers and her children. The men rode ponies or rode in wagons.

It took a day to reach Yellow Medicine. The stores and houses had not been burned as they had been at the Lower Agency. Farmer Indians were living in the houses to protect the property of their white friends who had fled to St. Paul.

Little Crow promptly informed them they would have to leave, that he intended to have the buildings set aflame. As soon as the buildings were empty, Little Crow ordered them put to the torch. Afterwards, he sent braves to speak with the Sisseton and Wahpeton who had opted not to go to war.

They rode into the camp of the "friendlies" and told them that, if they did not join the fight, they would be killed. The threat did not sit well with those threatened. After Little Crow's braves left, word was sent to other camps of the Upper Sioux to meet and come prepared for war. They did not intend to go to war against the whites; they were going to war against their brothers, the Lower Sioux.

The Upper Sioux—three hundred strong and painted for war—rode into the "hostiles" camp. They jumped from their ponies and formed a line. The leader of the friendlies spoke to Little Crow and his men: "You have started a war that you cannot win and that we want no part of. And when the fighting goes badly, you bring the war to my people."

The brave was passionate in what he said. He implored Little Crow to give up his captives and to stop the fighting.

When he had finished speaking, one of Little Crow's men stepped over the line and stood behind the speaker. Then another came over, bringing with him his two women captives. Only a few went over to the friendlies' side, but it was enough to dishearten Little Crow. He knew from the beginning there was no way to win, but he had held out hope that they could fight long enough to get the whites to offer a new treaty, one that would be more favorable to the Dakota. However, he must not let his men know his thoughts. Boldly he spoke, "We will not give up the fight. We will wage war until this valley is ours once again. Now you and the traitors who have deserted their brothers . . . go!"

It was not a big victory for the friendlies, but it was a start. They knew that if they did not want to be thought of as hostiles, they would have to secure the release of more captives and turn them over to the whites. Then and only then could they avoid being tarred with the same brush as Little Crow and his men.

After the confrontation with the Upper Agency Indians, Little Crow called a council. It was decided he would take two hundred men, go north and raid two settlements, Hutchinson and Forrest City. Big Eagle would go south with two hundred braves to New Ulm, which had been abandoned after the second Indian raid for fear of a massive third attack.

Big Eagle and his men would claim the spoils of war. The Indians intended to strip the town bare before burning it.

Chapter Forty-One

ON THE WAY out of camp, Big Eagle sees Yellow Hair talking to a woman captive and turns his pony in that direction. When he reaches him, he says, "Come with us, we are not going to fight. We go to bring back much needed supplies from New Ulm."

Without addressing what Big Eagle has said, Yellow Hair introduces the woman, "This is Sara Wakefield. Chaska and his mother have been protecting her and her children from some of the more troublesome braves. You know the ones that I mean. The ones that are drunk every night."

Nodding to Missus Wakefield, Big Eagle informs Yellow Hair that he must speak with him. Before walking away with Big Eagle, Yellow Hair tells Sara that, if Chaska is not around and she needs anything, to send word through Chaska's mother, and either he or Fighting Woman will come.

"Now, what can I do for you, my friend?" asks Yellow Hair.

"You must come with me. You cannot stay here with the women," exhorts Big Eagle.

"I can do anything I please. I think we will all be dead before long. The whites are bound to come after us sooner or later. With the number of men they have, and the feelings those men will have toward us after they have seen the dead farmers, their wives, and their children, we will not stand a chance."

"Ride with me. The whites cannot get here for five sleeps, even if they left today. We will be back in two. Besides, the pony I gave you is getting on in years; he needs a little exercise."

With a sigh, Yellow Hair says, "Alright, ride ahead. I will catch up. First, I must tell Suni that I am going with you."

• • • • •

The relatives of the dead settlers wanted their people buried; it had been two weeks since the initial assaults.

Advised that the area was free of Indians, Sibley sent out a detail accompanied by an armed escort. They totaled one hundred and sixty men.

The patrol first went to the river crossing and found Marsh's soldiers stripped and scalped. They buried them and proceeded to the Lower Agency where they interred thirty bodies before heading westward. Along the way, they found entire families lying dead in and around their homesteads. By nightfall, the number buried totaled one hundred and sixty-six.

With rations for only two days, they decided to camp overnight and take a different route back the next day while looking for more bodies to bury. The closest locale with water was a place the whites called Birch Coulee. The Indians called it The Valley of White Trees. That is where the soldiers set up camp for the night.

• • • • •

Riding Catcher-of-the-Wind hard, Yellow Hair joins up with Big Eagle and his braves an hour later. Seeing his approach, Big Eagle leaves the column and rides back to meet him. "I did not think you were coming."

"I was worried about Suni and the boy. But you know her, eleven winters of motherhood and she has not mellowed. She said now that Little Thunder is grown, she should go on a few raiding parties. When I started to object, she laughed and told me she was only funning me. That is some daughter you have, Big Eagle."

"She is no longer my daughter. She is your wife. I had to put up with her foolishness for eighteen winters. You have had her for only twelve. Come and tell me of your sorrow in another six winters." Both men laughed and rode to the head of the column.

Yellow Hair is exhilarated to be out riding his pony in the warm sun. Just to have something to say, he asks his father-in-law, "What is the plan?"

"The plan is to get food. Little Crow has three thousand people depending on him. He is worried about the war, he is worried about feeding his people, and he is worried about the captives. He told me he would like nothing better than to turn them all over to the friendlies of the Sisseton, but he knows the young braves will never stand for it."

"So we are going to New Ulm to get food?"

"Yes, but first we will go to the Agency to see if any stores are left. It is on the way. The scouts are down there making sure it is safe. If not, we will circle around and go straight to New Ulm. Little Crow told me he would rather have food than a few more soldier scalps. Tonight we will camp above the Agency and tomorrow morning go in. If it is cleaned out, as I expect it is, we will make for New Ulm and be there by the time the sun is overhead."

Late in the day, the scouts meet up with the column. Huha duta (Red Legs) reports to Big Eagle. "We saw soldiers, about one hundred fifty in number. They are making camp in The Valley of White Trees."

"Are they looking for us?"

The other scout, Ziŋtkála ho'ta (Gray Bird) answers, "We do not think so. They were riding through the valley like they never heard of an Indian before. This would be a good chance to wipe them out."

That last statement gets Big Eagle to thinking. He looks at Yellow Hair and says, "We could ride around the soldiers; that would be easy. But then on our way back with the wagons fully loaded, it would not be good if we were to run into them. We have more men than they do. We know their whereabouts, while they have no idea we are close by. What does that suggest to you?"

"It suggests to me that you are thinking of attacking them. But why?"

"We know the fight is coming to our village. Why they have not moved against us before now is a mystery. They cannot sit on their tails much longer. They have double the fighting men that we do. If we can whittle down their numbers . . . then when the fight does come, we will have that much better of a chance to win or at least fight to a draw."

Yellow Hair is shaking his head slowly as he says, "We already know the war is lost. It was lost before it began. So what are you talking about?"

"What I am talking about is what Little Crow and I have discussed many times over the last few days. Yes, in the end, we cannot win out over the *Wasichus*. But if we can fight to a draw, we can ask for a council of peace and demand a new treaty, one that will not let the traders touch our gold, one where we can set up our own stores. Just last night, Little Crow said that you would be the perfect choice to go East and buy our supplies and have them brought out here. You used to be a *Wasichu*; you know how things work in the white world. So let us rub out these soldiers now that we have the chance."

"I don't know," said Yellow Hair.

"Think of this. One of those soldiers, if left alive, may be the one to ride into our village and club Little Thunder or shoot Suni. We are going to attack them regardless of what you do. But you are Dakota and I thought you might want to act like a Dakota."

Damn him! The old fox has framed it so now I must fight.

With a sigh, Yellow Hair says, "Lead the way, O Great War Chief."

"We will attack before sunrise and we will make short work of these soldiers," says Big Eagle enthusiastically.

Shortly after midnight, Big Eagle and his men cross the river, ascend the bluffs, and see the white tents of the camp reflecting the light of a billion stars. It is on flat and open ground and will not be easy to defend.

The plan is to surround the camp and attack before daybreak, while the soldiers are sleeping. There are pickets posted, but they are too close to the camp to do much good.

The night is cool and Yellow Hair is lying in the tall grass observing the camp when Big Eagle crawls up beside him. "We are going to take out the watchers with arrows so as not to alert the soldiers that we are here. Then we will attack from all four sides. We should get most of them on the first assault."

"Do you want me to take out a watcher? I have my bow on my pony."

Big Eagle shakes his head and says, "No. With that new gun of yours, you can reload faster than the rest of us. I want you and the others that have guns like yours to place yourselves evenly around the camp. When you hear my call that will be the signal to start firing and keep firing. Braves with shotguns will be crawling under your fire to get close enough to shoot the defenders at point blank range."

In the early hours, just before sunrise, everything is going according to plan. That is, until one of the pickets notices something and fires at the rustling grass. He does not hit anything or anyone. However, the camp comes awake and the Indians that had been sneaking up on the pickets rise and shoot their arrows at the rapidly retreating men, killing two. Then all hell breaks loose. The Indians start firing into the camp and a number of soldiers are killed on the first volley, as are a great number of horses.

The Indians try rushing the camp, but are repulsed. They try a second time, but the defenders keep them at bay. One brave is killed and one wounded.

Assessing the situation, Big Eagle calls his men back and tells them to keep a constant barrage on the camp. "Keep them pinned down." As an afterthought, he orders the horses shot so that the soldiers cannot get a message back to Fort Ridgely.

For the rest of the day, the Indians continue to fire on the besieged camp. They have plenty of ammunition and food, and water is readily available. Late in the afternoon, the Indian women, who were on the far side of the river, cross over and prepare food for the braves.

The Indians have it good compared to the soldiers who are lying in shallow ditches, hastily dug to provide protection from the Indians' gunfire. Many are behind dead horses; some even use the bodies of dead comrades as breastworks. As the day progresses and the sun heats up the prairie, the bodies of the dead—animal and man—bloat and become malodorous.

After the braves have eaten and rested, Big Eagle realizes that he has not seen Yellow Hair since they rushed the camp for a second time. He goes from brave to brave asking if anyone has seen him. The answer is always the same, "No." Finally, he sends a man to search where Yellow Hair was last seen. "Be careful, keep on the ground. If you find him, call out and I will come to you," instructs Big Eagle.

After a few minutes, Big Eagle hears the call of the Red Bird, but he knows it is the brave's signal, for a Red Bird sings only at morning time. He crawls through the tall grass and finds the brave next to a recumbent Yellow Hair.

"What is wrong with him?"

"He has been shot in the shoulder, but look here on the side of his head."

Big Eagle moves over to see what the brave is pointing at and sees the bullet mark that left a bloody crease along the left side of Yellow Hair's head, just above the temple. Obviously put there by a ball shot from a musket. They know he is alive because they can see his chest rising and falling.

Big Eagle muses more to himself than the man kneeling next to him, "Either he is too hard-headed to die or the ball was almost spent. But, thank *Wakaŋ Taŋ'ka*, he still lives!"

They decide to wait until dark before moving him. In the meantime, they attend to his shoulder wound.

Chapter Forty-Two

ABOUT THE TIME Big Eagle first noticed that Yellow Hair was missing, a small detachment of soldiers left Fort Ridgely to investigate what was purported to be the sound of gunfire. The sound from the morning's battle at Birch Coulee had traveled over the prairie and through the valley.

The men were back within the hour reporting that, as soon as they left the fort, the sounds had ceased. They believed it to be an aberration, an unknown phenomenon of the prairie. However, the sound resumed and persisted throughout the day. In the afternoon, Sibley sent out another force comprised of two hundred and fifty men.

The scouts told Big Eagle of the soldiers headed their way and he gave the order, "Take twenty men to the soldiers, but do not let them see you. Make noise; make them think that you are many. Fire at them from a safe place and see if you can drive them back to the fort."

A few hours later, the braves returned. "We made them think that a thousand Indians were bearing down on them and they ran back to the safety of the fort."

When it was full dark, Yellow Hair was carried off the prairie and put into a wagon. He was still unconscious. Big Eagle ordered two of the women to take him back to the camp at Yellow Medicine and deliver him to his wife.

Big Eagle was concerned. He knew the shoulder wound would heal, but he did not understand why Yellow Hair should still be unconscious from a wound that did not even penetrate his skull. However, he would have to worry about that at another time.

Right now, I have a battle to conclude.

He had his men sleep in shifts. Those not sleeping were to fire into the soldiers' camp throughout the night.

The commander of the aborted rescue party reported to Sibley that half the Sioux Nation had set upon them, but they did get close enough to the besieged burial party and clearly heard gunfire. Sibley gave the order for his entire command of fourteen hundred men to prepare to move out.

• • • • •

Daylight dawns on the beleaguered camp—the second day of the onslaught; the soldiers are down to the last of their ammunition and the stench from the dead is overpowering. They had run out of water the day before. The cool, clear water of the river is out of their reach. They are preparing to die and have no appetite for breakfast this day. If they were Dakota, they would have a big, fine morning meal and then say, "It is a good day to die." But they are not Dakota. They are *Wasichus*.

After a restful night, or as restful as a night can be with constant gunfire nearby, Big Eagle decides that it is time to finish off the soldiers. He rings his men around the camp and gives the order to move in slowly with continuous fire.

As the Indians close in, a brave appears on a small rise out on the plain and signs to his fellow braves. Big Eagle reads the sign and understands its meaning. He orders his men to break off the attack and go into the woods. When they have assembled, he tells them they are going back to Yellow Medicine. "The *Wasichus* are coming. They outnumber us ten to one and they have their big guns with them. We will leave."

What the scout has seen are the wagons and men of Sibley's militia. Those few of the burial party that are left alive will have to wait for another day to die.

So ends the Battle of Birch Coulee. Big Eagle's force sustained one dead and four wounded, including Yellow Hair.

Sibley arrives and finds thirty-three dead, sixty-one seriously wounded, another fifteen with minor wounds and all the horses dead—ninety-two in number. The dead are quickly buried and the wounded are loaded onto wagons.

Before leaving and taking what is left of the burial party back to Fort Ridgely, Sibley pens a message to Little Crow and leaves it on a stick placed in the ground. He tells him that if he wants to talk peace, send word and they will meet.

Little Crow's mission to raid the towns of Hutchinson and Forrest City does not go well. The people of those towns, having gotten word of the uprising and hearing that Indians were seen close by, erected stockades. They are impressive, ten feet high and a foot thick with gun ports cut into them. The Indians do not even try to storm the towns after seeing how well they are fortified. Instead, they turn their ponies for Yellow Medicine.

• • • • •

Big Eagle stands looking down at Yellow Hair, who has regained consciousness and is sitting up, drinking an herb concoction given to him by Looking Elk.

"How do you feel?"

"Someone is beating a drum inside of my head. Besides that, I feel fine."

Suni tells her father, "He is not fine. He has a hole in his shoulder, and if he stands, he is weak. You are fortunate, Father, that you returned him to me alive. Now let him rest."

"Well, as long as he lives. And by the way, where is my grandson?"

Yellow Hair laughs and says, "He wanted to know all about the battle at the coulee. I could not tell him much because I slept through most of it. So he went out to find someone who could tell him a good war story."

"You tell that little warrior to come to my lodge and I will tell him the true story. Of course, I will have to tell him of his grandfather's great bravery in directing the battle."

Suni has heard enough, "Father, you leave. You can wear out Little Thunder with your tales of bravery, but Yellow Hair needs to rest. Now go."

Having long ago become accustomed to obeying his daughter, Big Eagle leaves the tipi.

When they are alone, Suni kneels down, takes the bowl from Yellow Hair's hand and says, "Now you rest."

"*Rest?*" repeats Yellow Hair. "I just woke up. I am going out to see what is going on. Like our son, I too want to know how the battle went."

"Then you should have asked Father when he was here. You lay there. Little Thunder can tell you all about your battle when he returns."

Like his father-in-law, Yellow Hair sometimes finds life easier if he just accedes to his wife's wishes, so he lies back down and in no time he is again asleep.

• • • • •

Sibley was placed in command of putting down the uprising the day after Little Crow attacked and burned the Lower Agency. For the next month, rather than engage the Sioux, he bombarded Governor Ramsey with missives imploring him to send more supplies and more men. Even when he had a fighting force of fourteen hundred, he commanded in a dilatory manner. The only time during that thirty-day period he led his men outside of Fort Ridgely was to rescue the burial party at Birch Coulee.

For every letter that Sibley sent to Ramsey, Ramsey sent one to Washington beseeching the War Department for help—all to no avail. The recipient of *his* missives was the Secretary of War, Edwin M. Stanton. However, Stanton was busy with the war, and for the most part ignored Ramsey's pleas for men and supplies.

Receiving no assistance from Stanton, Ramsey sent a letter directly to President Lincoln asking for help. To accent his plea, a telegram followed. And Minnesota's congressional delegation, two of which held positions on the powerful Military Affairs Committees—one in the U.S. House of Representatives and the other in the Senate—had not been remiss in their duty. They were pressuring Lincoln to send relief to Minnesota with veiled threats of congressional interference concerning the war.

On 6 September 1862, President Lincoln decided he would finally have to do something concerning the Sioux uprising.

● ● ● ● ●

Upstairs at the White House, against the window wall, sits a man at a mahogany desk. There is a knock at the door and immediately thereafter, a man walks into the room. "Mr. President, Secretary Stanton is here to see you. He is your 11:00 o'clock appointment."

"Thank you, John. Please show him in."

A stout gentleman enters the room. He is balding, wears spectacles, and has a beard streaked with gray, almost to mid-chest.

"Thank you for coming, Edwin. I know you have your hands full with the war."

"We both have our hands full with the war, Mr. President."

"True, true, but now tell me about this Indian business in Minnesota."

"Well, Mr. President, it seems the savages have taken to killing the white settlers. To hear Governor Ramsey tell it, the entire state is up in flames. I sent him the Third Minnesota Regiment. They were prisoners in Tennessee, but were paroled and, as you know, that means they cannot go back to fighting in the war."

The President stands from behind his desk and stretches, stifling a yawn. He walks over to a sofa that sits against the far wall. "I think we will be more comfortable over here. Pull up a chair and let's discuss the matter."

Once seated, the President says, "I too have heard from Governor Ramsey. I have also been hearing from the Minnesota delegation. Not that they have overtly threatened me in any way, but you know Congress. And I can ill afford to make enemies right at the moment. So my question to you, Edwin, is what can we do to help the people of Minnesota so that my friends in Congress will direct their energies elsewhere?"

"I do not know what to tell you, Mr. President. You know as well as I do how the war is going. Those damn rebels could overrun Washington at any time. Just look at what happened at Bull Run. And to be quite frank, Mr. President, if Washington falls, the Indians will be the least of Minnesota's worries."

Mister Lincoln leans back and stretches out his long legs. Clasping his hands behind his head, he says, "You know, Edwin, I've been thinking. We both know that we cannot divert supplies and men from the war effort. However, I must be seen as doing something."

"Yes, Mr. President?"

"The general that I had to relieve of command, the one from Bull Run; what was his name?"

"Major General John Pope, sir."

"Yes, that's it. I think a battle-hardened veteran from the regular army is just what Governor Ramsey needs to direct the campaign against the Indians."

"I believe you are right, Mr. President."

"Please take care of it, Edwin. Now, if you will excuse me, I have a lot of work to attend to before Mary comes in and makes me stop for the day. That woman thinks I work too hard. I try to tell her that next to our fighting boys, I am doing nothing more than taking up space."

Stanton does not respond to the President's last remark. He knows the war has taken its toll on the man. Mister Lincoln has aged considerably in the two years since being elected.

He says only "Yes sir" and walks out of the room, leaving the long-legged gentleman leaning back on the sofa, staring up at the ceiling—thinking of battles to come.

Thus was Maj. Gen. John C. Pope installed as Henry Sibley's commanding general.

Chapter Forty-Three

THE DAY AFTER POPE'S APPOINTMENT, Little Crow received Sibley's message—the one left at the coulee. He summoned a council to discuss a course of action. Should they negotiate for peace or continue the war?

Red Middle Voice spoke of the vengeance of the whites. "If you think that stopping the war and giving up our captives will save our lives, you are mistaken."

Shakopee spoke next. "Ever since the first time we dealt with the White Man, he has robbed and cheated us. He has killed many of our people and starved our families. We may regret what has happened, but the matter has gone too far. I say we fight until we have to die, and that we kill as many whites as possible."

Yellow Hair attended the council because he would write the reply to Sibley. When all had spoken for or against continuing the war, the men crafted a consensus letter asking Sibley to convey to Governor Ramsey the reasons for the war, i.e., Galbraith, Myrick, and the starving people of the reserve. Yellow Hair wrote the letter, and Little Crow dispatched it in the care of two mixed-bloods.

Again Little Crow wanted to put some distance between himself and Sibley's fourteen hundred men.

The Mdewakanton and Wahpekute, who had waged war on the Americans, folded the tipis and marched north. When they reached the Sisseton village of Maza duta (Red Iron), the chief and all his fighting men were waiting for them.

Red Iron informed Little Crow that he was not welcomed to camp on Sisseton land. In fact, he told the Lower Agency Indians that they could not even pass through Sisseton land. "You started this war, and now that you are losing, you come here. The whites are sure to follow, and when they do come, they will not ask who is Sisseton and who is Mdewakanton. They will kill us all."

A few of Little Crow's braves wanted to fight it out with Red Iron's people, but Little Crow would not allow it. Instead, the Mdewakanton and Wahpekute set up camp to the south.

While Little Crow was having trouble with Red Iron, the mixed-bloods he had sent to Sibley did more than just deliver his message. They told Sibley of the dissention between the friendlies and the hostiles. Until then, Sibley had thought the Sioux were united in the war against the Americans. When he heard what the mixed-bloods had to say, he decided to take a harder stance with Little Crow than he had planned. The note he sent back was terse and to the point:

"You *must* release the captives that you have taken before we can talk of peace."

Little Crow's reply was just as terse and to the point. "The Mdewakanton band alone has one hundred fifty prisoners. I want to hear from the Governor personally before I will even think of giving up the captives." He ended by telling Sibley that if the Sioux were attacked, it might not be so good for the prisoners.

Yellow Hair wrote Little Crow's latest dispatch. It was given to a captive, the mixed-blood Tom Robertson, to deliver. However, because it was getting dark, it was decided that he would leave in the morning.

That night, Wabasha, the chief who had spoken for peace the first night in Little Crow's lodge four weeks earlier, visited Yellow Hair.

"Come in, Wabasha," bid Yellow Hair.

"Where are Fighting Woman and the little one?"

"They are with Big Eagle. He likes the company of Little Thunder, and Fighting Woman worries about Big

Eagle getting enough to eat. She went along to prepare a meal for him."

"That is good because I wanted to speak with you alone."

Noticing the worried look on Wabasha's face, Yellow Hair said, "Please sit down and tell me what is on your mind."

"You know Little Crow has been opposed to me concerning this war since the beginning. Now he has got himself and all of us into trouble. He is trying to involve us all in the murder of the whites. Thinking if he presents a united front to Sibley, he will have more bargaining power. If he succeeds, all he will have accomplished is to bring down the wrath of the soldiers on all alike, regardless if they killed whites or not."

"You are right, old friend. Some did kill whites, others fought only soldiers. Still others, like you, did not fight at all. I am afraid that when the soldiers come into our village, we will all pay the same price for this war."

"You speak the truth. Do you want to see Fighting Woman and Little Thunder killed for what the younger braves have done? Have you seen the bodies? Women and children split up the middle like a buffalo. Skulls crushed with rocks. If the whites did that to the Dakota, I would lead the war party seeking vengeance. When the whites come riding into our villages that is what they will be after—vengeance. It will not matter if you are man, woman, or child; all the Dakota will be marked for death."

"I think you should tell me what is on your mind."

"Tomorrow, Robertson leaves with Little Crow's letter. I want him to take two letters. Sibley has to know that not all the Dakota made war on the Americans and that some of us are trying to save the prisoners. I need you to write that to him. I want him to know that we who have been against this war from the beginning will meet him at any place of his choosing and we will bring as many of the prisoners as we can steal away."

Yellow Hair leaned back and looked to the top of the tipi.

Wabasha makes sense. Maybe there is a way to save some of the Dakota, Suni and Little Thunder included.

"There is only one problem. If I write what you say and Little Crow or one of the war chiefs found out about it, you and I would be killed before we could pull our knives."

"Yes, Yellow Hair, I ask much of you. But I *too* have a family, and if I must die, I would like them to have a chance at life. If we keep to the path we are on, all Dakota will perish from this earth."

"I would like to discuss this with Big Eagle, but I know he would advise against it. So I will write what you tell me and give it to Robertson. But if Robertson refuses to carry it, there is nothing I can do."

Yellow Hair wrote Wabasha's words and gave the message to Robertson, who agreed to deliver it even though it would mean his life if he were caught.

Sibley received the two letters and replied to each in turn. To Little Crow he wrote: *Until you have released the captives, there is nothing for us to discuss.*

To Wabasha he wrote: *Any Indian who has not taken part in the uprising will have nothing to fear if they come to me under a flag of truce, bringing the captives.*

For Little Crow, there was no alternative. He had to fight on. His young braves would never give up their captives.

Wabasha knew he had to secure the release of more captives if he was to save his people.

Sibley knew that the time to engage the enemy was at hand.

On 19 September 1862, Sibley mustered his fourteen hundred men and marched forth. The single column stretched back for miles. It took him four days to get to the shores of Wood Lake; hence, the name of what would be the last battle of the war. Little Crow's scouts followed and reported on the movements of Sibley and his militia every step of the way.

As Sibley's troops bedded down for the night, Little Crow and his chiefs held council. It was not a council to determine war or peace; the purpose of *this* council was to come up with a plan of attack. Red Middle Voice and Shakopee were there, as well as Mankato and the other chiefs who had, weeks earlier, spoken for war.

Little Crow spoke first. "We should attack tonight while they sleep. We can overrun them before they know what is happening. Those we do not kill will scatter to the four winds and we will not see them again."

Shakopee and most of the other chiefs agreed that a night attack was best.

So intent were the chiefs to get the battle started that the council was about to break up without taking a vote on Little Crow's plan when Big Eagle spoke up.

"There is another way. Will you hear me out?"

It was the way of the council to listen to every voice. The chiefs sat back down to listen to what Big Eagle had to say.

"At yonder camp are soldiers; there are no women and children. When attacked, they may run into the night and then they may not. If they do run, they will still live and be able to attack us on another day. I propose a new plan, one that will insure that we kill or capture as many soldiers as possible.

"When Sibley moves out, he will have to take the Yellow Medicine Road. He marches without outriders and does not use scouts. Just north of Yellow Medicine, the road winds through an area that has a ravine on one side and a bluff on the other. If we were to wait in ambush at that place, we could attack from both sides. There would be nowhere for them to run. We can kill them or take them prisoners. If we held Sibley and his men as prisoners, then Ramsey would have to give in to our demands.

"White Men look down on those who attack women and children and hold them for ransom. When we defeat their fighting men, they will respect us. With many captives, Ramsey will meet with us. He will not demand, as Sibley has done, that we release the captives before he will parley. That is all I have to say. I am done."

There was silence as Big Eagle sat down. The chiefs started to speak among themselves. After a moment, Little Crow asked for quiet and said, "What Big Eagle says is true. We do not want any soldiers to get away. Let us go to the place of which Big Eagle speaks and await Sibley and his soldiers. Let us go now and kill our enemies!"

These were seasoned warriors, not young men. There was no whooping and shouting as they left the council fire. They were just ordinary men going off to kill other ordinary men.

Chapter Forty-Four

JUST BEFORE DAWN, in one of the tents assigned to Company G of the Third Minnesota, three privates are doing what soldiers have done since men first met across an open field and battled one another with clubs. They are discussing the merits of the food provided them.

"You know, I think we ate a lot better when we were prisoners down in Tennessee," says Bill Landmeier, looking to his two tent mates for affirmation.

Hubert Miller throws a rolled-up sock in Landmeier's direction and says, "Billy Boy is always complaining about the food."

"Well, this tripe Colonel Sibley gives us leaves much to be desired," responds Landmeier.

"You two fight it out . . . I'm going to wash up," says the departing George Spencer.

Once George is gone, Landmeier presses his point. "Do you remember when we were down south how we used to forage farms for chickens and eggs and whatever else we could find to supplement the grub the army gave us?"

"Yeah, I remember, and I also remember the trouble we got into. Do *you* remember Captain Connolly putting us on picket duty for a week straight the last time he caught us leaving camp without permission?"

"Yes, but Captain Connolly is still a prisoner down in Tennessee. He ain't gonna do nothin'. By the way, why did we get let go but not the officers?"

"That's easy. They're the brains of the outfit, we're just cannon fodder. The Indians should be a welcome relief next to those Johnny Rebs. Those boys are crazy!"

"They are at that, but what about something to eat?"

"What do you mean?"

"I mean, let's get George and go foraging. The Yellow Medicine Agency is only three miles up the road. Word is that it's abandoned. Think of all the grub just sittin' there waiting for us."

"You might have a point, Bill. We could be up there and back before anyone misses us."

"Sure, sure. Get your boots on. I'll find George and meet you at the wagons. I think we'll need at least one wagon to bring the goods back. What do you think?"

"I think you're touched in the head. I'd settle for a few potatoes I could roast."

Hubert and Bill find George and talk him into leaving camp to go foraging. It was not a hard sell.

Meanwhile, one half mile from where Bill and Hubert were discussing dietary matters, Big Eagle and Yellow Hair, along with eight hundred Dakota, are lying in the tall grass of the prairie waiting for Sibley to break camp and continue his march.

Getting a little tired of waiting, Yellow Hair observes, "I thought armies broke camp at sunrise. Sibley seems to be on more of a pleasant stroll than at war. It took him four days to cover what should have taken him one day. Do you think he is afraid to face us?"

"I do not know. Maybe . . . wait . . . look! There is a wagon leaving camp. Only one wagon and it is coming our way. What is Sibley up to?"

"They cannot be scouts. Not in a wagon."

"They are coming over the prairie right at us. If they keep going, they will run over some of our braves."

As soon as Big Eagle finished speaking, a brave off to the right jumps up and fires at the three men in the wagon, hitting one in the leg.

Thanks to three hungry soldiers, the element of surprise is lost. Sibley and his men now know the Indians are nearby.

A battle ensues in which the Dakota cannot breech Sibley's defenses. At the end of two hours, the Battle of Wood Lake is history. The Dakota are the losers. They retreat north, back to their camp.

Little Crow now knows that the war is at an end. He has tried to take Fort Ridgely—twice. His people have tried to take New Ulm—twice. They tried to take towns to the north. Except for Redwood Ferry and Birch Coulee, the Dakota have won not a single battle. Little Crow must add Wood Lake to his losses—Wood Lake where eight hundred of his best warriors suffered defeat at the hands of the whites. They say that the world will end not with a bang, but with a whimper. Wars also end in that manner.

• • • • •

Little Crow returned to his camp where one last indignity—one last defeat—awaited him. The friendlies had taken the captives.

The younger braves wanted to go to the friendlies' camp and reclaim their prisoners, but Little Crow said no. He knew there would be little purpose to it; the fight had left him. He announced that, at dawn of the next day, he would be leaving for the West and anyone who wanted to go with him was welcome.

On small things are wars won and lost. If not for three undisciplined soldiers, Sibley's force would likely have been defeated that day, and the history of the Dakota might have been quite different indeed.

Little Crow left the village early the next morning and headed west. He was accompanied by two hundred of his people, along with those who had fomented the war: Red Middle Voice, Shakopee, and the four young men who had started the ball rolling when one of them discovered a hen's egg.

Perhaps the beginning of the end was that day in 1805 when Lieutenant Pike came to parley with Little Crow's grandfather. Or it may have been the day in 1679 when Duluth walked into White Dog's village. Hell, it might even have been that hot summer day in 1492 when a certain Italian approached the Spanish Court in search of funds to find a new trade route to the East by going west.

Whenever its beginnings, the end of a way of life for the Dakota came on 23 September 1862. Or as the Dakota would phrase it, during the Moon of Black Cherries in The Winter Of Distress.

The Aftermath

Chapter Forty-Five

SUNI AND YELLOW HAIR stood and watched as Little Crow and his band headed west. Turning to her husband, Suni asked, "Do you think he will return someday?"

"I do not know. Perhaps."

"What happens now?"

"We wait. Sibley will be here soon. Then he will do as he wishes. It should not be too hard for those who did not join the war. Wabasha has heard from Sibley, and he has promised not to punish anyone who did not commit murder."

Everyone expected Sibley to arrive in a matter of hours. He was camped only a half-day's ride from the village. The Indians were fearful lest Sibley exact his revenge on them because they had let the hostiles get away. The captives were apprehensive lest Little Crow return, and having had second thoughts, kill them.

Both the whites and the Indians wanted a return to the life they had known before the war.

One of the frightened Indians was Chaska, he who had saved Sara Wakefield and her children. He was fearful of the White Man's retribution and he implored Sara to intercede with Sibley on his behalf.

"Do not worry. No one will harm you. I will tell Mister Sibley what you and your mother have done for me and my children."

The Indians and the captives waited all that day for Sibley to arrive. As each hour passed, both groups became more distraught. Finally, the sun started its descent over the far horizon and still there was no sign of Sibley.

The tableau of Indians and whites gathering in the center of the village was repeated the next day. Some wore a mask of fear, some of hope, and some were resigned to their fate—whatever it might be. At the end of the second day, Sibley still had not shown.

On day three, no one gathered in the center of the village. Scouts were sent out to report on Sibley's movements, or lack thereof. At mid-morning, they reported that at last Sibley was on the march and should arrive by noon. The scouts were correct. At noon—precisely at noon—Sibley and his troops appeared, but did not enter the village. Instead, they set up camp five hundred yards to the south.

No one knew what Sibley was up to. Was he planning an attack? Was he going to let the captives stay with the Indians indefinitely? What was he doing? For two long hours, the people in the village looked across the prairie to the camp with its cannons pointed at them.

At long last, Sibley, dressed in his finest regalia and with his entire retinue, rode into the village.

After making the captives wait three days, he was now in a hurry. He was put off at having to stand in the hot sun while the chiefs who had not gone to war made their welcoming speeches.

Sibley himself had a speech to make. What he said is of no importance, except for the fact that he named the camp he had just established "Camp Release."

With speeches made, hands shook, and niceties adhered to, the soldiers escorted the prisoners out of the village.

Sara Wakefield walked across the open space that separated the Indians from the soldiers, accompanied by Chaska who she introduced to Sibley.

"Mister Sibley, I would like you to meet Chaska. He saved my life when another Indian tried to shoot me. He and his mother have protected me and my children throughout our tribulations. The hostiles wanted to kill us on any number of occasions. If not for him and his mother, we would all now be dead."

"Fine to meet you, young man," said Sibley as he reached out to shake Chaska's hand. "I can't thank you enough—you and your mother—for what you have done for Missus Wakefield and her little ones. Please shake hands with my officers." As Chaska shook the officers' hands, the weight of dread lifted from his shoulders.

• • • • •

The next day the hammer fell.

"**THEY MUST BE EXTERMINATED**," shouted the headline in the Minnesota Pioneer.

"**THEY FOR ALL TIME TO COME HAVE FOREITED ALL RIGHT TO PROPERTY AND LIFE**," pronounced the St. Cloud Democrat.

Letters poured into Sibley's command, and they all said the same thing, "Kill the Indians, every last man, woman, and child!"

General Pope also had his say. In a letter to Sibley, two days after the release of the captives, he wrote, *"It is my purpose to utterly exterminate the Sioux ..."*

A common cry arose. *"Annihilate the Sioux!"*

It did not take long for those involved to know which way the wind was blowing. Sara Wakefield went in search of Chaska and when she found him, she implored him to take to the plains. "I do not like what I am hearing. There is talk of punishing the whole tribe." Chaska acknowledged that he had also heard such talk and told her that they had already rounded up a few men.

"Then flee. Get out of here!" pleaded Sara.

"I am no coward," said Chaska. "I will stay."

That evening Sibley arrested sixteen men. One of those men went by the name of Chaska.

Chapter Forty-Six

"*YELLOW HAIR*, what has happened to you?"

"I painted my hair black so I could get near the soldiers and they would not know that I can speak English."

"Why?"

"I wanted to know what they are planning to do with us."

"Did you learn anything?"

"Yes. Now listen to me good, Suni. I do not want any argument."

"I will listen to you if you will first wash that war paint out of your hair. I do not like you with black hair."

"Alright, but while I am doing so, you get Little Thunder. I want him to hear what I have to say." The seriousness of Yellow Hair's countenance coupled with his tone of voice worried Suni, but she nodded her agreement and went to find their son.

When he reentered the tipi, Yellow Hair found his wife and son waiting for him. He sat down next to Suni and took her hand in his.

"I was pretending to do some work near where the soldiers are gathered. I wanted to hear what they were talking about. When I first got there, they stopped their talk and called out to me. I acted as though I could not understand them. Once convinced I spoke no English, they resumed their conversation."

"What were they saying?" asked Suni.

"They are going to arrest all the men, but not just yet. Sibley is afraid that if he did so, none of those out on the prairie would give themselves up. He has sent word out that no harm will come to those who return on their own accord, but those that stay away will be hunted down like dogs."

Little Thunder started to say something, but Yellow Hair cut him off. "Hear me first, son, before you speak."

"The soldiers think that, in four or five sleeps, Sibley will move us all to the Lower Agency where he will put the men on trial. They were saying that anyone who picked up a rifle or was at a place where whites were killed will be hanged."

The news deeply distressed Suni, but she said nothing.

Yellow Hair continued. "But what worries me the most is that everyone in our band will be held as prisoners. I fear they may kill all the Dakota . . . old men, women, and young children."

Not able to sit still, Yellow Hair stood and paced back and forth within the confines of the tipi. "You and Little Thunder must leave here. Go as far west as you can; go to our brothers, the Lakota."

Suni could stand it no longer; she would speak. She stood and took her husband's hand to stop his nervous pacing.

"We will not leave you. All of us go or none of us go. There is no reason for you to stay."

Putting his arm around his wife, Yellow Hair said, "We will all go, but I must make a diversion. Sibley has watchers, or pickets as the whites call them, around our camp with orders to shoot anyone trying to leave. Do not worry. I have a plan. Once you and the boy are away, it will be easy for me to slip out at night. You two must go first. We must think of Little Thunder."

At the mention of his name, the boy said, "I am not afraid of the *Wasichus*, I will kill them all!"

Yellow Hair responded to his son with love and tolerance. "I know that you are brave. But before you can go on the warpath, you must have your Vision Quest, and you cannot do so here. It is the intelligent brave who will have a strategy for the warpath, who will make plans for the attack and not just run into a musket ball or an arrow to prove his bravery. That proves nothing and wins no battles or coups." Ruffling Little Thunder's hair, as he was wont to do, he continued, "Always remember this, you are half *Wasichu*. Not all the *Wasichu* are bad people. You know and like Helen Carrothers, do you not?"

A tentative "Yes" from Little Thunder.

"What makes a man good or bad is not his blood, it is not that he is a Dakota or a *Wasichu;* it is what is in his heart. Now enough of this talk. We must make our plans."

Yellow Hair did not like deceiving Suni, but he knew she would never leave without him, or at least without the knowledge that he would soon follow. He also knew he would be lucky if she and the boy got away. There was no way he could escape. When brought to the Lower Agency, an escape would be impossible. It would have to be done before then. The next night was chosen.

Yellow Hair's plan was simple. He would crawl out onto the prairie and fire his gun, and would continue doing so until the pickets were drawn from their post. At that time, Suni and Little Thunder would walk their ponies into the darkness before mounting them and riding away.

Just after midnight on the appointed night, they went to the corral holding the ponies; there was no guard. There was no need, not with pickets surrounding the camp.

Yellow Hair gave Suni his knife. "Here, you will need this. I have brought it a long way; all the way from the world of the *Wasichus*. If nothing else, you can trade it for something you may need." He told Little Thunder that he was giving him Catcher-of–the-Wind to look after until they were together again. "Until then he is your pony," he told the boy.

To Suni he said, "I worry about you leaving with no food. It is a long journey to the land of the Lakota."

"Do not worry. Was it not I who taught you how to hunt? The prairie may not have many buffalo left, but there are many prairie rabbits. We will eat better out there than we have here for the last few moons."

She started to tell Yellow Hair something, but held back at the last moment. She did not want to add to his worries. There would be plenty of time when they were together again to tell him that he was once more to be a father.

With a fare-thee-well kiss to Suni and an exhort to Little Thunder to take care of his mother, Yellow Hair took one last look at his family before turning to go and do what had to be done.

He went to the other side of the camp and silently crawled out into the tall grass. He was careful not to rustle it or make any noise. When he had gone far enough so he would not be found immediately, he pointed his rifle into the air and fired. The first shot was to get the soldiers' attention. He took his time reloading; he wanted to cause maximum confusion and he knew one shot would not pull the pickets away from their post, but to fire too rapidly would only give away his position before he was ready to be taken.

He lay on his back looking up into the night sky and thought of the time he spent with Suni as they traveled to her village. On those nights, they looked at the sky together as she told him of the Dakota. She had saved his life then; he hoped to pay his debt to her this night.

He took out his remaining bullets and placed them on his chest, he wanted to be able to reach them quickly. He squeezed the trigger of his gun, reloaded and fired, reloaded and fired, reloaded and fired. Four shots in all. By now, the soldiers were running to and forth, asking each other where the shots were coming from and if anyone had been hit.

Yellow Hair smiled to himself at the disorder he was causing and looked down at the remaining bullets. With a sigh, he picked one up, loaded it into the gun and fired. Then he reloaded again and again getting off five shots in rapid succession. As the last shot still rang in his ears, a size twelve boot kicked into his left rib cage and the owner of the boot toppled over him and hit the ground—hard.

The soldier did not recover his wits very quickly. He sat up and looked incomprehensively at the Indian. The Indian, in perfect English, said," I guess you caught me."

Once Yellow Hair's words had sunk in, the soldier jumped to his feet, pointed his gun at him and shouted, "Over here! I got him over here!"

Within moments, soldiers surrounded Yellow Hair, some of them dressed in nothing more than a red union suit and a pair of pants held up by suspenders. Yellow Hair recognized the pickets and was heartened to see they were all there. Then a voice roared out of the darkness, "What in damnation is going on here? Move, make room, make room!" As soldiers parted, much as the Red Sea must have parted for Moses a long time ago, Henry Sibley walked into the middle of the circle of men that surrounded the single Indian with yellow hair.

"Sir, this Indian was takin' shots at us and we just now captured him," said a man of indiscriminate rank.

"Excuse me, sir," said Yellow Hair. "I shot at no one. I was merely doing a little night hunting."

"Hot damn! That Indian speaks damn good American," said a soldier at the back of the crowd.

Sibley admonished the soldiers, "You men get back to your post. When you are on picket duty, you are not to leave for any reason. If there is a disturbance, it will be handled. Your job is to keep people from entering or leaving the Indian camp. And you others, bring that man with you. I want a better look at him."

The soldiers brought Yellow Hair to Sibley's tent where he stood before the colonel for some time before Sibley deigned to speak.

"So, you are the famous Yellow Hair? The White Man who became an Indian. I've heard of you."

Yellow Hair knew there was nothing Sibley could do to him—nothing that mattered now that Suni and Little Thunder were safely away—so he decided to speak his mind. "And I of you Colonel Sibley; your reputation has preceded you."

"My reputation? What are you talking about? I just received my commission a month ago and this is my first command."

"I don't know anything about that. I refer to your days as a trader. Are you not the Henry Sibley, the Long Trader, as the Sioux call you, who has been robbing the Dakota for twenty years?"

Not accustomed to being spoken to in such a manner, Sibley turned beet red and told the guards to put the Indian in chains and send him to the Lower Agency at once.

As Yellow Hair was being led out of the tent, Sibley ordered the soldiers to wait a moment. He walked up to Yellow Hair, looked him in the eye and said, "I have always been a friend to the Red Man, especially the Sioux."

"Perhaps, Colonel Sibley. Except when you were robbing us at your stores, and now you are condemning innocent people to death. The women and children of the Mdewakanton have harmed no one, yet you plan to put them in a prison camp. Now, if you please, I have chains waiting for me and I hope a nice comfortable prison cell."

In spite of himself, Sibley liked the tall Indian who stood before him. "Just one more question. What were you shooting at out there?"

"Night birds."

"There are no night birds in this neck of the woods."

"Exactly! Now may I leave, Colonel Sibley?"

"Take him away."

It was one o'clock in the morning and Henry Sibley was tired. He had had a very busy day. The first order of business that day had been the appointment of a five-member Military Commission to try the Indians for their rebellion.

Being Henry Sibley, he appointed a commission with preconceived notions and foregone conclusions. All five members had fought at the Battle of Wood Lake, and one, a survivor of Birch Coulee.

Sibley singled out three hundred and ninety-six men to stand trial before his "impartial" commission. One of those men was Yellow Hair.

The remaining Dakota, those not prisoners, were moved to what was left of the Redwood Agency where the uprising had started.

Chapter Forty-Seven

THE SUN is not so overbearing now. It is the beginning of the Moon of Falling Leaves. There are no buildings to house the prisoners at the Lower Agency. Hence, they sit chained to one another out-of-doors within a makeshift stockade. Tomorrow is Yellow Hair and Chaska's turn at American justice.

Besides the three hundred and ninety-six prisoners, there are almost two thousand Santee Sioux living in their tipis adjacent to the stockade. They are also in the custody of the United States of America and guarded night and day. With their weapons taken from them, they cannot hunt. And even if they could, they are not allowed to venture from the improvised enclosure that surrounds their tipis. The Indians are given only bread to eat, and then only once a day.

The stockade door opens at noon and the Dakota women come in with their baskets filled with bread. It is time to distribute the only food the prisoners will see that day. Just as one of the women reaches Yellow Hair and is about to hand him his crust of bread, the guard yells out, "Hey, White Man, the colonel wants to see you! You can eat later." He cannot eat later, but that does not seem to bother the guard.

Yellow Hair is unshackled and escorted to Sibley's tent.

"Welcome, Yellow Hair, please come in." Sibley is acting as though it were a social visit. "You may leave us, private. Wait outside." Then to Yellow Hair, "Have a seat. I thought we might have a little talk."

Yellow Hair says nothing and remains standing. After three weeks of captivity with very little to eat, he has lost the flippant attitude he exhibited at their last meeting.

"I guess you're wondering why I had you brought here."

Still no reply.

"What is your name?" asks Sibley.

"My name is Yellow Hair."

"No, I mean your Christian name."

"My name is Yellow Hair."

Sibley is about to say something, but seeing the look in Yellow Hair's eyes, thinks better of it. Instead, he shrugs and says, "This little uprising has caused a national uproar. Half the country wants me to hang every Sioux in Minnesota and the other half are saying they had good cause for what they did. Hell, this business has pushed the war off the front pages of the nation's newspapers."

After lighting a cigar, Sibley continues, "I've newspaper men from all over the country hounding me daily. There's even a *woman* from a New York paper! And Mister Lincoln has gotten into the fray. I wanted to hang the prisoners upon their conviction, but I was ordered to stay my hand by the President of the United States.

"Tomorrow may be the last day of the trials and you are scheduled. When you are led into the court, all those newspapermen are going to start asking questions. They will want to know why a White Man is being tried. And that will open a whole Pandora's Box of other questions.

"So, I need to ask you a few questions off the record. I want you to know that anything you say here will not leave this tent."

Sibley has piqued Yellow Hair's interest. "What sort of questions?"

"Well, first off, I would like to know . . . did you take part in the murders of, or outrages upon, civilians?"

"No, Colonel. I do not make war on women and children."

Sibley looks relieved.

"Did you kill any whites?"

"Yes."

For reasons of his own, Sibley does not like that answer. "In what respect did you kill whites?"

"I am . . . or I was . . . a soldier. I fought other soldiers at the Redwood Ferry and at what you whites call Birch Coulee. I also fought at Wood Lake."

Sibley leans back in his chair and thinks for a moment. "I'm glad you did not kill farmers and their families or debauch women. If you had, I would have to put you on trial, but seeing as how you fought honorably, we can forgo a trial. I won't be able to release you just yet, but in time you can go back to your tribe."

"Why are you so anxious that I not be tried like the others? Is it that you do not want me talking to the newspapers and perhaps telling them how you and the other traders have been robbing us? You, and people like you, were the main cause of the war. Other men I am being held with did nothing more than I; still they are slated to die. And there is one man, Chaska, who saved Missus Wakefield and her children. Why are you not concerned about him?"

"That fellow Chaska . . . I met him, and Missus Wakefield told me what he did for her. I will look into his case. But as for you, I'm sending you to Fort Lincoln. It's up by Mankato. Do you know where that is?"

"Does it matter?"

"No, I reckon not. As soon as the trials are completed, all the prisoners will be brought there and that is where the hangings will take place."

"May I ask how many men, as of today, you plan to hang?"

As Sibley looks through some papers on his desk, he says, "Let me see. Ah, here it is. As of last night, the number is two hundred and sixty-two." He seems proud of the fact. "There are no trials today and there are forty-two cases left to be heard. No . . . make that forty-one. You have been reprieved."

"Do you plan on having one mass execution? Hang all three hundred men at once?"

Sibley ignores the query and says, "You will be taken in a covered wagon and kept out of sight. Yes, I know what you are thinking, that I don't want the reporters to get a look at you. That is true, but if the people of the towns that you will pass through saw you, I think your life would be forfeited in the blink of an eye. There are some hard feelings out there. You should read some of the letters I've received."

Sibley signals that the meeting is at an end by calling to the private standing outside his tent. "Private, take this man back to the holding area and send Sergeant Willis to me." To Yellow Hair, Sibley says, "Good-bye. It has been an interesting experience meeting you. And don't worry; when things have calmed down, I will see to it that you are paroled."

When brought back to the holding area, Yellow Hair seeks out Big Eagle to tell him that he is being transferred to a fort to the north. "But we will see one another again. Sibley told me all the prisoners will end up there."

Big Eagle looks to his son-in-law and tears well up in his eyes. "It does not matter what happens to me. I am an old man. I am happy that Suni and my grandson are safe. Thank you for getting them away. If I had a son, I would want him to be like you, Yellow Hair."

"I am proud to have you as the father of my wife. I will be leaving in a few minutes, but first I must find

Chaska and tell him something. I will see you in a few days."

Yellow Hair finds Chaska and tells him of Sibley's promise to review his case. "Do not worry; he remembers you and what you did for Missus Wakefield. Everything will be all right."

Sergeant Willis has his orders. Quickly and quietly, Yellow Hair is transferred to Fort Lincoln.

The last forty-one trials take place on 12 November 1862. In record time, seven hours and forty-three minutes, including an hour off for dinner, all forty-one men are convicted and sentenced to die.

In the end, three hundred and three men are sentenced to death. Colonel Sibley and General Pope are champing at the bit to get the hangings over with, but because the President has told them that he must first review the list of those to be hanged, Sibley and Pope are forced to cool their heels.

When Lincoln seems to be taking too long approving the list, Pope fires off a letter to the President telling him that they are all guilty and that there should be no pardons.

After a careful review of the charges, Lincoln approves the hanging of thirty-nine of the prisoners—those that took part in murder and rape. Those convicted of only participating in battles with soldiers will not be hanged, but they will not be released either. They are to be held for the time being.

Sibley belatedly remembers Chaska and writes to President Lincoln explaining that there is new evidence that the man did not commit any outrages.

Lincoln pardons Chaska; however, there are many men with similar names. When they go to remove Chaska from among the condemned, they remove the wrong man.

When the names of those to be hanged are published, Sara Wakefield is relieved that Chaska's name is not among them. There is a Chaskadon, but that does not concern her.

Chapter Forty-Eight

THE MORNING OF 26 DECEMBER 1862 is gray and overcast. A cold wind blows down from the North Country. But the weather does not dissuade the four thousand people who have assembled to see the show.

Off stage, in a room by themselves, with their ankles chained to the floor, sit the main actors. They number thirty-eight. Among them walks a man of the cloth, extolling the virtues of *his* god, the god of the *Wasichu*. There is no *Wichasha Wahaŋ*—no holy man of their faith to tell them that *Wakaŋ Taŋ́ka* will be waiting for them in the next world.

The minister stops in front of the one called Chaska. Seeing that the young brave is distraught, he says, "Have faith, my son; eternity is near. Accept Jesus as your savior and this day you shall be with Him in Heaven."

Looking up at the man in the black robe, Chaska says in a loud and clear voice, "I was taught there is only one *Wakaŋ Taŋ́ka*. It does not matter what you call it, Jesus will do for you, but I am Dakota and I will call the Great Mystery *Wakaŋ Taŋ́ka*."

The scaffold is high. Thirty-eight nooses hang from its crossbeams. The mechanism for springing the thirty-eight trap doors has been tested and retested until it works perfectly.

Soldiers enter the room and unshackle the men from the floor. The Indians know that their time is nigh and begin to sing their death songs. As they chant, their hands are tied behind their backs.

It is not a solemn procession to the gallows. The men are sanguine as they walk towards the thirteen steps that will lead them to a land of peace and good hunting.

The condemned stand on the platform, white hoods in place over their heads, but still they chant their death songs. The audience is kept from the gallows by a ring of soldiers one thousand strong.

Cheers erupt as William J. Duley walks into the throng. His wife and children were killed during the uprising. At first, he fought bravely, killing the chief Lean Bear. But when he was pinned down by gunfire, he ran, and he ran fast. He did not stop to ascertain if his family was still alive, maybe only wounded.

The captain of the guard holds a gold watch in his left hand. When the time is right, he will raise his right arm and point his index finger at the man who will cut the rope that will simultaneously release all thirty-eight trap doors. The man who will do the honors: William J. Duley.

The captain is watching the minute hand approach twelve. At exactly twelve noon he will give the signal.

The second hand ticks to twelve, the signal is given, the rope cut, and the largest mass execution to ever take place in the United States of America is now history.

A few days later, Sara Wakefield reads in a newspaper that an Indian had been hanged by mistake. His name was Chaska. He was executed in place of a man named Chaskadon.

An incensed Sara Wakefield immediately wrote Sibley and asked him how such a mistake could have happened.

Sibley could not be bothered to answer her letter. Instead, he delegated the task to a Mister Riggs. Riggs was the man charged with selecting the Indians to be brought to trial. He was chosen for the job because he had lived among the Sioux for thirty-five years, spoke their language and could tell one heathen redskin from another. Such as the difference between the names Chaska and Chaskadon.

Mister Riggs wrote to Sara, telling her that he could not explain how the mistake had happened and that it was regrettable, but no one was to blame.

No . . . no one is ever to blame, unless of course, one is an Indian.

• • • • •

It was now time to deal with the rest of the Dakota nation.

Governor Ramsey wrote the following:

"The Sioux must be exterminated. They must be dealt with harshly."

Galbraith, the Indian Agent who refused to distribute food to a starving people, said:

"They must be whipped, coerced into obedience. Many will be killed; more must perish from famine and exposure."

During the Moon of the Popping Trees, the remaining Dakota, two thousand in number, were taken to Fort Snelling, situated on the land Little Crow's grandfather had ceded to the Americans in 1805, and enclosed in a stockade for the winter. These people had done nothing wrong. Many of them had helped the whites during the uprising. However, in the winter of 1862, in Minnesota, being an Indian was a crime in and of itself.

It was a bitter and bleak winter; many died from the cold and starvation. And if that was not enough, measles ran through the camp, killing children and adults alike.

Come spring, there were thirteen hundred Sioux left alive. Those poor souls were shipped off to Crow Creek in the Dakota Territory. Crow Creek, next to Death Valley, was one of the most inhospitable places for human habitation within the continental United States. Nothing would grow in its soil.

Yellow Hair, along with those prisoners that had been reprieved by President Lincoln, but not released, was sent to Fort McClellan, two hundred and fifty miles to the south.

• • • • •

Little Crow had gone west hoping to enlist the help of the western Sioux to continue the fight with the Americans. When they refused, he tried the other western tribes. They would not even speak with him, so Little Crow and his followers, who were now down to less than twenty, went East. They were going back to Minnesota to live, perhaps to die, in the Big Woods.

By the time he reached the Big Woods, Little Crow was down to one follower—his sixteen-year-old son. The two were picking berries when two White Men spotted them. One of them took aim and shot Little Crow in the hip. As he fell to the ground, Little Crow reached for his gun.

While the first shooter was reloading, the other man fired at Little Crow just as Little Crow fired at him. Both balls struck home. The one that went into Little Crow killed him while Little Crow's ball only grazed the man.

When Little Crow's body was identified, it was brought to the town of Hutchinson, mutilated, and then thrown into the town's garbage pit.

Little Crow's son escaped that day, but was later captured and imprisoned for four years before being released.

Braves from a Chippewa band in northern Minnesota killed Red Middle Voice in the summer of '63 while he was trying to cross into Canada.

Bounty hunters kidnapped Shakopee from Canada in the spring of '64 and brought him to Mankato where he was tried and hanged.

Big Eagle was released in the spring of '64. He never left Minnesota.

General Pope wanted to make a statement to Washington. He wanted to get back into the war, and the only way he thought he could do so was to impress the War Department with his military acumen. To this end, Pope organized a campaign against the Sioux that had run to the plains.

Roaming the plains and trying to stay out of the White Man's reach were eight hundred Lower Sioux, four thousand Upper Sioux, and a like number of Yankton and Yanktonai.

Chapter Forty-Nine

IN THE SPRING OF 1863, General Pope summoned General Alfred Sully and Colonel Henry Sibley to his headquarters in St. Paul.

"Gentlemen, good of you to come. Please sit down."

After the three had seated themselves, Pope began speaking.

"I've finally gotten some cooperation from the War Department. I've been able to form two armies: an army of infantry made up of thirty-three hundred men and a cavalry unit of four thousand. Colonel Sibley, you will head up the infantry. General Sully, the cavalry.

"I believe the Sioux are in the Devil's Lake region in the Dakota Territory, planning more attacks here within Minnesota."

Pulling a cigar from the inside pocket of his coat, General Pope stopped speaking long enough to bite off the end and fire it. Once he had it burning smoothly, he continued, "The plan, gentlemen, is to catch the Sioux in the jaws of a vise. You two will be that vise."

Sibley and Sully looked at one another and smiled. There was nothing either man wanted more than to go Indian hunting. And with thousands of men at their backs, that made the proposition all the more attractive.

Pope recommended, "Colonel Sibley, you will head west in mid-June. General Sully, you will embark at the same time from Fort Randall and proceed north up the Missouri River Valley. The Sioux will be caught between your two forces."

General Sully asked a few pertinent questions.

"What are our orders concerning the Indians? I mean, are we to capture them? Or are we to destroy their villages and supplies and then leave them to starve? And what of the women and children?"

"Good questions, General Sully, and to the point," acknowledged General Pope. "Your orders are to eliminate the Indian menace by whatever means you deem necessary. If you return with no prisoners, then the people of the United States will not have to pay for their upkeep. As far as women and children are concerned, consider them hostiles."

Both armies left at the predetermined time, mid-June 1863, Sibley heading west and Sully going north.

Sibley had a few small encounters with the Sioux at Big Mound, Dead Buffalo Lake, and Stony Lake. In each occurrence, Sibley's forces came up against hunting parties, not warriors. He claimed a total of one hundred and fifty Indians killed in those battles.

After Stony Lake, Sibley awaited Sully at the Missouri River's eastern bank in the Dakota Territory. On August 1st when Sully still had not arrived, Sibley led his men back to Minnesota.

Sully, on the other hand, had not happened upon any Sioux. That is, not until the first week of September as he made his way back to Minnesota.

At a place known as Whitestone Hill, he came across a Minneconjou Lakota encampment of twenty lodges. Within the camp were Fighting Woman and Little Thunder.

• • • • •

Eleven moons earlier and eight hundred miles to the east . . .

A woman and child stand in the corral next to their horses. They are waiting for something to occur. What exactly, they do not know, but when it does happen, they hope it will pull the watchers away from their posts so they can escape.

After what seems like hours, but is only minutes, a single shot rings out. Hearing the shot's report, the boy starts to lead his pony out of the enclosure. But he is stopped by the woman. "Wait, we cannot go until the watchers are gone," she whispers.

A volley of shots resound in the night, and two of the three pickets stationed on that side of the camp leave their posts, running towards the gunfire. The sentinel closest to the woman and child remains at his station.

The woman looks at the boy and shrugs.

An additional five shots ring out, and the last guard follows his comrades.

The woman smiles at the boy and says, "Come, it is time to go. Your father has freed us." Leading her pony by a lariat, she leaves the corral accompanied by her son and his pony.

Making sure that no one is about, they walk westward until swallowed by the night. Once out of sight of the camp, they mount their ponies and head northwest to the plains of the Dakota Territory.

They travel by night and hide in the woods during the day. In the Minnesota autumn of 1862, it is a crime to be an Indian. Any White Man, or White Woman for that matter, has a perfect right to shoot an Indian on sight.

They do not start fires for fear of being discovered. They live off berries and what they can steal from farms. Once they reach the plains of the Dakota Territory, meat is plentiful in the form of rabbits and other small game.

In six sleeps, mother and son happen upon a small camp circle. A young man stands at the center of the camp. The woman and boy make their way toward him. He is short of stature, but powerfully built. What has attracted Fighting Woman is the fact that his complexion is light, as is his hair. In a way, he reminds her of Yellow Hair.

"I am Fighting Woman and this is my son, Little Thunder. We are Dakota. We come from the Blue Earth Valley and have escaped the *Wasichus* that are holding our people captive."

The young man replies, "I am Thašúŋke Witkó. I am an Oglala of the Teton Lakota. This is a Minneconjou hunting camp. We have heard of the Dakota's war with the *Wasichus*. Some of your people have passed here on their way to Grandmother's land to the north."

"We would like to rest. We have been running for six sleeps. It has been hard on my son."

Little Thunder does not think that the journey has been that hard. However, it would not be proper to contradict his mother, so he remains silent.

Generosity being a virtue of the Lakota, Thašúŋke Witkó offers the sojourners shelter and food.

"Come, I will take you to my grandmother's lodge. I am visiting relatives; my mother was a Minneconjou."

As they walk, Thašúŋke Witkó informs his guest that most of the men are gone off hunting buffalo. He and a few braves have stayed behind to protect the women and children from the Long Knives, who have been known to attack Lakota villages without provocation.

That night as they ate, Fighting Woman looks out on the prairie, and speaking softly to herself says, "This is the land where I found my Yellow Hair."

Little Thunder, sensing his mother's mood and in an effort to change the subject, asks Thašúŋke Witkó if he has ever battled the Long Knives.

"No, little brother. We try to stay out of their way."

Little Thunder looks disappointed, "My father has killed many soldiers. If they come, I will fight them too!"

Addressing her son with forbearance, Fighting Woman reminds him that first he must have a Vision Quest before he can go on the warpath.

"Yes," agrees Thašúŋke Witkó, "I have gone on the warpath many times, but not until I had my vision. You cannot go into battle until you know your protector. Be patient, little brother. The Lakota and the Dakota have many enemies. You will have your share of coups."

"Will you tell me of your vision?" asks Little Thunder.

His mother interjects, "It is not proper to ask a man to tell you of his vision. His vision is between him and his *Wichasha Wakaŋ*."

Amused, Thašúŋke Witkó says, "That is all right. Many know of my vision; one more will not matter." To Little Thunder he says, "I will tell you when we have finished eating. My grandmother has heard it many times." With a laugh he adds, "I think it will tire her to hear it once again."

The meal concludes and Thašúŋke Witkó tells Little Thunder to follow him. "I will tell you of my vision; we will leave the women to their duties."

The two walk until the camp is only a dark outline against the night sky and the flickering fires nothing more than small pinpoints of yellow light. The sky is clear and filled with stars. Even with no moon, the boy can see the young man's face as he speaks.

"I was of twelve winters when I had my vision. And, like you, I could not wait to join a war party. But I did not prepare as one should. I went to a place I knew of with many cottonwood trees. There I stayed for two sleeps without eating or sleeping, trying to have a vision, but one would not come. On the third day, I slept and had a dream.

"I saw a rider in a storm—his hair not braided. He wore a small stone in his ear, and a bolt of lightning painted on his left cheek. Hail covered his body. Although a warrior, he bore no scalps. People clutched at him, but could not hold him. The storm faded and a red-backed hawk flew over the rider's head."

Thašúŋke Witkó looks to the boy and asks, "Can you tell me what my vision foretold?"

Little Thunder is thoughtful for a moment. "Does it mean that you . . . no . . . I was going to say it meant that you would be a great warrior, but the rider had no scalps, so he could not have been a warrior."

"Very good. You were right in the first place. I will tell you what the vision meant. My father is a *Wichasha Wakaŋ*, and as you know, they interpret dreams and visions. His name is now Waglula, but before, he was Horse-That-Is-Spirited. He gave me his name after my first battle. He said my dream foretold that one day I would be a great warrior of not only the Oglala, but of all the Lakota.

"I was young and all I heard was 'great warrior'. A little ways later—I was of sixteen winters—I went on the warpath against the Crow. Like the rider in my dream, I wore my hair free, and I wore a red-backed hawk feather in my hair. I painted my face with a lightning bolt as I had seen on the rider.

"During the fight, I took two scalps before I was wounded in the leg. My father told me I received the wound because I took scalps. He reminded me that the rider of my vision bore no scalps. From then on, I have taken none. My father also said that no one could kill me but our own people and, even then, they will have to hold my arms. Now come, it is late and time for sleep."

Little Thunder wants to stay and hear more. "Will you tell me of your coups?"

"I do not call coup. I fight the enemy of the Lakota to protect my people, not for honors."

"My father never calls coup either. He says he fights to protect the Dakota, not for ponies or the praise of people."

"Your father is a fine man. Your mother has told me of how he saved you from the soldiers. Someday I hope to meet him, and together we can go on the warpath against soldiers that come into our country. Now it is time to return to the camp circle."

Horse-That-Is-Spirited delivers the boy to his mother and asks her, "When do you expect your husband?"

"He is following. He should be no more than one or two sleeps behind us."

"How will he find you?"

"The land of the Lakota is not so vast that he will not find us."

"You may stay with us for as long as you wish. I like that boy of yours." With a chuckle, Spirited Horse adds, "He listens to my stories without interruptions."

"When his father returned from a battle, Little Thunder would refuse to sleep until he had heard all about it. He would sit with his eyes wide, not saying a word."

"He reminds me of myself at his age."

"I was the same. I could not wait to go on the warpath, but for a girl it is not so easy."

"You, a woman, went on the warpath?"

"Yes, that is why I am called Fighting Woman."

Shaking his head, Spirited Horse says, "We have had women of the Oglala fight alongside men, but not many. You must tell me about your coups someday, but now it is time for sleep. You will sleep in my cousin's lodge tonight; he has no wife and is away on the hunt."

The next day, Fighting Woman is helping the women grind corn into meal, and Little Thunder is following in Spirited Horse's footsteps asking questions about war, when from the south comes a lone rider. It is Mahpiya Iyapat'o (Touch the Clouds), Spirited Horse's cousin.

Reaching the camp circle, he tells the people the hunt has been successful. There is much meat drying and many skins. "The camp has to move south; the women are needed to tan the skins. We are low on ammunition and we are going to trade skins with the Cheyenne for powder and balls."

As the women dismantle the tipis, Spirited Horse seeks out Fighting Woman and tells her of the new development, and proposes, "Why not come with us?"

Fighting Woman thinks for a moment before responding, "I thank you, but Yellow Hair will be coming along soon. We have arranged that I would stay near *Pa Sapa*. You are going south; he might not find us if we are not near the Black Hills."

Spirited Horse agrees that going south might not be a good idea. "Make your way to the Powder River. Stay to the right of the sun when it is in the western sky and you will come to the river. Follow it north. You should run into a band of the Hunkpapa who at times set up camp there. Their chief is a good man by the name of Tȟatȟáŋka Íyotake. He will care for you and your son until your husband comes.

"When you see Sitting Bull, tell him that Spirited Horse will visit him soon. Now I will ask my grandmother to fill a parfleche with food for you, then you can be on your way."

As mother and child ride out of the Minneconjou camp, the women are busy disassembling their tipis and the men are gathering their ponies. Little Thunder turns to take one last look at his friend Spirited Horse. Little did he know that the young brave waving farewell would one day be killed under a flag of truce in his thirty-sixth winter as his own people held his arms. History will know him as the great warrior Crazy Horse.

Chapter Fifty

FIGHTING WOMAN and Little Thunder traveled for three sleeps before they came across another band of Lakota. They were of the San Arc Lakota and they too welcomed mother and child into their village circle. Fighting Woman and Yellow Hair had agreed that she would follow the sun in a straight line, so when the San Arc broke camp and headed southwest, she and her son once again headed west.

A moon had passed since Fighting Woman and Little Thunder left the Minneconjou and Spirited Horse, and still Yellow Hair had not shown. Fighting Woman thought of going back to find her husband. But she soon put that notion from her head. She feared they might cross paths on the way and miss each other. She could not bring herself to leave Little Thunder, and she certainly was not going to take him back to Minnesota and the dangers she knew existed there. In addition, she was going to have a child and she did not want to have it in Minnesota.

For three moons, Fighting Woman and Little Thunder traveled the plains, staying with various bands as they searched for Sitting Bull's camp. When the winter snows came, Fighting Woman was great with child.

They spent the winter with a band of Yanktonai, and in the Moon of the Snow-Blind, Fighting Woman gave birth to a male child. She named him Ziŋtkála Zi—Yellow Bird in the language of the whites. He had his father's yellow hair and blue eyes. By the time Yellow Bird was born, Fighting Woman had made many friends among the Yanktonai. The medicine man offered to prepare Little Thunder for his Vision Quest when he was old enough, so she decided to stay with the Yanktonai and not seek out Sitting Bull's camp.

Every day she looked to the east for a lone rider that she knew in her heart would one day come from where the sky meets the earth.

Throughout the spring and summer, the Yanktonai moved from hunting ground to hunting ground, following the buffalo and drying meat for winter. Then, late in the Moon When the Cherries Are Ripe, they set up camp at Whitestone Hill, which is where Fighting Woman found herself and her children at the beginning of September 1863—as the whites count time.

• • • • •

Fighting Woman sits in the old man's lodge. His name is Siŋte Ska (White Tail). She crushes the leaves of plants that he uses in his art. White Tail is the medicine man of the Yanktonai band in which she now resides.

White Tail's wife, Wiŋohiŋea Maka—Earth Woman in the White Man's tongue—died last winter of the little spotted sickness. He has been alone since her death.

He had watched his wife die and been powerless to save her. None of his herbs or bark from the trees helped her. Not a lifetime of curing his people readied White Tail for the *Wasichu's* diseases. He and Earth Woman had one child, a daughter, but she had died before reaching her second winter.

White Tail offered his hospitality and his lodge to Fighting Woman and Little Thunder when they first arrived. It was his nature to help those in need. He thought he would enjoy having young people around. Even the early morning crying of Yellow Bird was as a song to his ears. On this day, Fighting Woman and her children have lived with White Tail for eight moons.

Having bundled the last of his medicines, White Tail looks to Fighting Woman and says, "Thank you for your help."

353

"I enjoy helping you."

"It has been pleasant having you and your little ones in my lodge. It reminds me of when I had a family."

Fighting Woman does not respond to the compliment. A single tear trickles down her right cheek.

"What is troubling you, my friend?"

"I too had a family. It has been twelve moons since I last saw my husband. I fear something bad has happened to him or else he would have found us by now."

"He will come; this is a big country and there are many bands. It takes time to search, but I believe he will find you before winter comes."

"Thank you for saying that, but I believe Yellow Hair has been taken by the whites and hanged. I have been thinking this for many moons now, but I could do nothing until Yellow Bird was born. Now that he is of seven moons, I can take him and Little Thunder back to the Blue Earth Valley and look for my husband. I do not think I will find him alive, but I must know of his fate."

"What of Little Thunder's Vision Quest? You know how he is looking forward to it."

"He is young. I think he will gladly put it off until we know of his father. No, tomorrow we leave."

"Stay five more sleeps. Tomorrow Little Thunder and I will build his sweat lodge, and I will tell him what he needs to know. Within four sleeps, he will have his vision and then you can go."

"Where is Little Thunder?"

"He is with the braves, helping gather the ponies for the night. You stay and look after Yellow Bird. I will go to him and explain of the journey he is about to take and why. I will also tell him that he will have his vision before he leaves."

"For Little Thunder, we will stay."

The next morning, Little Thunder walks with White Tail as the old man tells him the ways of the Lakota.

"I am Dakota," interjects Little Thunder.

"We are all of *Wakaŋ Taŋ'ka,*" replies White Tail.

"My father has told me that *Wakaŋ Taŋ'ka* lives in all things."

"Yes, your father speaks the truth. We are all of our mother the earth, and all things of our mother are of us. We are all ONE. From *Wakaŋ Taŋ'ka* comes the spirit that is in all things. Look to the rocks, the flowers of the prairie, the birds in the air, the bear in the hills, the elk and the little badger; look to all and you will see *Wakaŋ Taŋ'ka.*

"Have ears for the prayer of the old ones.

> *"Hey-a-a-hey! Hey-a-a-hey! Hey-a-a-hey! Grandfather, Great Spirit, once more behold me and lean to hear my voice. All things belong to you, the two-legged, the four-legged, the wings of the air and all green things that live. Day in and day out, forever, you are the life of all things.*
>
> *"From the west, you have given us the cup of living water and the sacred bow, the power to make live and to destroy. You have given us a sacred wind and the herb from where the white giant lives—the cleansing power and the healing. The daybreak star and the pipe, you have given from the east; and from the south, the nations' sacred hoop. You have shown us the goodness and beauty and the strangeness of the greening earth, the only mother.*
>
> *"Hear me, not for myself, but for my people; I am old. Hear me that they may once more go back into the sacred hoop and find the good red road, the shielding tree! In sorrow,*

I am sending a feeble voice, O Six Powers of the World. Hear me in my sorrow, for I may never call again. O make my people live!"[4]

White Tail finishes the prayer and looks to Little Thunder. "You must remember this, for you will one day be an Old One and you will pass it on as I have given it to you. Sit and I will sing the prayer once again and then again until you know it as I do. After that we will sing it together. Now listen."

It is 2 September 1863—as the whites count time.

---

[4] *Black Elk Speaks*, pg. 171. By John G. Neihardt. Published by University of Nebraska Press 1932.

Chapter Fifty-One

IT HAD BEEN a long, hard march . . . almost ten hours. Every damn minute of those ten hours, the dust choked you until you thought perdition itself could be no worse.

Generals ride at the head of a column and do not have to eat dust the livelong day. However, the rank of general brings with it the responsibility of looking after the comfort of your men. Well, not all the men, but certainly your fellow officers.

On the evening of 2 September 1863, three officers sit on folding chairs in General Sully's tent, smoking cigars and watching him pour whiskey into four glasses. Those invited are Colonel Hargrove, Major Guilford, and Major Cummings. Captains and lieutenants will have to wait until they make major before General Sully will deign to have them in his tent for a social occasion.

When the glasses contain a significant amount of the amber liquid, General Sully passes them to his guests, raises his glass, and states, "We haven't had decent bourbon since the beginning of the war, but here's to victory and good sippin' whiskey!"

Not knowing if he's referring to victory over the rebels in the south or over the Indians, the three officers raise their glasses in like manner and, to a man, exclaim, "Here! Here!"

The whiskey tasted mighty good to men who had been eating dust since early morning.

"Gentlemen," says the General, "it's a damn shame we have not encountered the enemy during this campaign. And now that we are headed for home, we may never have a chance to rid this land once and for all of the heathen savage."

Feeling the warmth of the alcohol, Major Cummings adds, "It's too bad we failed to meet up with Colonel Sibley. Perhaps he had better luck in finding Indians."

"*Luck?*" counters the General. "Luck has nothing to do with it. The savages knew we were coming, and for no other reason than the damn plume of dust we kicked up everywhere we went. Once they saw that, they headed for the hills."

As he refills everyone's glass, General Sully finishes his thought by rationalizing, "My orders were to eliminate the threat the Indians posed to Minnesota by whatever means possible. By driving the savages further west, I believe I have accomplished my mission."

At that moment, the guard outside sticks his head into the tent and says, "Excuse me, General, but the head scout is here and would like a word with you."

"By all means, show him in."

Secretly, the General is gratified for the distraction. Major Cummings' remarks have hit a raw nerve. He had so wanted to engage the Sioux to prove his mettle to General Pope and the War Department. General Sully hopes, as does General Pope, to get back in the war before it's over, and the quickest way to achieve that goal is with victories on the field of battle.

The scout enters the tent and stands silently before the four officers. After a few moments, the General asks his name. He has been told the man's name on any number of occasions, but he can never seem to remember it. Perhaps General Sully does not remember because he just does not like Indians. If fact, if they were not necessary for scouting and tracking, he would have none in his command. He thinks this one is a Crow. Granted, a Crow is better than a Sioux— marginally. But they're all dirty savages with greasy hair and, for his part he'd rather not associate with any of them.

"My name is John Black Moon."

"And what is it you have come to tell me?"

"We have found a small camp of Sioux about five miles southwest of here; sixty lodges in all. We saw the men leave in a hunting party. They will be gone two or three days."

With a broad grin on his face, General Sully turns to his officers and says, "This is indeed good news!" He turns back to Black Moon and asks him how many hostiles were in the camp.

"*Hostiles*, sir?"

"Yes, man, hostiles! How many hostiles do you estimate in the camp?"

"None sir. The camp has about three hundred people in it, mostly women, children, and old men. A few braves are there to watch the ponies. The band is just hunting meat for the winter. As I told you, most of the men have gone away."

"That is all for now, but tomorrow before first gray light, you will lead a detachment of my men to the location of these 'friendlies'. You will be told whom to report to and when. You are dismissed."

General Sully turns his attention to his guests, "I think we'll call it a night, gentlemen. I have some planning to do."

As the men stand to leave, Colonel Hargrove asks the obvious question. "Sir, will we be participating in the attack?"

"No, I don't think more than a few companies will be needed. I'll send Captain Murray; he heads the Nebraska Second."

General Sully wants to use Captain Murray for two reasons. The first being that Captain Murray has been posted out here in the Northwest for a number of years and has had contact with the Sioux. It is in his record that, as a lieutenant, he has even met with Little Crow. The other, and far more compelling, reason is that in Captain Murray, General Sully has a man who will obey orders without question.

Before Major Cummings leaves the tent, the General asks him to tell Captain Murray to report immediately.

General Sully does not want his senior officers to be involved in tomorrow's raid because some might call what he has in mind to be out-and-out murder. He wants no witnesses to the orders he is about to give the good captain.

Within minutes, Captain Murray reports as ordered.

"Captain, how many men make up the Second?"

"Two hundred forty-eight, sir."

"How about the Iowa Sixth?"

"I'm not sure, sir. It's about the same."

"Lieutenant Wells came down with something and Doc says he'll be out of commission for a few days. I want you to take over the Sixth until Wells is fit to resume command."

"Is that all, sir?"

"No, not by a long shot. We've found some Sioux camped nearby. You and your men are to proceed to their camp before first light and engage the enemy. John What's-His-Name, the scout, will lead you there."

"What are my orders, sir?"

"Your explicit orders are to engage and neutralize the menace by whatever means you deem necessary."

"Could you be a bit more specific, sir?"

"Captain, are you an Indian lover?"

"No sir!"

"Damn any man who sympathizes with Indians! I have come to kill Indians. And I believe it is right and honorable to use any means under God's Heaven to kill as many of the damn savages as I can."

"Yes sir!"

"Listen up, Captain. If the braves are dead, they can't fight. If the women are no more, they cannot spawn heathen children. If the children are dead, they cannot grow up to slaughter innocent whites." Taking a deep breath, General Sully continues, "If their food supply is destroyed and their tipis are gone, the ones that remain extant on this earth will expend their energies finding food and shelter instead of making war on innocent whites. Do I make myself clear, Captain?"

"Yes sir!"

"Alright, you're dismissed. Just one more thing. I do not want to have the burden and the expense of housing and feeding prisoners."

Snapping off a brisk salute, Captain Murray turns and exits the tent, knowing full well what the General wants. He wants all the Indians dead.

In the hours before dawn, 3 September 1863, five hundred soldiers and nine Indian scouts assemble just outside of General Sully's encampment on the plains of the Dakota Territory. Leading the men is Captain William A. Murray of Boston, Massachusetts. He is a graduate of West Point. His mission this day is to kill—without warning—innocent men, women, and children, but mostly women and children.

Chapter Fifty-Two

CAPTAIN MURRAY loves his wife, Mary, with all his heart. The first years of their marriage were the happiest of his life. Now—ten years later—Mary has withered. She has become a drawn shell of the beautiful young girl she once was.

For years they have tried to have a child, to no avail. As each succeeding year passes and it becomes more evident that they are not to be blessed with children, Mary has gone within. She follows William from posting to posting like the good military wife that she is, but she is slowly dying, and the Captain knows it. These are his thoughts as he enters the Yanktonai village this day.

Captain Murray does not know that the men of the village had left the day before to hunt buffalo. It would not have mattered to him if he had known. He is an ambitious man. His orders are to destroy the village and kill as many of its inhabitants as possible. He plans to execute those orders to the best of his ability.

The few braves in the camp try to fight off the raiders, but they are too few and their weapons are antiquated and no match for the breech-loading rifles the soldiers use.

Captain Murray stays on the edge of the camp as his men go from lodge to lodge setting them ablaze. If a woman or child emerges from a burning tipi, they are immediately shot—if they are lucky. He witnesses women being opened with a knife, as one would gut a fish. Children have their brains knocked out of them with the stock of a rifle.

The captain is as thorough as he is heartless. From atop his white horse, he directs his men to kill the poor souls who try to reach the ravine to the south. By the end of the one-sided "battle," more than two hundred Yanktonai Lakota, mostly women and children, lie dead and mutilated.

A woman cut open and her unborn child ripped from her. Many scalped. Women with their private parts cut out that some of the soldiers wear on their hats. One soldier takes a man's testicles to use the sac as a tobacco pouch. Fingers and ears cut off the bodies for the jewelry they carry.

Children who had their brains beat out of them lay on the ground with the gray jelly seeping from the wounds. Suckling infants to old men lie dead on the prairie.

One would think it impossible for men to butcher and mutilate other human beings as the soldiers have done at Whitestone Hill. The massacre lasts four hours and when there are no more Indians to kill, Captain Murray orders his men to destroy the meat stock and kill all the horses.

His last order, to kill the Indians' horses, is easier said than done. They are three hundred in number. At first, the men assigned to the detail try cutting the horses' throats. But when the horses smelled blood they got skittish, and the smell of the White Man makes them even more so. In the end, the Lakota ponies are shot.

Captain Murray passes a tipi not yet put to the torch and hears a baby's cry. For some unknown reason, the wail draws him to it as a Siren's call. He dismounts and, with gun in hand, enters the tipi. As he does so, Fighting Woman runs at him with Yellow Hair's knife. Before she gets within striking distance, Captain Murray lifts his revolver and shoots her through the right eye. The bullet exits the back of her head, taking with it a large portion of her skull.

He hears a noise behind him and sees Little Thunder running at him, also holding a knife—the business end pointing in his direction. The boy, for his trouble, receives a bullet to the head, although it does not exit his skull.

Captain Murray takes stock of his surroundings. It is now that he sees the reason for his being in that particular tipi. It is an Indian baby, but no, this baby has yellow hair and blue eyes! He thinks of Mary and how taking care of a child will bring the bloom back to her cheeks. He wraps the child in the skins on which it lies and hefts it into his arms. He plans to tell General Sully that, before she died, the mother confessed to stealing the baby from a white couple.

Captain Murray orders a passing corporal to set fire to the tipi he has just exited. The corporal's name is Alfred Cooper and he notices the yellow-haired baby in the captain's arms. The Captain's first reaction to Corporal Cooper's interest in the child is to turn and walk away, but, after a few steps, he stops and calls to the Corporal, "When you have finished here, report to me."

It will be at least two months before they get back to Minnesota, and during that time, someone will have to care for the child.

• • • • •

Every massacre has its survivors. So it was with the Battle of Whitestone Hill, as the whites called the massacre. The survivors, eighty-six in number, hid in the ravines until the killing, looting, and destruction was over and the invaders had left. Then, one by one, they emerged from their hiding places.

One of those who had escaped death that morning was White Tail. Being an old man, he could not sleep and arose early, before the daybreak star was alone in the sky. He left his lodge, walked east for a while, and then sat down upon a small hillock to await the sun.

He sat looking at the few remaining stars in the sky when, off to the northeast, he perceived a line of dark shapes that appeared to be moving toward his village. He knew what he saw must be men on horseback. Could it be the hunting party returning early?

As he sat watching the men approach, the sky lightened to gray, and he saw the fork-tail flag of the Long Knives.

He knew this would not be good for his people, for he remembered what happened eight winters earlier to his cousins the Brûlés. That was when the horse soldiers under the command of "Squaw Killer" Harney (General William S. Harney), also known by the Lakota as "Mad Bear," attacked a peaceful camp and murdered men, women, and children at Blue Water Creek on 3 September 1855—as the whites count time.

Yes . . . another 3rd of September.

White Tail, when he realized what was about to happen, ran to warn his people, but he had to run down a ravine and back up the other side, and by then it was too late. When he crested the rise, the soldiers were firing into the lodges and setting them afire. At that point, all he could do was sink into the tall grass and watch the slaughter of his people. The people he had nurtured and cured of their ailments for so many winters.

When the soldiers had gone, White Tail walked down to what was left of the village and joined with the other survivors.

What they beheld was heartrending; the bodies of their friends and relatives lay dead and mutilated. The remains of the lodges were still smoldering. The meat that had been hunted and dried for winter, burning in a fire at the center of the camp circle. All their ponies dead.

The women keened over the bodies of their loved ones. Old men and boys walked the camp as though in a daze.

White Tail looked about him, and in a loud voice he said, "We are Lakota! We must not perish. We must live to tell others of this day. You women get off your knees; there will be a time to mourn, but now there are things we must do."

Pointing to the fire, he continued, "Right now our winter meat is burning. Save what you can. It is all we have until our hunters return. You men and boys do not walk as shadows. Search the lodges, or what is left of them. Find knives; we need to cut meat out of the ponies before they bloat in the sun."

While the people were busy with their tasks, White Tail went to where his lodge had stood. Pulling up the burnt skins of the collapsed tipi, he found the half-charred remains of Fighting Woman and Little Thunder and sadness filled his heart.

He saw the knife in Fighting Woman's hand. She had spoken of how Yellow Hair had given it to her the night she and Little Thunder escaped. He bent over and removed it from her hand. From around her waist, he removed the sheath that she had made all those winters past. Putting the knife in its home, he promised himself that he would one day return it to Yellow Hair and tell him what had happened to his family. He did not look for Yellow Bird for he had seen the soldier carry him away.

White Tail covered his friends with half-burned buffalo robes and then searched for his medicine pouch. He had to attend to the wounded.

The dead no longer had need of his art.

Chapter Fifty-Three

Two Weeks After The Events At Whitestone Hill, at the far end of the large room, in a corner, sits a man. Very little light shines through the small, barred windows that are set seven feet above the earthen floor. The room houses forty-eight men. Every one of them has a shackle on his right ankle. Attached to the shackle is a chain, three feet in length. At the end of each chain, a forty-two-pound iron ball, black in color, resembling a cannonball. If a man wants to move more than three feet in any direction, he must first stoop down and pick up the ball. Then, cradling it in his arm, he is free to go where desired, although slowly.

These men are the incorrigibles, the ones who will not conform to the rules. They are the troublemakers—all but one. The man in the far corner is with the others because his keepers do not want the world to know of his existence. If his part in the recent uprising were known, questions would be asked. Embarrassing questions.

The door of the room opens. A shaft of light falls in among the men who shield their eyes from the invasive brightness. The black silhouette in the doorway shouts, "YELLOW HAIR . . . YELLOW HAIR! Where are you, you miserable savage?"

The man in the far corner stands. He says nothing. The figure standing in the light shouts for him to come forward. "The Major wants a word with you. That is, if you're not too busy."

Ignoring the guard's sarcasm, Yellow Hair picks up his ball and chain and walks to the front of the iron and wood cage that has been his home for ten moons.

Once outside, and once his eyes adjust to the brightness of the daylight, he sees before him a soldier with a smile on his face. What the soldier sees is a White Man over six feet tall, with yellow braids down his back, reaching almost to his waist. He wears White Man's clothing—a shirt and pants. The prisoners are forced to wear the clothes of the hated White Man.

"I am Major Nelson. Before he left for the West, Colonel Sibley entrusted me with a task, a pleasant task I might add. I am here to fulfill that duty." Holding an envelope, Major Nelson says, "I assume you can read. This is for you. It is from Colonel Sibley."

Blinking in the bright sunlight and not quite understanding, Yellow Hair bends to put the ball on the ground, straightens, and accepts the proffered envelope. Inside he finds a single sheet of paper:

Sir,

As promised, I am setting you free as of this day. I am away, but Major Nelson will act in my stead.

If you will take the advice of an older man, you will cut your hair and dress as a White Man. Even though it has been a year since the uprising, feelings in Minnesota still run high.

If you elect not to take my advice, I would then urge you to leave the State of Minnesota. I do not want to free you only to have you killed by irate citizens. However, do as you will.

Major Nelson will see to your release.

Colonel Henry Sibley

Yellow Hair finishes reading Sibley's missive and looks to Major Nelson. "Now I can go to my family."

In response, Nelson tells Yellow Hair to follow him to the blacksmith's shop where he will have his shackle removed. To get to the shop, they must pass through the main yard where the two hundred and twelve men not deemed incorrigible are kept.

Entering the yard, Yellow Hair says to the Major, "I must say good-bye to a friend." Nelson starts to object, but then says, "Well, don't be all day about it."

Cradling the ball in the crook of his right arm, Yellow Hair sets out to find Big Eagle. His eyes search the yard and settle on his friend off to the left—talking with two men.

Big Eagle sees Yellow Hair coming his way and goes to meet his son-in-law. The men in the yard do not wear shackles and chains.

When they converge, he slaps his hands onto Yellow Hair's shoulders and says, "It is good to see you. I did not know if you were alive or dead."

"As you can see, I am alive."

"I heard that you were in the wooden building with the iron bars, but no one I spoke with had actually seen you."

"Well, I have been more dead than alive these last few moons, but now I am reborn. I am to be set free this very day! And I wanted to say farewell, at least until we meet again."

"I am delighted for you."

"I only have a short time. There is a soldier over there who will not allow me more than a few words. I am going to Suni and Little Thunder. I will tell them that you are fine, in good spirits, and that you will join us when you can."

"Yes, tell them that, but I am an old man. If I ever get out of this place, I will stay close to the Blue Earth Valley where I was born. That is, if the whites will allow it. I have heard talk that our people have been sent west, away from here."

"I have heard very little where I have been."

"Tell Suni that her father fares well, and tell the little one that I will finish the stories of my coups when next I see him. I think it better that he believes we will be together again than to know otherwise."

"I will tell him what you wish. Now I must go, my friend."

Yellow Hair stands with his right foot on the blacksmith's anvil. The smithy works to remove the shackle while Major Nelson tells him that as soon as the shackle is off, he will escort him to the gate, and then he will be a free man.

Once the shackle is removed, Yellow Hair looks to his ankle. It is discolored and bleeding. The Major and the smithy have the decency to look away in embarrassment.

As he is walking out of the shop, Yellow Hair notices an old forage cap hanging from a nail, and seeing that the smithy wears a hat of his own, asks to whom the cap belongs.

"A young trooper who got hisself a new Sunday-go-to-meeting bowler left it. Said I could cut holes in it for my horse's ears and she could wear it."

Tentatively, Yellow Hair asks, "May I have it?"

"I reckon so. I ain't got no use of it."

Yellow Hair thinks that it might come in handy if he is to get out of Minnesota in one piece, because he is not about to cut off his braids.

At the gate, Major Nelson extends his hand and Yellow Hair accepts it. After they shake, the Major wishes him well and the gate is closed. Yellow Hair is now free and the master of his own destiny for the first time in twelve moons.

The first thing he does is to put his braids up under the hat. He has a plan, and if he hopes to get to Suni and his son, he will have to pass for a White Man, at least temporarily. It should not be too hard, seeing how he is dressed and the fact that his skin has not seen the sun for a long while. With his braids hidden, the only thing Indian about him are his moccasins, which he hopes not too many people will take note of.

• • • • •

The few people that Yellow Hair passed as he walked the road paid him little or no notice. He was not concerned with his fellow sojourners. He was happy to be out in the fresh air once again. He looked up at the sky and was amazed at the blue color. Had it always been such a beautiful hue? He also gave heed to the clouds as they moved across the blue background. It was all wondrous, not only what was above him, but what he beheld as he walked. The large oak trees with their cool shade, the birches with their white bark that is so useful in the making of canoes, the green grass of the prairie; all given to us by *Wakaŋ Taŋ́ka* and our mother the earth.

After a few miles, he turned his mind to solving the problem of obtaining a pony. Of course, he would have to steal one. And it could not be just any old horse. He needed one that was strong and had grit, because he intended to ride hard and fast. He had to get out of Minnesota before someone cottoned to the fact that he was an Indian. And once he had the horse, he would have to put miles between himself and where he got it. If caught, he would be right back in prison, or worse. Horse thieves were usually hanged in that neck of the woods. As he pondered these thoughts, he heard the clop, clop, clop of a horse coming up behind him. Without turning, he knew it was a White Man's horse with iron on its hooves. A Dakota's pony does not make that sound.

The horse drew abreast and Yellow Hair saw that it was a big, strong bay stallion. The man riding it looked to be a farmer. He eyed Yellow Hair and nodded, before saying,

371

"Morning." Yellow Hair answered in kind, and the horse and rider moved on down the road.

That is the horse to take me to Suni.

But he knew that within a few minutes, horse and rider would be down the road and out of his life. He would have to look elsewhere for a pony. Then, quite unexpectedly, the rider turned off to the left and approached a farmhouse. Behind the house stood a barn, unpainted . . . its gray, weathered wood making it look older than it probably was.

The man dismounted and led the horse into the barn. Yellow Hair stopped walking and looked about for a place in which to conceal himself. Opposite the farmhouse, on the other side of the road, stood a field of corn that was nearly ready for harvest. The stalks were seven and eight feet high. He walked in among the corn a few feet and sat down. From where he sat, he could not be seen from the road, but he could still see the house and barn. About ten minutes later, the man came out and entered the house.

Now Yellow Hair knew where he was going to get the horse that would take him to Suni. All he had to do was stay hidden until nightfall. It would be a long wait; the sun had not yet reached overhead and he was hungry. But that was not a problem. He was surrounded by *wamnaheza.*

After finishing off a few ears of fresh corn, he moved further back among the stalks and lay upon the ground. He watched the clouds pass by and tried to discern what their shapes reminded him of . . . a game he had played as a child.

Without meaning to, he slept.

Chapter Fifty-Four

YELLOW HAIR awoke to find that pinpoints of white light—imbedded in a vast blackness—had replaced the blue sky and white clouds. He took a moment to take in the wondrous sight of a billion stars before he stood from his prone position. He started toward the road, but stopped to relieve himself after only a few steps. When he had finished, he proceeded to the edge of the cornfield and saw that there was a solitary light shining from one of the farmhouse's windows.

While waiting for the light to go out and whoever was in the house to fall asleep, Yellow Hair picked a few more ears of corn, for he was hungry again. The *Wasichus* did not feed their prisoners very well.

He did not relish what he was about to do. But he had to get to his family and this was the only way. Stealing had never been his custom. Since becoming a Dakota, the Christian principles taught to him as a child had only been reinforced by a people who had never heard of Jesus or Christianity—at least not until the *Wasichus* appeared.

Standing among the corn stalks, he thought of his first days with Suni when he had been so ill, and how she had cared for him. How she taught him the Dakota tongue and the ways of the Dakota. He thought of Little Thunder, his boy-child who would one day grow into a man. He wondered what kind of life the boy would have. Would he be a great hunter and warrior? If so, it would have to be among the Lakota.

Yellow Hair was torn in his thoughts. On the one hand, he wanted Little Thunder to grow up in the ways of the Dakota. On the other, he did not want him killing for coups.

To protect his family and people, yes, but to kill for glory and honor, no.

The light in the farmhouse eventually went out. A short while later, he crossed the road and approached the barn where the door stood open. There was just enough light from the stars for him to make his way about. He saw the horse in his stall, with the saddle hanging from the gate.

Before he did anything, he wanted to calm the horse. He knew horses owned by White Men were skittish around Indians. Maybe it was his white blood, but the horse accepted him right away. He put the blanket and saddle on and placed the bit in its mouth. As he started to lead the horse out of the barn, he suddenly stopped in his tracks. He had no weapon and no tools. How was he to eat until he found the Lakota? Might there be something of use that he could find in the barn? Backtracking a few steps, he tied the horse to a post and started his search. Pickings were slim; he found an old knife with a dull blade, a strip of rawhide, and a small axe, that was all.

While walking the horse out of the barn, Yellow Hair kept a watchful eye on the farmhouse.

Once on the road, he mounted the horse that he intended to call Suŋktaŋka Tanʹka—Big Horse, as the whites would say—and rode toward Mankato. After traversing the town, he and Big Horse crossed the Minnesota River and headed for the land of the Lakota.

He rode through the night until the sky lightened to gray. Unlike Suni and Little Thunder, he had no need to hide by day. As long as he kept his braids up under his cap, he could pass for a White Man.

He eventually came across a small stream shaded by poplar trees. He stopped to rest and to make a hunting club. He found a flat rock on which to sharpen the knife. When it was honed to an edge, he took the axe and went in search of a branch that would suffice as a handle for the club.

374

After a short exploration of the available trees, he found what he was looking for. He cut the forked branch from the tree and stripped it, creating what looked like a boy's slingshot with a two-foot-long handle. The opening at the top would accommodate a rock six inches in diameter. All that was left to do was find an appropriate stone and fasten it to the stick with the rawhide, which he did. Then he dipped the business end of the club into the stream. As it dried, the rawhide would shrink and the rock would be securely fastened to the handle.

He cut some bark from a lone cottonwood and gave it to Big Horse. When the horse was well fed and rested, Yellow Hair continued westward.

He was itching to try out his new club. When a rabbit darted out onto his path, he urged Big Horse forward at a fast gallop. The horse seemed to sense what Yellow Hair had in mind and rapidly closed the distance between themselves and the hare. Coming abreast of the rabbit, Yellow Hair leaned over to wallop it on the head, but fell to the ground instead. It had been more than a year since he'd ridden a horse and much longer since he had hunted rabbits. He was a bit rusty, to say the least.

Big Horse slowed, turned, and trotted back to where Yellow Hair sat on the ground. With Big Horse standing over him, Yellow Hair said, "Why don't we forget about rabbit hunting for today. There's plenty of sage for you to eat and I may acquire a taste for it myself if I don't find some food soon."

Picking up his club, he remounted Big Horse. "Let us go. Suni and Little Thunder are waiting for us."

Once again, the two headed west.

They traveled for two sleeps without seeing another soul—white or red. Then, just before sundown of the third day, Yellow Hair saw smoke off to the northwest. He was too hungry to worry about whether it came from a white settlement or an Indian camp circle. He spurred Big Horse onward.

The distance was greater than it had looked, and by the time he and Big Horse crested the last ridge, it was dark. However, the fires that he saw within the camp circle filled his heart with joy.

Yellow Hair entered the camp still dressed as a White Man. He walked Big Horse to the center of the circle and removed his hat. When his yellow braids fell down his back, a murmur arose from the people who had gathered at the approach of the White Man. Then a brave rushed toward him, and Yellow Hair drew his knife. But the man stopped and raised his hands, shoulder level and palms outward to show they held no weapon. He said, "Yellow Hair, it is I, Long Claws!" Indeed, it was Long Claws from the Soldiers' Lodge.

Recognizing his old friend, Yellow Hair put the knife away, and a wide grin appeared on his face. "It is good to see a friend in this country."

"It is good to see you too, Yellow Hair."

By now, the people were crowding around them.

Long Claws said, "Come, let us go to my lodge. We will smoke the pipe and talk."

"Do you think I might also have something to eat?"

"Yes, of course. Leave your pony here." He turned to a group of young boys and told them to take care of his friend's pony. "Water him and remove the White Man's saddle."

As they made their way to Long Claw's lodge, the people they passed slapped Yellow Hair on the back and, in general, made him feel right at home.

When they had settled in, and after the pipe had been passed between them, Long Claws asked of news from home.

"What has happened to our people who stayed?"

"First, may I have something to eat?"

Long Claw called to his wife to bring them food.

Between mouthfuls, Yellow Hair addressed his friend's question. "Do you not know about the trials and the hangings?"

"Hangings? What hangings? I know nothing of what happened after we left the Blue Earth Valley."

"When did you leave?"

"The day after Little Crow left. When Sibley failed to show that first day, we decided it might be better if we were not around when he marched into our camp. We had intended to stay on the prairie until we heard that everything was all right. But when word came to us that some had been arrested, we moved farther west. Now tell me of the hangings and what you have been doing."

Yellow Hair told of his arrest, of the trials, and of the hangings. He spoke of Sibley and how, because he had once been a *Wasichu*, Sibley hid him from view during the trials and then released him. He told about Fighting Woman and Little Thunder escaping and finished with what he had heard about their people being sent to a reserve somewhere in the West.

"I know the place!"

"What place would that be?"

"Where our people were sent," replied Long Claws. "It is called Crow Creek. We went there two moons ago. We thought we might stay. But when we saw how our people were living, we left. The agent is a very bad man."

"What are you and your band doing now?" asked Yellow Hair.

"We have been trying to keep out of Long Trader's way."

"Sibley? Is he out here?"

"Him and another soldier-chief. They both have about three thousand men and many wagon guns. I heard that they wiped out an entire village over by Whitestone Hill. I do not know if it's true, but it sounds like something the Long Knives would do."

"I have another question; I have not asked it before because I know if you knew anything, you would have said something when I first arrived, but I must ask it."

Long Claws expectantly waited for his friend to continue; however, when Yellow Hair hesitated, he ventured, "What is it that you desire to know?"

"Have you heard anything of Fighting Woman and Little Thunder?"

"No, I am sorry. I have not."

The two friends spoke into the night. The next day, Yellow Hair resumed his search for his family. He had discarded his White Man clothes. He was given leggings, a breechclout, a deerskin shirt, and a buffalo robe that he rolled up and tied to his saddle. Long Claws advised that he should not be riding a horse with a White Man's saddle.

"If soldiers come upon you, they will know that you stole the pony."

"If I am asked, I will tell them I traded many buffalo skins for the saddle and horse."

For the next two moons, Yellow Hair went from band to band—the Sans Arc, the Brûlé, the Minneconjou, among others, searching for his family. He did not come across any more Dakota. However, he did spend a few days with a band of Cheyenne.

Chapter Fifty-Five

IN THE MOON OF FALLING LEAVES, the weather was turning cold. Yellow Hair had doubts if he would be able to continue his search during the winter, but he had made up his mind to look for his family for as long as possible. If winter snows kept him from moving about, he would carry on his quest at the first sign of spring.

As he contemplated his limited options, he came to the top of a bluff. Looking to his left, southwestward, he saw the familiar smoke of a camp circle. In the two moons he had been on the plains, he had learned to discern the difference between Lakota smoke and the smoke from the soldier camps. The smoke from a Lakota camp was wispy and not as thick and heavy as that from a *Wasichu* camp.

It had been many sleeps since he last enjoyed the hospitality of the Lakota. And even though his rabbit-hunting expertise had improved, he was getting tired of eating rabbit every night. With a sigh, he spurred Big Horse in the direction of the camp. He sighed because he knew it would be just one more village where no one had seen or heard of his family.

He slipped his horse at the edge of the camp and dropped the reins; Big Horse would be content to partake of the prairie grass, dry though it was. A tall man approached. He was smiling, and when he reached Yellow Hair, he said, "*Tanyáŋ yahi,* my friend. I welcome you to the camp circle of the Oglala. I am Worm. I am the *Wichasha Wakaŋ* of our band. Our Chief is Ošota, but he is away. Will you come to my lodge and smoke the pipe and eat?"

"Yes, I am weary; food and rest would be good. I am Yellow Hair."

"Yes, I know who you are. My son has spoken of you."

"Your son?"

"His name is Horse-That-Is-Spirited. He has met your wife and child."

Yellow Hair's eyes widened with expectation; his whole demeanor changed as he asked, "He has? Where are they?"

"I do not know. He met them at his relatives' camp about this time last winter. When he returned, he spoke of the woman who had coups. He told me of her husband with the yellow hair. Come, we can talk of this in my lodge. My son is not here now. I think he is out hunting, but I never know. He will return within a sleep or two. Then you can ask him where your people have gone."

Horse-That-Is-Spirited returned two sleeps later. When he entered his father's lodge and saw the man with the yellow hair, he knew him immediately. "I am Spirited Horse and you are Yellow Hair."

Yellow Hair asked about his family.

"They should be with Sitting Bull, near the mouth of the Elk River where it meets the Powder. That is where I suggested they go."

"I will start for them first thing in the morning."

Spirited Horse and Yellow Hair found they had much in common; neither called coup in battle and neither took scalps. Both wanted to be left alone and only fought in defense of their people. Spirited Horse did not hate the whites; when he was a child, he had played with their children as the whites traveled the Holy Road.

"Holy Road? What is the Holy Road?" inquired Yellow Hair.

"It is the road that the whites take to the big water that lies over the mountains."

He was speaking of The Trail. The same trail Yellow Hair had traveled when he was a *Wasichu*.

During their short time together, Yellow Hair and Spirited Horse forged a true friendship. Spirited Horse told Yellow Hair what he did during the times he was away from the village.

"I go to kill the whites that invade our land. I do not make war, but I kill as many as I can, one at a time. I kill most with my gun, but I leave a Lakota arrow in them so the whites will know that it was the Lakota that killed them; that it was the Lakota protecting their land."

Yellow Hair was of mixed feelings about what he had just heard. He knew what happened to the Dakota when the whites moved in. The same thing would eventually happen to the Lakota. Spirited Horse had every right to try to keep the whites from stealing his land. Of course, the Lakota took the land from the Crow, and the Crow took it from the Nez Perce. Yellow Hair did not bother to tell Spirited Horse that, over the course of time, the whites would prevail and take the Lakota's land.

Instead, he said, "You are crazy to go out by yourself to kill *Wasichus*. I do not judge what you do. But you should have someone with you to help if something goes wrong or if you are wounded."

"People do call me crazy for what I do, but the whites cannot kill me. Only my own people can do that."

The two shook hands the next morning in the cross-arm way that denotes respect and friendship.

Yellow Hair's parting words to Spirited Horse were, "If I find my people with Sitting Bull, then that is where you can find me. Come and see us. From what you have told me about your talks with Little Thunder, I am sure he will be happy to see you again."

"I plan to see my cousin Sitting Bull soon. He also refuses to sign the White Man's treaties and sell our land. It will be good to see Little Thunder and Fighting Woman."

With a smile he added, "She has not yet told me of her coups."

Crazy Horse told Yellow Hair how to find Sitting Bull's camp. And as his son had done, Yellow Hair turned to take one last look at the man as he rode out of camp. However, unlike Little Thunder, Yellow Hair would live to see his friend again.

Chapter Fifty-Six

FOR TWO SLEEPS, Yellow Hair kept moving, stopping only to rest Big Horse for an hour or so. He did not have to hunt because Crazy Horse had given him plenty of dried buffalo meat.

On the third day, he came upon a village of forty lodges comprised of three hundred people. He wanted to get to Sitting Bull's camp as soon as possible. His family awaited him there. But he needed sleep, so he decided to go into the village.

As he neared the camp circle, he saw women run to their children and herd them into lodges. Men stopped what they were doing; some picked up guns.

Something was amiss.

Yellow Hair did not dismount. He stayed on Big Horse and waited. He did not have long to wait. Three men with muskets came toward him, with other men—having retrieved their weapons—falling in step behind them. When they reached him, they surrounded him and Big Horse. In poor English, one of the men sneered, "What you want, White Man?"

Yellow Hair realized that they had mistaken him for a *Wasichu*. He threw back his head and laughed. In perfect Lakota, he said, "I am Dakota. My name is Yellow Hair."

While the men spoke among themselves as to what to do about the strange man on the large horse, an old man pushed his way through the crowd. Standing next to Big Horse, he spoke. "This is my friend, Yellow Hair, husband of Fighting Woman and father to Little Thunder. You all knew them. Now go about your business. I would speak with my friend."

The men started to disperse, and Yellow Hair looked down at the old man.

"You know Suni and Little Thunder?"

"I knew Little Thunder, but who is Suni?"

"I meant Fighting Woman."

"Yes, I knew them. They lived with me for a while. Get off your pony. We will go to my lodge and I will tell you what you want to know."

"I am on my way to Sitting Bull's camp to be with them and I cannot stay long. I came only to ask if I may sleep a little while next to one of your fires."

"They are not with Sitting Bull. Come, I will tell you where they are."

Yellow Hair slipped his pony and addressed the old man in the formal way, "*Lekši*, you know my name. May I ask yours?"

"My name is White Tail."

When they were seated within White Tail's lodge, but before either man could speak, a young boy of twelve winters bounded into the tipi. He stopped short at the sight of Yellow Hair. White Tail told the boy that the man was the father of Little Thunder.

White Tail explained that the boy's name was Hinháŋ Gleška (Spotted Owl). "He was a friend to Little Thunder." To Spotted Owl he said, "His pony is on the edge of camp, go and attend to him. Yellow Hair and I have words to speak."

After the boy had left, White Tail apologized for the reception he received when he came into the village. "My people have good reason for being suspicious of anyone with white skin."

Reaching into a parfleche that hung from the center lodge pole, he drew out a knife that rested within a deerskin sheath with an image of the sun painted on it. He handed it to Yellow Hair and said, "This is yours."

Yellow Hair took the knife and looked to White Tail. "Yes, it is mine; I gave it to Fighting Woman. How is it that you have it? Did she leave it behind?"

Taking a deep breath, White Tail said, "That boy, Spotted Owl, lives with me. We are not related. His parents, little sister, and three brothers were killed by the Long Knives two moons ago at Whitestone Hill."

"I am sorry to hear that, but what has that to do with Fighting Woman and this knife?"

White Tail then went on to tell Yellow Hair of how Fighting Woman and Little Thunder had come to his village and decided to stay. How he had taken them into his lodge, how he loved them as though they were of his own family. He told of the band's decision to split into two camps to hunt the buffalo for winter meat. He told of sitting in the grass at Whitestone Hill and watching the soldiers kill women and children.

White Tail did not tell about Yellow Bird being taken by the soldier chief. He thought that knowledge would be more than Yellow Hair could bear. No, it was better for him to believe that all his family had died at Whitestone Hill. In fact, he did not tell of Yellow Bird's birth. It would have been one more sorrow for the man to carry. Only two knew the fate of Yellow Bird, himself and Spotted Owl. When White Tail had finished speaking, Yellow Hair looked at the knife in his hand, and for the longest time said nothing.

White Tail was about to go outside and leave him to his own thoughts when Yellow Hair stood and said, "I thank you for being so kind to my people."

Still holding the sheath with the knife in it, he walked out of the tipi.

White Tail followed and watched as he gathered Big Horse's reins from Spotted Owl. With a word of thanks to the boy, Yellow Hair rode west toward the setting sun.

While they looked at the receding figure, Spotted Owl asked, "Will he come back?"

"I don't know," was the reply. White Tail continued, "You told me you saw the soldier chief hand Yellow Bird to another soldier?"

"Yes, I was in the bushes down in the ravine when the soldier chief rode to where I was hiding. I was afraid; I thought he had seen me, but he got off his pony and sat on a boulder holding Yellow Bird. A little while later, a soldier came down and met the soldier chief. Then the soldier chief handed Yellow Bird to the soldier and they talked."

"If you saw the soldier again, would you know him?"

"Yes, he has only one eye."

"One eye! What are you saying?"

"He had only one eye. The other one was covered."

Spotted Owl was speaking of an eye patch. Cooper had lost the sight in his right eye the previous year in a fight with a half-breed over one of the fort whores.

White Tail took Spotted Owl by the hand and they started for their lodge. While walking, he said, "I have not told Yellow Hair of his other son, and I do not want you telling him or anyone else that Yellow Bird lives. One day we may tell him, but for now let him grieve for two, not three."

Chapter Fifty-Seven

YELLOW HAIR sat high up on the bluff as the sun touched the prairie in the west. He saw nothing and thought of everything. Why did fate declare that he was to have no family? No, it may have been fate with his first family, but it was the horse soldiers—the Long Knives—that took Suni and Little Thunder from him.

I have tried to see Wakaŋ Taŋ̓ka in everything and everyone, but how can Wakaŋ Taŋ̓ka live in the hearts of the Long Knives? How?

At length, he stood and spoke to the wind. "The first thing I need is a gun. Not a front-loading musket. I need a repeater like the soldiers have."

Yellow Hair held hatred deep within his spirit. It would now be his lot in life to kill as many soldiers as he could. He would kill until he was killed.

He followed the trail back to the Yanktonai camp, sought out White Tail, and asked "Where is the nearest soldier fort?"

"There is a soldier camp not much more than one sleep from here."

"A camp? What are they doing?"

"I do not know. They came into our country, set up camp, and that is all we know. Our scouts are keeping an eye on them."

"Will you tell me where I can find this camp?"

"Spotted Owl can guide you there. He knows the place. But what do you want with soldiers? You should stay far away from them."

"I need a gun and I thought they might give me one."

White Tail started to say something, but seeing the look in Yellow Hair's eyes, he desisted.

Yellow Hair and Spotted Owl headed east as the sun rose from the floor of the prairie. Before long, Yellow Hair asked, "You were a friend to Little Thunder?"

"Yes, we would hunt prairie chickens together. He was good with an arrow."

Yellow Hair smiled a sad smile at the memory of making Little Thunder his first bow.

Spotted Owl added, "We were going to have our Vision Quest soon. He talked about it all the time. White Tail was going to prepare us."

Though he wanted to hear more of Little Thunder, Yellow Hair became silent, for his heart was heavy. In such a manner, they traveled onward.

At mid-day of the second day, Spotted Owl said, "We are here. The soldier's camp is over the next rise."

Telling Spotted Owl to stay where he was, Yellow Hair slipped his pony and, keeping low, made his way to the edge of the bluff. When he looked down the other side, he saw white tents set up in two rows of eight each and an animal corral made of circled wagons. The soldiers were going about their soldier business, cutting wood, bringing water up from the creek, and starting fires. There were also soldiers on guard duty; they were ten in number and were evenly spaced around the camp. When he turned to his left and looked north, he saw a small assemblage of men—soldiers and non-soldiers—about a quarter of a mile away. Wanting a closer look, he moved along the ridge until he was above them.

After studying the scene for a few minutes, he knew what they were doing. Four soldiers and three men not in uniform. Of those three, one held a long stick, another stood by what looked like a short spyglass, and the third held papers in his hand.

He had seen men like that in Concord. They were surveyors, and the soldiers were guarding them. What they

388

were surveying he did not know, but at least he could tell White Tail what they were doing. It looked as though the *Wasichus* were intent on staying in Lakota country.

He made his way back to Spotted Owl and gave him a message to bring to White Tail.

"Tell White Tail that those men are marking the land for the whites. It usually means they are going to build something, probably a fort. Tell him that I thank him for what he did for Fighting Woman and Little Thunder. And I thank you, Spotted Owl, for being Little Thunder's friend. Now go."

"Are you not coming back to the village?"

"No. When I am done here, I am going to Sitting Bull."

"Then I want to go with you."

"No, my friend, White Tail needs you. I will see you again. But for what I have to do, you cannot be a part of. Now go."

Spotted Owl did not like it, but he got on his pony and rode away. Yellow Hair pulled his buffalo robe from Big Horse and spread it out; he would sleep until nightfall. It must be dark for what he had in mind.

He awoke as the sun was going down. The western sky was a fiery red with orange and purple clouds hugging the western horizon. But he took no note of the wondrous spectacle. He was intent on what he was doing— sharpening the blade of his knife on a flat stone.

Before it was completely dark, he looked down at the soldier camp once again. He wanted to know where the watchers would be. There would be no moon that night, which was good for what he intended, but finding a man at night on a moonless prairie would be difficult unless he knew approximately the man's location. He lay in the grass with only his eyes above the ridgeline, getting his bearings and memorizing each man's station.

He knew the pickets were fresh. He would have to wait awhile, until late in the night when boredom and tiredness had set in.

In the early morning hours, he crept over the rise and made his way down toward the camp. The grass was dry; he had to be careful not to rustle it as he moved. As he drew near the man he had selected, he smelled tobacco smoke. Raising his head just above the grass, he saw a dark outline against the star-filled night.

It was lucky for him that the watcher was smoking his pipe because Yellow Hair had misjudged the man's position. If not for the waft of tobacco smoke, he would have blundered right past the soldier.

He pulled his knife from its home, and on hands and knees moved forward. When he was but a few feet from his prey, Yellow Hair brought himself up on one knee, and without hesitation, sprang before the man could react. He plunged the knife deep into the side of his enemy's neck, burying it to the hilt, and thought of Suni. The man did not die instantly. But he could not cry out—the knife had severed his vocal cords. A second thrust to the heart finished him.

Yellow Hair laid him on the ground and picked up his gun. Damn! It was a musket. He went through the man's pockets. He found a tobacco pouch and some matches. The matches he kept; the tobacco he left.

Not every soldier carried repeaters. Even at the height of the war, the army was slow to purchase them. Spencer, the inventor of the repeater, traveled from fort to fort, selling his gun to individual militia brigades. The men voted whether to purchase the gun or not. The cost of a Spencer was $35.00, double the cost of a musket and two months' pay for the common soldier.

That night, Yellow Hair had to kill four men to get two repeaters and ammunition. He also took two holstered revolvers. Before he went back up over the bluff, he set fire to the dry grass in the hope that more soldiers might die before daybreak.

He rode for three sleeps before he crossed the Black Hills and came to the Bighorn River. He followed it to the Elk or, as the whites called it, the Yellowstone. Following the Elk northeast, he crossed the Rosebud.

Shortly thereafter, three riders approached from the east. When they met, one of the men asked, "Where are you going, White Man?"

Before he replied, Yellow Hair held the man's eye for a moment, then he said, "I am not white, I am Dakota! I come in search of Sitting Bull."

"What business have you with Sitting Bull?"

"That is between me and him."

"We are *akicita*. We protect our people."

"Do you think one man can harm the great Sitting Bull?"

"Come, *Dakota*, we will take you to our chief."

When they came into the camp, the people stared at the man with the yellow hair. The same thing occurred in every Lakota village he had visited. Being the object of so much scrutiny took some getting used to. The Dakota of the Blue Earth Valley knew him well; he had been with them twelve winters when the trouble started. They took him as one of their own.

They reached the center of the circle and Yellow Hair was told to wait. Two of the *akicita* stayed with him. The leader dismounted and walked to a nearby tipi. Saying something that Yellow Hair could not hear, he lifted the skin and went inside.

A few minutes later, he emerged and signaled Yellow Hair to come. He got off his pony and after pausing to remove a small leather pouch and one of the two rifles, Yellow Hair advanced toward the tipi.

The *akicita* soldier barred his way. Pointing to the gun in Yellow Hair's hand, he said, "You will not need that."

Yellow Hair smiled and handed over the rifle, saying, "You hold it. It is a gift for Sitting Bull." Taking possession of the gun, the *akicita* motioned Yellow Hair to enter.

When his eyes had adjusted to the dim light inside the tipi, he saw a man leaning against his backrest and smiling sardonically at his visitor. Yellow Hair stood where he was and waited for the man to speak.

"*Háu*. Come in, Dakota, and sit down. You are welcome in my lodge," said Chief Sitting Bull.

Yellow Hair saw that the man's eyes were black in color. His eyelids drooped on the outer edges, giving him a world-weary countenance.

"I have come far to meet the great medicine man Sitting Bull. I have brought a new kind of gun as a gift. It fires eight shots without reloading."

Sitting Bull's eyes widened; he reached out and took the repeater from the *akicita* soldier. He ran his hands over the gun, sighted it, and said, "You must show me how it works. But first we will smoke the pipe."

After the pipe had been passed between them, Yellow Hair spoke of the troubles in Minnesota, how he had come to be in Lakota country, and about the soldiers killing his wife and son.

"I am sorry for what happened to your family. We have heard of Whitestone Hill. We have also heard of your troubles in the East. Last winter, Little Crow passed through and asked us to join in his fight against the white soldiers, but as long as they leave us in peace, we will not go on the warpath."

"What do you call Whitestone Hill? Is that leaving your people in peace?"

"What happened at Whitestone Hill happened to the Yanktonai; we are Hunkpapa."

"You are all Lakota. Before long, the same will take place in your village. But enough of this talk. Come, I will show you how to rapidly fire eight shots."

Yellow Hair handed Sitting Bull the leather pouch when they were outside and said, "This is what the soldiers carry. It contains forty cartridges."

It took but a few minutes for Sitting Bull to become proficient at loading and firing his new weapon. As not to waste the precious ammunition, they stopped after three firings. Yellow Hair went over to Big Horse, removed one of the holstered revolvers hanging from the saddle horn, and presented it to Sitting Bull. "This also is for you, my friend."

Next to ponies, guns were the most prized possessions of the Lakota. That day, Sitting Bull invited Yellow Hair to live in his lodge. That day, Yellow Hair made a fast and life-long friend.

In the evening, after they had eaten and the women and children had left them alone, Yellow Hair said to Sitting Bull, "These new guns need a special kind of ammunition. You saw those metal cartridges."

"Yes, I know. But we can trade for what we need."

"I do not think so. These guns are new. I do not think the traders will have cartridges for them. But we will see."

"If the traders do not have what we need, perhaps the Slota will."

"The Slota?"

"A band we trade with from the North, Grandmother's land. They are half-breeds . . . half French and half Indian."

Yellow Hair felt certain there was only one way to get cartridges for their guns, and that was to take them from the soldiers. However, he refrained from saying anything more.

When the time came, he would tell the chief of the plan he had devised.

Sitting Bull and Yellow Hair hunted elk and deer together in the Black Hills. One day, as they dressed a kill, Sitting Bull told Yellow Hair why *Pa Sapa* were sacred.

"These hills were given to the Lakota by *Wakaŋ Taŋ'ka* as a storehouse, so that in time of want, we would always have a source of food."

For two moons they sought to obtain cartridges for their guns. They tried three different traders. Two of which wanted to trade for the guns themselves. The Slota had been and gone. They had offered three muskets, lead, and powder for one of the rifles.

After the Slota left, Yellow Hair told Sitting Bull there was a way to get all the cartridges they needed plus enough powder and lead for the other guns in his band.

"First, I must cut off my braids. And I will need some White Man clothes."

Sitting Bull looked to Yellow Hair and asked, "Is it necessary to cut your braids?"

"They will grow back. If we succeed, we will have cartridges for a very long time. Listen to my words, my friend; have ears for what I have to say. The soldiers must resupply from the East. They bring their supplies up the river by boat and then load wagons for the trip to the fort the whites call Randall. From there, the supplies are transported to the other forts when needed."

Sitting Bull asked, "How do you know this?"

"I have camped above Fort Randall and observed the boats, the fort, and the comings and goings of the soldiers' wagon trains. I have noticed that there is always one wagon that is last. It is kept apart from the others. I believe it is the wagon that carries the powder and ammunition. They keep it separate so that if it blows, only the driver will be killed. They do the same thing at their forts. The building farthest from all the other buildings is the one that holds the powder and lead." Yellow Hair added, "You should send out scouts to let us know when the next wagon train leaves the fort.

"Now here is my plan."

Chapter Fifty-Eight

26 MARCH 1864:

Twelve miles from Fort Abercrombie—a column of wagons driven by soldiers out of Fort Randall:

"Captain . . . over there. Look!"

"What is it?"

"It looks like a White Man being pursued by the whole damn Indian Nation. And he's comin' right this way!"

"Sergeant, send a detachment to meet and protect him."

"Yes sir."

Coming down the hill, Yellow Hair, dressed as a White Man, was fifty yards in front of one hundred yelping, whooping warriors. From all appearances, he was running for his life.

The Indians saw the soldiers coming their way and broke off the chase. Yellow Hair did not slow down until he reached the safety of the column. A private rode up to him and said, "The Captain's compliments, sir. He asks that you join him at the head of the column as soon as you are able."

In his best Yankee accent, Yellow Hair responded, "I am able now. 'Lay on, Macduff.'"

"The name's Casey, sir."

"Yes, of course it is. That was just my little joke. I'm feeling a bit light-headed. Please lead on."

Getting abreast of the Captain, Yellow Hair said, "I am mighty glad to meet you. My name is Ariesen, Jacob Ariesen, from Concord, Massachusetts."

"I am pleased to meet you, Jacob. My name is Will Farmer, Captain, US Army. But tell me, what are you doing out in this god-awful country all by yourself and being chased by Indians?"

"It's kind of a long story. I was up in the Hills panning for gold when I was set upon by the savages. Thank God my horse was saddled. I had only time enough to get him and myself out of harm's way."

"You'll be safe enough now. With the odds a little more even, it seems the fight has left them."

"I reckon you're right, sir."

"I see the rest of my boys are coming back. We'll be underway in a few minutes. You need anything?"

"Just some water for me and my horse and we'll be fine."

That night, after they made camp and as they ate, Yellow Hair was downright talkative, telling the soldiers around the fire that he had come out West to seek his fortune. But after almost losing his scalp, he thought he'd go back to Massachusetts and join his father's bookbinding business. "It's rather boring work, but it sure beats having your scalp handed to you."

The men laughed, and all tended to agree with that thought.

Bedding down, Yellow Hair chose a spot as close to the out-lying wagon as possible without arousing comment. Posted sentries were on duty—their attention directed outward. A short while after midnight, he heard a coyote's howl, then its mate's answering bay. Yellow Hair knew then that his "pursuers" were in place and ready.

Calmly and deliberately, he rose from the ground, picked up his saddle and walked over to the wagon that he believed held what he was after. It was too dark to see what was inside. And besides, the contents were covered with a long piece of canvas. It *had* to be the powder wagon; why else would it be off by itself? He placed his saddle below the driver's seat and went to get Big Horse. This would be the most dangerous part of the whole endeavor, hitching up

Big Horse. But all went well. Soon he was flapping the reins and saying, "Go, boy, go!"

You had to hand it to Big Horse; he liked to run, even when pulling a wagon. He was gone like a shot and passed the pickets before they knew it.

One picket, a little quicker on the uptake than the others, leveled his rifle and shot in the general direction of pounding hooves. A bullet buzzed Yellow Hair's left ear. The shot woke up the entire camp.

Within minutes of Yellow Hair bolting, the soldiers—realizing what all the commotion was about—had their horses saddled and were ready to give chase. They felt certain they would overtake the renegade in a matter of minutes. After all, he was running in a heavily laden wagon pulled by only one horse.

Soon, Yellow Hair heard the hoof beats closing in behind him. He chanced a look over his shoulder and saw a dark line against the stars—a dark line that was getting nearer by the second. Turning back, he noticed more dark forms in front of him. Two clusters of Lakota, one on either side of where he was headed. They let him pass, then closed ranks and charged the oncoming soldiers.

The two forces collided, but firing a weapon was out of the question. It was too dark and neither side wanted to risk killing or wounding its own. And the risk was great that someone would hit the wagon and blow them all to kingdom come.

It was hand-to-hand combat, at which the Lakota excelled. There were many coups called that night. In the confusion, Yellow Hair made his getaway.

As it turned out, they had made quite a haul. The wagon contained twenty-four, two-foot high-barrels of five hundred musket rounds each. Lead ball, a powder charge, and wadding, all packaged together for quick loading—by musket standards. There were also five boxes stamped

Spencer Repeating Rifle Co. Boston, Mass. Each box held a thousand rounds of metallic cartridges.

Sitting Bull had the musket ammunition distributed to the men of his band. The cartridges were divided evenly between himself and Yellow Hair, seeing as how they were the only ones who owned repeaters. Yellow Hair took his allotment to the Black Hills where he hid it in a small cave. The cartridges would be safe and dry there. The opening was small and narrow; to enter, he had to lie on his stomach and twist and turn his body until the crevice widened a few feet in.

He returned from secreting his cache to find his friend sitting outside his tipi. Sitting Bull smiled and asked, "Where did you get the White Man clothes?"

"There was a man in *Pa Sapa* looking for the yellow iron. He was kind enough to give me the clothes off his back. Right down to his boots."

"You killed him?"

"No, I left him in a red union suit tied to a tree. He has probably worked himself free by now."

"A union suit?"

"It is something the whites wear to make themselves look ridiculous."

The following day, Yellow Hair said goodbye to Sitting Bull and left the camp to go about his business—the business of killing soldiers. He would watch a fort from high ground until he was sure of the soldiers' routine. When they came out to cut trees for firewood or to tend the livestock, he would aim his rifle at the first man he decided had to die that day, then swing the Spencer on the other men, dropping as many as he could with his allotted eight shots.

He had become proficient with the rifle . . . and with the killing of men. He averaged three men per eight shots. By the time the soldiers in the fort could mount a patrol to chase him, he was long gone.

Eventually, word got back to the villages about the strange, fair-haired one killing their enemy. It was not long before the people of the Lakota were calling him Hokšíla iyé tuwe kté or He-Who-Kills-Soldiers.

At the beginning of the Moon When Cherries Are Ripe, Yellow Hair heard that Sitting Bull was camped at the mouth of the Little Missouri, by a place called The-Hunting-Ground-Where-They-Kill-The-Deer. Today it is known as Killdeer Mountain. Seeing as how he had not laid eyes on his friend since right after the Great Ammunition Steal, he decided to go north for a visit.

It was good to see Sitting Bull again. The chief had heard of Soldier Killer and surmised it must be Yellow Hair.

"You are getting well-known among the Lakota, and it is not only by the Lakota that you are known. The soldier chiefs have offered six American ponies to any Indian who tells where you can be found or brings you in—dead or alive. It is all the same to them. They believe Soldier Killer and the one who stole their powder and ammunition are one and the same."

"It is nice to be wanted," responded Yellow Hair.

"This is serious, my friend. You have nothing to fear from us Lakota in the North. But those to the south that have signed the White Man's treaties and gave their land away may cause you trouble. We call them Loafs-Around-the-Forts. They will sell you out to gain favor with the whites."

"I will be careful. Now tell me, how has the hunting been?"

Sitting Bull started to tell of a great bull buffalo he had taken down with only one shot when a commotion from outside his lodge interrupted the story. "Let us go and see what the excitement is about," said Sitting Bull.

Once outside, they learned that people were setting up their tipis nearby. Sitting Bull asked a brave who they were.

"They are from the East, some Yanktonai and Dakota."

Yellow Hair heard the word Dakota and said, "I think I will go over and see if anyone I know is among them."

He walked through the Dakota camp looking for people he knew, but the band was from the Yellow River Agency. Although a few faces were somewhat familiar, he did not see any old friends. He learned that they had left Minnesota right after the trouble, and had been moving ever since, trying to stay out of the way of the soldiers.

As he started back to the Lakota camp, someone behind him cried out, "Yellow Hair!"

He turned to see Spotted Owl running towards him with a big smile on his face. "I heard you were here. It is good to see you. You cut your braids!"

"Slow down, little friend, catch your breath. It is good to see you also. Is White Tail with you?"

The smile faded from Spotted Owl's face and he looked to the ground as he said, "He has gone south. His spirit left his body in the Moon When Ponies Shed."

"I am sorry to hear that."

"Do not be sad, Yellow Hair. He was happy to go. Before he left, he told me he saw his wife, and she told him she and their child were in the spirit land waiting for him. That when he joined them, he would be young again and there would be good hunting and plenty to eat."

"I am glad for him, but what of you?"

Again, Spotted Owl gazed downward. "I live alone in White Tail's tipi. It is hard because I have no woman to set it up and take it down. And my pony does not like to drag it."

Clasping the boy on the shoulder, Yellow Hair said, "How old are you now? Thirteen winters? I think you are a little too young to take a wife. A wife is much more than someone to put up and take down your tipi. But come with me, there is someone I want you to meet."

As they walked, Yellow Hair asked Spotted Owl if he had had his Vision Quest yet.

"No, we were too busy moving and keeping out of the way of the Long Knives. Then White Tail took sick."

Yellow Hair thought of how badly Little Thunder had wanted to have his vision. As they made their way into the Hunkpapa camp, he said, "I know of a medicine man who might prepare you for your vision."

Arriving at Sitting Bull's lodge, they found him outside talking with the headmen of the Dakota and Yanktonai. Yellow Hair held back until the men had left, then he walked Spotted Owl over and introduced him to the chief. He told Sitting Bull of how the boy's family had been killed at Whitestone Hill. He spoke of the two boys, Spotted Owl and Little Thunder. How they had looked forward to the day they had their vision. He concluded with, "Helping Spotted Owl will be like helping Little Thunder. He needs a medicine man, a holy man, to prepare him. I thought you might do it."

"Yes, it will please me to help the boy. He will live with me while we prepare."

"I thank you, my friend."

"No need, it is the way of the Lakota."

That night, Spotted Owl did not have to erect his tipi. He slept next to Yellow Hair in Sitting Bull's lodge.

Chapter Fifty-Nine

THE NEXT MORNING the camp was in great turmoil. The Long Knives were coming.

"They are only one sleep out and headed this way," reported the scouts.

The people were worried, but their chiefs calmed their fears.

"The soldiers cannot be looking for us. We have done nothing to provoke the soldier chiefs' wrath."

However, as a precaution, the entire camp moved back into the hills.

On the second day, word flew through the village that the soldiers were now nearby. There was a flurry of activity as the warriors selected their best ponies, tied the tails for war, and assembled at the foothills. The women gathered their children. The old men positioned themselves for a good view of the fight . . . if there was to be one.

Sitting Bull, his uncle Pteché Tópa (Four Horns), Yellow Hair, and Spotted Owl rode up a small hill to watch the advance of the soldiers and saw that they were spread out in a long blue line. The infantry preceded the horse soldiers, who were followed by the wagon guns.

The Dakota and the Yanktonai filed into a ravine to the east, where they intended to ambush the Long Knives as they passed.

The Lakota waited for the Bluecoats to draw near. They did not know if the soldiers would attack or not. At length, a man called Šúŋka Háŋska (Long Dog) called out. "Let me go close to them. If they shoot, then we will know they are here for war." He spurred his horse toward the soldiers. When he got within rifle range, he turned to his right and galloped along their line. Immediately, the soldiers started firing at the solitary man. Three hundred guns let loose and not a bullet touched him. Now the Lakota knew the soldiers were there to fight. The Yanktonai and the Dakota had never thought otherwise.

Back on the hill, Yellow Hair turned to Spotted Owl and said, "Return to the village and help protect the women and children."

"No, I will fight!"

"The women and children need your protection. Now go."

Reluctantly, Spotted Owl turned his pony toward the camp.

After he was on his way, Sitting Bull said to Yellow Hair, "That is how I was when I was young. I could not wait to call my first coup."

"It is different today, my friend. Spotted Owl's bow is no match for the repeaters the soldiers use."

"Yes, that is true. We have many soldiers to kill, so let us get to it. It is a good day to die!" Sitting Bull charged down the hill with Four Horns following closely behind.

Yellow Hair took a moment to think of Suni and Little Thunder before he drew his revolver from its holster and shouted, "It is a good day to die!" and followed Sitting Bull and Four Horns into battle.

It was not much of a battle. The Lakota were in a defensive position from the very start. The wagon guns and the repeaters of the soldiers were just too much for the Indians. The soldiers were driving them back toward their camp, but the Lakota fought bravely in the face of superior firepower in order to give the women time to strike the camp and get to safety.

The Dakota and Yanktonais' tactic of ambushing the soldiers from the ravine failed. The soldiers knew they were there and fired into the arroyo, killing thirty men.

Yellow Hair found himself in the thick of it, off on the left flank. He emptied his revolver twice. How many soldiers he killed, he could not say. The air was thick with smoke from the guns; it was hard to see friend or foe. As he paused to reload, the air cleared momentarily and he found himself staring down the barrel of a long gun owned by Private Jeremiah T. Jones of the First Minnesota Volunteers. Private Jones stood his ground and, shaking in his boots, pointed his rifle at Yellow Hair. Private Jones was only seventeen-years-old.

At that moment, Yellow Hair knew with certitude that he was a dead man. As he sat high up on Big Horse, contemplating eternity, an arrow flew past his knee and embedded itself into Private Jones' chest. Private Jones cried out, dropped his gun, and placed both hands on the shaft of the arrow in an effort to extract it. However, he dropped dead to the ground before that task could be accomplished. Yellow Hair swung his head around and saw a smiling Spotted Owl.

He said to the boy, "Come with me. We must make a stand to give the women time to get away." He whipped his horse to a gallop and headed west toward the foothills. After the first few strides, he looked over his shoulder and saw that Spotted Owl had not moved. Turning his horse around, he rode back. When he reached the boy, he said, "What is wrong? Come with me."

Spotted Owl pointed behind Yellow Hair and said something that Yellow Hair could not make out. He turned to see what the boy was pointing at, but saw only soldiers forging ahead toward the Lakota camp. He asked in a loud voice, "What are you doing?"

Spotted Owl kept pointing at the same place and exclaimed, "Over there! Over there!"

Once again, Yellow Hair looked to where Spotted Owl pointed and saw nothing but a line of soldiers. Finally,

Spotted Owl shouted, "Over there . . . that is the soldier chief from Whitestone Hill. He is the one that told the soldiers to kill our people."

Yellow Hair jerked his head around for a third time and saw the man who was responsible for the death of his wife and son. An officer on a white horse with his sword drawn, urging his men onward.

Heedless of the bullets flying by, Yellow Hair steadied his horse, drew his rifle, and took careful aim.

Time slowed down.

The man, of course, was Captain William A. Murray of Boston, Massachusetts. A year earlier, he had become the father of a beautiful, fair-haired son. The boy was back in Minnesota with his mother. Mary, sweet Mary. She has her life back because of the child, and that has made Captain Murray very happy. He has plans for his son. One day he will follow in his father's footsteps and go to West Point. On graduation day, Captain and Missus Murray will be the proudest parents in attendance.

The bullet ripped into Captain Murray's right side, traveled left, and came to rest in his heart; the heart that so loved his wife that he stole a child after killing its mother.

Yellow Hair watched the Captain fall from his horse, never relinquishing the grip on his sword. It was as though he was looking at many individual photographs, each picture representing a fraction of a second in time. It seemed to take forever for the man to go down. When the Captain finally lay dead upon the ground, time telescoped back to normal.

Something is not right, but now is not the time to worry about it.

He looked to Spotted Owl who once again had a large smile on his face.

At least someone is enjoying himself.

"Come. If we do not hurry, we will be cut off from the others."

Together, they set off for the foothills. When they arrived, Yellow Hair told the boy in no uncertain terms that he was to go to the camp and help the old men move the ponies. Spotted Owl started to protest, but Yellow Hair stopped him before he could utter a word.

"Your arrows are no good against an enemy that fires his guns from far away." Softening his voice, he added, "You have two coups; you killed an enemy and you saved a fellow warrior's life. That is very good for your first battle. There will be many battles and many more coups in your future. But for now you must do what I tell you."

Saying not a word, but smiling because he knew that Yellow Hair would tell of his coups at the Kill Dance, Spotted Owl turned his pony and headed back to camp.

The Lakota held off the soldiers as best as they could and made them fight for every inch of ground. Nonetheless, they were forced back into the hills.

With the soldiers right on their heels, the Indians passed through their camp and saw that the tipis had not been moved and the meat supply had not been saved. The women had not had enough time to do anything more 'than gather their children and run.

The braves met up with the rest of their band about ten miles upriver where they thought they would be safe. They had no way of knowing that the orders from the soldier chief were to take and destroy the camp, not to pursue the Indians.

To Spotted Owl's great disappointment, there was to be no Kill Dance. The people had work to do. For the next few days, the men would have to hunt the buffalo for meat and secure new skins to cover the lodges that would have to be built. The women and young girls would cut the pine lodge poles while the old men and boys tended to the ponies.

Within a few days, the people would have meat and lodges once again. They would not take handouts from the whites as their brethren had done at the agencies to the south. However, before the hunt, before the poles could be cut, the people of Sitting Bull's band needed to rest.

Yellow Hair lay on his buffalo skin looking at the stars and thinking of the man on the white horse. He wondered why his death did not set him free from the sadness that he held in his heart. For eight moons, he had lived to kill the men responsible for the murder of his family. Short of that, he killed anyone who wore the hated blue uniform of the Long Knives. Now that he had killed the man most responsible, he felt nothing. And what was worse, the hate he had felt when he first learned of Suni and Little Thunder's deaths was rapidly dissipating.

Was it because he understood the workings of the army? Whoever the man on the white horse had been, he was only carrying out someone else's orders. Yellow Hair could not go up the chain of command killing everyone who had had a hand in the events at Whitestone Hill. Where would it stop? With the Secretary of War? With the President?

For now, he would remain with Sitting Bull. He would stay to look after Spotted Owl. With a look to the sleeping boy and a sigh, Yellow Hair turned on his side in the hope that he would be able to sleep and, with sleep, obliterate his demons . . . at least for a few hours.

Early the next morning, the makeshift camp was fraught with activity. The Yanktonai and the Dakota were each going off in their own direction. The Dakota went north. The Yanktonai traveled southwest.

At mid-morning, the Hunkpapa scouts brought back word that there were buffalo to the west, on the other side of the Elk. There were also stands of lodge pole pines in the area. Therefore, the band packed up what little they had and moved toward the buffalo.

Yellow Hair stayed with the Hunkpapa until the end of the Moon of the Snow-Blind. He stayed the winter because he wanted to be on hand for Spotted Owl's Vision Quest. He also had things of his own to work through. He had come to the conclusion that killing for killing's sake was not going to free him. He did not think he was ever going to be free from his torment. It had been almost two winters since he first heard of Suni and Little Thunder's deaths, three since he had last laid eyes on them. And he missed them every day of his existence. Sometimes he wondered if White Tail had actually seen his wife as he lay dying. Yellow Hair also wondered if his mother had seen his father before she died.

Did White Tail's wife and my father say those things about being together in the spirit land? Could it be true that one day I will be reunited with Suni and Little Thunder?

He stayed until the snow receded. He wanted to cross the mountains and go to the Big Water. He wanted to see California, the land his father was taking him to when fate intervened and he became a Dakota. Furthermore, there was a price on his head. Someday, somewhere, someone would take a shot at him to collect the bounty. He did not want to stay with Sitting Bull any longer because his presence, if the Long Knives knew he was there, might give them an excuse to raid the village.

A few days before his departure, he retrieved what was left of his ammunition in *Pa Sapa*. He packed as many rounds as he could carry and gave the rest to Sitting Bull.

On the day of his departure, Spotted Owl presented him with a bow and a quiver full of arrows that he had made himself. In return, Yellow Hair unbuckled the holster holding his revolver and handed it to the boy.

Spotted Owl had wanted to go along, but Yellow Hair told him he had to stay and help defend the Lakota homelands. "Sitting Bull will need many braves in the coming moons. I am going away because I do not want to fight anymore, but there will be many battles and plentiful coups for you."

Sitting Bull walked up as Yellow Hair spoke those words. "So, you do not want to kill soldiers anymore?"

"I will if I have to, but I remember what an old friend once said to me when I first became a Dakota. He said the older he became, the less he hated. He was right. It is hard to hold on to hate."

"Your friend was wise. There is no hate in my heart. If the whites would stay off our land, and if the soldiers would not attack us, I would make war only on the Crow. Not from hatred; we fight the Crow because that is the way it has always been."

Nodding to his two friends, Yellow Hair said, "It is time for me to go." He reached out to Spotted Owl and shook hands in the crosswise fashion of true friendship. Then he did the same with Sitting Bull.

Mounting Big Horse, he said, "Look for me in one . . . maybe two . . . winters."

But he would not see his friends again in one or two winters. It would be much longer than that before the three of them sat together again and smoked the sacred pipe.

He rode southwest until he intersected with the Holy Road, or the California-Oregon Trail, as the whites called it. The same road he started on fifteen winters earlier. It was clearly marked by wagon wheel ruts if nothing else, but occasionally he came across a marker telling him he was on the right track.

There was snow still on the Green Horns, and at one point, he passed within one hundred yards of the cave that held the mortal remains of Big Jim Cody.

He eventually crossed the mountains and descended to the sea.

Chapter Sixty

FIFTEEN HUNDRED MILES to the east, in St. Paul, Minnesota, a woman sits in her rocker doing needlepoint. Every now and then, she looks up from her work and gazes—with love—at the sleeping figure on the bed before her. Hearing a knock upon the door, she puts down what she is doing and walks into the outer room. She opens the door to a familiar face.

"Why, Corporal, it is so nice to see you."

"I don't want to disturb you, ma'am, but I heard you was leaving for Boston and I thought I'd come over and say good-bye before you go."

"That was very mindful of you. Please come in. I'll make us some coffee if you'll tend to the fire in the stove."

"I don't want you to go to no trouble on my account, ma'am."

"Don't be silly. I was just thinking of making a cup for myself. Now, you get the wood from the back porch and I'll get the coffee on the stove."

The two sit in silence while they wait for the coffee to heat. After a few minutes, the Corporal clears his throat and says, "I was hoping to see the boy. Is he around?"

"Yes, he's sleeping in the next room. He's been running around all morning like a holy terror. I just got him settled down a little while ago, and not a minute too soon. I don't think I could have kept up with him a moment longer."

"He's a little whirlwind alright."

Again there is silence until the woman says, "My husband told me how you cared for William Jr. after he rescued him from the savages."

"It was my pleasure, ma'am. By the time we got back, I was quite fond of the little tyke."

"He's fond of you also. And not only because of the presents you've brought him."

The coffee is ready. As the woman stands and reaches for the pot, she says, "Now tell me, Corporal, there is something on your mind; I can tell by your manner. You didn't come here just to say good-bye."

"No, ma'am, I didn't. As I've said, I'm quite attached to the little shaver and I was wondering if I could come and visit you folks when you're back in Boston. I don't get back East all that often, but I'm from New York and I still have kin there. I thought maybe I could stop in on occasion and see how the boy's progressing."

"Why, that's very sweet of you, Corporal. Of course you may. My father's a ship builder. Have you ever heard of the *Chandler Ship Company*?"

"Yes, ma'am, they're a pretty big outfit."

"Well, that's my maiden name . . . Chandler. I'll be living with my parents. I'll give you the address before we go."

"Thank you, ma'am."

"If you ever decide to leave the army, my father can always use a man who's as good with his hands as you are. That cradle you made for William Jr. when he was a baby was a beautiful piece of work."

"I've always had a knack for working with wood, but I'm afraid the army's my life. Tell me, will William Jr. be going into the family business?"

"It's a bit early to speculate on that. My father hasn't laid eyes on him yet and already has him running the shipyard. He and Mother had only girls, so Father thought he would have no one to take over the business. We're fourth generation ship builders, you know, so an heir was very much on Father's mind."

"Ship buildin' ain't a bad business to be in, but the Captain told me on more than one occasion that he wanted the boy to follow him to West Point."

"Yes, I know. We discussed it also. However, I think we will all have to wait and see what William wants."

With an embarrassed smile, the man says, "Reckon I better be leaving and get out of your hair."

"It's always good to see you, Corporal."

As an afterthought, the woman adds, "I know that because of the difference in rank, you and my husband were not close, but he always spoke highly of you. He told me if not for you, William Jr. might not have made it here. He said it was an arduous trek for grown men, let alone a small, helpless baby.

"I will expect you to visit us when we're back in Boston. And thank you for everything you've done for William Jr."

"That's alright, Missus Murray. And you'll see me for sure the next time I get back East. You two have a fair journey."

With that kind wish, Corporal Alfred Cooper takes his leave.

Chapter Sixty-One

YELLOW HAIR reached the continental coast and met the Ulseah, or the people of *Whosshee*, as they called themselves. Things there were not much different; the Americans were moving Indians off their land, sometimes at the point of a gun—sometimes without even the pretense of a treaty. The only two tribes left in relative peace were the Ulseah and their neighbors to the south, the Sayonstla, who were also known as the Siuslaw. They were left alone only because the whites thought their lands worthless.

While with the Ulseah, Yellow Hair was known as Ikdah tu (Tall One). He learned to trap the sea otter and traded their pelts to the men who came by sea expressly for that purpose. Within two winters, he was a wealthy man—in Indian terms. That is when the trouble started. Otsehis (Black Stone) had a daughter by the name of Takmiya (Eagle Woman) and he wanted Yellow Hair to purchase her to be his wife.

Yellow Hair repeatedly said no, that he was not interested in a wife. Black Stone took his attitude as an offense. It looked like there would be a showdown of sorts between the two, but one day the village awoke to find that Yellow Hair was gone.

Instead of going south into California, as was his original intent, he traveled north. He had heard that the Indians who lived under the protection of the Grandmother, Queen Victoria, were treated with respect. This he wanted to see for himself. He and Big Horse crossed into Canada and ultimately ended up with the Haida where he learned to carve totems.

He learned that there were two kinds of totems: the memorial, which celebrates the death of a family member, and the house pole, where animals represent members of the clan. He preferred carving house poles because they presented more of a challenge.

Although he became proficient in the craft, he never accepted payment for his work. He would allow the family to feed him while he worked on their pole, but that was all. He did not want to make the same mistake he had made while with the Ulseah. Rich men attract all sorts of trouble to themselves.

Yellow Hair stayed with the Haida for many winters, but he knew in his heart that he was only biding his time. There was something in his future that he would have to confront before he could be reunited with Suni and Little Thunder.

While he was in Grandmother's country, things only got worse for the Sioux on the northern plains of America. There were many other massacres like Whitestone Hill. The whites called it a battle when soldiers entered a village at dawn and killed men, women, and children as they slept or as they ran for their lives. However, when Indians killed only soldiers on a field of battle, the whites called it a massacre.

•••••

A lone rider nears the fort. The sentry on the walkway, just below the parapet, calls down to his Sergeant, "An Indian approaches."

"Only one?" asks the Sergeant.

"Yup . . . I mean yes, Sergeant."

"Damn. What could he want?"

The Sergeant is rightfully concerned. Just last week there was an attack on the wood train and four men were killed. He looks up to the guard and asks, "Is he armed?"

"He's holding an old musket, but he doesn't seem to be in any hurry."

"Can you see anything else out there?"

"No, he's the only thing moving."

The Sergeant orders the private at the gate, "Open up and let's see what he wants."

The massive door swings inward as the Indian reaches it.

With a careful and all-encompassing look at the interior of the fort, the Indian enters. He is met by the Sergeant. Tom Bower is his name. Having had the forethought to send for an interpreter, Sergeant Bower asks, "What do you want?"

"We are camped up at the Tongue in the Powder River country. I have come to ask for lead and powder so that I may hunt. My family is hungry for meat."

"Are you a friendly?"

"I am a friend of the White Man. I do not make war. I hunt."

What harm can a little lead and powder do? Isn't it better to make a friend than an enemy?

Turning to a private on his right, he tells the man to get a ration of ammunition—forty rounds.

While waiting for the private to return, the Indian's eyes never stop moving. They take in everything—the thickness of the walls, the number of men on duty, and where they are posted. He makes note of the wagon guns. He counts the buildings.

The private comes back with the ammunition and hands it to the Indian, who says, "My family will now have good hunting." He does not mention that his "family" is six thousand strong, two thousand of them warriors. Now that he has reconnoitered the fort, he will report to the chiefs. They will decide the best way to kill the Bluecoats who inhabit the hated fort known as Fort Phil Kearny. The Indians know it as Buffalo Creek Fort.

The scout's people are camped on the Tongue River. They consist of Northern Cheyenne, Arapaho, and Lakota Sioux. Within the Lakota are bands of Minneconjou, Oglala, Hunkpapa and Brûlé. The chiefs are, among others, Maȟpíya Lúta (Red Cloud) and Tamílapéšni (Dull Knife). Also in the camp is a young war chief by the name of Crazy Horse.

Three sleeps later, the chiefs and headmen of the tribes assemble to hear the report of the scout. He tells them of the heavy fortifications and the wagon guns, and that to try to take the fort would result in the loss of many braves.

He finishes his report and is sent on his way. It is time to come up with a plan for taking the fort and rubbing out the soldiers. Each chief, in turn, stands and gives his thoughts on the matter. This process takes hours and when the last chief has spoken, there is quiet in the council lodge.

A young man stands and says, "I know how we can get at the soldiers."

The older men look at him and one says, "As a courtesy, you were allowed to attend this council, but we have serious matters to decide today. You young men want to charge the fort and throw your lives away. I ask you, what good is that? Afterward, the fort will still be there."

The young man says nothing, but remains standing, looking down at the older men.

There is silence in the lodge until a voice rings out, "We will hear what he has to say. We must have ears for all points of view." It is Apáhaka (Hump), a Minneconjou chief and uncle to Crazy Horse.

The young man thanks his uncle and then speaks, "When we attacked the woodcutters outside the fort, I noticed a place that we could hide two thousand braves. If they were there, ready for ambush, we could have a few braves attack the woodcutters again. But this time do it closer to the fort so the gunfire can be easily heard by those inside. When soldiers are sent out to investigate, we can decoy them to where our warriors will be hiding. It is a perfect place, steep hills all 'round, and no way out if we surround them."

Crazy Horse finishes speaking and once again there is silence in the council lodge. After a few moments and a few whispers among the chiefs, he is asked to elaborate on his plan.

Chapter Sixty-Two

THE DAY: 1 DECEMBER 1866, as the whites count time. It is very cold and there is snow atop the ground.

Colonel Henry B. Carrington sits in his office at Fort Phil Kearny reading the latest dispatch from the War Department when there is a knock on his door. Without looking up, he calls out, "Enter."

The Sergeant looks nervous, but says what he has come to say. "Sir, we're getting low on wood."

"What? We just had a detail out there last week."

"No sir, that was two weeks ago. We lost four men then."

"I know how many men were killed, Sergeant!"

"Yes sir. But with the weather we've been having lately, we're using up wood at a faster pace."

"Then organize a detail and send it out, and I want an officer to lead it. Get that new man, Grummond."

"Yes sir."

As an afterthought, the Colonel asks, "Any Indians lurking about?"

"No sign of any, sir."

"Well, make sure the detail is properly protected."

"Yes sir."

Subsequent to leaving the Colonel's office, the Sergeant makes his way to the officers' mess where he finds Captains Fetterman and Powell in conversation. As he nears their table, he overhears Captain Fetterman state, "Give me eighty men and I'll ride right through the entire Sioux nation."

Captain William J. Fetterman is a veteran of the war. He served under Ulysses S. Grant and he thinks Colonel

Carrington's methods in dealing with the Indians are too passive.

The Sergeant approaches the table. "Excuse me, sirs. I'm looking for Lieutenant Grummond. The Colonel wants him to head the escort of a wood-cutting detail."

Captain Fetterman orders the Sergeant to get the men together and informs him that he will see to Lieutenant Grummond.

After the Sergeant has gone, Fetterman says to Powell, "I don't know about you, but I'm tired of sitting on my backside. This may be an opportunity for some action. I'm going to the Colonel and ask to take Grummond's place."

Captain Powell does not think much of the idea and says so. "It's freezing out there and all you'll be doing is watching men cut wood and freezing your . . . your fingers off. They'll be close enough; if we hear gunfire, we'll be out there pronto. Then you'll have your action."

"Maybe you're right. Even so, I'm going to ask the Colonel to allow me to lead the relief party if one is needed."

"Alright, Bill, but I'm going to sit here and have another cup of coffee . . . and don't forget to give Grummond the good news," says Powell somewhat sarcastically.

• • • • •

Ten miles away, two thousand braves wait in makeshift shelters for their scouts to relay word that a wood train has left the fort. The council had adopted Crazy Horse's plan and the warriors readied themselves by painting their faces and tying war ribbons to their ponies' tails. They left the next day for the three-day trek to Buffalo Creek where they now wait for the signal that will send them into battle.

At mid-morning, the lookouts see the first flashes of sunlight off the hand-held mirrors the scouts use to relay messages. It is as fast as the singing wires—or the telegraph, as the whites call it. The messages say that a wood train has left the fort.

The braves separate into four groups. The two largest, each a thousand strong, go where the ambush is to take place. The Cheyenne and Arapahos conceal themselves on the west side of the depression, and the Lakota on the east. The other two groups are made up of ten men each. One will attack the wood train; the other will be the decoys that lead the soldiers to their doom.

Within minutes, they are mounted and on the way to their appointed positions. Crazy Horse and the decoys secrete themselves just below the rim of Lodge Trail Ridge on the far side from the fort. The two main forces split up. Some take positions behind boulders, while others, still mounted, hide below the ridges. The men who are to attack the wood cutters ride to catch up with their quarry.

The Indians fire the first shot thirty minutes before noon. The party that attacked the train does try to kill soldiers, but their priority is to draw the Bluecoats out of the fort.

Hearing the gunfire, Captain Fetterman rushes to Colonel Carrington's office, and without bothering to knock, goes in to inform the Colonel that a relief party is needed.

"Yes, Captain, I am aware of that. I heard the shots. I want you to take the 18th Infantry and the 2nd Cavalry and go to the aid of the wood train. They're both at only half-strength, but that should be sufficient to chase away the Indians; there's never more than a dozen or so. Under no circumstance are you to cross Lodge Trail Ridge. Your orders are to bring the men of the wood train back to safety."

Displeased because he cannot pursue the Indians, Fetterman dejectedly answers, "Yes sir."

From his place of concealment, Crazy Horse watches Fetterman and his soldiers come out of the fort at full gallop. Then he settles in to await their return.

By the time Fetterman reaches the wood train, the Indians have disappeared. That annoys him to no end. "The base cowards! I warrant there isn't an Indian in all of Dakota Territory who has the courage of one White Man!"

Lieutenant Grummond rides up to Fetterman and tells him there is a man wounded and he should be brought back to the fort.

"Alright, Lieutenant; I'm to bring you all back and then we'll see what the Colonel wants to do about the wood situation."

A little while later, Crazy Horse sees the soldiers returning. He and the other decoys mount their horses and prepare to antagonize Fetterman and his men.

"What's that up there on the ridge, Captain?"

"Where, Lieutenant?"

"Up there on Lodge Trail Ridge. Wait . . . I'll be damned. I believe it's the Indians that attacked us!"

"Well, there's nothing we can do about it. I'm ordered not to go over the ridge. They're out of range, but have your men fire a few shots at them anyway. Let's see what happens."

The soldiers fire but, as expected, the shots have no effect on the Indians. They continue to wave their guns and shake their fists at the Bluecoats below.

"Those sons-of-bitches!" exclaims Fetterman. "Hand me your glass, Lieutenant. I want a better look."

Putting the glass up to his eye, Fetterman's whole demeanor changes and his back goes rigid. He raises himself in his saddle, then sits back down. He hands the glass back without saying a word. Naturally, the Lieutenant wants to know what Fetterman saw, so he raises the glass to his eye and sees three of the Indians standing on their horses, leggings pulled down, shaking their bare rear ends toward the soldiers.

That is the last straw for Fetterman. He tells the Lieutenant to see that the detail gets back to the fort. "I'm going to teach those redskins a lesson they'll never forget."

"With your permission, sir, I'd like to accompany you. I'm itching to teach a lesson also."

With permission granted, Lieutenant Grummond turns to Sergeant Bower and gives the same order, "See them back to the fort."

"Ah … ah …"

"What is it, Sergeant?"

"I've got an itch, too, sir."

"What do you think, Captain?"

"Alright, Lieutenant, but let's get a move on before the whole dang detail volunteers. Corporal Littlejohn, see the detail back to the fort. Bugler Metzler, sound 'Charge.'"

With the acquisition of Grummond and Bower, Captain Fetterman's command now numbers exactly eighty-one soldiers.

When Fetterman and company start up the hill, Crazy Horse and the other decoys retreat a bit. Not too far, just enough to keep the soldiers interested. They stay on the crest until the last possible moment, then descend to the other side. Keeping just out of reach of the soldiers, they pretend to be running for their lives.

It is just noon as the soldiers come down the far side of Lodge Trail Ridge. The cavalry overtakes the men of the infantry. At the bottom runs Peno Creek. The soldiers reaching the creek is the signal for the Indians to attack; by then, all the soldiers, infantry and cavalry, will be too far into the trap to escape.

As soon as the first soldier splashes across the creek, the Arapaho and the Cheyenne pour out of their hiding places on the west, and the warriors behind the ridge top come down to join in the fight. On the east, the same thing takes place, and before the soldiers know what is happening, they are in hand-to-hand combat. The infantry is the first to be wiped out. The cavalry makes it to the protection of nearby boulders and turn their horses loose. It is there that they make their last stand. There are so many braves trying to get at too few soldiers that the braves get in each other's way.

Near the end of the battle, the warriors on the outer edge stop to watch an amazing sight. The young bugler, Metzler, who had not yet reached his majority, stands with many arrows sticking out of him. But he fights on. He uses a musket as a club, and when that breaks, he takes the bugle hanging from his belt and starts to clout any Indian that gets near him. One by one, the Indians back away. They respect a brave enemy. This boy has fought with courage, with more courage than any other soldier. At least ten arrows pierce his young body. As the braves pull away, he looks about wondering why the fighting has stopped. He does not know it, but he is the last man standing, and the Indians do not want to kill him. But too late, he is already dead; he throws his bugle at the nearest brave as he falls to the ground.

The trap had been sprung at noon. Half an hour later, all eighty-one of Fetterman's Bluecoats were dead.

The Indians strip the soldiers of their clothing and collect their weapons. The Arapaho warriors round up the infantry's horses. The Cheyenne and Lakota disfigure the bodies. That is, all but Adolph Metzler's. They tenderly remove the arrows from his body and cover him with a buffalo robe.

As they mutilate the bodies of the other soldiers, the Cheyenne think of Sand Creek and the Lakota remember Whitestone Hill and Blue Water Creek.

In the irony of all ironies, the man who said that, if given eighty men he would march "right through the Sioux Nation," now lies dead of a self-inflicted gunshot wound. He took his own life rather than face his enemies as his teenage bugler had.

The battle came to be known as the Fetterman Massacre by the whites. However, to this day, the Northern Cheyenne, the Arapaho, and the Lakota refer to it by its rightful name, "The Battle of One Hundred Slain."

Ten winters will pass before the Cheyenne and the Lakota have another victory so complete. During that time, the United States pursues its policy of taking the Indians' land. Year after year, soldiers are sent onto the plains to subdue the Lakota bands that prefer hunting to sitting around a fort accepting handouts from the White Man.

Hunters are labeled unfriendly. That means not only are the men of the tribe fair game, but their women and children are as well.

Chapter Sixty-Three

IN THE SUMMER OF '76, two men look out of an office window and watch a young boy apply tar to the seams on the hull of a ship.

"He's a good worker. Of course, I have him only during the summer months when he's out of school."

"You must be very proud of him."

"I am, Mister Cooper."

"When I saw your daughter this morning and she told me he was here, I thought you might have taken him into the business."

"No, I'm sorry that is not the case. My daughter insists he go to school until his eighteenth year."

"Then what?"

"Well, he says he wants to go to West Point. But I think it's more his mother speaking than him. She's been selling him on the idea since he was knee-high to a grasshopper."

"How old is he now?"

"Fourteen. I understand you were with my son-in-law when he came upon him."

"I can remember when I could hold him in the crook of my arm."

"I never wanted Mary to marry a military man. There were so many rich, eligible men calling on her back then. But when I look at that boy, I guess everything worked out for the best. Now, if I can only change his mind about going to West Point, everything will be perfect."

"Well, as Missus Murray once told me, it's up to him to decide."

"Right you are, Mister Cooper. Or is it Corporal Cooper? My daughter told me you were a corporal in her husband's outfit."

"It's Mister. I topped off at sergeant a few years back. I was getting a little long in the tooth for soldiering, so I mustered out last month and secured myself a license to trade with the Indians. But first, I wanted to see some kin back here. And I wanted to see how the boy was doing."

"Are you going to say hello to him?"

"I don't reckon so. He won't remember me. I just wanted to see how he was getting along. Now if you'll excuse me, I have a train to catch."

"Certainly, but next time you come East, you must stop in for dinner. I want to hear all about how you and William found my grandson."

"Yes sir. It will be my pleasure."

Cooper thinks to himself as he walks out of the boatyard that Mister Chandler would *not* like to hear the story of how William Jr. became his grandson. It is a story that has given Cooper nightmares. A story he has been trying to forget for nigh on fifteen years.

• • • • •

A few months before Cooper met with Mister Chandler, and three thousand miles away, Yellow Hair packed up his tools for the last time. He had decided to go home. Well, the last home he had known—he wanted to see Sitting Bull and Spotted Owl once again.

He told no one he was leaving; he just left the village and never returned. In the twelve winters he spent with the Haida, he had kept mostly to himself. Of course, he had made friends, but he would allow no one to get close to him. It seemed that every time he let someone into his heart, they were taken from him. He was half convinced that Sitting Bull and Spotted Owl were dead. Still, it felt right to make the journey. Something was pulling him back to the plains of America.

He stayed in Grandmother's country until he was over the mountains. Then he angled south and crossed the Medicine Road (the US-Canadian border) north of where the Milk River separates from the Missouri. Shortly thereafter, he came across a small band of Sans Arc Lakota and inquired of them if they knew where Sitting Bull was camped.

"We are on our way to Sitting Bull's camp. Many are there and many more are coming," answered the headman.

Yellow Hair asked why so many were going to Sitting Bull.

"Sitting Bull has sent out runners to all the bands and tribes telling us the Long Knives were coming to kill us and that only by uniting could we be safe."

The whites are still killing us Indians for our land. Back in the Blue Earth Valley, they tried starvation, and look what happened. The people rose up, and more whites died than Indians.

He decided that he would ride along with the Sans Arcs.

Two sleeps later, they crested the last hill and Yellow Hair beheld the great camp for the first time. Two thousand lodges stretched out along the Rosebud River. Each band had its own camp circle. The Cheyenne, who had joined the Lakota to fight the Long Knives, occupied the place of honor to the north. Then the Sans Arc, the Minneconjou, the Oglala, and the Brûlé. The Hunkpapa anchored the camp. Next to the Hunkpapa were small camp circles made up of Dakota, or Santee Sioux, who had been driven out of Minnesota fourteen winters back. Camped with the Hunkpapa were Blackfeet and Two Kettle Lakota. The Arapaho camped with the Cheyenne. The big camp ran for miles, and within it were the finest horse soldiers in the world.

When they reached the camp of the Sans Arc, the people Yellow Hair had been traveling with broke off. He continued on to the Hunkpapa village and went looking for Sitting Bull. Not an easy task given the large number of lodges.

He stopped to ask a woman who was building a fire where he could find the chief.

Without looking up from what she was doing, she answered, "He is gone."

"Gone? Gone where?"

"On the warpath."

Yellow Hair thought he must have misunderstood. The camp certainly did not look to be on a war footing. Everyone was going about their business in a calm manner. This was not a village that feared soldiers would attack at any moment. He was about to ask his question again when someone behind him said, "Yellow Hair?"

He turned to see a man and a woman standing a few feet off to his right. They were both of about twenty-five winters.

Taking a few steps in their direction, he asked, "Yes, I am Yellow Hair. How do you know me?"

The man smiled and said, "Yellow Hair, it is I, Spotted Owl. But now I am called Šaké Matȟo. "

With joy in his heart, Yellow Hair said, "It is good to see you, Spotted . . . I mean, Bear Claw."

"Bear Claw is the name Sitting Bull gave me because of my courage in battle. But come, let us smoke the pipe and talk." Pointing south, he added, "My lodge is over this way."

They started walking and the woman fell in step behind them. After a few paces, Yellow Hair asked, "Who is the woman?"

"She is my wife. Her name is Wakíŋyela Ská."

"She is beautiful, and the name White Dove suits her."

"Yes, she is beautiful."

They walked the rest of the way in silence. Once settled within Bear Claw's lodge, Yellow Hair asked if it were true that Sitting Bull was on the warpath.

"Yes. Last winter the Agent at Fort Peck sent out word to all the bands on the prairie that we had one moon to report to an agency or we would be considered hostile.

"At the time, we were camped at the mouth of the Powder, and to get to Standing Rock would have taken us, because of the deep snow, ten sleeps. Sitting Bull did not want to bring women, children, and the old through the snow. It was very cold and many would have died. Besides, our ponies were thin and weak; they could not drag our tipis. And we knew there was not enough food at the Agency to feed us. So Sitting Bull sent word to the Agent that, come spring when the snow melted, we would report.

"When spring came, our relatives at Standing Rock told us Three Stars was making ready to come after us. That is when Sitting Bull sent out word for the tribes to come together. We moved to the Rosebud to put distance between ourselves and Three Stars. But yesterday, the scouts saw him and about fifteen hundred soldiers coming our way. To protect the village, Sitting Bull and Crazy Horse took our warriors out to meet them."

"Crazy Horse is here?"

"Yes. He is here with his band."

"I would like to see him, but why are you not with Sitting Bull and Crazy Horse?"

"I was with a hunting party when they left. It takes plenty of meat to feed all the people. Besides, I have many coups. I do not have to prove my courage as when I was young."

Before Yellow Hair could say anything else, they were distracted by much noise outside the lodge. Braves were passing by singing of coups. They were celebrating their

431

victory over Three Stars (General George Crook) in what history refers to as the Battle of the Rosebud.

When Sitting Bull returned, Yellow Hair went to see him. At the sight of his old friend, the chief broke into a big grin. "Where have you come from? We thought you dead."

"I was in Grandmother's country, but I wanted to see you and Bear Claw again so I came back."

That night, Sitting Bull was in a talkative and expansive mood. He told Yellow Hair of the battle, and how they could have wiped out Three Stars if it had not been for his Crow and Ree scouts.

"They were in a small valley; the soldiers were resting on the grass. Most had taken the saddles off their ponies, and they did not put out watchers. But their scouts did not let their guard down. When we attacked, the scouts slowed us just enough to allow the soldiers to get organized. We still whipped them, but we have thirteen dead and a number of wounded."

After loading his pipe, but before lighting it, Sitting Bull said, "Our braves are ready for a fight, but, after today, it may be a while before they get one. Three Stars will not come back soon." Stopping to light his pipe, he continued, "I do not know how long I can keep the camp together. There are many to feed. A camp this size runs off the game and the grass is shortly eaten by our ponies."

Later that night, Sitting Bull told Yellow Hair they would be moving the next morning. "There are buffalo up to the Greasy Grass. By the way, do you still have your Spencer?"

"No, I ran out of ammunition years ago. I stopped using it and it rusted up on me. Besides, I like using a bow when I hunt."

"Yes, I know what you mean. The old ways are vanishing fast, my friend. I still have the revolver you gave me, though I gave the Spencer to my nephew Tȟakhíyuȟa waŋží. Now I have a Winchester. It is a good gun. I tell you this because today I took a Winchester off a dead soldier, and I can fire only one gun at a time." He leaned back, pulled out a .44 Winchester from under a buffalo robe, and handed it, along with a fully-loaded cartridge belt, to Yellow Hair.

"It is good for shooting either buffalo or soldiers."

Accepting the gun, Yellow Hair said, "I thank you, but let us hope that it is only buffalo I have to shoot up at the Greasy Grass."

Early the next morning, the great camp headed north. The column was a quarter mile wide and miles long. They traveled in the same order as they camped, the Cheyenne at the lead, then the Oglala, the Sans Arc, the Minneconjou, the Brûlé, the Dakota and at the end of the column, the Hunkpapa.

It was a remarkable sight. The pack horses dragging tipis or carrying the band's possessions. On the flanks were the pony herds—the wealth of a family. The men rode. The women walked, carrying either a bundle of belongings or an infant child.

The children ran in and out of the column playing the games that all children play. Then there were the dogs, hundreds of them. The *akicita* brought up the rear to protect the people, and to keep those who wanted to slip away from doing so. At the front of the procession rode Sitting Bull, Crazy Horse, and the other chiefs and war chiefs. Yellow Hair rode with Bear Claw and helped him move his ponies along. The scouts rode out in the four directions of the four winds, looking for any trouble that might be coming the column's way. And, of course, there was the dust . . . the ever-present dust.

The Cheyenne reached the Greasy Grass about mid-day. The Hunkpapa did not arrive until twilight was full upon the prairie. When all the camp circles had been set up and their fires were burning, Sitting Bull sent for Yellow Hair and Bear Claw. It was the evening of 24 June 1876—as the whites count time.

Chapter Sixty-Four

SITTING BULL TELLS YELLOW HAIR of his most recent vision.

"At first, I heard a voice say, 'I give you these because they have no ears.' I looked up into the sky and saw soldiers on horseback falling into our camp. Their heads were down and their hats were falling off."

Yellow Hair inquires as to what the vision meant.

"It means that the whites who make war on women, children, and old people are coming to us. Because they were upside down, they will be killed in our camp."

• • • • •

That same night, less than a day's ride to the east, another man sits around a fire speaking to Indians. However, he is no friend of the Indian. He is in Sioux country to kill as many Indians as possible. It does not matter if they are warriors or not. In fact, his tactics demand that he attack the women and children first. He has even written a book telling of this stratagem and has used the ploy before. He assembled his men before daybreak and had them fire into the tipis of peaceful, sleeping Indians— killing mothers, grandmothers, daughters, and anyone else that a bullet struck. His name is George Armstrong Custer. He is a lieutenant colonel in the United States Army.

The Lakota know him as Long Hair.

The column has marched all day. The men are tired, dusty, and hungry. As they tend their fires and prepare their meals, Custer sits in his camp chair and speaks to his Ree and Crow scouts. He tells them something he has not told another soul except his wife. He feels he is on the verge of greatness, and the next few days will cement his place in history.

"Now listen here, boys. When we find the Sioux camp, I need you to scatter their horses so they cannot get away. If we kill us enough Sioux, then I will be the next Great Father."

After taking a pull from his canteen, he continues. "We're supposed to meet up with General Terry and General Crook in two or three days. I need you to find the Sioux before then. If Terry and Crook get into the act, the newspapers will write about them. If we get to the Sioux first and wipe them out, then I'll become the Great Father, and I'll look after you. So tomorrow, I want you to fan out and find me those damn Sioux."

While he is speaking, a Ree scout rides into camp and approaches. Custer says, "What is it?"

"I have found the Sioux. They are west of here."

The news so excites Colonel Custer that he jumps from his chair and starts to pace back and forth. This is what he has wanted. He is so close to being the great hero of the Indian Wars, he can practically see himself in the White House. The public already loves him; all he needs is this one victory. It does not matter to Long Hair that innocent people must die for him to obtain his wish. They are irrelevant, as are the soldiers under his command. The only thing that matters is that he becomes the next President of the United States.

He asks the scout how far it is to the Sioux camp.

"Twelve, maybe thirteen hours," is the answer.

George Armstrong Custer believes that great men must make momentous decisions. He calls to his orderly and instructs him to ask his officers to meet him in his tent immediately. He is going to pull up camp so that he can attack the Sioux at first light. As not to miss his date with destiny, he will lead the Seventh westward into the night.

Just before dawn the next morning, Custer and his men are within ten miles of the great camp. It is here that he splits his force, sending Major Reno to attack from the south. He believes the Indians will run when Reno strikes. He wants to be in a position to the north, to kill the Indians as they flee.

• • • • •

While Custer and Reno advance toward their respective fates, the young boys of the camp drive their ponies to water; the women start fires for the morning meal.

Sitting Bull is in the council lodge when a brave comes and tells him there are many soldiers nearby. Running outside, he looks downriver and sees the column of dust. Through the dust, he sees the blue coats of the Long Knives.

Immediately, the great camp is thrown into a state of panic. There is no time to strike the tipis. Women grab their children and run north, away from the soldiers. The men run for their guns, mount their ponies, and go to meet the invaders. Their only aim at that point is to slow the soldiers' advance to give the women and children time to reach safety.

Yellow Hair was at the river watering Big Horse when he heard the cries and shouts. He looked up and saw Reno's column descending on the camp. He did not have his Winchester with him. He jumped on Big Horse and galloped to Bear Claw's lodge where he grabbed his gun and cartridge belt. By the time he joined the other braves, Reno and his men, for some inexplicit reason, had dismounted and were fighting on foot.

The braves were prepared to retreat if they had to. However, because of their greater numbers, it was Reno and his men who broke and ran. They made for the trees along the river to the northwest. The timber did afford some protection, but the Indians were relentless. They kept up their fire until the trees were obscured by the smoke from their guns. It was then that Yellow Hair heard someone shout out in English, "All those who wish to escape, follow me!"

Yellow Hair watched as the soldiers broke and ran for a second time. They were trying to make it across the river. It is not known what they thought their next move would be. It may be surmised that their only thought at the moment was to get away from the people they had come to kill.

Yellow Hair and the other braves pursued the soldiers to the river's edge. The banks were steep and about five feet high. He stood on the rim, firing at soldiers as they made their way through the water and as they tried to climb the far side. He was so intent on what he was doing that he did not notice the soldier lying just below him at the water's edge.

This particular soldier, in his haste to be rid of the Indians, stumbled and fell down the embankment, losing the grip on his rifle in the process. When he stopped rolling, he found himself on his back with his gun lying not two feet away. Because no one was shooting at him at the moment, he lay there catching his breath. It was then that Yellow Hair ran up to the edge and began firing at the soldier's comrades.

Thinking he would never make it more than a few feet with the fair-haired Indian standing over him, he resolved to eliminate at least that threat. But before he could roll over and pick up his gun, Yellow Hair turned his sights on him. At that instant their eyes met, one man held a gun, the other did not. Yellow Hair knew that he would kill the man. And the soldier was just as certain that he was about to die.

As Yellow Hair looked into the man's eyes, time slowed for the second time in his life. The seconds became minutes, the minutes became hours. The sound and noise of the battle retreated into the far distance until he and the soldier were the only two men in all the world.

Time also slowed for the man lying by the river. It was strange. One minute all he could hear were the sounds of war, the yelling of men, the explosion of gun powder as it sent a bullet or ball on its way. Then all of a sudden, everything was quiet. He could hear the water of the river as it splashed over the rocks on its way south. He could hear the incessant chatter of the birds that had been driven from their homes among the trees. He felt the warm sun upon his body. He looked at the sky. He had never seen it so blue. He took it all in while thinking about his wife and two sons back in Kansas.

Yellow Hair thought of *his* family as he stared down the barrel of his gun at a man who reminded him of a turtle on its back—helpless.

Helpless or not, the man had come to kill, so now he must die.

The man, whose name was Roberts, Private John J. Roberts, started to reach for his gun, but stopped.

Why bother? The Indian has me sighted. It is now my time to die.

CLICK

It was the sound of an empty gun. Yellow Hair was out of ammunition. Time rushed in and the battle once again raged all around them.

Private Roberts was stunned by his good fortune. The Indian's gun was empty! It took him a moment to understand that his life had been given back to him. He reached for his rifle, and while still in a prone position, fired.

Yellow Hair went down. Roberts jumped up and splashed into the river. He was halfway across when a bullet entered his back and severed his spine. He pitched forward, he felt no pain. He could not move his arms or legs. He lay face down in the water, but that was of no consequence. His lungs had ceased to labor.

He wished that he could reach into his coat pocket and pull out the picture he kept there, near his heart—the one of his wife, Anne, and their two sons, John Jr. and Samuel. He wanted one last look at them before he died. But that was not to be.

As Private Roberts' body started its journey downriver, Yellow Hair lay on top of the embankment, his blood soaking into the dirt. He would go to the spirit world; he would see Suni and Little Thunder, but not on this day. The bullet had gone through his left leg and plowed into his right thigh, breaking bone. Unlike Private Roberts, Yellow Hair felt pain.

All the soldiers that were going to make it across the Little Bighorn that day were across and gone. The others were floating in the river or lying on the far bank; the ones that were still alive were trying to reach a small bluff. That is when Sitting Bull rode up and shouted, "Let them go. Let them live to tell the other White Men what has happened here today." Some of his braves obeyed, others did not.

Bear Claw stopped his pursuit and turned his horse at the embankment. He followed the river looking for guns and other booty. He saw braves stripping the dead of their guns and clothes. Eventually he came upon his friend, Male Antelope. He was down at the river washing blood out of a pair of blue-colored pants. Bear Claw did not stop, but shouted "*Háu*" as he passed.

A few minutes later, he came across Yellow Hair and jumped from his pony. He knelt on one knee next to the recumbent body of his friend. He did not have to ask what was wrong. He could see the wounds and the blood pooling on the ground.

Without a word, he lifted his friend and put him across his pony. Yellow Hair had enough strength left to say, "Get my gun. Sitting Bull gave it to me," just before he passed out from the pain and loss of blood.

Bear Claw brought him back to his lodge where White Dove ministered to him. She knew of the healing ways; her father had been a medicine man.

Yellow Hair awoke as White Dove was probing for the bullet. She gave him an arrow to bite down on and continued fishing for the lead. When she had it out, she gave him a concoction to drink and, shortly thereafter, he fell back into a deep sleep. That was how Yellow Hair spent the remainder of the Battle of the Little Bighorn.

Later that evening, he regained consciousness and found White Dove sitting next to him. When she saw that he was awake, she smiled and asked, "Would you like to eat?"

He thought for a moment, "Yes, I am hungry. But what happened? How did I get here?"

"Bear Claw brought you. You had been shot."

"The last thing I remember was firing at soldiers in the river."

"All that Bear Claw told me was that he found you on the bank above the river."

"Do you know what happened to Big Horse?"

"Yes, he is with our ponies. Bear Claw brought him in."

Yellow Hair tried to raise himself into a sitting position and felt pain course through his entire body. With a grimace, he lay back down.

Leaning over to wipe the perspiration from his brow, White Dove said, "You were shot and the ball broke your leg bone. You will not walk for a little while, but then you will be fine. Now I will get you some food."

As Yellow Hair ate, Bear Claw came into the tipi and told him of the day's events.

"We ran the Bluecoats out of our camp and right across the river. What is left of them is dug in on that first bluff to the east. Our men have them surrounded, but they are dug in so good, it is hard to hit them. Sitting Bull said to let them go, but the young braves are having too much fun. We could have rushed them, but too many braves would have been killed."

In between mouthfuls, Yellow Hair had a few questions.

"How did I get shot?"

"You do not know?"

"I cannot remember."

"I did not see you get shot. I found you on top of the riverbank. It is too bad you were wounded; you missed a good battle, although we lost many braves."

"I remember most of it."

"No, not the battle to the south, the one to the north. We rubbed out all the soldiers."

Yellow Hair put down his food and asked, "What do you mean, to the north?"

"I forgot, you slept through that battle," said Bear Claw with a slight grin on his face. "After we ran the soldiers across the river, and our women thought it was safe to return to the village, a dust cloud was seen to the north. It was more Bluecoats, two-fifty, maybe three hundred, in number. Many braves ran to meet them.

"Sitting Bull told some of us to stay in camp to protect the women and children. He feared another attack from the west. I stayed, and tried to see the fight from the Cheyenne camp. But the smoke was too thick; I did not know who was winning. But as the smoke cleared, I saw that all the soldiers were down, but so were many of our braves.

"Someone said that it was Long Hair's outfit because they carried his fork tail flag, but no one saw him."

The Lakota knew Custer well. Years earlier, he opened the "Thieves Road" into the Black Hills. He was the one that announced to the Americans that there was the yellow iron within the sacred hills. He had met the Lakota many times, not in battle, but in the early morning hours when he would kill people while they slept—as was his way.

White Dove returned to take the bowl from Yellow Hair's hands. Turning to her husband, she said, "It is time for Yellow Hair to rest. You go and sit at the fires if you want to tell your war stories."

Bear Claw looked to Yellow Hair and said with a smile, "Now you know who is chief in my lodge."

Yellow Hair thanked White Dove for all that she had done for him, and within minutes he was asleep.

Thus, for Yellow Hair, ended the day of 25 June 1876—as the whites count time.

Chapter Sixty-Five

TWO DAYS LATER, it was decided that the great camp should break up, but first they would go up into the Bighorn Mountains. In four days' time, to celebrate the courage of the young warriors, there would be a Kill Dance, after which the bands would go their separate ways. It would be the wisest course of action. Most believed that the soldier chiefs would send a large force to punish them for their victory at the Greasy Grass.

Sitting Bull spoke to encourage the other chiefs.

"We have defeated the Long Knives three times now, once at the Rosebud and twice here at the Greasy Grass; perhaps now the soldiers will let us be."

No one believed that would come to pass, not even Sitting Bull.

Bear Claw made a pony drag for Yellow Hair and tied it to Big Horse. When it came time for White Dove to fold the tipi, Yellow Hair made his way to the drag as best he could, using his rifle for support. As he sat watching White Dove do her work, Crazy Horse walked up and looking down at Yellow Hair, shook his head.

"You *Wasichus* cannot keep out of the way of a bullet."

"You forget, my friend, I am not a *Wasichu*. I am Dakota."

"Yes, you are. I have come to say farewell until we meet again in battle against the Long Knives."

"I hope that it will not be for many moons."

"Why do you say that? Do you tire of the fight, Soldier Killer?" asked Crazy Horse, using the name applied to Yellow Hair so many winters past.

"I have not been called that for many winters. You say it because you think I do not want to fight the soldiers. I said I hope it will be many moons before we next fight the soldiers not because I do not *want* to fight, but because I want to be by your side when we do so. Because of this leg, it will be many moons before I am able to fight as a Dakota should."

Crazy Horse stepped forward and shook Yellow Hair's hands. "Your spirit will always be by my side, my friend." He turned and walked away without looking back.

By mid-day, the camp was on the move. A few bands slipped away and returned to their respective agencies. They did not want to be thought of as bad Indians and be punished for what had happened at the Greasy Grass.

The chiefs were right; the soldiers pursued all the Lakota that were not at an agency. The ones they did not slaughter outright were forced to give up their guns and ponies and live on a reservation. Sitting Bull and Crazy Horse held out the longest. However, after being guaranteed safe conduct, Crazy Horse and his three hundred braves surrendered. He was dead within an hour of handing over his rifle to the *Wasichus*. He was stabbed in the back by a soldier while two Loafs-Around-The-Fort Lakota held his arms.

Sitting Bull did not surrender. He and his band crossed the Medicine Road and went into Grandmother's country. By then, his band was not as mighty as it once was. Many had left and surrendered because of Bear Coat Miles (Col. Nelson A. Miles), who tracked Sitting Bull and his band relentlessly.

Yellow Hair and Bear Claw stayed with Sitting Bull.

The time in Grandmother's country was a good time for Sitting Bull. He made friends with the Red Coat chief and was accorded the respect he believed due the chief of all the Lakota. Only Sitting Bull's band and a few small bands that still roamed the American plains remained free.

After the Battle of the Little Bighorn, Sitting Bull was a famous man, and the Americans feared him. They did not want him free in Canada where he might bring the tribes together again and precipitate another Indian war. They wanted him back in America, on a reservation where they could keep an eye on him.

The Canadians also wanted him to return to America. There were not enough buffalo to feed the indigenous tribes, let alone the interlopers from America. However, unlike the American government, the Canadians would not use force against peaceful Indians. As long as Sitting Bull and his people obeyed the laws of the land and did not make war on other tribes, they would be allowed to stay.

Because food was in short supply, Sitting Bull and his men would go south into America to hunt the buffalo. But they had to be quick about it and get back over the border before the soldiers knew they were there.

His band had dwindled to sixty lodges. Many had gone back and surrendered at the Agency. It was bad to surrender your guns and ponies to the Americans, but at least you were given beef twice a month in exchange.

Sitting Bull was nearing his second year above the border when the United States sent a commission requesting him to return and surrender at the Standing Rock Agency. Even though the Red Coats were asking him to meet with the commission, he steadfastly refused. When the pressure became too great, he went to one whom he could trust to give good advice and talk with a straight tongue.

Yellow Hair was living with a small band of Santee Dakota that had gone north right after the uprising in '62. Without hesitation, Sitting Bull entered Yellow Hair's lodge and said, "Do you think I should meet with the Americans?"

Yellow Hair was in the process of sharpening his knife and did not look up. He did not think he should give advice to Sitting Bull. Hence, he said nothing.

Sitting Bull would not be put off. "You lived with the *Wasichus*; you know how they think. Can they ever be trusted? Have they, at long last, come to tell us what is true and will they then keep their word?"

Yellow Hair's leg had long since mended, but the injury left him with a pronounced limp. He put the knife aside and made his way over to his friend. Placing one hand on his shoulder, he said, "Do not trust anything they say. Have nothing to do with them."

Turning away from the great man, he limped back to where he had been sitting and picked up his knife. He resumed drawing the blade across the stone without saying another word.

Because of pressure from the Red Coats—and against his better judgment—Sitting Bull decided to meet with the Americans. When he entered the room where the meeting was to take place, he shook hands with the representatives of Queen Victoria. He pointedly ignored the Americans. He and his men sat on the floor facing the commission, whose members sat in chairs.

Sitting Bull listened with a stone face to what the head of the commission had to say. The chairman was Brigadier General Alfred A. Terry. The Lakota referred to him as "One Star." The same General Terry that was on his way to the Little Bighorn River two years earlier to kill the men who now sat before him.

One Star told the Lakota that the Americans wanted only peace, and that, once they turned themselves in at the Agency, they would receive a full pardon. Sitting Bull sat listening to what One Star had to say. He then stood and addressed the commission.

"White Men like to dig in the ground for their food. My people prefer to hunt the buffalo as their fathers did. White Men like to stay in one place. My people want to move their tipis here and there to the different hunting grounds. The life of White Men is slavery. They are prisoners of towns and farms. The life my people want is a life of freedom. I have seen nothing that the White Man has, houses or railways or clothing or food, that we want. What we want is the right to move in open country and live in our own fashion.

"For sixty-four years you have kept me and my people and treated us bad. What have we done that you should want us to stop? We have done nothing. It is all the people on your side who started us to making trouble. We could go nowhere else, so we took refuge here. It was on this side of the line that I first learned to shoot and that is why I came back here again. I would like to know why you came here.

"I did not give you my country, but you have followed me from place to place and I have come here. I was born and raised here with the Red River mixed-bloods, and I intend to stay with them. I was raised hand-in-hand with these people and that is why I shake their hands. That is the way I was taught. That is the way I intend to go on doing. See how I live with these people.

"Look at me. I have ears to hear with. I have eyes to see with. If you think me a fool, you are a bigger fool than I am. This house is a medicine house. You come here to tell us lies, but we do not want to listen to them. I do not wish such language be used to me, nor any such lies told to me in my Grandmother's house. Do not say two more words.

Go back home where you came from. This country is my country now, and I intend to stay here and raise up people to fill it. The country that belonged to us, you ran me out of it. Now you come here and want me to go back. I have come here and here I intend to stay. I want you to go back, and take it easy going back."[5]

Sitting Bull turned his back to the Americans and walked out. He would not be going back to America. At least not then, but in three years' time when the lodges of his band numbered only forty and his people were hungry, he would return.

When a second commission came to Canada and promised him that if he returned to America, he could live with his people wherever he wished, and with the Red Coats urging him to leave, Sitting Bull decided to lead his people home.

On the morning of the day that the Hunkpapa Sioux were to leave, Yellow Hair went to Sitting Bull's lodge. After being seated in the place of an honored guest, he told the old warrior the reason for his visit.

"My good friend, I have come to tell you that I will not be going back with you."

Sitting Bull showed no emotion, but simply asked, "Why not?"

"I do not trust the whites to keep their word. I have lived on a reserve and I did not like it. I know you must go; you are a chief, a leader. Your people will need you to look out for them. I am not needed anywhere. So I will stay with my Dakota friends."

"I will miss our talks. I will miss your friendship, but I understand. If I were not a chief and my life was my own, I too would stay. But my people are hungry and it seems that the only food for them is at the Standing Rock Agency." He added, "Yellow Hair, my old friend, we are getting to be old men. We both walk with a limp and our hair has gone gray."

"Yes, my friend, I feel old and tired. That is why I do not want to go to Standing Rock. I would like to die here among the trees. They remind me of the Blue Earth Valley."

The two men stood and shook hands. Without another word, Yellow Hair walked out of Sitting Bull's lodge. He then went to say good-bye to Bear Claw and White Dove. They were sad to hear that he was staying, but bid him well, as he did them.

Sitting Bull surrendered on 19 July 1881. He was the last of the Lakota to do so. When it came time to turn in his gun, he handed it to his son Sí kȟaŋǧí (Crow Foot) and told him to hand it to the soldier who was waiting to receive it. When it was in the soldier's hands, Sitting Bull said:

"I surrender this rifle to you through my young son. I wish it to be remembered that I was the last man of my tribe to surrender my rifle. I have killed enough White Men. I now wish only to live in peace with the White Man. Our ways are no longer. So I must ask you, how are the young men of my tribe—how is my son—to live? Who will teach him the White Man's ways?"

The Ghost Dance

Chapter Sixty-Six

THE DATE: *12 JUNE 1884.*

The place: The parade ground at the United States Military Academy at West Point, New York.

A woman and two men sit together in the reviewing stand. The older man is Chandler; the other is Cooper. The woman's name is Murray, Missus William A. Murray.

They are there to see Missus Murray's son graduate. Mister Chandler is the proud grandfather. Mister Cooper, an honorary uncle. All three are smiling. Mister Cooper must lean into Missus Murray to be heard over the playing of the band.

"You must be very proud of him."

"Oh, I am. I only wish his father could be here today."

"I believe he's looking down from Heaven."

"Yes, I believe that also."

"I want to thank you for inviting me. You know how I feel about William."

"It would not have been the same if you were not here."

"It was just lucky that this day coincided with my trip back East."

"By the way, how is your trading business going?"

"It's doing quite well, thank you. That is why I came back. I'm expanding and opening a second post at Fort Yates. I had to come back to secure additional suppliers and a more reliable freight company than the one I've been using."

"Did you say Fort Yates? That is where William is to be posted."

Their conversation is interrupted by the increased volume of the band, announcing the arrival of the cadets onto the field.

After the ceremonies, while the families are standing in the courtyard talking with the newly-minted second lieutenants, Mister Chandler addresses Mister Cooper.

"He looks mighty good in that uniform, if I do say so myself."

"That he does. Have you reconciled with the fact that he won't be going into the family business?"

"You never know. He might not take to the army. He's going out West to some hell-hole of a fort. Maybe he'll come into the business before it's all over."

"That's right. Missus Murray mentioned that he's been posted to Fort Yates."

"I believe that's the name."

"That's the hell-hole where I'll be opening my new post."

"My, my, I meant no offense. But to me, anything west of the Mystic River is a godforsaken hell-hole."

"No offense taken."

"Why, this is good news indeed! You can keep an eye on him and let me know if there's anything he needs."

"I'll keep an eye on him alright, but I don't think he'll be needing anything."

"Well, let's go meet his classmates' families and get it over with."

"I'm with you."

Chapter Sixty-Seven

NATURALLY, the United States did not honor its commitment to Sitting Bull. When he surrendered, he was not pardoned. He was arrested, sent to a military prison reserve, and held for two years. Upon his release, he went to the Standing Rock Agency and moved into a log house. A mile away lived Bear Claw and White Dove, though at the time they still lived in their tipi.

A year later, White Dove gave birth to a female child during the Moon of Changing Seasons. The infant arrived at night and under a full moon. As all men, of all cultures, Bear Claw was not allowed to be with his wife. That suited him just fine because, as all men, of all cultures, he preferred not to be present.

Shortly after he heard the first cry, one of the women came out of the tipi holding a small bundle in her arms.

"It is a girl-child," said the woman.

Bear Claw looked at his daughter bathed in the light of the full moon. He would name her Wakȟaŋheža haŋwí (Child-of-the-Moon). One year hence, a male-child was born to the Bear Claw clan. The boy was named John Bear Claw, for his father knew the old ways were gone. He wanted his son to succeed in the White Man's world. John would have his hair cut, go to the White Man's school, and learn their tongue.

Now that he was a father, Bear Claw thought back to Yellow Bird, Yellow Hair's son. White Tail had told him not to tell Yellow Hair of his loss because it would only make matters worse. That was when he was a boy. Now, as a father, he wondered if he had done the right thing. White Tail *did* say there may come a time when Yellow Hair should know of his son. Of course, it was of no consequence now. He would probably never see Yellow Hair again.

Around the time his son was born, Bear Claw heard that a trader had opened a new post at the fort, so he went over to see what was in stock and maybe do a little trading. He entered the store and walked around looking at the items on the shelves. There was only one clerk and he was busy dickering with an old Indian.

"I tell you, your five rabbit skins are not worth more than one pouch of tobacco."

"No, five pouches."

"One is all I can give you."

"No, four."

So it went until the Indian left the post clutching two pouches in his hands.

The clerk then turned his attention to Bear Claw.

"Help you with something?"

Bear Claw was about to say "Yes" when the door to the back room opened and a man emerged. Bear Claw was stunned. It was the one-eyed man who had taken Yellow Bird!

The clerk saw that he was staring at his boss. "Do you want to speak with Mister Cooper?"

After a second or two, Bear Claw found his voice, "No, I must go now."

He hurried outside where he mounted his pony and headed for home. He had a powerful lot of thinking to do and he wanted to do so while he smoked his pipe.

In the end, he decided that there was nothing to be done.

It might be different if Yellow Hair was here, but he is not.

It was the last day of 1884—as the whites count time.

Chapter Sixty-Eight

IN THE YEAR 1890, a Paiute holy man by the name of Wovoka (Wood Cutter) started a new religion. He called it Dance-of-the-Ghosts. Its tenets were that the Christian Messiah was about to return. He would come out of the West and all the White Men would be buried under the ground. Then all Indians, both living and dead, would inherit the earth. Things would be as in the old days, plenty of buffalo and game. The herds of wild horses would also return. However, because the whites had forsaken and killed him, the Messiah would come as an Indian this time. All that was needed to bring the Messiah back was to dance the Dance-of-the-Ghosts. Those that danced would be able to speak with their dead relatives.

The whites feared the Dance. The Indians at the agencies had stopped scratching at the earth, trying to bring forth food that would not grow in such an arid environment. Instead, they danced the Dance-of-the-Ghosts from early morning until late at night. Many told of speaking with the dead.

From the agencies to Chicago to Washington, the officials were worried that the Indians would once again go on the warpath. The settlers near the agencies were driven to fear by the newspapers writing that no white person was safe as long as the Indians danced the Ghost Dance, despite the fact that the religion preached non-violence; the people were only to dance for a short while until the Messiah arrived.

Word came from the Indian Bureau in Washington. The agents were to gather the names of all the "fomenters of the disturbances" and forward them to Washington. Because of his fame and notoriety, Sitting Bull's name headed the list.

Despite what the officials thought, Sitting Bull was a non-believer. The living could not commune with the dead as far as he was concerned.

Washington wanted Sitting Bull arrested, but feared his arrest would spark another Indian war. The local agent, Major James McLaughlin, known as White Hair to the Indians, decided to delay the arrest for the time being.

Meanwhile, word of the Ghost Dance spread north into Canada. At the time, Yellow Hair worked for the trader Jean Louis LeGare. Because he could speak English and most of the Indian dialects of the area, he was a valuable asset to LeGare.

At first, Yellow Hair gave the Ghost Dance no credence at all. However, as time went on and he spoke with more and more people passing through—people who claimed to have first-hand knowledge of friends and relations who had actually spoken with the dead—he wavered in his disbelief. He did not care about a Messiah or Indians inheriting the earth, but if there was a chance that he might speak with Suni and Little Thunder, then this religion would be worth investigating.

Yellow Hair was now an old man of sixty winters; his hair had turned completely gray. Big Horse had died some years back and he had no other pony. It would not be easy to travel to Standing Rock to see if there was anything to the Ghost Dance. Then fate stepped into his life once again. LeGare asked him to drive one of his wagons to Fort Yates. He had forty wagons leaving in a few days to pick up supplies. The goods came up the Missouri a few times a year and were collected by the trader Cooper and held for LeGare.

Yellow Hair jumped at the chance, not only because of the Ghost Dance, but because it was also a chance to see his friends Sitting Bull and Bear Claw. The LeGare train left Fort Walsh on, coincidently, the day Major

McLaughlin received orders to take Sitting Bull into custody without further delay.

While LeGare's train traveled south, McLaughlin decided on the best course of action for taking Sitting Bull. Rather than have the army do it, he would use the tribal police.

• • • • •

In the early morning hours just before dawn, forty-three men gathered outside McLaughlin's office. They wore blue uniforms like the soldiers did. They were known as Metal Breasts to the Indians because of the badges pinned to their chests. It was bitter cold and the men kept moving to keep warm. Their breath and that of their horses hung in the air like a fog. They were waiting for their leader, Lieutenant Bullhead. Most of them were young. They had replaced the older men who had resigned when ordered to arrest Sitting Bull.

At length, Lieutenant Bullhead showed and called the men to him. When they had formed a circle about him, he said, "You know what we have to do. We want to arrest him and get out of there before his Hunkpapa friends can come to his rescue." All the men nodded their heads in agreement.

Bullhead continued, "Five of us will go into the house and the rest of you will spread out to keep away anyone that shows up. I want Sergeants Shave Head and Red Tomahawk to go in with me, also Privates Weasel Bear and Eagle Man. Now mount up. We will proceed slowly; we do not want to wake people along the way with the hoof beats of our ponies."

All was quiet that cold, crisp morning as they rode from settlement to settlement. In time, they came to where the Hunkpapa lived. They reached Sitting Bull's house, dismounted, and fanned out to encircle it. Bullhead looked to the four men he had selected to accompany him into the house and nodded.

He pushed open the door and took a step inside, stopped to light a match to get his bearings, and then went to where the old chief lay asleep. Another match flared and someone lit an oil lamp. The Metal Breasts saw that Sitting Bull was not alone; one of his wives lay next to him. Ignoring her, two of the men grabbed hold of Sitting Bull and pulled him to his feet.

"Get dressed," barked Bullhead "You are going with us."

Stunned and still half asleep, Sitting Bull said, "I will go with you, but first I must dress." While the first two continued to hold him, a third Metal Breast picked up articles of clothing and threw them at him. They were in a hurry to leave because they could hear the sounds of his neighbors outside. As the people arrived and saw the police, they knew that their chief was being taken away.

Again, the Metal Breasts grabbed Sitting Bull, now dressed, and led him to the front door. Before going outside, Bullhead ordered Red Tomahawk to pull the men together at the front of the house and form a semi-circle. He directed his men to move quickly. "We are going out into that crowd. Keep him moving and talk to no one. Wait, I forgot! You, Eagle Man . . . go outside and tell one of the men to find Sitting Bull's horse and tell him to be quick about it. That damn crowd is growing by the minute."

While they waited for the horse, a nervous Bullhead spoke to Sitting Bull: "You do not have to be afraid. We are only bringing you to White Hair so he can tell you of a new home he has for you nearer the Agency. It will be easier for you to help your people if you are near to White Hair."

That was a bald-faced lie. It was a story McLaughlin had concocted to get Sitting Bull to go with the police with minimal difficulty.

Within a few minutes, Eagle Man returned and said that the horse was outside.

"Now we go," said Bullhead, and the five men exited the house, bringing Sitting Bull with them. As soon as they were outside, the other Metal Breasts surrounded them. They tried to get to their horses, but the people would not move out of the way. Bullhead and his men made only a few paces before they were stopped by the shouting crowd.

"Sitting Bull, do not go with them!"

"You will not take him!"

Women wailed to the frozen night sky and children cried out as they clung to their mothers.

Sitting Bull stopped, and turning to Bullhead he said, "I will not go with you."

Five Metal Breasts surrounded him. They in turn were surrounded by thirty-eight other Metal Breasts who themselves were encircled by the Hunkpapa people. Like the calm before a storm, that is where the matter rested. For a moment, no one spoke, all was quiet. Then, like the parting of the Red Sea, the Hunkpapa people moved aside and allowed a solitary man through. His name was Oyúspa kiŋ matȟó (Catch-the-Bear). He got close to Bullhead and calmly said, "Let him go."

A chant rose up from those out in the darkness. "Kill them! Kill them! Kill them!"

The Metal Breasts were beginning to show fear. They licked their lips and looked about for a means of escape. By then, most of them did not care if Sitting Bull was arrested or not. They stole glances at Bullhead, hoping he would do the smart thing and release Sitting Bull. But Bullhead was not about to let him go. He had been charged by White Hair to bring him in, and to not do so would be his shame.

461

Catch-the-Bear wore a gray blanket about his person. Without warning, he threw it off and raised the rifle he had hidden beneath. The shot, when it came, startled the people. Bullhead was hit, and as he went down, he got off one shot before hitting the ground. His bullet lodged in Sitting Bull's back.

Standing next to Sitting Bull was Red Tomahawk. When he saw Bullhead go down, he fired point-blank into Sitting Bull's skull, killing him instantly. Then all hell broke loose. Guns came out from everywhere. Three Metal Breasts and two Hunkpapa were killed in the next thirty seconds.

The Metal Breasts retreated to Sitting Bull's house where they barricaded themselves behind its thick log walls. By the time the army arrived, seven Metal Breasts lie dead. Including Lieutenant Bullhead and Sergeant Shave Head. On the Hunkpapa side, eight were dead besides Sitting Bull, including Catch-the-Bear, the man who had fired the first shot.

A few days later, LeGare and his train arrived at Fort Yates. As his men attended to the wagons, he went into the post. When Cooper saw him, he rushed over and shook his hand, saying, "My friend, it is good to see you, but you should have been here days ago."

"I know. I did not plan on spending Christmas Day on The Trail, but we had a little trouble on the way down. Nothing to speak of, we ran into more mud than expected. On the way back, the ground should be frozen."

Changing the subject, Cooper said, "I've got something special put away. Let's go to my office and have a dram."

"Sounds like a good idea, but first I want you to meet someone. And I've got a favor to ask of you."

"A friend? Well, any friend of yours . . ."

"*Très bien*, I'll be right back."

Less than a minute later, LeGare returned with Yellow Hair, and introduced him to Cooper. As the two men shook hands, Cooper was taken by Yellow Hair's eyes. They had not lost their sky-blue color over the years. In fact, they were, if anything, more pronounced. For his part, Yellow Hair was a little disconcerted by Cooper's eye patch.

After the introductions, LeGare told Cooper that Yellow Hair had come to visit friends, one of whom was Sitting Bull.

Cooper looked at the two men and said, "You mean you have not heard?"

"We have been traveling. We have heard nothing."

"Sitting Bull was killed a few days ago."

It took a moment or two for the words to sink in and for Yellow Hair to find his voice. "That is not possible; the Lakota are not at war."

Cooper told them the story of Sitting Bull's death, and finished with, "I am sorry for your friend's demise, Yellow Hair."

"He still would like to see a friend of his by the name of Bear Claw. Do you know him?" asked LeGare.

"Yes, he trades with me."

"This is the favor I wanted to ask. Do you have a horse that Yellow Hair can borrow? I will vouch for him and be responsible."

"Of course, I'll take you out to the corral now. I have a sorrel he can use."

"Thank you, my friend. There is one more thing. How does he find Bear Claw?"

"Come with me, I will tell you while I saddle the horse."

Fifteen minutes later, after thanking Cooper for the use of the horse, Yellow Hair was on his way to Bear Claw's lodge. Cooper had informed him that Bear Claw now lived in a log house and how to find it.

463

As Yellow Hair rode out, LeGare yelled, "Be back in six days—the first of January. That is when we leave for home."

Yellow Hair came upon Bear Claw's house as the sun started its slow descent from its zenith.

It was a modest affair, thirty feet long and twenty wide. There were no windows, only a door in front. On the north side, attached to the edifice, stood a lean-to where the fires were built and the meals cooked.

Two small children came running from around the back, followed by Bear Claw with a load of firewood in his arms. At first, he did not notice the rider. But the children did, and stood silently staring at Yellow Hair as he came on.

Bear Claw looked to see what his children were fixated on. When he saw Yellow Hair, he let out with a whoop and shouted "*Háu.*" Letting the wood fall to the ground, he ran to meet his friend. "It is good to see you! I never thought I would see you again."

"It is good to see you also."

Pointing to the children, Yellow Hair asked, "Are they yours?"

Bear Claw smiled proudly and answered in the affirmative. "The girl's name is Moon and the boy is John."

"They are good-looking children. Where is White Dove?"

"She is at a neighbor's. She will return soon and then we will eat. But come inside, we will smoke the pipe and talk of old times."

As Yellow Hair was tying the horse to a post, Bear Claw asked, "Did you hear about Sitting Bull?"

"Yes, but you must tell me what happened."

Bear Claw told what little he knew of Sitting Bull's death, then asked of Yellow Hair, "Why did you come to Standing Rock?"

"I wanted to see you and talk to someone about the Ghost Dance."

"After Sitting Bull's death, all the Ghost Dancers fled to the badlands because they were afraid of the soldiers. For some reason, the Dance scares the whites."

"What about you?" asked Yellow Hair.

"I have no time for such foolishness. If it is true about us Indians reclaiming the earth, then me and mine are in a good position. And if it is a false religion, then I have a family to feed; I cannot be wasting my time dancing all day and all night."

"That is smart thinking. But the only thing that I want to know is do they really speak with their dead relatives?"

"I do not know. I have heard that they do. Many Hunkpapa are Ghost Dancers and some have told me that they have spoken with the dead."

Yellow Hair decided that he would have to go to the badlands and speak to the Ghost Dancers themselves. But when he mentioned it, Bear Claw told him, "You do not have to do that. People from Pine Ridge brought the Dance here. There are many Dancers over there, I hear the whole reservation Dances. They can tell you what you want to know."

Yellow Hair decided to go to Pine Ridge in the morning.

They ate when White Dove returned. Afterward, Bear Claw and Yellow Hair went for a walk. They did not speak until they had gone about a mile from the house. "What is it, my friend?" asked Yellow Hair. "Something is on your mind. I saw it on your face when I first arrived. What is bothering you?"

The sun was just hitting the rim of the earth; shortly it would be dark. Bear Claw said, "Let us sit here and watch Ta'kuwakaŋ as he leaves our world. There is something of which I must speak, but I do not know how to begin."

They sat and gazed at the setting sun. When blackness and twinkling stars had replaced the orange and pink of the sky, Bear Claw told his story.

"There is something I have held inside since Whitestone Hill." He went on to tell Yellow Hair that Little Thunder was not his only son. How Fighting Woman had given birth to a boy-child with blue eyes and hair the color of corn. A boy she had named Yellow Bird. He told of how, on that day of slaughter, the soldier on the white horse took Yellow Bird.

Taking a deep breath and still not looking at Yellow Hair, Bear Claw continued, "White Tail said for you to know about Yellow Bird would only add to your suffering and that I should say nothing."

Bear Claw finished his narrative and was glad it had gotten dark. He did not want to look into the eyes of his friend. He was afraid he would see hatred there. But when Yellow Hair spoke, his voice was soft and contained no anger.

"I understand. You were only a boy and your family was wiped out that day. Perhaps White Tail was right—the news is hurtful, and it is better that you waited." He reached over to his friend and clapped him on the shoulder. "But why have you told me this now?"

"I now have children."

Bear Claw hesitated for a moment before going on. Then he blurted out, "The man who took your child is at Fort Yates."

"What are you talking about? I killed him. It was you who pointed him out to me. The officer on the white horse, remember?"

"I remember; he is the one that killed Fighting Woman and Little Thunder. He took Yellow Bird, but he gave him to another soldier. I saw it. I was in the bushes not twenty

466

feet away!" Bear Claw then told Yellow Hair of the soldier giving the baby to the man with one eye.

"Are you telling me Cooper has my son?"

"Do you know him?" exclaimed Bear Claw.

"I met him today. He seemed like a decent man, not a murdering child-stealer."

"Yes, I deal with him. He always treats us Indians fairly. He gives us credit when we need it and never demands payment before he will give more credit."

Yellow Hair stood. "Let us go back. I must speak with him tonight. Do you know where he lives?" He was six paces down the path and Bear Claw had to hurry to catch up. When he did so, he told Yellow Hair that Cooper lived above his store.

As Yellow Hair saddled his horse, he said, "I will see you again before I return to Canada." He added, "My friend, you have done no wrong. White Tail was right. There is a time for everything. If you had told me about Yellow Bird back then, I do not know what I would have done, but I do know it would not have been good." With a final farewell, Yellow Hair rode off into the darkness.

It was too dark to see the path, so he gave the horse his head and let him find his own way back to the fort. He was in no hurry; he had some thinking to do.

Bear Claw said that Cooper was a good man. Can any man that took part in Whitestone Hill be considered good? If I find out that Cooper had a hand in the killing of Suni and Little Thunder, will I then kill him?

At the trading post, Yellow Hair saw a light on upstairs. The store itself was dark and sure to be locked up for the night. He continued around to the back where the corral was located, and saw the stairs he had not noticed earlier in the day.

He unhurriedly made his way up to the second story. Maybe Cooper would tell him the boy was a long time dead. Children die all the time, from disease, accidents, any number of things.

He knocked twice before he received a response. "Yes, yes, I'm coming." Cooper opened the door and saw the Indian he had lent his horse to. "Yellow Hair, I did not expect you back for a few days. Did something happen to my horse?"

"No, but I must speak with you. It is important."

"Then come on in. I was working late, doing some bookkeeping; we can talk in my parlor." They seated themselves at a table littered with invoices and bills of lading.

Cooper asked, "What's on your mind?"

"There is a question that I need answered, and you are the only man in the world that I know of who can answer it."

"I'll answer your question if I can. What is it?"

"Where is my son?"

The question perplexed Cooper.

"I don't know what you're talking about. It's late and if this is some sort of joke . . ."

Yellow Hair stared the man dead in his one eye and said, "You were at Whitestone Hill and you took a baby away from there. The man who gave you the baby, I killed a long time ago. And I might kill you this night, I have not yet decided."

Cooper heard the words "Whitestone Hill" and he seemed to shrink into himself. He hung his head and shook it back and forth, while Yellow Hair sat opposite him, his right hand on the handle of his knife as it rested in the sheath that Suni had made.

After a while, Cooper unbowed his head and returned Yellow Hair's stare. "My God . . . in my dreams I've relived that horrible day for almost thirty years now. The only good thing to come of it was the baby I carried away."

Tears were starting to form in Cooper's good eye, but Yellow Hair was unmoved. He sat looking at Cooper, waiting for him to answer his question. He wanted to know what had become of his son.

His unwavering gaze had an effect on Cooper. He wiped away the tears that ran down his cheek and sat erect. Squaring his shoulders, he said, "I believe you are his father. I see the resemblance in your face. But before I tell you of your son, I want you to know that I killed no one that day. If I had had any guts, I would have just ridden away, but then they would have said I deserted during battle and I would have been shot on the spot. *Battle?* Hell, it was a slaughter!"

There was a glass of amber liquid sitting on the table. Before continuing, Cooper raised it and drank down its contents in one swallow. When the glass was empty, he resumed his story.

"We were ordered to kill everyone and destroy the village. I could not bring myself to kill defenseless people, so I got off my horse and went from tipi to tipi setting them on fire. But I always looked inside first to ascertain if it was empty or if the people inside were dead or alive. In a few, I found people hiding, mostly mothers sheltering their children. If I found live people in a tipi, I did not set it afire. I'd just go on to the next one.

"Well, as I was heading to this one tipi, the Captain comes out holding something. He called to me and ordered me to set fire to the tipi he had just come out of. As I got near to him, I saw that he was holding a baby. At first, he turned, like he didn't want me to see it. But then, he turned back around and told me to report to him at a nearby draw. I waited until he rode off and then went inside the tipi. I thought that if there was someone in there, I'd have to get them out because I'd been ordered to burn that particular tipi and I would have to do it."

Up until that point, Yellow Hair showed no emotion, but now there was something—a look in his eyes—that made Cooper think he had just spent his last day on earth. Nevertheless, he had started telling his story. And after all the years of holding it in, it was soul-satisfying to lay it out to another human being. Even to *this* man who had every right to strike him down dead where he sat.

"When I went inside and my eye adjusted to the dim light, I saw a woman lying on the ground with a large knife in her hand." Out of decency and perhaps a little fear, Cooper did not tell Yellow Hair that half her head had been blown away. He continued, "And there was a boy across on the other side of the tipi. They were both dead."

Yellow Hair gripped the handle of the knife until the knuckles of his hand showed white. Interrupting Cooper, he quietly said, "She was my wife and he was my son." Cooper looked to the glass on the table, then remembered it was empty.

Yellow Hair saw the glance.

"If you want a drink, it will have to wait until after you tell me what I want to know. What happened to Yellow Bird?"

"Was that his name? I came to love that boy. But let me tell it in the order that it happened so you will understand."

Yellow Hair nodded and told him to go on.

"Well, when I knew there was nobody alive, I set fire to the tipi. Then I went to the draw as ordered and found the Captain sitting on a rock holding the baby. As I approached, he stood and held the baby out to me. I accepted the child and he told me he'd been taken from white settlers. The Captain said the Indian woman admitted it before he shot her. He then ordered me to take care of the baby until our return to Minnesota. It was to be my only duty.

"He also said that if the child did not make it back to Minnesota happy and in one piece, I'd be court-martialed. After the first day, I didn't need the threat of a court-martial hanging over my head. The little one was perfect, he never cried once. When we were on the move, I carried him in the crook of my arm, and he would play with the ends of my kerchief. Day after day, I held him and he would look up at me with those piercing blue eyes of his. Like yours. By the time we got back to Minnesota, I couldn't have loved him any more than if he were my own flesh and blood. I was hard-pressed to give him up, but I had no choice in the matter."

Cooper stopped talking and Yellow Hair slowly removed his hand from the knife. He did not think he was going to need it after all.

The lamp was growing dim, so Cooper reached over and gave it a little more wick and waited to hear what Yellow Hair would say.

"You have not told me what has become of my son. Do you know if he still lives?"

Looking to gain a little time while he decided how to tell Yellow Hair of his son, Cooper said, "I don't usually talk this much; it has made me kind of thirsty. Mind if I pour myself a drink?"

"Help yourself."

"Would you like one?"

"You know that Indians are not allowed liquor."

Cooper shrugged, poured himself a stiff drink, and brought it back to the table. This time he did not gulp it. He sipped while Yellow Hair patiently looked on. Finally, he said, "Your boy is alive and doing well. I've been in touch with him and his mother over the years."

At the word "mother," Yellow Hair rose to his feet, pointed south, and shouted, "His mother's bones lie out on that prairie somewhere!"

471

Cooper immediately realized his mistake and told Yellow Hair that he was sorry. "It's just that I have come to think of the woman as his mother. If it means anything to you, she loves him as though he were her own."

Yellow Hair sat back down and said, "Continue."

"Well, what I'm getting at by taking the long way 'round is that I also hold him dear, and I wouldn't want to see him unhappy. I was thinking that if you came out of nowhere and told him you were his father and that he was half Indian, it might not sit so well with him. I don't know, I'm just saying."

In spite of himself, Yellow Hair was beginning to like this man Cooper. His concern for Yellow Bird was admirable. He decided to put the man's mind at ease. "I only want to know of him. If he were here at the fort, I would not approach him. I would like to see him, but it is unlikely I will ever find myself in Minnesota again."

Yes, thought Cooper. *He is the father. That is the way a father would speak.*

He decided then to tell Yellow Hair who and where his son was.

"Your boy is not in Minnesota. He's right here at this fort. He just made captain. He's in the 7th Cavalry, and he's a fine lad."

Yellow Hair sat silent for a moment and then asked, "What is his White Man's name?"

"It's William, William Murray."

"Will you point him out to me tomorrow?"

"I will point him out to you, but not tomorrow. The Seventh is on patrol and aren't due back for a few days."

Yellow Hair was disappointed that he would have to wait, but at the same time, he felt great joy. A part of Suni still lived.

"I have never been one for liquor, or firewater as my friends call it, but this calls for a celebration. I do believe I will avail myself of your offer and have a little of what you are drinking."

A friendship was forged that night. The two sat together and talked until dawn. Cooper told Yellow Hair about Yellow Bird, West Point, the ship-building grandfather who wanted William to take over a very profitable business, and about the woman who called herself his mother. For his part, Yellow Hair told of his origins in Concord, his journey on The Trail, and his becoming a Dakota.

When there was a lapse in the conversation, Cooper asked, "You said you killed the man who killed your people and took your son. The man is dead, but how do you know you killed the right man?"

"A friend of mine was hiding in the bushes when the man gave Yellow Bird to you. Both of you were distinctive, him with his white horse and you with your eye patch. Two years after Whitestone Hill, my friend pointed him out to me during a battle. I raised my long gun and shot him and had the pleasure of seeing him go down."

"He *was* a son-of-a-bitch alright, but I never told his wife or William that."

"'William'. . . I will have to get used to thinking of him by that name."

Yellow Hair did not want to hang around the fort waiting for his son to return. He told Cooper that he was leaving and would come back in two days. In the meantime, he had some business down at Pine Ridge.

Before the sun cleared the horizon, the two men shook hands and Yellow Hair was back on the sorrel headed south. Maybe he could talk to Suni. If he could, he would tell her what had become of their son.

His thoughts were of family as he made his way. If Little Thunder had lived, he would be thirty-eight winters. Yellow Bird was twenty-eight winters. Of course, they would have been given new names after their Vision Quests. By now, both would be fathers. Those thoughts so occupied his mind that he did not see the band of Indians as they came in from the northwest.

At length, he heard them. He looked to his right, their paths would intersect. Thinking they might be Ghost Dancers, he rode over and spoke to the man driving the lead wagon.

"*Háu*, I am Yellow Hair. I am on my way to the Pine Ridge Reservation; do you know how far it is?"

"Not far, we will be there by morning."

"You are going to Pine Ridge?"

"Yes, we are going there to be safe. Because we dance the Ghost Dance, the soldiers want to arrest our chief and send the rest of us east to a camp on the Missouri. We are coming in from the badlands where we went after Sitting Bull was killed."

"Who is your chief, and what is your band?"

"We are Minneconjou, but there are some Hunkpapa with us. Our chief is Heȟáka Gleška.

"Where is Spotted Elk? I have come a long way to learn of the Ghost Dance. I would like to speak with him."

"He is sick, maybe dying. Ride with us and when we get to Pine Ridge, you can speak with Matȟo Waŋáȟtake. He brought the Dance to us from the prophet Wovoka."

Yellow Hair joined with the Minneconjou and continued south. As they passed Porcupine Butte, he said, "My eyes are not as good as they once were, but is that not a line of Bluecoats off to the southeast?"

474

Chapter Sixty-Nine

MAJOR WHITESIDE (Samuel M.) of the 7th Cavalry was in an irritable state of mind. He was not pleased about being sent all the way out to the badlands to bring in Spotted Elk and his people.

What is all this hoopla about some dance? It's been fourteen years, hell fourteen and a half years, since the Little Bighorn. The Sioux are a beaten people; why not just let them be?

He was brought out of his reverie by his half-breed scout and interpreter, John Shangreau.

"Sir, there are Sioux ahead of us. I reckon they number 'bout three, four hundred. I think they are Spotted Elk's people."

"Are they painted for war?"

"No sir. Some in wagons, others on foot. Mostly women and children, best as I can see."

"Well, let's get this over with."

"Yes sir."

When the Lakota saw soldiers coming their way, they knew that it did not bode well. Soldiers always meant trouble.

Major Whiteside brought his men on. When they reached the lead wagon, Shangreau asked if they were of Spotted Elk's band. When the answer came back "Yes," Whiteside asked where he could find Spotted Elk.

"Third wagon back."

Yellow Hair kept his eyes averted and his ears open. If there was trouble, he could always tell them he was from Canada and that Cooper, the trader, would vouch for him. But for now he wanted to see what the soldiers were up to.

Major Whiteside rode to the wagon that held Spotted Elk and found him lying in the back, blood seeping from his nose. He was dying of pneumonia. Through Shangreau, Whiteside asked why they were on the march.

Spotted Elk replied, "We are on our way to see Red Cloud at Pine Ridge."

"Why did you leave your camp at Cherry Creek?"

"When Sitting Bull was killed, we knew you soldiers would come for us next."

Major Whiteside sighed. To Shangreau he said, "Tell him he is under arrest and we are going to disarm his men."

Shangreau hesitated. Instead of conveying the message, he advised the Major, "If you try to take their guns out here, there is going to be a fight. Many women and children will be killed, and most likely some of your soldiers. It would be best to get them into a camp, and when they are surrounded, they will have little choice but to give up their weapons."

Whiteside thought for a moment.

"Alright, tell Spotted Elk that the 7th Cavalry will escort him and his people to Pine Ridge, but first we will make camp at Wounded Knee Creek."

The Lakota called the place *Čhaŋkpé Ópi Wakpála*.

Spotted Elk replied that they could get to Pine Ridge without the soldiers' help.

"Tell him that the Seventh would consider it an honor to escort a chief of his standing."

Spotted Elk did not believe that for a minute, but was too weak to argue and lay back down.

During the talk between Whiteside and Spotted Elk, Yellow Hair stayed close enough to hear their words. He knew the band was to be disarmed and arrested, but if he told what he knew, many people would die. He decided not to say anything. Besides, his thoughts were on something else he had heard. So, this was the 7th Cavalry? Then his son must be among the soldiers and he certainly was not going to precipitate a fight in which the son he had never seen might be killed.

While riding to Wounded Knee Creek, Yellow Hair sidled up to a soldier and asked him if he knew of a captain in the Seventh by the name of William Murray. At first the soldier was taken aback by Yellow Hair's command of the English language, but then said, "What's it to you?"

"He is a friend and I want to say hello."

"Didn't know the Captain had any Injun friends."

"I am only half Injun."

"Yeah, I reckon I can see that. He's with Colonel Forsyth's detachment. They're not with us. I believe they're out on some other patrol."

Yellow Hair thanked the man and rode back to the Lakota.

The sun was getting low in the sky by the time they reached Wounded Knee Creek. Because it was late, Whiteside decided to disarm the Indians the next morning. Although he did take precautions.

He deployed his two Hotchkiss guns on a small rise overlooking the Lakota camp. Hotchkiss guns were capable of firing forty-three rounds per minute and were accurate up to a range of two thousand yards. Whiteside also set out a line of pickets surrounding the Indians' tipis to make sure that no one escaped during the night.

The soldiers, both officers and enlisted men, thought it a good day's work. They had captured the dreaded Spotted Elk and his band. That Spotted Elk was near death and his band was made up mostly of women and children—120 men and 230 women and children—did not dampen the celebrations that night.

Yellow Hair decided that, in the morning, he would go to the soldier chief and tell him he was no Ghost Dancer and that he had to return Cooper's sorrel back to Fort

Yates. He knew if he were arrested with the others, his chances of laying eyes on his son would be slim indeed.

He need not have worried. Fate was about to bring father and son together.

During the night, the remaining companies of the 7th Cavalry Regiment arrived, commanded by Colonel James Forsyth. They also carried two Hotchkiss guns, which the Colonel had deployed on the bluff along with the first two guns. One of his junior officers, Captain William Murray, led Company K.

The Indians were issued hardtack for breakfast the next morning. Shortly thereafter, they were told to form a single line; their guns were to be taken from them. The Lakota looked about and saw the big guns pointed at them from above and the soldiers surrounding them. Once again, they had been lied to by the White Man.

Chapter Seventy

ALL ONE HUNDRED AND TWENTY MEN, one hundred and twenty-one if you included Yellow Hair, formed a single line. Each man was to place his weapons—knives, tomahawks, and war clubs, as well guns—in a pile as they advanced to the front of the line.

Yellow Hair was farther back; at the head of the line stood two soldiers with an officer off to one side. The Indians were to place their weapons on the ground between the two soldiers. Slowly the line moved forward. When Yellow Hair progressed to near the front, he saw the large pile of guns, but he had no intention of giving up the Winchester Sitting Bull had given him. He already had his knife safely hidden on his person. When it was his turn to place his rifle onto the pile, he would tell the officer his story and see what developed. If necessary, he would tell them that he was a White Man, and upon close inspection, he would be believed.

Yellow Hair was fourth from the front of the line when it stopped moving. The young man at the front, Šuŋgmánitu sápA (Black Coyote), raised his gun in the air and shouted, "I paid much for this gun. I will not give it up!"

Colonel Forsyth, who had been standing nearby, heard the shout and addressed the officer in charge. "Captain Murray, what is the trouble?"

That was all Yellow Hair had to hear. He looked to the soldier called Murray and saw that what little hair stuck out from under his cap was the color of corn. He looked at his face; it was the face of Suni, but masculine. Yellow Hair thought him handsome.

A soldier approached Black Coyote and made a grab for his gun. In the ensuing struggle, a shot rang out. Black

Coyote's gun had accidently discharged. At first no one made a move. The entire camp was quiet. Then, without warning, the Hotchkiss guns started to rake the tipis, going through their skins as though they were not there. The people inside the tipis, those that were not killed instantly, ran out in panic. The Lakota men who had given up their guns ran towards the pile in an effort to retrieve them, but most were cut down by the fire from the Hotchkiss guns. The few who still had possession of their guns began to fire at the soldiers.

Hearing a gun cock behind him, Yellow Hair turned to see a Hunkpapa brave leveling a revolver at William. With reflexes he had not possessed for many winters, he raised his rifle and clubbed the brave just as he fired. The bullet went wide and missed its mark. The brave did not object, for by then he had taken a shot to the forehead, fired by one of the Hotchkiss guns.

Yellow Hair turned to see if William had been hit, but he was not there. He looked around trying to find him, but bullets were flying every which way, so he ran. He ran as best he could, considering his limp, to a ravine that was off to the west. Without slowing, he jumped over the lip and almost landed on a dead woman sprawled on the incline. Next to her was an infant, still alive, oblivious to the horror going on around him.

He plucked up the child and made for the bushes at the bottom where he found a woman and a small girl hiding among the scrub. The girl was crying and the woman was shaking from head to foot. Yellow Hair handed the infant to the woman and said, "Do not worry, Mother. Neither you nor your child will die this day." He made sure that his gun was fully loaded; he was prepared to shoot the first soldier that stuck his head over the rim of the ravine— providing that it was not William.

They were the only ones in that area, but one hundred yards to the north, men, women, and children were huddled at the bottom while soldiers stood above and shot down at them. Every once in a while he could hear someone shout, "Remember the Little Bighorn!"

The Seventh was getting its own back that day.

While that was going on at the ravine, the men behind the Hotchkiss guns continued to fire at anything that moved. Unfortunately, for some of the soldiers in front of the guns that meant them as well. In the frenzy, soldiers were killing soldiers as well as Indians.

Not all the Lakota ran to the ravine. Some ran to the open prairie in an effort to escape death. None of them had weapons; they were just running for their lives.

A few of the soldiers made for their horses and, as if they were on a buffalo hunt, ran down the fleeing people. As they approached their prey, they would cock their revolvers and fire. If they missed, they would turn their horse for another try. One trooper was heard to exclaim, "Great fun, I betcha I get more than you!" When the carnage was over, Lakota bodies were found as far away as five miles, which led some to speculate that the soldiers toyed with the Indians to prolong the hunt.

Back at the ravine, when targets became scarce, one of the soldiers on the rim started to make his way in Yellow Hair's direction. His name was John Dinneen, a private in the Seventh. That morning he had killed fifteen unarmed people, ten of whom were women and children. Now he was looking for more "turkeys." That is how he thought of the cowering Indians. At one point, he yelled to his compatriots, "Come on, boys, it's just like an old-fashioned turkey shoot and I'm a-gonna win me a prize!"

Dinneen made his way toward Yellow Hair's location, searching the bush for Indians. He walked slowly and purposefully; he did not want to miss any "turkeys."

Because of his slow progress, the tension built within the woman and girl. Finally, it became unbearable for the girl and she bolted from her hiding place.

Dinneen saw her and smiled to himself. Under his breath he said, "I oughtta git two points for this one. Them small ones is hard to hit, especially when they're movin' so fast."

As he raised his rifle to his shoulder to take aim, Yellow Hair stood, sighted Dinneen, and fired.

The bullet, though aimed for the man's heart, plowed into his left shoulder before he could fire at the girl. With a shout of pain, Dinneen dropped his gun. The look of astonishment on his face made Yellow Hair smile. He cocked his gun for another try at the man's heart, but Dinneen turned and ran before he could sight him.

Yellow Hair looked for the girl, but she was nowhere to be seen. Looking down at the woman, he said, "Do not worry, she got away. She is safe." He did not know if it were true, but it was the only thing he could say.

Private Dinneen's wound was not life-threatening, although, because of nerve damage, he did lose the use of his left arm. But other than that, he lived a long, if not particularly fruitful, life. He—along with twenty-two other "brave" men of the Seventh—was given the Congressional Medal of Honor for his bravery at Wounded Knee. His citation read in full, *"For conspicuous bravery in action against Indians concealed in a ravine."*

Yellow Hair looked up the ravine for anything in a blue coat that moved. The big guns were still firing, but the report of the small arms fire had moved off into the distance. Yellow Hair's eyes never left the rim. Soon, he saw a blue hat at the top. Thinking he would get the man before he came any closer, he sighted his gun and squeezed the trigger. The hat flew off to reveal yellow hair. A face appeared over the rim. It was Yellow Bird who had become

William. The surprise of seeing his son, and the consternation of knowing he had almost killed him, propelled Yellow Hair to his feet.

One thing had to be said for William; he was no coward. He did not run when his hat was shot from him. He stood his place as a soldier should, pointed his gun at Yellow Hair, and said, "I do not want to kill you. Drop your gun."

Yellow Hair could only stand there, staring into his son's face. Yes, he was Suni's child alright.

Yellow Hair is no longer in a ravine at Wounded Knee Creek. He is back on the prairie travelling with the woman who calls herself Fighting Woman. She has just saved his life. He sits in their camp while she hunts rabbits and birds. He remembers right after they were married how much in love they were. How they made love under the oak trees when they were supposed to be hunting. He is thinking about the day Little Thunder was born and how proud he was to have a son.

The bullet, as it plowed into his body, brought Yellow Hair back to the present.

He was lying on his back, looking up at the bluest sky he had ever seen. As the cottony clouds rolled by, he said, "Suni, you see that one? What does it look like to you?"

"I'm sorry, mister; I didn't want to shoot you. You should have put the gun down when I told you."

Yellow Hair's mind cleared. He looked at William, his son, standing over him and said, "It is all right, I was somewhere else for a little while. Where am I hit?" Then he felt the pain. It was a gut shot—a slow and torturous death.

Yellow Hair looked into the eyes of his son, and he so wanted to say, *"Son, I love you."* Instead, he said, "Please do something for me."

"If I can."

"The woman over there in the brush . . . she and the baby have done nothing wrong. Will you give them your protection now that I am no longer able?"

"Yes, of course."

"And leave me your revolver . . . you can take my rifle; it was given to me by Sitting Bull."

Wincing in pain, Yellow Hair gritted his teeth and continued. "I will not recover from this wound, but now that I have had my wish fulfilled, I am ready to go south and join my family. In fact, I have two families waiting for me. I am many winters late in getting to them."

He held up his knife, "For your kindness, I want you to take this. It was in the war way back with Andy Jackson and it has seen many a war since. It will bring you luck. It is what you whites call a family heirloom and I give it to you."

Not understanding about the knife, but knowing why Yellow Hair wanted the revolver, William accepted the knife and placed the revolver on the ground within easy reach.

"Won't you let me get our doctor? He may be able to save you."

"He will not see me until your wounded have been cared for, and by then I will be dead."

To the woman, Yellow Hair spoke in the Lakota tongue. "Go with this man. He is a good man; he will see you to safety."

With Sitting Bull's rifle in hand, William helped the woman as she struggled up the steep incline of the ravine, holding the baby. Just as they reached the rim, Yellow Hair shouted, "*Damakota!*—I am Dakota!"

They heard a shot and William turned to look back.

What he saw was an old gray-headed Indian, lying dead, with a smile upon his face.

484

Thank you for reading *Yellow Hair*.

If you enjoyed the story, please leave a review online where you purchased the book.

And if you would like to share your thoughts on the book or just chew the fat, please visit me at www.andrewjoyce76.com and click the "Contact" button.

Andrew Joyce

About the Author

Andrew Joyce left high school at seventeen to hitchhike throughout the US, Canada, and Mexico. He wouldn't return from his journey until decades later when he decided to become a writer. Joyce has written five books, including a two-volume collection of one hundred and forty short stories comprised of his hitching adventures called *BEDTIME STORIES FOR GROWN-UPS* (as yet unpublished), and his latest novel, *YELLOW HAIR.* He now lives aboard a boat in Fort Lauderdale, Florida, with his dog, Danny, where he is busy working on his next book, tentatively entitled, *MICK REILLY.*

Books by Andrew Joyce:

REDEMPTION: The Further Adventures of Huck Finn and Tom Sawyer

MOLLY LEE

RESOLUTION: Huck Finn's Greatest Adventure

YELLOW HAIR